KU-734-376

Jacky Gillott was educated in Lancashire and at
University College, London, where she read English.
She worked for the *Sheffield Telegraph* and her
journalistic career later took her to radio news and
subsequently to ITN, where she worked as a news
reporter. She has presented 'Newsdesk' on BBC radio
and also broadcasts frequently on various arts
programmes. She does freelance work for many
newspapers and writes book reviews for *The Times*.
She is married, with two children.

Jacky Gillott's first novel, *Salvage*, which received
much critical acclaim when it was published in 1968,
is also available in Penguins.

Jacky Gillott

War Baby

Penguin Books

Penguin Books Ltd, Harmondsworth,
Middlesex, England
Penguin Books Australia Ltd, Ringwood,
Victoria, Australia

First published by Victor Gollancz 1971
Published in Penguin Books 1974

Copyright © Jacky Gillott, 1971

Made and printed in Great Britain by
Hazell Watson & Viney Ltd,
Aylesbury, Bucks
Set in Linotype Pilgrim

For John

If the worker and his boss enjoy the same television programme and visit the same resort places, if the typist is as attractively made up as the daughter of her employer, if the Negro owns a Cadillac, if they all read the same newspaper, then this assimilation indicates not the disappearance of classes, but the extent to which the needs and satisfactions that serve the preservation of the Establishment are shared by the underlying population.
– HERBERT MARCUSE, *One-Dimensional Man*

I do not like the masses in the flesh.
– HAROLD NICHOLSON

Characters

GARBIE, *alias Beryl Veronica Pendleton*
DOTTY, *her mother*
RIKKI, *her father; missing, presumed dead*

The Rotherbrook Relatives

JACK PENDLETON, M.P., *Garbie's uncle*
CISSY PENDLETON, *his wife*

QUENTIN
ROBIN } *– their pre-war children*
VICTORIA

EDWARD } *– their post-war children*
THOMAS

TREVOR
JEAN
BILLY } *– evacuee children staying at Rotherbrook*
JOYCE

OLD MRS PENDLETON: *Grandmother, otherwise Rikki's and Jack's mother*
EMILY: *later Quentin's wife*
GERALD BUCKINGHAM: *later Victoria's husband*

The Dagenham Relatives

BETTY BEAZLEY, *Dotty's sister*
ARNOLD BEAZLEY, *Aunty Betty's husband*
COLIN BEAZLEY, *their mongol son*

Outside Influences

FREDDY: *nothing known*

MRS CRABBE, *Garbie's teacher*
NANNY, *a countrywoman*

Patients

PEG
DAISY
ETHEL MACREADY
MRS CRICHTON-SMITH
VIV JAMES

The Thursday Group
(*A political group on the Right of the Left*)

SIDNEY HERZOG
DENTON CALDWELL
HUGH BENNETT
BEN DIGBY

1 23 December

'See what Santa Claus 'as brought!'

'Something new is it?'

'Must be bad to bring 'em in at Christmas.'

The two women peer like puppets over the white strip of their sheets, heads threaded on the same stiff string as their gaze follows the new arrival.

'They like to clear the beds come Christmas.'

'So they don't 'ave to put as many sixpences in the puds!'

They crack and rattle with laughter.

'Young.'

'Is it young?'

'That's right.' The string is jerked to make the head nod on its wooden joints.

'Bit of competition for you then eh, Peg? Got your mistletoe in your locker!'

(The heads waggle.)

'Passion pants yourself! Them young doctor students, they're not safe near your bed. Your tongue near mops the floor it's hanging out so bad.'

'They're drawin' the curtains.'

'Hey, you've farted again, I can tell.'

'No, it's Sister done it. Here she comes, pinchin' the cheeks of 'er bum nice 'n tight.'

'You don't fool me Daisy Coltart.'

'There she goes, tight-arsed old boot. No wonder she's single. A feller'd need a power drill to get in there.'

'You're losin' your self-respect Daisy. You know what they say about losin' your self-respect.'

'I'll bet the bloody turkey's stuffed with bleedin' supposi-tories.'

'You'll be telling me next it's sage and onion I'm getting a lungful of. Honest, Daisy, we'll all be dead afore Christmas. Gassed. I bet you made a fortune in the 14–18 war selling your secrets to the Kaiser.'

'Up your Kaiser an' all! I wonder what she's got?'

'I'm gettin' a crick in me neck wonderin'.' Peg's head drops back on the bosomy white pillows. 'Keep us posted!'

Her short, square-cut hair is nearly as white as the linen and the skin of her face is brown and seamy, like a dried fig.

Enamel rattles on enamel. Staff nurse's footsteps make a supercilious squeak on the lino. A cloud of lint and mouth-wash goes by. Further up the ward, in the far corner, Mrs Crichton-Smith begins, quietly, to cry.

The faded chintz swings on its rings.

'We'll soon have your clothes off! Have you got someone to take them away?'

'Of course I've got someone.'

'We'll make a parcel. Can't trust the post. I'm putting these books in your locker. Lord save us, have you been robbing the local Library?'

'It's part of my work. To do with my *studies*.'

'Oh yes? Well it's not *True Confessions* is it? Crikey, *The Nature of Politics, Logic and Sexual Morality* . . . that's a bit on the saucy side . . . you'll not have time for much of that in here!'

Garbie, lying flat on her back, forces a thin smile towards the ceiling. It is cracked, shiny and eau-de-nil in colour. They haven't managed to reach the dust on top of the large, opaque light bowls.

A strong pair of arms smelling of pink soap is busy ordering her belongings. The photograph of Dotty, framed unevenly in black passe-partout, is placed on top of the locker while another pair of hands pull off her thick khaki woollen socks.

'Do you want to keep your knickers on?'

'Please.'

'Right you are then. What a nice warm nightie!' Sister's navy-blue top half is angled across her vision behind limp, yellow Viyella.

'Put this in your mouth.'

'I haven't got a temperature.'

'Never mind, pop it in.'

Antiseptic flows under her tongue. She doesn't like strangers touching her (although she's submitted herself gladly to their care), and she refuses to look at them. They are touching her things.

At Rotherbrook, the unpacking always used to be done by some tiptoeing secret agency, closing the doors behind them like eggshells. The house will be full of the smell of burning pine and cinnamon by now. And in the cupboards, where her cousins keep their old fishing tackle and bats, there must be irregular heaps of red, white and gold wrapped parcels. How disappointed they will be she can't be there.

'Normal!' proclaims Sister, shaking down the mercury. And leaning over to replace the thermometer in its place above the bed, she reveals bleached stains in the navy armpit. 'We'll be glad of any help with the decorating,' she says, pressing her clip board to her breast. 'Everybody does something.'

She vanishes in a flurry of chintz.

'Pain? Waterworks? Bowels? We'll take name and other details later.' She is given a chart of her own.

It was all quite pleasant. She needn't worry about anything now.

'Chocks away! Sister's out – it'll not be long.' Daisy gives Sister a faint and windy wolf whistle.

The two women wait patiently for the curtains to be drawn back. It's better than a matinee. Under the skimming weight of bedclothes their joints grow slowly into monstrous shapes.

The curtains are slapped back and the two women jerk with expectation as Nurse Bagley clips away.

'Flat on 'er back,' hisses Daisy, cheated. 'Flat on 'er back! What a diddle eh? Give 'er a wave, just in case.'

Two curved claws rise like heraldic beasts, pause and withdraw. 'Never mind,' Peg tries to comfort her friend. 'The padre'll be along sometime. He'll give you a cuddle.'

'If 'e gets 'ere afore they put me away in men's orthopaedic.'

'Don't let it get you down duck.'

'Those bloody pills,' grumbles Daisy. She's losing her hair and has grown a moustache.

'I'll 'ave a tool as long as your arm by Easter.'

Peg grins till her lips disappear behind black gums. 'I can smell dinner,' she says.

The damp, floury odour of mashed potato drifts to each bed in turn. Ethel Macready, trembling upwards out of her anaesthetic, catches it in her nostrils and cries faintly for a bowl to be sick in.

Mrs Crichton-Smith dries her tears and fetching a grubby damask napkin and some solid silver cutlery out of her locker, sits up in patient readiness, a knife and fork firmly upraised in either hand.

Cased in plaster up to her neck, Viv James thinks of the damn good dinner she'll have tomorrow when they let her out.

They like to clear the ward at Christmas sending home all who can reasonably go, or all who have somewhere to go, so six of the twelve beds lie smoothly empty looking as though their occupants have only newly died.

Pink, yellow and green paper chains, pinned to the picture rail, slump between the beds like sausage strings. A large cardboard bell, speckled with silver dust hangs on a red ribbon from the centre of the ceiling. Someone has stuck cotton wool balls on two of the windows like they do in butchers' shops. Christmas could have been over two weeks ago.

Garbie thinks she will make paper roses – they always said at school she was good with her hands. Mrs Crabbe, her best remembered teacher (though it must be twenty-five years at least since she sat in her class), was very keen on the creative side. Mrs Crabbe was able to find a mean talent buried deep somewhere inside all her pupils or able to lie and lie until each of those boys and girls believed they had a talent.

She will make paper roses.

Garbie knew anyway, that she was different, but the other children wouldn't listen, wouldn't believe her. They screwed up their toffee mouths and rolled their eyes when she told them about her relatives in the big house with servants and a proper gong for mealtimes. It had a bathroom on the first *and* second floor. The children ate their tea on their own in the nursery and there was dinner as well later, after you were ten. Altogether there were eleven bedrooms and a garden you couldn't even see the end of from the sitting room windows. Out of sight was a dark and neglected lake where frogs sang in the evening. And on the centre of the lawn a black walnut tree, two hundred years old like the house.

There was a fat pony in the paddock and gloomy paintings in the hall of her great-great-great grandfathers and, most wonderful of all, a small library with folding mahogany steps to reach the top shelves.

The other children tugged their caps round backwards, and made their ears waggle while touching the tips of their noses with their tongues. Anything to show they weren't listening, weren't believing. They put a stinking dead bird in her satchel and cut off her plaits on the school bus so she had to go home with clown tufts of hair under her hat, and her mother, playing an unchanging game of patience, turned over the cards with yellow fingers and failed to notice till she climbed into bed with her six hours later when she gave a single, piercing scream.

'Dotty by name, dotty by nature, your mother!' observed Dotty's sister Aunty Betty after the incident. Garbie went to live with Aunty Betty and Uncle Arnold after the incident.

'Goodness knows . . .' said Aunty Betty as she beat a cake or polished the brass fender or knitted an egg cosy, 'Goodness knows what she was dreaming of when she *had* the accident.'

The accident was tremendous and awe-inspiring. Better than

anything Garbie could have imagined. Her mother had fallen in front of a tube at Aldgate East on her way to work at the zip factory and been cut neatly in three pieces like a Cornish pasty.

For weeks after the children at school stopped pulling faces. They stared with a shiny admiration. They couldn't speak to her about it, but one or two asked for her autograph.

She had learned of the incident from Aunty Betty who came to meet her from school, her face reddened and streaming with weeping. 'Poor little love! . . .' she wailed as she pounced from the place where she'd been crouching alongside the tall black wall. '. . . All alone in the world and Dotty cut off in her youth! . . .'

She broke forth into a fresh spasm of tears so contagious, Garbie joined in

'Can I come and live with you Aunty Betty?'

'Of course, my precious.'

So there was nothing to complain of really. Aunty Betty and Uncle Arnold had a proper little house all of their own on the estate at Dagenham and a mongol son called Colin who was expected to die at fourteen, which gave Garbie two interesting and anticipatory years of watching. For true enough, the very day after his fourteenth birthday, he swallowed a wheel off one of the toy cars he'd been given as a present and choked to death.

After that the house got quieter. The only thing Garbie found at all difficult to put up with (and it was a minor thing really) was her aunty's insistence on calling her Beryl.

'Right-you-are!'

Garbie's attention is caught suddenly by the pausing planet of a face overhead.

'I'll have your details now.'

'Details?'

'Details. Blimey, we've had you here an hour and a half already and not got your number. Good thing you're not a terminal eh? Might have let the opportunity slip!' The nurse grins and breathes hard on her biro to make it write.

At the end of the bed Mrs Crichton-Smith, who has been loaded into her wheelchair for a little exercise, sits, listening.

'Got them pinned back?' calls the cheery nurse.

'Eh?' says Mrs Crichton-Smith.

'Tuned in?'

'Pardon?'

The nurse does a trial squiggle with her biro. 'Right-i-ho then!' she says. She's a plump girl with buttery hair. 'Name?'

'Beryl Veronica Pendleton. But I answer to Garbie.'

'Garbie? What kind of name's that when it's at home?'

'It's a ... it's a family name ...' She puckers the greyish skin round her mouth into a simper. 'It's what I'm used to.'

'What's it mean?'

For a moment she can't think. Then recalls her cousins and the pony and trap Aunty Cissy used to drive. She was allowed to drive with her round the country lanes, one of the elect Cogs Corps who collected rubbish. The G.I.s waved as they went past and said, 'There goes the garbage girl!'

It was an honourable title.

'It's just a name,' she says, glad to have had a name imbued with that meaningless kind of affection things do have in families. Even if Nanny had banged the boys' heads together when she'd heard them using it.

'Date of birth?' The nurse has lost interest.

'First of the first thirty-five.'

'Nearly your birthday then?'

'I suppose it is, yes.'

'Your ...' the nurse counts using her fingers ... 'your thirty-fourth.'

'Doesn't time fly!' shouts Garbie. 'How old would you have said I was?'

The nurse gazes down at the indeterminate, putty skin, and thin yellow hair and the pink, catarrhal nose.

'Not a day over twenty-six,' she decides and looks for the next question.

'Home address?'

'33a Pitt Street, N.1.'

'Where is that near?'

'Close to the prison. Halfway between Pentonville and Holloway.'

'Oh, very smart.'

'It's very convenient for town,' says Garbie politely.

'Religion?'

'Now that's a tricky one. Nothing you could put a name to.'

'It's the same with everyone these days,' says Nurse Dodds writing down C of E. Somebody's bell rings, but she ignores it.

'Height?'

'Five ten.'

'Weight? We can't weigh you lying down.'

'Eight three about.'

'How do you do it?' asks the nurse enviously,

'It's a matter of metabolism.'

'With me, it's chips.' Nurse Dodds giggles. 'I'm starving myself for Christmas so I can have a real binge.' She closes her eyes and sucks in her lips to capture the thickening odour of potato and greens.

Garbie thinks of Biafran babies, eyes and bellies freakishly bulged by kwashiokoor. The silent, weeping anger begins.

'Any serious diseases?' the nurse is saying.

'What?'

'Any serious diseases, operations, anything of that nature ...?'

'Oh.' She thinks hard. 'Nothing you could really boast about. I've never been in a hospital before.'

'It's not too bad.'

'Oh it's very nice,' she says rapidly and hears herself add, 'I'm very grateful.' The words act dangerously on her system. It makes one eyelid quiver. 'It's very nice *indeed*,' she repeats.

'It's not where most people choose to come for their holidays, but it's all right. They do you a good Christmas dinner and you get the carol singers round.'

'Oh it's very, very nice. Very comfortable ...'

The bell rings again, more insistently 'All right, all right ...' sighs Nurse Dodds, and she writes something down with squinting care. 'Next of kin?'

Garbie thinks about it, her pulse accelerating The nurse doodles.

'We've got to ask. Just in case.'

Garbie's mind dives disloyally between her connections trying to establish her true roots Not that really, there's any question of choice.

'Cissy and Jack!' she decides.

The nurse blinks.

'Jack Pendleton M.P.' She says it loudly, challengingly. 'The Right Honourable ... Rotherbrook, Sussex.'

'That's not much of an address,' says Nurse Dodds, reluctantly impressed.

'It's enough.' Garbie breathes strongly through her nose.

'Is that your Dad?'

'Uncle ...'

'Ah.' Her shoulders relax. 'I went into the House of Commons once ...'

The bell shrills long and angrily. Nurse Dodds takes the time to check her watch and says resignedly, 'I'll have to see who's the bright spark on the buzzer ... Supper's up in ten minutes.' She withdraws and orders Mrs Crichton-Smith to get back to her own bed.

Born as one of those who hath not, Garbie had been given, not quite the kingdom of heaven, but a good deal more (as Aunty Betty said), than she had any right to expect. And Garbie was deeply aware of what she owed in gratitude both to Aunty Betty herself (who was utterly frank about the debt) and to the Pendletons (who never mentioned it at all).

It was Freddy (dear Freddy) who'd confused her about this debt she owed. He was fond of repeating that gratitude brought a man to his knees. Women, he never referred to, but Garbie took his meaning.

Gratitude, he said, was distasteful and downright dangerous. It spelt a slavery of the spirit. (He had a wonderful way of putting things. Even when you didn't understand entirely, the drift was plain enough.)

Freddy said the day was nigh when the grateful would rise

up and Garbie agreed with him although it was, she found, a conviction that slithered away from her whenever she visited Rotherbrook. She admired and loved Uncle Jack, Aunt Cissy and her cousins. It would have been rude to say anything to them about the grateful rising up – although she had, on occasion, tried.

With Aunty Betty it had always been quite different. Aunty Betty wasn't particularly nice, but she was straightforward and that, in a way, was a virtue. Her priorities were very clear. Cleanliness of every kind came first. Clean speech, clean ears, and a clean mind and a nice, bright brass strip round the front doormat. Washing your hands after you'd been to the toilet.

Aunty Betty's delight at the arrival of pre-packed meats in the supermarket was spoilt only by the marked increase in price, for economy too, was high on the list of priorities. She could mend or darn anything. She knew fifty ways with eggs. She was at her best during the immediate post-war period when faced with the task of making something edible out of snoek and soya flour.

If Aunty Betty's mouth ever shut like a mousetrap you knew immediately it was because you'd done something that was either wasteful or dirty.

There are blander mouths in the world that leave you guessing.

Outside the windows the sky is swollen dark yellow with snow.

'Soup?' cries a nurse with exploding red hair and freckles the size of saucers. She is holding a little Aladdin's lamp that steams from the spout.

'Can you sit up?'

'No.'

'All right then.'

'I'm not allowed.'

'You can manage this yourself. It's a feeder. Just pour it down.'

She is frightened of spilling it over her face. But it doesn't spill. She has to suck quite hard to ease the thin liquid past lumps of barley wedged in the spout. The rest of the ward is quiet except for other gentle sucking sounds and the hurried scrape of a spoon.

Turning her head to the left, Garbie can see, two beds away, the pebbly profile of the woman who's had her operation. Two orange tubes snake out of her nose. Her mouth is open like a desert waiting for rain.

The red-headed nurse returns with a plate she puts down on the locker. She grunts as she cuts the grey strips of liver into tiny pieces. Garbie watches as best she can out of the corner of her eye.

'Where is this place exactly?' she inquires.

The nurse stops, giggles and raises her white eyebrows. 'Where *is* it? Where *is* it?' she repeats and laughs. 'It's Rawley of course.'

'Yes, yes, but where is it exactly?'

'Rawley? It's *Rawley*.'

'But how far from London?'

'Rawley, Surrey. About thirty miles ... didn't they say?'

'You can't see in the ambulance. I wanted to go to the Royal Free. That's where I live.'

'This is the annexe. It's got clean air and all that. It's supposed to be better for you but there's not a cinema within seven miles. I'm trying for a transfer.'

'Oh.'

'Do you like the movies?' The nurse fights with a lump of gristle and gives it up.

'Oh, when I'd the time to spare you couldn't get me out of the Rex. Or the Odeon, up at Highbury ...' Garbie is genteel in her enthusiasms. She speaks nicely. There is a pause in which the nurse places her plates of scraps on a shelf at face level. Garbie gazes at it and remarks, 'It's a bit far for my friends.'

The nurse pours salt on the edge of the plate. 'Got a feller?'

'You could say ...' The smile spreads like a pool of oil on Garbie's face.

'Got a car?'

'Not exactly. A bike.'

'Ah well ...' observes the nurse (her short pink nails are impossibly clean). 'There's no point in London. Not now.'

(There are angels in Oxford Street with flutes and trumpets and the hems of their robes dipping lightly in the ochre tide of traffic fumes.) Might Freddy come?

'Oh well, he'll come to see you likely.'

'If he can.' Awkwardly, she pursues a scrap of curling meat through the mashed potato with a fork. 'If his work *allows*.'

'What is he? Uncle Holly at Selfridge's?' The girl pushes her fist against her nose and giggles.

'I'm not free to say.'

The eyes pop. 'Go on!'

'I've said too much already.'

'You could have fooled me!'

Fascinated, the girl lingers, re-arranging the jug, glass and Dotty's photograph on top of the locker and glancing sidelong through her white lashes. Garbie ignores her. During the longish pause, the liver turns to a tasteless fibre between her teeth.

'Peaches and custard, treacle tart, ice-cream?'

'Ice-cream please.'

She is hungry not having eaten for nearly thirty hours. The pain in her back had pushed electric tendrils down her thighs preventing her legs working properly. During the long night and succeeding day she had lain under blankets trying to keep warm as the other people in the house came back from work, thawed frozen food in their frying pans and went out again to their sprinkling of parties. She had lain shivering and imagined it. Red wine or sweet white in hired glasses, French bread lacerating the roofs of their mouths, a ribbon of shrill interference on the tape recorder. She had slept in spasms, hunger nibbling her stomach and pain biting her back.

Beside her bed had leant a bulky orange paper sack full of presents for her relatives and an overnight bag ready packed to go away for Christmas. She'd had to leave the presents behind but the overnight bag had come in handy.

The ice-cream arrives, a round, waxy disc like a nightlight.

'It's like a rock. I'll knock it about a bit for you!' cries the nurse with red hair. She is a friendly girl.

Shortly after supper when the ladies are meant to rest quietly for half an hour and gather their strength to receive visitors (or not to receive them as the case may be), Mrs Crichton-Smith knows she has wet her bed.

She doesn't like to call out because it's against the rules and would disturb the others, but now it dawns like a light over her shame, that having broken one rule, the others barely matter. The sense of liberation is almost too great to endure. She yells at the top of her suddenly powerful voice.

Discreetly, feet run.

They are quite kind in a bullying sort of way. They tell her she is a dirty girl with a wink and a pinch. Sister tells her how important it is to maintain one's standards.

'What's the point?' sighs Mrs Crichton-Smith, '... in here?'

'It's the same here as everywhere else,' Sister insists, not meeting the old lady's eye.

They lift her and the anchor of plaster around her hip back into the sterile bed. Sister pulls up the bedclothes and fussing, tucks them in kindly.

'People do things because other people care,' she whispers. 'You'll get along nicely if you just stick to what other people do. If you want anything just ring the bell. Now, now,' she adds gently, 'there's no call to start your crying again.'

But Mrs Crichton-Smith can't think of anything else to do.

Peg and Daisy swing into line and trundle their wheelchairs across the ward, hands like shiny lumps of plastic striking the wheels forwards.

'Race you Peg!'

'You've got your choppers in!'

'Well, I'm going visiting ain't I?'

They split formation and arrive on either side of Garbie's bed, heads jerking and twisting at mattress level.

'Hello darlin'!'

'And a Merry Christmas!'

'How do you do.'

'Are they going to operate?'

'It's just my back thank you. I've just got to lie still.'

'She's got herself a slipped disc Daisy.'

'That's what it'll be.'

'How's a young girl go getting herself a slipped disc I wonder?'

They both erupt with mirth.

'She's got a filthy mind,' says Daisy. 'You mustn't mind her.'

'It just happened,' answers Garbie politely, her mouth stiffening with terror.

'One thing's for sure, you don't go getting it from saying your bedtime prayers.'

Garbie turns her head from one to the other. The one with a moustache has hardly any hair. She can see all the domes and depressions of her skull amidst the grey tufts of wool. She would like to join in their joke.

Peg cranes her neck with its dry, turkey flap to examine the belongings on top of the locker. 'Do you smoke?' she inquires.

'No thank you.'

'Oh.' Disappointed, Peg turns her head away.

'I see your name's Beryl.'

'I had a niece called Beryl. Well, I still have,' says Peg.

'What do you do here?' Garbie strains for the proper conversational level.

'Fat as butter she was. She got done for shoplifting. What d'you say?'

'What do you do here?'

'Well I'm a lady pianist and she does the conjuring tricks.'

Daisy heaves with laughter and sticks her two cramped hands on the side of the bed.

'Here!' she cries.

'Look at our hands! That's the joke.'

'Got any sweets Beryl?' asks Peg.

'Sorry.' Guilt prickles.

'Take no notice. She'd have your bedsocks off you if she could. Wouldn't you you old bugger!'

Peg grins and re-adjusts her plate with her tongue.

'Well, only one more shopping day to Christmas,' observes Daisy.

'Yes.'

There is a silence.

'It's a good thing,' says Garbie carefully, 'that I got my cards off early.'

'Have many to send did you?'

'Three hundred and fifty-three.' She is modest about it.

'Three hundred and fifty-three! Did you hear that Peg? Three hundred and fifty-three!'

'That's a lot of cards,' says Peg. 'It must have cost you a good bit.'

'Five pounds two and fourpence, with postage.'

They think about it.

'You must know a lot of people then.'

'Oh, quite a number.' She smiles sideways through the yellow strands of hair. '*Quite* a number.'

The bait is taken. 'How's that then? Do you work in a shop? Never had so many friends as when I worked in a shop. In the chippie. Except p'raps when I was behind the bar for a bit up the Cat and Fiddle when my sister Alice was having her fourth, I liked that . . .'

'It's my political connections,' says Garbie. 'I'm in regular contact with a lot of M.P.s and committee chairmen.'

'M.P.s eh?' Daisy muses, 'I'd write meself if I thought I'd get one to come and warm me bedpan, but they'd not come.'

'You're dead right there Daisy. You'd not get one coming to take me to the pictures either eh?'

'Take you to the pictures Peg. They'd have all the usherettes out on searchlight duty!'

They crow with glee. Peg's blue tongue protrudes like a starling's.

Garbie feels the custardy warmth of their breath and tries again. 'My uncle's in the House.'

'That's good, your aunty'll know where to find him then!'

Their pipes wheeze anew.

'Laughing hurts my back,' explains Garbie lamely.

'I'll say this for the National Health though ...' Peg rolls her tongue back in her mouth to check the coughing, 'I've got a nice warm bed and three good meals a day and that's a bloody sight better than they'd give you in the Sally Army, eh Daisy?'

Her friend shrugs. 'These fucking pills,' she mutters.

'She lets it get her down,' hisses Peg leaning close to Garbie's ear. Then, shouting to her friend: 'You don't want to let it get you down!' *Sotto voce* again: 'She thinks she's a sex change.' Shouting: 'You'd be worse off without!'

'That's right.' Garbie agrees.

'Anyway,' yells Peg, 'I might fancy you, you never know!' Daisy snorts.

'You've got to be grateful ...' The custard mouth sways close to Garbie's cheek. 'I say, you've got to be grateful ...'

A small flurry of agitation ripples across Garbie's mind as she stares at the cracked ceiling and tries to square the thought with Freddy's philosophy. The surface ripple subsides without revelation. There *are* reasons even, why she dare not think of Freddy at all. (It's almost a relief to let both him and his philosophy escape.)

The two old women watch her face working with interest.

'It'll be a spasm,' comments Daisy knowingly, and she blows her nose on her dressing gown sleeve. 'Well, Beryl,' she calls, raising her voice, 'When'll we have the pleasure of meeting your uncle?'

'Constituency work is very pressing at this time of the year.'

'Because things here aren't all they might be.' The left eyelid comes down like a theatre curtain.

'What's she saying, what's she saying?' Peg falls against the side of the bed in the effort to catch what her friend is up to.

'They beat some of the old things up in the toilets.'

'You what?'

'Or leave them sitting there hours on end 'cos they can't get theirselves up off the seat.'

'Oh, she's making it all up,' Peg pushes herself back off the mattress into her wheelchair. 'She makes things up when she gets bored. You don't want to take any notice.'

'No smoke without fire!' cries Garbie excitedly. 'This could call for further investigation.'

'You're completely at their mercy!' persists Daisy, carried away now. A blob of spittle has appeared at the corner of her mouth. Her eyes are filling with tears. Garbie stares, feeling more at ease with a situation than she is able to feel with people.

'How am I to know what's in them pills?' whines Daisy. 'I wish they would bloody well leave me alone. You can't even fuckin' well die without some student trying to give you the fucking kiss of life.'

Garbie is used to people speaking violently *in extremis*. She doesn't flinch. 'Let me take the matter up for you,' she says firmly.

Daisy ignores her.

'Give her a couple of ticks and she'll be over it.' Peg pushes a claw round the top of Garbie's locker to see if she can find anything of interest.

'I won't let it rest!'

'I shouldn't interfere.'

Peg's jaws move round twice on a fluid axis, then she yells across the bed: 'Don't give me that you old sod! You'd go without a week's hot dinners just to get the kiss of life!'

Garbie cannot understand their laughter.

There was always something about Garbie's offers of help that caused a tremor of withdrawal, a stiffening in the circle of shoulders. She understood instinctively people's natural embarrassment at the idea of being helped but refused to let their reservations get in the way of what was right. Freddy had explained how certain things had to be done on behalf of people, for their own good. One had to risk rejection.

'One mustn't be afraid,' he said, 'of making enemies.' But then, he'd been talking about revolution which was his overriding interest in life.

Freddy was compulsive on revolution.

'The forerunners of rebellion,' he explained, 'are rarely popular people. Martyrdom is what creates popularity and Western democrats generally speaking are not fool enough to imprison or execute the very people who threaten them. Not unless they are really pushed ... Mockery and indifference are the weapons they prefer to use ... and why not? People often *do* vanish if you ignore them ...'

His conversation was prone to abstract turns. When the lion roars, he said, you pull a face of comic fear to make the crowd laugh and then throw a scrap into the jaws to close them. The components of democratic control are comedy, benevolence and confidence in the ultimate operation of law. With these you can tame.

Garbie had nothing to say in answer to all this but devotedly she pressed herself to running errands, lending her bus fare home to people in greater need, volunteering for committees when nobody else could be found to do the job and always ready to work overtime in the office if it meant somebody else could leave early. People were constantly taken aback by her generosity.

(Even at this moment, people all over the country, a number of them men and women in high places, were asking their secretaries to send off one further card to a Miss G. Pendleton 'care of Rotherbrook, Sussex'.)

'But I *like* doing things for people,' she would say when bewildered acquaintances protested that she shouldn't have done this or she shouldn't have done that, and overcome by this rare survival of Christian charity they would, perhaps, ask her round to tea.

The invitations were always gladly received. It was the event itself which often proved delicate and difficult to handle. Garbie lacked a mastery of the finer minutiae of conversation, finding it a struggle to invent a response that matched its preceding query. Certain words just skidded away from the main currents of a person's conversation and took her with them. She was aware that the gears of communication didn't always enmesh quite accurately and found it safer on the whole to stick to large topics where she could oppose statement with statement.

At Rotherbrook there were always topics adrift like so many small craft on the sea and if one seemed in danger of capsizing, it was always possible to strike out sideways for another.

With Freddy it was different. Detached from the rest of the noisy, clumsy crowd they could wind patterns of their own.

It was almost a year since they'd met. It was New Year's Eve, just a week less than the year.

She'd glimpsed him before, here and there. Sometimes here in the transport café sitting at a formica-topped table with his hands in their fingerless gloves clasped round a large enamel mug of tea. He was tall and thin and unsubstantial, like a larch tree, and he wore a very long overcoat frayed round the buttonholes.

She'd gone out into the bitterly cold night to get a carton of milk from the machine outside the café and through the steamy window she noticed him sitting alone. She'd only gone in to ask them to get her sixpence unstuck from the machine but Harry, who had the keys, had just nipped out the back to put some anti-freeze in the van and Lily said she'd better have a warm cup of something on the house while she waited.

The café was only half-full. Normally the lorry drivers would growl at her and push their caps back on their heads. She would look offended and swallow excitement. Tonight they were quiet. Fat bubbled in the huge chip pan.

Lily filled the teapot as big as a tanker and strained both arms holding it up to pour out a cup. 'Got a party lined up for tonight, duck?'

'I thought I might go down to Trafalgar Square later.'

Lily laughed, all kindness and surplus weight. 'You want to get yourelf a feller before you go down there duck. I wouldn't fancy a fountain tonight – they'll have to break the ice to throw them in. No thanks. Go and sit yourself down lovey and I'll get Harry out the back. I'll bet he's nipped down to the Plough for a quickie.'

She pushed past the tables. 'Eh,' whistled a driver with a day's growth of grey beard on his face and waxy deposits in his eyes. 'Eh, are you from upstairs?'

'Gerroff, you daft bleeder,' nudged his mate. 'You can tell just by looking.' They turned their backs on her. She sat at the thin man's table.

He stared at her, his fingers clasped tightly round his mug. He had a neat, whitening moustache and deeply socketed, pale, yet bright, blue eyes. He had the fine lines and the pallor of the sick. Under his soft brown trilby, he had tied a brown scarf round his head and knotted it beneath his chin. He stared.

'Cold out,' she said.

He nodded thoughtfully and pushed the sugar container towards her. She rubbed the sleeve of her coat against the steamed window and looked out at the narrow black houses opposite. The windows were oblong and weakly ochrous because of the cheap light bulbs that were used. Or the thin, brown paper blinds. Bedsitterland. Not the bedsitterland of Belgravia and Kensington, but the bleak country of the night shiftworkers, bus conductresses, West Indians with six kids to keep happy in a single room and the feckless ones, out of nick for a short spell.

'It's not right,' she couldn't help saying and swallowed her hot tea rapidly.

Lily came back from the yard, blue nosed and blowing her lips. 'He must be off down the Plough,' she said. 'Can you hang on a bit or shall I let you have half a pint?'

'Give him five minutes,' said Garbie and sucked more gingerly at the hot strong tea. It tasted like iron.

She watched the thin man as Lily wandered their way, removing plates and wiping the neck of the sauce bottles with a damp cloth. Winter or summer Lily wore her blouses with a deep V that showed a fine and benevolent cleavage.

'Will you be wanting anything else, sir?' she asked of the thin man. (Half-playing, half-serious to call him 'sir'.)

'No thank you very much,' he replied courteously. He spoke, Garbie noted, *nicely*. Maybe he wasn't a methie after all. The fingers protruding from his amputated brown wool gloves were yellowed by nicotine, but not dirty.

'As you like.' Lily flicked her cloth.

The thin man placed a monocle to his eye and leant towards Garbie. 'What,' he inquired in a reedy voice, 'is not *right*?'

She gave him a suspicious look in case he was trying to pick her up. Brutally she stirred her tea, then looked again. He was waiting.

Clearing her throat of spiky phlegm she rubbed the window a second time with her sleeve and nodded hurriedly at the windows opposite.

'Ah.'

'They deserve better,' she muttered, face down.

'Ah.' He continued staring through the steamy vista.

She looked for Lily, bolted her tea and felt her face grow rough with eczema. 'I must be off!' She leapt to her feet, tangled herself in a chair and dragged it a few feet across the floor with her.

'I shall come with you to Trafalgar Square,' he said quite calmly.

Lily, smiling, a driver's hand looped on her waist, nodded encouragement. 'That's right,' she called.

'I suppose it's all right.' Garbie clutched her lapel and adjusted her shoulder bag.

'Of course it's all right,' said the thin man rising. 'This is a very special night. A superstitious night moreover ... one should never see the New Year in on one's own.'

She ran a loose tongue over her lips. 'It'll be my birthday at midnight.'

'I knew it was special.'

The city was full of sharp distant sounds and glittering frost.

She knew from the delicate way he took her arm that he was a real gentleman.

They caught a 4a which sped down the City Road, swaying dangerously because it was empty. They had to grip the seat in front and Garbie laughed.

'Yes, they deserve better!' he cried suddenly. 'But not more of the same!'

'Absolutely not,' echoed Garbie already loyal.

'Greed deceives!!'

'Greed does!' She was becoming wildly excited.

'Leads to a surrender of freedom!'

They clung to the cold metal rail as the bus swung their bodies far to the right. 'An end to surrender!' piped Garbie, eyes bright with incomprehension.

'Attagirl!' cheered the thin man and began singing 'Keep right on to the end of the road!' conducting himself vigorously with one hand and hanging desperately on to the rail with the other as they swept through the derelict streets of the City.

'So . . . keep right on to the end!'

The floodlit skull of St Paul's rose between concrete rectangles. They plunged down Ludgate Hill and lurched into Fleet Street, bright and busy with light from the newspaper offices.

As they roared past, the thin man broke off his singing and shouted out headlines. 'Peer claims showgirl wife is man', 'Priest elopes with heroin addict', 'Superfly has transplant'.

The sound of her own laughter obsessed her. The conductor, playing a dull note on his machine, took no notice of them.

People were gathered more thickly on the streets. They walked in twos and threes, arms together. Their faces shone with cold and delight. Outside Rhodesia House, the police stamped their boots on the pavements and smiled in secret.

He took her arm and they leapt from the bus.

'I'll show you where I work!' he shouted becoming swiftly separated from her. And when she caught up, he marched off again with long strides towards the National Gallery over the far side of Trafalgar Square. He cut through the crowds like a knife. She had to run.

He stopped suddenly by the railings in the north-west corner. 'Here!' He flung his arms wide.

'Here?'

'Sometimes.' He laughed. (He laughed like a girl.) 'I'll show you!'

He fumbled in his pockets and then with surprising agility dropped to his knees and began to draw with some chalk on the pavement. He worked quickly, choosing from a range of coloured chalks he cradled in his left palm. People gathered round squeezing together for warmth. He drew broad-leaved jungle plants, a passion flower, macaws and yellow monkeys with flat faces.

Leaning back on his heels, he flung his arms wide. Coins spun and rattled to the stone.

They counted them together. 'Twelve shillings and tenpence,' he said. 'You shall have a buffet supper for your birthday.' And he took her to the jellied eel stall alongside St Martin's. It was then he said his name was Freddy. She said he could call her Garbie because that's what her friends called her though Beryl Veronica was her proper name. He hooted at Beryl Veronica. 'I'm an orphan!' she cried sharply to stop him. Her bony face showed the cold quickly and her eyes which were weak, tended to water.

'An orphan!' he repeated, taking both hands and trying to smile under the blinds of her face. He was pleased by the fact. 'So we're both casualties of war. Well that's splendid, orphans need looking after! They should look after one another.'

'War?'

'The world's war.' He drew her arm through his sinewy arm and marched her deep into the body of the crowd as though he were taking her into deep seas.

She held tightly on to her handbag.

People were singing and blowing trumpets and loosing a flurry of balloons towards the stars. Bodies, wedged hard against one another, surged forward with excitement when the rockets popped red, white and green overhead. As the bells began to strike away the old year, a great roar arose, swelled and broke and made the stars waver in their steady places.

A piper appeared in a white glare of light between the lions. He blew his windy, Highland note. A hundred thousand throats opened up in song.

> 'Should auld acquaintance be for-got
> And never brought to mind!
> Should auld acquaintance be for-got
> For the sake of auld lang syne . . .!'

Drunken, discordant, joyous, they sang and sang. And when, finally, the sound trailed raggedly away, Freddy began to sing

Happy Birthday. She couldn't hear him but she knew from the movement of his lips that that's what it was.

It was the beginning of a New Year.

The most important year of her life.

2 War

The earliest recollection Beryl had of the war which killed her father was of being dragged through a hole in the fence to the air raid shelter in the next door garden while a siren whooped and wailed.

The shelter wasn't large and had to hold all the people from two buildings – eight families there must have been in all. Her mother, who left her during the day with one of the other women while she went off to work in an aircraft components factory, would sit beneath the one table with Beryl in her lap, moaning a little and rocking gently backwards and forwards.

She remembered peering out from beneath the table at the neighbours' children who were left to clamber about and play or sleep in what little space there was.

The other men and women talked amongst themselves with a quiet, even cheery wakefulness. She was embarrassed by her mother.

After the All Clear, they would sit at the window of their upstairs room and watch the fires of London redden the sky. Once, a bomb had dropped nearby and where, one minute, three identical houses had stood neatly side by side there was a huge smoking crater crammed with splinters and the powder of people's belongings. Somebody put a hand over her eyes as she was led past.

When she was six and three-quarters, word came from Rotherbrook that she was to go there. She didn't know whether her mother were unwilling to go or hadn't been invited, but she was sent alone. She sat in a carriage amongst strange children, a label tied to her arm.

It was hard to believe that grass could stretch so far or the sky be so uninterrupted. Space, passing beyond the window, blew and ballooned about her until she felt herself slipping from the curving edge of the world. She had to be put forcibly off the train, her small fingers torn from the safe barrier of the door.

She was collected by Aunt Cissy who had a pony and trap waiting. She tried to make the child stroke the pony's nose but she was afraid to. Aunt Cissy was sweet and powdery and hypnotically pretty. She kept smiling down at Beryl, her head lost in the occasional dazzle of sun, but the child, clutching a pillowcase, containing her clothes, forgot to smile back.

Bumpily they trotted past trees still heavily leaved. The air was crisp and gold. She smelt earth and animals. She smelt silence. She saw a cloud of black birds settle on plough land and feared her relatives would speak a language she didn't understand. Her aunt's face and hands were brown and the skin of foreigners, she knew, was brown.

Aunt Cissy's jogging head was lowered to meet hers and whisper: 'Don't mention Daddy to your grandmother. Poor grandmother's not well.' The trap bumped violently over a rut in the road and Aunt Cissy's smile was knocked a little awry. 'We shall be at the house soon. There are lots of other children.'

The house was huge, like a hotel. It was pale, creamy yellow and square with white edges and great white globes on each corner of the roof. A plant with pale buttery flowers grew round the door which had been left, to Beryl's horror, wide open. A sparkling ball of tears stuck in her throat.

As the trap was led away behind the house, two large curly dogs bounded out of the door. She screamed and buried her face against her aunt's legs.

Two strong hands held her but she could smell the hot, meaty breath of the dogs and a wet nose pushed against the back of her knees.

'They like you!' she heard her aunt say. But one of them had her pillowcase between its teeth.

'Say hello to Brutus and Caesar!'

Aunt Cissy gave up and tried to lift her but both dogs and Beryl hung on to the pillowcase.

'Drop it Caesar, there's a good boy! Drop it.'

Then more voices, younger and giggling: 'Drop it! Drop it!'

The dogs let go and she shot up in her aunt's arms, her legs dangling like a puppet's.

Below, a group of children formed a ring, staring upwards while the dogs ran round in excited, wagging circles.

'Quentin, Robin, say hello to your cousin!'

Two boys, one about eight, one about ten moved forward from the little group. The taller of the two had long, black hair which fell in a slippery forelock.

The other boy was plumper and more like his mother. The tall one shook his hair from his eyes and said, 'How do you do,' in a small, distant voice.

She stared down.

'You're an evacuee!' cried the younger one catching sight of her label. He sounded indignant.

'Beryl's your cousin, darling.'

'She's an evacuee,' the small boy repeated to his brother, then turning back to his mother demanded angrily, 'Which room is she going in?'

'Tea first. Take Beryl's luggage will you Quen?'

He took the pillowcase stretched out to him as though it were a dead cat.

Nanny came to them in the hall and seized Beryl from her aunt's arms. 'Oh, what a peaky thing!' She set the child down and fell on her knees in front of her. 'Let's get some of these things off so the air can get at you.' And she unfastened the pixie hood, the navy raincoat, the pink cardigan, the brown cardigan and the tartan scarf. 'Deary me, it must be winter all year long in London.' The hugely magnifying lenses of her glasses flashed and capsized with laughter.

During nursery tea, formal introductions were made. She was shown to the other four children and they were shown to her. There was Trevor, Billy, Jean and Joyce. Trevor and Jean were brother and sister, aged ten and nine respectively. Billy had impetigo and a cast in one eye and Joyce, who was the same age as Beryl, had a funny little old face and a runny nose. They all came from Stepney and had been living at Rother-

brook for over three months. Trevor was their leader. He had
two broken front teeth. The only other child was her youngest
cousin, an eighteen-month-old girl with yellow curls and enormous brown eyes, called Victoria.

Quentin was not as strong as Trevor but he was far cleverer;
he could already wound with his tongue.

'We're all one big family,' pronounced Aunty Cissy when
she delivered Beryl to Nanny at the tea table. 'Move up a little,
Robin.'

Robin squeezed himself one inch further along the bench,
and buried his face in a mug of milk.

'That's right, you sit alongside of me,' crooned Nanny putting Victoria on her lap and then moved herself into an uncomfortably small space so that Beryl could sit between her
and Robin. The four Stepney children sat on the opposite side
their faces blank as pebbles.

'Billy's playing with himself again,' observed Quentin.

Beryl's eczema flared and spread.

'Have a sandwich dear.' Nanny dropped a small white square
on Beryl's plate. She glared at Quentin and then at Billy.

There was something slippery and unpleasant in her sandwich. Beryl tried to make her mouth look as though it were
moving without actually chewing or swallowing anything but
Nanny wasn't fooled by her.

'What is it? What is it? Not eating!' she squawked and,
picking up the bitten remnant of sandwich, wagged it in Beryl's
face drawing her own plump downy face close to the child's.
The wheedling smile exposed grey, gold and yellow teeth. 'You
do want me to love you. You don't want to make me cross ... ?'

The child stared. She swallowed the slippery pulp.

Nanny had a wonderful way with children.

They were all bathed together, the girls. Clear, hot water
came out of the taps. They were each lathered in turn with
a huge cake of yellow soap which smelt of surgeries. Nanny
rubbed it over Beryl's hair too and dug into her scalp with
powerful fingers. 'Keep your eyes closed!' she commanded too
late, but the child was crying already in a mewing, restricted
way. Jean and Joyce, splashing one another disconsolately,

ignored her until Nanny went out to fetch their nighties, then Jean inquired of her if she'd weed in the bath. Beryl didn't want to answer these girls who were not her cousins. Joyce, dug her toe nail into Beryl's leg and smiled.

'Your eyes can't *still* be stinging,' reproved Nanny, her glasses misting abruptly as she came back into the bathroom. Her hair was beginning to escape from the neat roll girdling her skull.

So Beryl squeezed back her tears into the great inner vessel of her misery and submitted to the strange, stiff nightie, with its scorch marks and hot cotton smell.

They were told to leave the plug in so Trevor and Billy could get in the same water, which was covered with little floating putty planets of scum. Then they ran down the chilly passage to their room and were made to kneel beside their camp beds. Beryl, copying the others, peeped through her fingers to see what they did and muttered in the same sober, meaningless way.

On the white chair beside her bed, the old pillowcase had been emptied and folded. Awaiting her cue from the others, she climbed into bed and while they bounced and shrieked, she sneaked the pillowcase beneath the sheets and pressing it to her tummy with one hand, she stuck her other thumb in her mouth, turned her back to the others and lay in a stiff, sickle shape between sheets that smelt faintly of old ladies' cupboards.

Her hair was pulled into two thin, taut little plaits so that there were always a few hairs making her wince at the nape of her neck. Her clothes were washed and softened into colours that London water had never penetrated. She was given proper gloves with fingers and forced to eat fresh vegetables, exotically strange to her. She was always the third in any group, which-ever one she went to, the Stepney girls, the Stepney boys or her cousins, and they always knew more secrets than she. Yet the tearful inner whine of wanting to see her mother grew weaker and weaker.

'When we're sure the bombing's over you can go home,' said Aunty Cissy.

'You just be grateful you're in a nice safe place with plenty of food,' said Nanny.

'You just be grateful.'

She found a way of pleasing her cousins.

'And the bombs just blew up the house like that,' she cried, flinging her hands wide apart. 'And arms and legs and heads fell all over the floor and blood ran down the stairs and a woman with bits of glass stuck in her face ran down the street screaming and a man was running behind her with all his clothes on fire. He just burned up as he was running, just burned up into bits of ashes.'

'Did you see Jerry? Did they shoot him down,' cried Quentin, leaping up and down with excitement and hurling grenades at the walnut tree.

'Oh yes, I saw him looking down out of his plane laughing and then whizz! bang! . . . it exploded and all the different pieces of him flew in the air and fell on London. They found his head with the smile still on in the garden next door.'

'*Wizard!*' shrieked Quentin and directed his machine gun along the advancing line of infantry before flinging his arms open and falling dead.

The Stepney children sat on the grass picking their noses in suspicious absorption. They'd been badly bombed too but never as badly as that. And if they tried to pretend they had you could always tell it was a lie.

'You're just a dirty liar,' sneered Beryl scornfully when Trevor said he knifed Jerry with his own bare hands. 'You tell awful stories. You'll burn in hell!' And she advanced on him with dreadful rolling eyes.

'Liar yourself,' he muttered without any trace of conviction.

Those were the best times. She was quite willing to be a Junkers pilot herself and be shot down, or brought in for questioning. Sometimes she was allowed into the trenches behind the bean poles to nurse her cousins' wounds. Jean and Joyce seemed more interested in practising handstands or dressing up.

Things would break up when Trevor and Billy, sick of firing

mortal shots and discovering their opponents wouldn't fall down, threw themselves bodily into battle.

These fights were often violent and sometimes bloody. Billy was easily defeated which meant that Robin and Quentin together could bruise Trevor quite badly. When it was two against one like that Beryl suffered spasms of guilt at cheering her cousins on. 'Bash him! *Kill* him!' she cried feebly, her knuckles to her mouth and a thin trickle of pee escaping down the inside of her leg.

Once she felt her plaits seized and twisted round so that her head swivelled to a gallows angle.

'Bleeding watch out,' hissed Jean quietly and with a short, final tug, let her go.

Aunty Cissy, a white blur at the drawing room windows waved and smiled at her lively family, and wished Jack could be here to see them all instead of steaming towards Suez in a troopship.

All the previous summer Cissy had worked for E.N.S.A. trying to bring some amusement to the clouded faces of soldiers back from Dunkirk. Every small town and village seemed full of them – men sickened by talk of glory and idiocies of their officers. They had disturbed that blue and dazzling summer far more than the reports of parachutists landed on the Sussex downs, more than the disappearance of quiet, modest families to internment camps. It had been a relief to sit with other women of the W.V.S. making home-made bombs in the church halls.

Looking out across the lawn at the children playing their boisterous games, Cissy felt hopefully that she was doing her bit.

It was still a time of suspicion. Albert Thoroughgood, a veteran of Flanders and now of the Home Guard sat in a ditch bordering the leafy lanes winding into the village and, holding his shotgun in a menacing manner, stopped strange cyclists to ask for their identity cards.

Mrs Hogarth at the Post Office kept a sharp eye and a sharper ear open in an effort to discover who it was might have let Lord Haw Haw know Rotherbrook's church clock had stopped at a quarter to three.

Colonel Naseby-Smith wound his way up Barley Beacon every evening at ten and sat, gas mask beside him, observing through his field glasses strange lights in the night sky.

It was not a time for those who did not belong.

Beryl was arrested by Robin as a suspected Fifth Columnist and taken to his superior officer Quentin. She was locked in the potting shed for an hour and twenty minutes until everybody could be assembled for the trial. Trevor and Jean did double duty as witnesses and guards, holding the prisoner's arms firmly above the elbow.

'The prisoner is accused of behaving in a manner likely to arouse suspicion,' announced Quentin in his cold little upper class voice. He had one of his father's belts strapped diagonally across his grey jersey like a Sam Browne.

Beryl felt fingers pinch her arms and began to cry.

'Oh do shut up,' groaned Robin who sat beside Joyce on a packing case. Joyce was twisting a grey, lace-edged hanky round and round her fingers looking frightened. She sniffed and looked away as Beryl's face puckered out of shape. Billy stared out of the little ivy-darkened window by the door fulfilling his sentry duty.

'Have you got anything to say?' persisted Quentin in his merciless voice.

Tears flooded any prospect of words. What could she say when she didn't understand? She was not yet seven.

They stared at her. Stared at one another. Then stared at Quentin in the hope of some leadership.

'You've infiltrated,' said Quentin eventually, having remembered the wonderful word.

'She's what?' Trevor frowned at his leader and meeting a blank gaze, mumbled. 'Yeah. Oh, yeah,' and tightened his grip on Beryl's arm.

Though nobody knew the dictionary meaning of the word, it pulled at grudges in all their minds.

'She eats with her mouth open.' Robin.

'She cheats.' Jean.

'She sneaks.' Billy.

'She's a nuisance.' Joyce added falteringly to the list.

'You're an alien.' Quentin hit on a more official term.

Indistinctly she sobbed, 'Your Mum's my aunty.'

That seemed to enrage her elder cousin whose face purpled. 'You're *not* on our side!' he screamed.

Trevor decided to twist her arm behind her rather than merely hold it. Then fear, rage, pain and panic combined to make her scream and fight.

Robin leapt towards her and clamped a hand over her mouth. It smelt of white mice. '*Shut up* or we'll kill you!'

'It's nearly tea time,' whimpered Joyce, her eyes pink with gum but nobody heard her. They were waiting for Beryl's tears and struggles to subside.

She became quieter as Robin's hand closed over her nose as well as her mouth, and finally stood still, gazing beseechingly at her cold, fierce cousin.

'We shan't kill you,' acceded Quentin generously, pulling at his belt. 'You shall be deported back to London.'

An uncertain tremor passed among the others as they wondered how this might be done. Billy concentrated on the view from the window hoping no one would ask him. There was a sense of shifting and Robin dropped his hand from Beryl's wet face turning to hear what his brother would say.

'She can't *walk* . . .' said somebody.

'Of course not stupid!' Quentin didn't even bother to look who'd raised the point. 'Between us we could save up for a ticket.'

'Will you let go of me please?' whispered Beryl through salty lips. She was freed and stood humbly, bewildered, while her future was considered. She didn't understand, but there was a terrible grief lodged in her ribs. It stuck there like a dead bird.

'She's too little . . .'

'She'll have to keep saying,' decided Quentin, pushing his fingers abruptly through his hair. 'She'll have to keep saying that she wants to go home. You tell my mother,' he repeated to his cousin, 'that you want your own mother. And then they'll send you away.'

'I don't know,' muttered Beryl, meaning she didn't understand. Her lower lip trembled.

Dimly, the gong summoned them to tea, all but Beryl and Quentin leapt in response. The shed door flew open and sun poured in making the dust dance.

'Do you understand?'

'Yes.'

'Do you promise?'

'Yes.'

'Because if you don't we'll do something much worse.'

'Yes.'

'Ah Nanny!'

Cissy stopped the countrywoman as she carried linen across the landing. 'Nanny, does little Beryl seem homesick to you?'

'Homesick! What would she be homesick for? Hasn't she got all a child could want? She's a funny little creature, that's true, but no, Mrs Pendleton, nothing to fret yourself over.'

'I'm wondering if my mother-in-law may have said something to her.'

'I keep them clean apart, ma'am.'

'Well then, we must try and be kinder.'

And Cissy, preoccupied with other states of war, went for a practise run on her bicycle to see if she could improve on her record between Rotherbrook and Pidditch, the distance she would have to cover if the telegraph wires were ever cut down.

Old Mrs Pendleton sat in her drawing room on the first floor and stared out at the Stepney boys swinging from the walnut tree. She was in a state of rage. She was always in a state of rage. Generally her rage was directed towards the German race who started wars that took her menfolk from her. But sometimes it was directed towards her younger son for letting the family down.

She doted on Rikki and had often, over the years, laughed

long and bawdily when news reached her of his ticklings and kissing. She had been hard pressed to conceal her pride when he was caught at the age of thirteen with a maid some six years his senior. The maid was sacked. But the woman Dotty was a different matter. She came from the village where the nature of gossip was hard to control. She worked in the pub. She refused to leave when pregnant and Rikki seemed powerless to make her.

When she'd heard there was to be a child, old Mrs Pendleton's hair dropped out in the space of a fortnight and the scratchy red wig she now wore only aggravated her rage. She found to her fury that she no longer belonged to an age where mistakes of this kind were ignored to a point of polite oblivion. Unable to expel the girl, she helped, indirectly, to expel Rikki who disappeared, bound for the Far East. She didn't want that either. Nor did she welcome Jack's insistence that now Rikki had gone the child should be cared for by them.

Eventually Dotty had returned to London and old Mrs Pendleton submitted, ungracefully, to the sending of occasional parcels containing outgrown clothes and a few discreetly bought National Savings Certificates. But bringing the child to the house like this, however, brought her rage to a point which went beyond enjoyment. Had her body only been as strong as her spirit she would have built barricades across the lawn and patrolled the wire herself.

As it was she had to try and content herself by watching at a low, crouched level from her window, waiting her opportunity to direct a fossilizing beam into the child's straying eyes.

She resented the child's skinny, yellow unspectacular looks. A sallow, nothing child, the dry, evaporated dust of Rikki.

From time to time she shouted at Cissy (and convinced herself) that this experience would kill her. She saw yellow fumes surround the child and on dull days believed this poisonous glow would seep through the house, along the passages and into the unprotected labyrinths of her brain while she slept.

During the night she kept her bedside lamp on. During the

day she summoned Quentin to her room and loosed thin streams of spittle in his ear.

'Are you sure you're really trying?' asked Quentin, exasperated. It seemed to him ages since he'd set his scheme in operation and nothing had come of it.

'I want my Mummy,' whined Beryl obligingly.

'Damnation!' seethed Quentin turning away from her and kicking furiously at a tussock of grass. He sent an army of red ants streaming off in battle order.

'Would you like me to do a double somersault?'

'No thanks.'

'Would you like to have one of my elastic bands to chew?'

'*No!*' He paused. He relented. 'Oh, all right, I'll have one for my catapult.'

Gratefully she untwisted a band from her plait.

'I tell you what ...' said her cousin, amicably. (He was always more charitable when they were alone together.) 'You can be our prisoner of war.'

'Thank you,' said Beryl, flattered.

'I'll report it to the other officers.'

'Yes, please.'

There was a meeting of officers in the loft over the harness room. They agreed she could start by cleaning up.

And so, as autumn grew chill, she swept their floor, polished their shoes, built little smouldering fires, found matches to light them with, took the blame when caught and allowed them to take her knickers off so they could have a good, close look.

Cissy, kissing her sons goodnight, touched their clean, pink faces with her fingers and smiled. 'I'm so glad,' she murmured, 'to see you looking after your little cousin so nicely. She seems so much happier at last.'

And she kissed them both again fondly on their burning faces.

By November Cissy was finding it increasingly difficult to keep the house warm. She shooed the family into fewer and fewer rooms. They all ate a high tea together in the breakfast room and the children were allowed at last to bring their toys in the drawing room. Being more nearly under her eye as a result, their behaviour towards one another became less openly cruel. Billy broke a vase, but otherwise the arrangement worked quite well until they were hit in slow and steady succession by chicken pox.

For Beryl, to be ill at Rotherbrook was unlike being ill anywhere else. It meant having your pillows piled so high you could sit without sliding. It meant hot drinks and little trays with everything you needed on them including a salt and pepper all to yourself. It meant there was always someone to answer when you called and it meant being regarded in a special, extra way. Illness, the child understood, exerted a tyranny of privileges.

Dotty's way was quite different.

Dotty complained she couldn't go to work if Beryl was ill and then took her down to the surgery on the corner and sat inside its dark green light to get a bottle of something.

Then she dressed her daughter in her own old brown tartan dressing gown, spread a rubber sheet beneath her, asked Mrs Tilly to look in from time to time, and went off to the factory. 'We need the money,' she said.

She left a raw carrot (to help Beryl see in the dark) and a pan of cold porridge on the gas ring.

Only once was the child really afraid. There was the early, warning howl of dogs telling her that planes were on the way. She heard the engines steadily approaching and then the tearing sound of a bomb falling before the explosion. Afterwards there were bells, bells of all kinds like the keening of women.

Mrs Tilly came to see her.

'It's a good way off,' she said gently, parting the curtains a little to let a sliver of grey light illumine the angles of furniture. 'What's been passing through your queer little head today?' She thought Beryl an odd scrap.

'My dad in the jungle ...'

'Your dad ... In the jungle is he?' Mrs Tilly gave a small breathy laugh.

'It's so hot there you sweat till you're wet all over. That's what eyebrows are for.'

'What are they for?'

'That.' The reason escaped her. It was something to do with sweat. It said so in one of Dotty's books.

Dotty's books were magazines filched, borrowed and bought from anywhere. They lined and carpeted the small brown room. *Picture Post*, *National Geographic*, *Girl's Crystal*, *Doctor's Weekly* ... Dotty would sit for hours turning the familiar pages, letting the child in on her absent dreams. Their world was full of the strangest things – Yap islanders with blackened teeth, princes, pagodas and the dragons of Bhutan.

'The jungle eh?' tittered Mrs Tilly.

'It's full of snakes. As long as trains and poisonous. And flowers that eat insects.'

'Go on!'

'It's true!'

'You're a funny one.'

Mrs Tilly wished the child would cry. It wasn't natural to be left alone like this and not do. Her own had swung on her skirts and clung on to their dummies till they went to school. She couldn't touch this child. If she'd *cried* perhaps she might have been able to, but not otherwise. There was something funny about the eyes she thought, that made you keep your distance. She could not, just could not, stretch out instinctively and cuddle the little girl.

'You're a funny one,' said Nanny who was paid to look after the children. She wiped her face and plaited her hair and read her stories.

Her bedspread heavy with books, Beryl found she could read. It was quite sudden and mysterious. Quentin, who was the next to go down with chicken pox, demanded she read to him, however haltingly.

'Golly, you are *slow*!' he kept sighing, but he didn't want her to stop.

And so to the astonishment of Mrs Horseforth – who was meant to come in daily to teach the children but was so baffled by the vast range in age and ability that she resorted chiefly to reading out loud for hours at a time – Beryl began to flash through her Beacon Readers, books III, IV and V in a way that caused quite a stir.

A whisper went round. 'The child has real ability.'

Old ranks eased open. They were delighted. It was a relief to find virtue in the child, especially for Cissy who was troubled spasmodically by guilt. She neglected the children she knew, devoting herself mainly to running the house and garden. She kept two dozen chickens and a sizeable vegetable patch, did all the cooking herself and spent what time was left attending to W.V.S. duties in the passionate hope that anything she could do, might, in some indirect fashion, help keep Jack alive until all this was over.

The boys, she knew, should be away at school but she was frightened of losing her sons as well as her husband, she put the decision off and prevaricated in her letters.

As Christmas approached and the worst of the chicken pox subsided Cissy was seized by a growing anger (brought on by the season of family gathering) that she, at thirty-three and sexually at her peak, should be without the man she loved to madness. It gave her a wild kind of energy.

The Stepneys were restored to their families for a brief holiday, but no reply was received from Dotty. Extravagantly, Cissy used up the petrol supply to drive to London and track her down.

'I think she's got a man friend,' said Mrs Tilly guardedly when questioned by Cissy. Cissy's hair seemed to drift in electrical wisps.

'I rather think I recall her saying she'd be spending Christmas at Frinton. No, I don't have no address.'

But a parcel with an indistinguishable postmark arrived for Beryl from her mother. It contained a pink doll's brush, mirror and comb and though Beryl had no dolls of her own, she was proud of her present and kept it by her.

Pheasants, bagged illicitly by an unknown admirer, hung in the larder. One of their own little fir trees from the woodland was brought into the drawing room to save lighting a fire in the hall. Cissy allowed herself more than her usual number of dry sherries and staggered, a little drunkenly, round the children's bedrooms in the dark, muddling some of the presents which led to bitter argument in the morning.

'Hush now!' Nanny cried, bursting in on the battle. 'Nothing's to be allowed to spoil today.' And quite involuntarily her eyes rose briefly upward in the direction of old Mrs Pendleton's sitting room above.

For old Mrs Pendleton wouldn't be kept away for Christmas. She demanded to be carried downstairs by Cissy and Potterton who was at least as old as she was and was nearly killed by the effort.

The children tried not to be seen peeping and the dogs slunk away.

Old Mrs Pendleton's gaze went round the table like a radar beam. Her appearance was alarming.

Once (three years ago when she'd been told she'd never walk without sticks again) she ordered Potterton to take all her outdoor clothes and burn them in full view of her bedroom window. Potterton, who was terrified of the old lady, had carried out the order before anyone could prevent it.

She wore, together with the violently ginger wig, swinging jade ear-rings and a pink and black silk kimono. She'd gone to some trouble with her face which was separated into starkly red and white areas.

Her eye went round the table once, then twice on its silencing axis.

Even Quentin turned away to concentrate on his mother's hopelessly inadequate carving, flicking the barest glance at his cousin who sat on his mother's left hand.

Cissy, head down, sensed a moment of imminent explosion and struggled to say something meaningless. Too late.

'So *this* is the child then!'

Old Mrs Pendleton gripped the edge of the table, her rings clashing savagely. Everybody but Beryl turned to look at her. The little girl studied the stuffed bowel of the bird in front of her.

'That's not fair!'

Cissy stood rigidly, the colour sweeping from her face, carving knife and fork raised aggressively in her hands. The two women stared at one another.

Robin began a tearful kind of tittering. Nanny began putting potatoes on people's plates. This subdued activity went on beneath a taut canopy of white fire.

The old woman's fist came down on the table scattering spoons and forks across the rich mahogany. A dog rose from the fire, growling. 'Quite deliberately ...!' she cracked on a series of unsteady registers. 'Quite deliberately you've tried to defy me!'

A worm of interest stirred in Beryl.

She gazed at the old lady. She continued to gaze as the full venom of expression was turned on her. She didn't realize that she was the object of anger.

The jade ear-rings swung like Chinese lanterns.

'That's just not fair,' repeated Cissy, frozen into her pose. The carving knife trembled slightly. 'This is *Christmas*!'

'So!'

'Sprouts?' inquired Nanny and without awaiting the answer, placed three noisily on Mrs Pendleton's plate.

'The season of goodwill eh? Goodwill towards whom?' She flashed and sparkled, an outrageous piece of pantomime. 'This is my house!'

'You're spoiling it for the children.' Cissy was being brave. She resumed her carving with murderous vigour.

'*My* house!'

Beryl felt hungry.

'I want the bastard out!'

Robin's smothered giggles touched an hysterical note.

'How dare you!'

Cissy was quivering. She had never dared to speak to the old woman like this.

Beryl couldn't understand why Nanny was picking her out of her chair and carrying her from the room. She hadn't done anything naughty. She began to struggle but Nanny's strong arms closed round her. Hot tears spurted. 'I want my dinner!' she screamed. '*Lunch!*' hissed Nanny, and swept from the room.

Later, Nanny brought her a plateful of food to the nursery.

She cut it all up in little bits although Beryl could manage perfectly well by herself. Nanny speared things with a fork and seemed angry so she swallowed everything obediently, without enjoyment and stared at the grey hairs on Nanny's chin to avoid her eyes.

She was visited like an invalid by everybody. There seemed a great deal of weeping which surged through the house at intervals throughout the day like a distant tide. They were not cross with her, but it was all very muddling.

A sense of wounded importance flowered in her.

A few weeks later, Cissy received two letters. One from Jack, four months out of date, telling her of a desert battle won, clearly El Alamein. The other was from Dotty. It had been written with a failing fountain pen and lacked full stops. It seemed to say that Dotty was in danger of being conscripted into the Navy and needed to prove she was a mother.

There was news on the wireless of two air raids in London, but everyone knew the blitz had been over for almost a year. Even the people who slept in the Underground only did it out of habit.

Cissy decided Beryl should go home.

The news brought no joy. Beryl had grown used to the dogs although they made her sneeze. The house, draughty, uncarpeted though it was, brimmed with a noisy activity that made her feel included by life. But she said nothing and submitted weakly to the extra scrubbing Nanny gave her before leaving. It was a scrubbing meant to *last*, said Nanny fiercely, working away down the parting line of the pink scalp.

3   1943–45

The London she returned to was in ruins.

The houses, amputated from their neighbours, stood nakedly exposing mass taste in wallpapers and fireplaces. Shops, though their windows were boarded up, were still in business. Mr Spiggott, the corner grocer had a notice on his window which said: 'You can't see from the outside so come inside and have a look!'

In the streets, queues of blue-faced women stretched right round corners and became confused with other queues waiting for buses that had long ago deserted timetables. The people were tired; many wore black. The gayest sight of all were the exotic bands of soldiers wandering the streets. There were black men by the score.

Dotty had a new boyfriend, a Pole, and a new job as a hospital cleaner. (She had panicked unnecessarily about the Navy.) The components factory had moved to some spot outside Oxford and tried to take her with it, but Dotty had had a bellyful of the country and preferred the city which had life as well as death.

It meant she worked shifts, sometimes nights so she was more often home during the day. Except that then she wanted to go to bed. Sometimes she took Beryl into bed with her. Sometimes Maxy.

He was a jaunty little man with a huge grin, gold teeth and a clumping boot. His foot had been blown away from the ankle and when he left his funny boot off and used a crutch instead he could swing about like a monkey. His English was frightful but he bought books and chewing gum for Beryl and was always giving her threepenny bits to go out and play.

She came home from school in Stoke Newington at about half past four. The little ones came out at a quarter past three but she had to wait in the playground for the juniors to finish so she could go home on the buses with one of the bigger girls, Madge Duckworth. It was Madge who turned a blind eye when Stanley Ball and Pattie Stevens cut Beryl's plaits off.

'Oh my giddy aunt!' cried Beryl's teacher Mrs Crabbe the following day. '*What* has happened to your hair?'

'Please Miss. Nothing Miss.' She wriggled her head on one shoulder and pulled at the cracked, singed curls Dotty had wound round the tongs.

'Ah!' breathed Mrs Crabbe and clutched the wounded head to her stomach which was as yielding and richly covered as a Rotherbrook cushion. Beryl could tell Mrs Crabbe about her cousins and be believed. She let her draw pictures of houses with gardens that held fictional trees and horses.

'That's right! Get it all down!' urged Mrs Crabbe, cherishing the child's vital imaginative experience. And her fingers fluttered, each one adorned by a different stone. She made the children repeat the names after her.

'Cornelian!'

'Topaz!'

'Onyx!'

'Sapphire!'

'Rose quartz!'

'Garnet!'

'Moss agate!'

'Pearl!'

They were very fortunate at Cross St Elementary School to have Mrs Crabbe looking after the little ones. She was a widow who stood out among the bitten grey vistas of Clapton and Stoke Newington because of her long amber beads and the Indian silk scarves she wore (two or three at a time), twisted around unusual parts of her person. She thrilled her children to breathlessness and worried Mr Vincent sick. But then, times

54

were desperate as he whimpered to his Deputy Head.

Mrs Crabbe's mission in middle age was to bring colour into the lives of poor children.

'There's too much grey in the world!' she cried in a rich contralto which she also used, more unreliably, for singing. She liked to sing 'What is Life' with a very wobbly initial 'Wh.a.a.a.t ...' while the children painted or sewed. Occasionally she would struggle along the street behind her portable gramophone which she wound up vigorously, rattling like a bead curtain, so the children could listen to Elizabethan songs sung by the counter tenor Alfred Deller. 'I'm here to teach you the best *kind* of envy ... a longing for *quality* in life my dears!' She flashed and sparkled like a beacon in their lives.

'What do I want you to learn, dears?'

'Envy?'

'No, no, no!'

'Beauty?' squawked the East Enders.

'*That's* better!'

Extraordinary gobbets of knowledge poured from her chalice. Mrs Crabbe, who had never taught before she was fifty and never even thought about it as she'd travelled the world with her late husband Ernest (a big noise in asbestos), had received a call shortly after Ernest collapsed from cirrhosis in Rawalpindi. Perhaps the voices who'd made the call intended that Mrs Crabbe should stay in India to teach poor children, but she'd preferred to return to England.

'It's not the usual qualification ...' faltered Mr Vincent.

'I have a *gift.*'

And so it was.

Her closest attention was claimed by the quiet ones like Beryl. The ones on the silent perimeter of the classrooms. These, hypnotically, persistently, she coaxed into confidence until they emerged from their shells delicate and transparent like small hermit crabs.

Dromedaries, dodos, dragon prows and ice palaces. All were true.

'I've had a letter from a mother inquiring about singing

peacocks, Mrs Crabbe . . .' Mr Vincent waved a sheet of lined paper. 'It's caused quite a family argument.'

He laughed uncomfortably. 'Er ... do peacocks *sing* exactly ...?'

'To those who have ears to hear.'

'Yes, I see.' He met her brilliant smile and gave his pencil sharpener a turn.

'We are,' he observed, 'in the *fact* business . . .'

'My children are not short on fact, Mr Vincent.'

They were not. Their grasp of political and military affairs was rare in seven and eight year olds. Mrs Crabbe devoted half an hour daily to current events.

The war became more than London rubble, absent fathers, coupons and the sound of sirens, to Form Three. The Germans were driven out of the north of Africa. The Allied forces were in Sicily. By August, the Russians were pushing the Germans back from yet another frontier. They listened with shiny eyes, hair prickling with excitement. And intertwined with these events across curved oceans, they were taught of expectations at home.

'We are growing wise ... we must learn to care deeply for one another and to fight for one another ... the sick, the old, the have-nots.'

The phrases, with their rippling repetition made a distant sense. It was *their* world which was to be re-furnished. The bulldozers were already thrusting into the rubbish.

'I'm not here to make you *happy* ...!' Scarves cracked like patriotic flags. 'Not *happy* ...! Only to teach you to expect better ...'

Acts of Parliament were going to work like wands. They would all wake one day and find themselves warm, well-fed and educated. The children dwelt on the dreams. Some of them couldn't imagine palaces but Beryl knew exactly how it was to wake with a pony in the field beneath your window and have someone else to wash your face for you with a soapy flannel and warm water.

'Not *happy*!'

Mrs Crabbe faced her rows of pale children with their

scabby knees and knuckles and she probably told them the names of things but they forgot and remembered only that they had once sat there and she had made them a firm promise.

'The poor, the deprived and the half-alive will be brought to a new dignity.'

Even the men in the buildings talked buzzingly about it. They said simply 'When this bloody war is over ...' But a child passing and hearing them, knew what they meant. One of Mrs Crabbe's children anyway.

Maxy and her mother were often asleep when Beryl crept in. Dotty, whose breathing trouble had been inherited by her daughter, lay with her mouth open, rattling faintly with phlegm. Around her nose, the skin was a greyish colour. Her closed eyes looked like bruises. Maxy, on the other hand, slept neatly and quietly, his bald head, fine sun-streaked hair and tranquillity, making him look like a large baby.

She could reach the tap and fill the kettle but dared not light the gas. So she sat and waited, reading in a whispered monotone to herself till the tiny vibrations of her presence woke them up. The room smelt of sour bodies.

She liked the way Maxy woke. Instantly and with a delighted shout of welcome for the new day (or night). He whirled his strong brown arms and let her wrinkle up the blankets to examine his smooth shin stump of a leg.

'Maxy's looking after me while your dad's away,' Dotty explained, turning the bottom of her hair under with curling tongs to make herself look like Veronica Lake. She stared at herself in the yellow, freckled mirror and thought she was beginning to look more than twenty-eight. She pinned a spray of artificial lilies-of-the-valley, to the shoulder of her brown jumper and added, 'When you see your Aunty Betty, you'd better not say. She's funny about foreigners.'

'When's he coming home?' asked Beryl, meaning her dad, whom she'd never seen.

'When this bloody war's over,' Dotty lied. She didn't expect Rikki to come and claim them. She'd have to say he'd been killed whether he had or not, but he very likely would be. He was a crazy bloke. She'd not had a letter for over two years.

Anyway ... That was life.

'You speak quite nice now,' she observed, nodding at her daughter's reflection over her shoulder in the mirror. 'It's important, speaking nice. And you're a better colour than what you was ... Would you like to go back there?'

'It wasn't bad.' Dotty worked hard at her face. Beryl thought she looked lovely. Her mother flexed the strap of her canvas shoulder bag and stood, staring dreamily beyond her daughter. 'Yes, well ...' she murmured, and wished she'd got a bottle of scent she could dab on.

'We're going to the pictures,' she said suddenly. 'It's an A.' Beryl went on scribbling in the tracing book Maxy had given her. 'This bleeding war,' said Dotty.

She knew Maxy would be gone one day and she wanted as much of him as she could get now, never mind his funny leg.

'Give us a kiss,' she lowered her cheek absently to the child.

Dotty smelt of stale oversweet powder and dandruff. It was hard to see that at eighteen she'd had a sleepy kind of desirability and a slenderness that hadn't sharpened off into ill-fed angles. Women like Dotty lose their youth very quickly.

'When you're a bit bigger, you'll be able to go to the pictures,' she told Beryl good naturedly. *She* went whenever she could. If Maxy was away somewhere and the child was still at school, she'd set the alarm to go off to a matinee. She'd seen *Brief Encounter* four times, *Now, Voyager* six times and *Gone with the Wind* no less than nine times.

'When can I go?'

'When you're bigger.'

'When's that?'

'Oh, I don't know! Ten years, twelve years maybe, I don't know.' She lost interest and brushed a scattering of powder off her lapel.

'Oh.'

'I'll bring you some chips back when I come.' Dotty tried to make amends. She stood tapping her foot and fidgeting with any button or strap that came within her grasp. She'd forgotten what she was waiting for. She yawned enormously revealing a jawful of rusting teeth.

Then she remembered she'd arranged to meet Maxy outside the Rialto. 'Right, I'm off!' she cried, stumbling forward in her flapping peep-toe shoes.'I should keep on saying your prayers ... you never know.'

And Beryl left alone, kept tracing in the light of the gas fire until it guttered out. Then, as her mother had told her never to light it on her own, she got into bed to keep warm, putting her dressing gown over her clothes and going to sleep until Maxy and Dotty returned at ten o'clock with a bagful of chips for her. Dotty made her get out of bed and undress properly in front of the fire while Maxy laughed and tried to tickle her.

A curtain had been hung on a clothes line across the room between her bed and theirs, but the sounds couldn't be completely kept from her.

When the creaking and grunting began again, Beryl pressed one ear against the hump of her shoulder and crushed her knuckles against the other. It was a sound she'd never heard until she'd lived in the country a little while and now she knew it came from animals.

Maxy, who was a kind man in many ways, with a wife and children adrift somewhere in Central Europe, pitied the child. Long after he'd grown bored with Dotty, he continued to come simply because he felt somebody should take an interest in Beryl. He couldn't explain this to Dotty, because his English wouldn't reach round so complicated and diplomatic a conversation but he decided, inside himself in his own language, that Garbie should have a pet.

He arrived one Saturday morning when the room was curiously light with reflections from the snow outside and came in full of stamping noises and laughter as he unbuttoned his greatcoat with one hand. In the other he swung a package wrapped around in newspaper.

'Ber-r-yl!' he called, rolling the 'r' in her name affectionately. 'See!' Gently he put the package down on the table and delicately began to peel away the newspaper.

She flew to the table speechless with rapture as he showed

her the little cage with its rustling ball of hay in one corner. He crouched down so that his eye level was the same as hers and putting a thick arm round her, pressed her face to his. The skin was rough, icy and burning all at the same time. 'You love him, yes?' he urged, grinning and nodding eagerly. She sat on his good knee and stared in the cage waiting for the lump of hay to resolve itself.

'Allezoop!' Maxy tapped the side and a white mouse shot out, bunched up and quivering. Its ears swivelled backwards and its pink nose moved hysterically to detect the enemy.

'What d'you say, Beryl?' said Dotty coming up behind them eating a thick slice of bread and dripping.

'Thank you, Maxy.' Then, fearfully: 'Is it all right, Mum?'

'I s'pose.' Dotty shrugged, and ran her tongue over her upper teeth to clear away scraps of dough. Then, laughing in her cracked way, she too, dropped to her knees and gazed with them at the trembling creature. 'Eh . . .' she breathed. 'What a little korker,' and busily she began to roll pellets of her bread and stick them through the wire. The mouse shot back in its hay and stayed there all morning, but Dotty couldn't be taken away from it. She pulled a chair up to the table and stretching her elbows either side of the cage, stared hopefully until it was time to go to work.

Both of them gave up all their cheese ration for the mouse, breaking it into daily crumbs because they couldn't think what else it would eat. It was called Maxy after its donor and died a week later because Dotty forgot to give it anything to drink.

They couldn't invite Maxy to the funeral as he'd vanished. Dotty said he must have joined that long march of men to the south coast. The second front it was. Then she remembered Maxy couldn't have marched anywhere on his stump, and was so overcome with hysterical laughter she quite forgot to be either sad or angry at his absence.

In school, under the passionate eye of Mrs Crabbe, the children watched the events of the year mount climatically.

There was a sense of something afoot throughout spring and

early summer; secret movements of men and vehicles, curious structures on the south-east coast, a shortage of trains. Without ever speaking to one another, total strangers felt bound by a colossal secret and smiled at one another with the pleasure of keeping it.

Tensely, at Aunty Betty's bullying insistence, Beryl knitted a slow succession of khaki balaclava helmets for her father in the steaming jungles of Burma until the bubble burst.

And when, finally it did burst, it was D-Day and she could put her knitting needles down; there was no need for anyone to keep up any kind of pretence a moment longer. People were able to laugh openly.

The excitement was greatly added to by Mrs Crabbe's continual promise of a performance to come. A double act it was, Beveridge and Butler. Again and again, she spoke of the pair, conjurors or jugglers they seemed to be. Their stomachs tight with excitement, the children waited for the next new thing to happen.

It came, to everyone's surprise, out of the clouds. In the middle of poetry writing, they paused, ink dripping in slow blobs from their lifted pens and stared upwards at a weird spluttering in the sky.

Beads and scarves flying in wild pennants, Mrs Crabbe flattened her class beneath their desks.

The menacing new bombs burst out of the clouds like locusts. By the time the school had gathered to sing Lord Dismiss Us With Thy Blessing, Mrs Crabbe's class was the smaller by twelve children. Two were dead, three injured. The others had been whisked for the second, even third time, out of London into the safe, dull valleys of Wales or the Lake District.

Dotty, gazing up at the dangerous sky, said she was blowed if she was going to be done out of her holidays again and it would take more than a bloody doodle bug to stop her.

When Beryl saw the sea for the first time it was just a sliver of silver squeezed between mud flats and an ill-tempered sky. Once a day, the tide crept in, swift and cunning, arriving in circuitous curves that made it hazardous to walk out too far across the mud in case one got cut off. And then, having left its excremental fringe of bottles, jellyfish, pulped cardboard and gritty pebbles, it slid back up the estuary to Europe.

All the same, it was the seaside, far enough north to be free of barbed wire, full of new, stinging smells and winds so strong it made the few stunted trees grow flat to the ground. The sand was dark and damp and made very good sand-castles.

Beryl's pockets became misshapen and heavy with shells.

She and Dotty were there by courtesy of Uncle Ted, an A.R.P. warden who'd winked at Dotty when she was sweeping under his bed in the hospital. He'd had flying shrapnel lodged in his skull. 'Now I've got a tin head,' he said tapping it to amuse her. It didn't sound any different to any other head to her. 'I get terrible headaches, but you've got to stay cheerful.'

He seemed cheerful in patches to Beryl. For long periods of time he'd say nothing but sit gazing at his watch on its chain weeping silent, involuntarily tears which left gummy smears at the corner of his eyes. Without him, though, Dotty would never have been able to afford the holiday.

'My dad's in the jungle. In Burma,' Beryl told him.

'Well, I bet the weather's an improvement on this!' he hooted, winking frantically. His winks, like his tears seemed out of control.

'He's socking the Japs.'

'There's only one way better to spend your time!' he shouted and stuck a hair-backed hand up Dotty's jumper.

'Oompah! Oompah! Stick it up your jumper!' He tickled Dotty till she was weak with laughter. 'Oh! You are a caution!' she wept, happy.

They were sitting in a hollow of the sand dunes with their collars turned up and the coarse grass, flattened by the wind, striking at them from time to time.

'You'll get sand in your watch!' shrieked Dotty.

'That's nothing to what you'll get!' And his winking became so rapid he had to look the other way.

He smelt of sweet, cheap hair oil and beer. He always seemed to have a bottle of beer in one pocket or another. Sometimes, both pockets of his long, navy blue raincoat. He'd brought his gas mask with him on holiday and carried it down to the beach with him every day. Beryl collected pebbles in it.

Dotty had bleached her hair a lighter shade specially for the holiday and bought Beryl a black woollen swimming costume two sizes too big through the W.V.S. clothes exchange. She kept urging her to get into it and go for a swim.

'It's too cold!' Beryl resisted. But she knew what was expected of her. She clambered to her feet, sliding through the soft sand of the dune and went down to the nearly empty beach to pop seaweed.

'If it's nice tomorrow I'll take you in!' shouted Uncle Ted in a friendly way.

It was nice, but the tide was due in at seven-thirty in the morning. Still, Uncle Ted, loyal to his word and a little guilty, left Dotty snoring at the boarding house and took Garbie down to the sea, wrapping her costume neatly inside the towel like a swiss roll.

She changed behind a deserted beach hut while Uncle Ted stood guard and then he carried her over the pebbles so she wouldn't hurt her feet and put her down gently at the edge of the water while he rolled up his trouser legs. It was a clear fresh morning, the high blue arc of the sky free of cloud and the sea less depressingly slatey than usual.

'Off you go then!' His white arms in their shirt sleeves shooed her on as though she were a wayward hen. But her toes sank into the squelchy sand and her knees stuck together in fear that she might be sucked in up to the ears.

'There's nothing to be afraid of. I'm watching you.' He felt quite gently disposed towards the child when her mother wasn't there. He saw that the sagging costume drooped below her faint little nipples. He waded in, holding her small, cold hands.

'There!'

The water swirled round her ankles leaving a lacy scum as it drew back a little. And then again, it lapped forward a little higher. She watched, fascinated, her skin growing accustomed to the temperature of the sea.

'Lie on your belly!' shouted Uncle Ted and splashed her so

that her skin shrivelled and goose pimples broke out on the back of her arms. Paper seagulls slid blithely on the air currents overhead.

Then she lay on her belly stirring up murky grains of sand and Uncle Ted snapped his braces with satisfaction. He showed her the gestures to make with her arms and stood there, like a performing porpoise, his bare legs white as fish meat.

He bent and slid his hands under her, his face puffing and red, one eye winking boisterously. She found the courage to move her arms as he had showed her.

'Good girl!' he roared and it was the first praise she'd ever heard that she knew was truly meant.

'Now kick your legs.'

He was covered with salty spray, but he hung on and even waded out deeper, supporting her skinny body on his broad palms. 'Keep going chick!' Her neck was aching with keeping her head up out of the water and she'd never been happier. Great slugs of salt water gushed into her mouth stinging the rough patch of impetigo. And then, with one breathless, final kick, she made Uncle Ted overbalance and he sat down plop! in the water, vanishing momentarily in spectacular spray. When he emerged, he was laughing, he wasn't cross and he was still hanging on to her.

'Whoopsadaisy!'

He heaved them both up and out and carried her on to the beach.

He stood there, hands on hips, drenched, laughing. Shirt and trousers clung to his huge, firm stomach. Garbie heard her own thin, reedy laughter.

'What'll your mum think of me!'

They pranced along the shoreline, flapping their arms and the wind dried the salt in a crusty bloom on their skins. They passed a woman walking a dog and she laughed at them too because they seemed so happy although she could only see their outlines black against the early glitter of the sea.

'Let's get that wet costume off!' The wool was so heavy with water the legs hung down to her knees. He held her close to him, rubbing briskly with their scratchy towel which smelt of feet. He rubbed and rubbed until her blood sprang hot to the surface and then he put her on his knee to dry her hair and made her head shake till she thought her teeth would drop out.

'Now what goes on first?'

She stood naked, shivering while he sorted out her clothes. He held out her pants, his hands stretching the elastic as wide as it would go so she could just step in. He patted her bottom gently and hugged her to his damp shirt. She didn't mind his winking any more. His cheeks were bright red with the tributaries of broken veins.

'Now give your Uncle Ted a kiss,' he said and she smelt his hot grown-up breath heavy with fragments of the last day's food and drink. His mouth was hard and circled with barbed-wire bristles.

'Do you like your Uncle Ted?'

'Yes.'

'D'you like him more than your other uncles?'

She thought hard of Uncle Arnold and there seemed no comparison. 'Oh yes,' she nodded.

'Then we'll have to have another swimming lesson eh?' He drew back his lips over mauve gums in a querying smile.

'Hey! Te-ed!'

Dotty was stumbling over the pebbles towards them, waving, her yellow hair streaming in the wind.

Beryl felt herself dropped.

'Hello duck!' He waved back to Dotty. 'Now get your things on sharpish,' he said in a quite different voice to Beryl pointing at her things on the ground.

'Look what the little bugger's done to me!' he yelled jovially as Dotty staggered closer and he indicated his wet clothing.

'Oh yes.' Dotty nodded vaguely and screwed her eyes up against the sun. 'Now, do you want your breakfast or don't you?'

'Do I want my *breakfast*!' he roared and slapped his wet stomach. 'Do *I* want *my* breakfast!'

Beryl was bundled into her clothes and dragged up the dunes. When they reached the pill box at the top and drew breath, she tried to slip her hand into Uncle Ted's, but he pulled away and lumbering into the pill box stuck out a hand from one of the slits with two fingers pointing at her. Then making a sound like a machine gun he fired at the enemy. Obediently, Beryl fell down and her mouth filled with sand.

Bewildered as she was, she always tried hard to do what was expected of her.

'How would you like another little holiday with your cousins? I'd let you go on the train on your own. Uncle Ted's got a bit of woodwork in mind for me, so you'd be better out of the way. Anyway, your Aunty Cissy's sent a letter.'

Dotty meant well. And houses were being bombed every day. It was better for the child.

Beryl helped Robin and Quentin move pins across the map of France and she went out in the trap, collecting for the Cogs Corps. Now she was older she was allowed to take Victoria for walks. She said she liked being called Garbie, it didn't matter.

They sent her home when the blackout ended, smelling of Germoline and wearing a pair of Robin's shorts. Uncle Ted hadn't got round to putting the shelves up, though he'd left a hammer and nails behind. Dotty said he'd been called away urgently and yes, she could be Garbie if she wanted. Men come and men go, she said, as though it were an immutable law of nature.

'Can I have the hammer?' asked Garbie.

'Why not?' said her mother. 'Waste not want not.'

'Will he come back?'

'He'll not miss the hammer.'

'He said he'd teach me to swim.'

'They say all sorts,' grinned Dotty, wiser in her way about promises than anybody else ever was.

Occasionally Aunty Betty came over to see them. Not often, because she didn't like leaving Colin with Uncle Arnold for long. And she didn't trust Dotty to find her way to Dagenham.

'I just don't know how a person can leave a bed unmade!'

'You don't call this a tea towel do you Dotty!'

'Is this vest supposed to be *washed* . . .?'

'Oh, Dotty, there is a limit!'

She came to a rest finally, and then in silence, lips compressed, while Garbie and her mother sat watching, she unpacked rock cakes, a couple of new flannels, a tin of Spam and fudge that she made from soya flour and Camp coffee essence. Then she settled, her bottom only reluctantly on the chair edge, and had a go at her younger sister.

It always ended with Dotty in tears because she wasn't a bad woman. She just found it difficult to keep her mind on more than one thing at a time.

Betty was kindness itself; 'Sometimes,' she said, 'I think you're a bit gone up here.' And she tapped her perspiring forehead. Dotty wondered how her sister got so fat with rationing as it was.

Downright mental, Betty meant, but she wouldn't go so far as to be cruel. It was only for the best. She knew there were places you could go if you were just a bit touched,

'Just a bit touched, that's all. Not *barmy* or anything.' (Not fit to be left on your own.)

Arnold had told her not to interfere, which was bold of Arnold, but Betty could see good reason – and she worried about the child Beryl.

'Have you been leaving that child alone again?'

No reply.

Aunty Betty breathed heavily and took a small hanky from her sleeve. Its hem was stiff with starch. It must have scratched her nose to blow it, thought Garbie.

'There'll be a nasty accident one day . . .' She stuffed her hanky back in her sleeve and flexed her shoulders. 'There's a time and a place for plain speaking . . .'

Dotty stared at her, thin and bruised in her old brown dressing gown.

'I'd take her myself, but how can I with Colin and coupons . . .? What about those rich relations of yours?'

'I like her here. She's company.'

'Company? What kind of company do you give her I'd like to know?'

Garbie crept into the fatty warmth of the brown dressing gown and hid her face.

'I can keep a job,' said Dotty proudly reaching thin yellow fingers down to her daughter.

'Who can't in wartime?'

'I can keep a job!' repeated Dotty indignantly. It was a great pride to her. A compulsion almost, that whatever else happened and however bad she was at the job, she always managed to get there on time. She never lost her temper either. Garbie had never seen her mother angry. She sat mutely between the two women, weak with a sense of protection towards Dotty and frightened by a treacherous worry that Aunty Betty might be right.

'And another thing,' declared Aunty Betty, breathing hard on her glasses, 'a child of that age needs friends of her own. And fresh air. And ...' (her body took on a critical shape) 'and *love.*'

'I do love her!' Dotty's voice trailed out of her weeping, a thin whine, 'I bloody do!'

'You don't know the meaning of the word!' Aunty Betty knew. She had devoted ten years of her life to a dribbling child she couldn't display to the world. She, who had raised a million teaspoons to his lips and sat him on his pot ceaselessly without complaint, she knew. 'You wouldn't know love if you saw it!' she shrilled.

And Garbie, her stomach exploding in bitter flakes of fear, wondered if her mother did know. She tugged feebly at the hem of the dressing gown in hope of an answer. But her mother, smeary with tears of shame and defeat, wailed: 'Fetch us a fag, Garbie!'

'And *"Garbie!"* What kind of heathen name is that! She's got a perfectly good name I helped you choose. What's wrong with Beryl eh? Tell me that!'

'She likes it. It's hers.'

'She likes it does she? What do you like about it eh, Beryl?' Aunty Betty coaxed a big smile that rose and hid her eyes behind a crescent of fat.

'I like it,' said Garbie stubbornly, and paused. 'My cousins give it me.'

'But what's it mean dearie ... *Garbie*?' Encouragingly, she bent her head, roofed by a home perm, towards the child.

'I like it.' One of her intestines bubbled apprehensively.

Aunty Betty seized on the murmuring signal as if she'd found a murder clue. 'When did the child last eat? When did she eat!'

They worked it out. Four hours and thirty-seven minutes before she'd had an iced bun. Aunty Betty wasn't defeated, she'd read her Ministry of Food pamphlets. 'It's not a properly balanced diet!' she cried, victorious. 'I'd take her myself, but how can I . . ?' she sighed again. Then rising to her feet, she sacked the room like a Visigoth.

She ripped sheets from the stained green mattress, then finding the only other pair were still damp, she had to return the originals, gingerly brushing them free of tea leaves. She went spreading, stretching, patting till Garbie and Dotty sneezed at the dust. Mouse droppings were discovered in the food cupboard. Black grease was stripped from the stove. A dishcloth smelling of fungus dropped in a bucket.

Dotty curled up in an armchair crying quietly, while Garbie sucked her fingers and watched to see what would be uncovered next.

'Where's your pride?' A bundle of dirty washing was found under the bed. 'What kind of example's this meant to be?' (Slipping two dresses back on their hangers.)

'Come here, Beryl!'

The child submitted herself to her aunt who, flushed with effort and triumph, pressed her nose to the navy blue cardigan. 'I thought so!' she said, jubilant. 'She *smells*!'

Garbie began her suppressed mewing note. She wept for shame; two kinds of shame. Shame that her mother should let her smell. Shame that her Aunty Betty should find out.

'It's downright wicked!' Breath came down Aunty Betty's nose in short, incendiary bursts. 'You'll be having the Inspector round here before you know what.' She picked the child up, wiping her eyes briskly. 'Ugh!' she exclaimed, to drive the point home.

Flinging herself on the newly made bed, Dotty began a fresh episode of watery grunting and choking. The point, thought Betty, was made (although the visit followed pretty faithfully the pattern of all earlier visits). She sank on the bed still clasping Garbie and patted Dotty's back.

'I don't like doing it, believe me. You've got to be cruel to be kind.' And with this act of partial forgiveness she sighed and said, as she had said many times before, that it was all the fault of the young devil who'd got Dotty to fall for a baby in the first place. She was pleased by her broad mindedness. And she had reason to be for Aunty Betty clung to respectability like a sinking Catholic clings to his crucifix. Respectability was the measure by which she selected her clothes, her tone of voice, her films, her furniture. Colin was an unlooked-for error, but like all narrow people she was rich in sentiment and sentiment blended with a sense of duty produced what her neighbours would describe as a wonderful mother. She worked at motherhood accepting the pain with joy as if she were wearing a crown of thorns.

Aunty Betty told people (when pressed) that the experience of bringing up her son had made her a better human being.

Towards Dotty she felt an ambiguity she couldn't admit to. It didn't matter that her sister had offended every rule in Aunty Betty's book, the fact of the matter was that the person responsible for Dotty's little lapse, was in a manner of speaking, a gentleman. Aunty Betty's moral values skidded from one side of a turbulent deck to the other.

Little Beryl, though the image of her mother (poor mite), had breeding. There was no knowing when breeding would tell. The best solution was to play safe. Reward, as Aunty Betty perfectly understood, was the prize of the next world, but there was no point in any sensible person sniffing at the lottery of this. She had made up her mind that if one day, little Beryl grew into a rather grand person, she, Betty Beazley, was not going to be forgotten.

Aunty Betty didn't want money or a paid-for holiday or anything like that; simply to be remembered as someone who'd done her honest best for the child.

'Well now,' she said, all this smoking faintly in the back of her mind, 'Well now!' And holding her breath, she kissed the child, promising to knit her an angora jumper in whatever colour she liked.

'Pink,' said Garbie.

'Very pretty dear, very tasteful. Say thank you.'

'Thank you.'

Aunty Betty straightened her bulky body and glared at Dotty. 'Now then!' was all she breathed, but it was enough.

As her footsteps grew fainter on the stairs, their tears dried and they fell on the little packets Aunty Betty had brought. Dotty would put up with almost anything for the sake of a good feed.

She was particularly fond of fudge.

'Always remember, whoever you are .. ' urged Mrs Crabbe as she faced her shrivelled class on that last day of term. (She had one hand pressed to the side of her nose to stop weeping, the other placed in a deathly way between her breasts ...) 'Always remember, like the rose bay willow herb, life can spring from chaos.' She let her gaze droop over them all like a slow sunbeam. 'Never,' she cried. 'Never be afraid of holding the very *highest* expectations for yourself and never be afraid to fight if that's what it takes to achieve them.'

Smiling like a Madonna, she shot them full of militancy, her small children, 'The *best* ... the *finest* lives, are those lived in a state of war! ...' She looked down from her perilous peak for a fine pause and then, dramatically, hung her head. 'A quick prayer, children, very quick before we sing Onward Christian Soldiers ... a quick prayer for Mr Churchill, Mr Butler and Sir William Beveridge ...' And rapidly she muttered through her hopefulness in a way that meant little in any particular sense to her class of eight year olds but left a general sense of the important that many of them could recall years afterwards without ever knowing why.

Perhaps because Mrs Crabbe, comical as she began to look down the long retreat of years, did really, truly care.

4   Post-War

She was ten when she went to live with Aunty Betty and Uncle Arnold and Colin and was one of the first batch of children, six months later, to fail the 11 plus.

She failed it because there were so many possible answers to all the questions and anxious to please, to do the right thing, she tried to get them all down and was only a third of the way through each page when the invigilator, glued to his watch, told them all to turn over.

So Mr Butler and his magic Act let her down.

She went to Starhill Secondary Modern and Aunty Betty secretly wrote away to Rotherbrook for money to buy her a brown utility blazer, gymslip and hat (bought large enough to allow plenty of room for growing). She was the only child in her class who wore uniform. All thirty-five of them were doomed to spend the next four years together having their heads crammed with the kind of things that had once been the prerogative of small boys in stiff collars and straw hats.

The war was over. Life was rosy and it was Mr Attlee's turn to do tricks.

'What do you expect? . . .' said Aunty Betty as they sat round the dinner table in Atwood Avenue and stared down at the shrunken cubes of meat and cheese. The family loaf was smaller and greyer. 'What do you expect with Labour? Poor Mr Churchill, it's plain ungrateful.' 'Give them a run for their money,' murmured Uncle Arnold who was shortly going to be a white collar worker. Aunty Betty cut all the tails off his shirts and made new fronts and cuffs with them. She made fishcakes from snoek which Beryl slid under the tablecloth for the cat to eat. An occasional food parcel arrived from Rotherbrook containing tins of anchovies and almond paste.

In many ways, life was easier for Aunty Betty. During the paralysing heat of that summer she was able to let Beryl look after Colin in the garden while she had a rest or picked her way round the impoverished shops. All the same; 'It's a judgement,' she declared firmly when the great tide of winter ice locked itself about them. 'It's all in the Bible. Just like frogs and boils.' And she gave Beryl the job of cleaning out the grate that winter telling her to save all the ashy bits that might just burn again. 'They do say,' she whispered darkly, 'that people are eating one another in Poland.'

Beryl thought of Maxy and wondered whether he would eat or be eaten. He'd have a job running away.

Uncle Arnold sent her down the road with a shovel to follow the milkman's horse in the hope of some manure for his garden. 'She *likes* horses,' he said.

'All these airs and graces!' tutted Aunty Betty, tying a bib round Colin's neck, 'It's the one thing that gets me down.'

At Rotherbrook it was perfectly normal to want to wade through the deep meadow grass where two Shetland ponies, as round and black as moles waited to be spoiled and stroked.

In Dagenham it was a disturbing interest. 'Where would we *put* it!' exclaimed Aunty Betty throwing her fat, red hands in the air when the child asked if they could have a pony. Torn between horror at Beryl's lack of money sense and a gnawing idea of how grand it would be to have a horse on the lawn, she gazed out of the window at the burnished oblong and pictured it all, a shining racehorse with red, open, nostrils grazing daintily at the turf while the neighbours peered enviously through the knot holes in the fence.

'I suppose it's out of the question ...?' she murmured to Arnold, 'Just a donkey perhaps ...?' But to Beryl she said sharply : 'Give, give, give and all you want is more!'

Beryl knew that Dotty (given a square foot of grass) would have found a pony somehow and dared to point this out. There was an angry spluttering in Aunty Betty's sinuses. 'I daresay she would've! But she hadn't the first idea how to look after a child, let alone an animal. It'd have starved to death in no time!'

Beryl remembered the white mouse and fell silent.

Obstinately, she pursued her interest and cantered round and round the doctored square of turf herself, whinnying gently, until a worn circle became visible from the lounge windows.

'We'll have to put a stop to it!' (What would the neighbours make of this queer capering?) 'It's not natural.'

So Beryl stopped going to school by bus and went instead, on horseback. The people who lived in Atwood Avenue, Lightwood Avenue and Starhill Gardens got quite used to the brown hat bobbing in its unnatural rhythm above the privets every morning and afternoon. Some of them, those who weren't on an early shift, set their watches by it or gulped their tea down and grabbed their macs as the brown hat galloped by.

Smartly, head tossing, she trotted on unaware of her oddity on a housing estate. Through the horse she made friends.

'Give us a ride! Give us a ride!' shouted the children at school and leapt on her bucking back. They had to hang on like grim death to prevent their heads from being split open on the asphalt playground.

The interest spread like wildfire. They held rodeos in the dinner break and two boys from the year above started a book. Every day they studied the form in the *Mirror* and the *Express*, made their selections and offered their own odds. Some of the children had suspiciously large sums of money on them and did rather well. Harry Butler became so good he sold tips to the newsagent until the headmaster got wind of it and started an inquiry.

'You want to look for a nice sloping pastern and well-sprung withers,' advised Beryl seriously. They listened to her intently. She became confident, even a little superior using her expertise as a bargaining counter in friendship. Nobody minded her rashes, her sniffing or the double sties on her eyes because nearly everybody suffered from the same kind of thing at Starhill Secondary Modern. Even the teasing about her school uniform dwindled away.

'Do try and walk *properly*!' hissed Aunty Betty as Beryl

cantered and snorted alongside her elbow on their way to the ironmonger's. 'You'll have everybody looking.'

'Do you know who won the Derby in 1893 Aunty Betty?'

'I do not!'

'Hyperion!' shouted Beryl rearing up on her hind legs, not quite sure whether she was right, but absolutely certain Aunty Betty wouldn't know either.

'Why don't they teach you some proper dates!' Her teeth were as tight as mousetraps.

'What good's it going to do a girl knowing all that queer stuff?' She changed her shopping bag to the other arm and walked rapidly ahead of her niece. 'That'll not help you get a good job!' she cried out and then pausing, until the untamed palomino stallion caught up with her, she lowered her head to whistle: 'You just wait ... you just wait till you go to your relations. They'll not stand for this funny business!'

And she made it her duty to run up one new dress for Beryl every time she went on the train to Sussex because Aunty Betty would rather burn in hell than be seen to be neglectful. Inside the suitcase her vests and liberty bodices were angularly ironed and white. Each sock had an exquisitely darned heel and there was a petticoat made from parachute silk. But Beryl was made to travel in her school uniform because Aunty Betty thought that smartest. 'And since they helped pay for it, it's only right they should see how you look.'

Beryl tried to interest Colin in horses but he got over-excited and Aunty Betty smacked her. 'Play nicely with him,' she ordered, which meant letting him pull her hair and run his fingers over her face. Beryl didn't mind. She tried to teach him to read and waited with a distant kind of curiosity for his fourteenth birthday.

After Colin choked to death Aunty Betty lost interest in things, including Beryl.

With a silent, furious energy she lost herself in polishing her house and tending a little shrine she made for her son on the sideboard. There was a photo of him in a silver frame showing his poor, flat, dribbly face studio-lit and softly tinted and in front of it a heavy crucifix on a polished red granite base which had holes for violets and a Gothic inscription reading 'In Memoriam'.

The flowers were changed every day. Primula, petunia, rosebud, dwarf chrysanthemum and lily of the valley marked the seasons in the holes provided and Uncle Arnold's back ached continually from digging and sowing and planting his little garden to provide for the shrine. The two grown-ups rarely spoke. Aunty Betty seemed to blame Uncle Arnold. The house grew as lonely and immaculate as a coffin.

Beryl sat with a book on her lap watching Aunty Betty spend hours on her bandaged knees before the shrine. At first Uncle Arnold stood behind his wife's squat, kneeling form and muttered about it making no sense brooding, but the icy rebuke he met drove him out to his garden. He seemed to find in that small, overworked square, a satisfaction that took his mind off the things that might have worried him inside the house.

Beryl followed close behind him and he smiled at her to show he was sorry about being so awkward and gave her a packet of love-in-a-mist seeds to sow. He let her cut up worms occasionally as long as she promised not to tell her Aunty, but he was so unused to dealing with normal children that his willingness to try was defeated from the start.

Beryl would follow him along the flower bed, he thrusting a fork into the earth to loosen it, she, shaking the precious stuff free from each clump of weed, then dropping the weed into a bucket with its handle missing. When the bucket was full it was too heavy for her to carry in her arms and Uncle Arnold had to stop his digging to carry it down to the end where he kept his compost and his canes and his upturned flower pots.

'I'll fill it to here,' Beryl would say, indicating a line inside the bucket, three-quarters of the way up. 'About there.' So, she meant, so that you won't have to stop your digging and carry it for me.

'Never you worry,' replied Uncle Arnold. 'Just top it up, there's a good girl.' They never looked at one another.

If ever they had anything at all to say, they never looked at one another to say it. Their heads swinging away from one another in downward arcs, they had their brief discussions.

'Pass me the trowel would you?'

'Can we grow strawberries Uncle Arnold?'

'Strawberries?'

'Could we?'

'Give us the trowel, Beryl ... they're a lot of trouble ...'

And then a silence disturbed by soft grunts of exertion and the dazzled flight of butterflies.

'They're my favourite, strawberries.'

'Are they?'

'Yes.'

And they thought about them, eyes making an idle search of the loam.

'Yes, well ... you have to dig them up every three years.'

'Every three years?'

'Yes ... that's right ... and the baby birds get caught in the netting.'

Besides, Uncle Arnold had to keep his small beds full of things that would flower at all peculiar seasons of the year starting with the witch hazel, a clear, lemon bloom for January.

And so their afternoons would fade away in a sinking warmth.

'Can we ... ?'

'Yes? ... is it strawberries again?'

'Can we have a bonfire?'

And they'd stand together, gazing into their small blaze, the air round them darkening and sharp with the scent of scorched green wood until the heat lay in a saucer of white ash and it was almost time for bed.

Slowly even this much speech evaporated in the effort it took Uncle Arnold to stay in this world. He was reduced to desperate nodding, smiles, which Beryl knew were meant for her in the simple way that children do know, although the nods and smiles veered off along their parabolic curves.

Aunty Betty scolded him continually for his lack of attention to things, though nobody knew what these 'things' were. He did his work scrupulously both at home and in the factory;

but he seemed to inhabit a world of incommunicable thought and feeling to which the nods and smiles were last desperate signals of meaning.

Eventually, all that filtered through to Beryl as she grew, was her uncle's sense of discomfiture. He no longer wanted her there beside him in the garden because of his shame. He kept his face turned away as though it were disfigured by its silent mouth. It was all so gradual that it never struck anyone as odd. It wasn't a thing you could call a doctor for.

'He likes to be left to himself,' was the only diagnosis, and everybody accepted the ordinariness of that and left him alone and it wasn't till years later when Garbie finally came to understand – years after Uncle Arnold had died of despair in a gaunt and brutal mental hospital – that she understood he was frightened of being alone, frightened of what it was about himself that made the people around him suppose he should want to be alone. It wasn't until then, years after he'd died, that she came to see they'd had something in common, and that the sad uncle had himself seen this and tried to communicate it to her through his nods and smiles, but it was a symptom of their mutual sickness that he could not.

When she understood this, it terrified her and then she cried a long time for the sorrow of it and grasped why it was that something affectionate in her responded to the memory she had of him; although he had so successfully erased himself in life, she was barely able to remember anything particular about him after death.

'You're growing into a young woman now,' began Aunty Betty, wretchedly twisting the hem of the gymslip she was letting down.

'Can I go out and play?'

'You're growing into a young woman now,' repeated Aunty. And her heart sank. 'Fifteen next birthday, and I don't know what ...'

'What Aunty?'

'I don't know.' She'd meant to talk about periods but couldn't find a starting point. There was a little book to put beneath Beryl's pillow.

The girl was growing and there was still no sign.

'You'll have to be thinking about a job,' she said.

'Can I go out and play later?'

'You'll be bringing home some money at last,' Aunty Betty hadn't meant to sound mean. It was a fair return that's all. She bit off the thread. 'How's your shorthand and typing coming along?'

'I'd rather do something else.' Beryl crept her fingers along the arms of the chair and stared at them.

'What then?'

Beryl shrugged and pulled her mouth down.

'As long as it's somewhere where you can keep your hands clean.' There were three faded bands on the gymslip now, but never mind. It only had another nine months to last her out. 'I'd like to see you in an office,' said Aunt Betty. 'A nice insurance office. Not down at the works like everybody else.'

'Uncle Arnold's down at the works.'

'Your Uncle Arnold's white collar.'

Her period began four months later. It was the early spring of 1951 shortly before Easter. She was to go to Rotherbrook for Easter and for every Easter, Whit and Christmas thereafter for there was no longer any reason preventing her. Old Mrs Pendleton after falling asleep with a lighted cigarette and burning herself as she'd once burnt all her clothes, failed to recover from ten obstinate weeks spent in an oxygen tent.

It should have been a familiar business, stepping off the train and searching round for Aunty Cissy's head absurdly and unnaturally high the other side of the fence (because she was standing up in the trap) but a thin wind tore at the black, budded twigs and everything felt different.

She picked up the suitcase full of a child's clothes and shyly went to meet her aunt. They bent their heads close with a careless embarrassment.

'I know I'm not meant to say such things ...' cried Cissy, 'But haven't you grown! It must be six inches at least!'

'Five and three quarters.' Garbie liked to be precise. It steadied her.

'Oh! Well . .' The correction threw Aunty Cissy. She collected the reins together with more flapping and clucking than necessary. 'Move over boys!' she urged the two youngest, Edward and Thomas (now aged three and four and born in a burst of love after Jack's return). 'Make room for Garbie.'

They eyed her with directness that would have been insulting in anyone older.

'Are you going to stay with us?' inquired Edward in a clear, high copy of Quentin's voice.

'Where are you going to sleep?'

Garbie met Thom's hazel gaze. He seemed at least as old as she. She turned away and saw the thorn coming into flower along the lane. At the cross roads there were still sandbags heaped into tidy piles beneath the signpost.

'Why don't you take your hat off dear?' Cissy flapped the reins over the swaying skewbald back.

Obediently, Garbie removed her hat and cradled it on her lap trying to hide her knees with it. Already the hot gymslip had become too short.

Out of the worn arms of her blazer two knobbly wrists bloomed into purplish hands with swollen finger tips bitten down so far, little more than the painful crescents remained. Aunt Cissy had noticed them out of the corner of her eye.

She had noticed the unexpected growth, the sudden awkward arrival on the frontiers of womanhood. It made her think more urgently of the future, of things that must be done.

'Oh darling,' she said, keeping her eyes on the road ahead, 'Shall we get your nails to grow this Easter? Would you like that?'

Instinctively, Garbie folded her fingers into tight fists and refused to let Edward open them again though he tried. She squeezed her brown suitcase between her legs and remembered (for the first time with mortification) that she had once arrived with a pillowcase containing her clothes.

Quite suddenly her inside contracted, the back of her nose dried and a sudden tickling began somewhere between nose and throat. A tremendous sneeze shifted every organ in her body and a childish spray of urine dampened her knickers.

She sneezed again. And again.

'Poor darling!' shouted Aunt Cissy above the clipping hooves. 'So you're still allergic to horses ... what a rotten shame for you!'

Her eyes began to stream.

Quentin's legs protruded from beneath an old, yellow Wolseley Hornet he'd been given for his eighteenth birthday. At the sound of hooves on the gravel he wriggled out an unending length of leg and rose to his feet. He waited for them, leaning against the bonnet, a spanner in one hand, the other pushing away a loose fall of the overlong, dark hair.

They stopped and clambered down.

'How do you do,' he remarked unsmilingly.

Confused Garbie blurted, 'I do very well. How do *you* do?' And knowing it was wrong, blushed.

'I do very well too,' he remarked with a lopsided shadow of amusement. Still, he didn't move away from the bonnet of his car. The younger boys began kicking gravel at one another and Garbie looked away.

'See to Belinda for me darling,' called Cissy, stepping down from the trap.

Quentin eased himself off the car bonnet.

'Look!' said Cissy anxiously. She drew her slender son towards her. 'See how tall she's grown.'

Quentin stared expressionlessly.

The knees and wrists growing uncontrollably out of her brown uniform became as big as boulders.

'Tea!' cried Cissy sharply, sensing danger and aware that rebuke would profit no one.

Tea was a meal taken on rare Sundays in Dagenham.

Tea was served on the terrace behind the house on a marble-topped wrought-iron Regency table surrounded by comfortable wicker chairs.

It was pleasantly warm for early April, one of those blue,

drifting days when the sun's warmth seems to encourage a pale flush of green on the wintering trees. Large waxy blossoms of magnolia grew over the creamy yellow walls of the house which overlooked, on its south-western side, a deeply plunging slope of grass planted here and there with rhododendrons, azaleas and ericas. Towards the tangled woodland at the end grew a golden rush of daffodils and then, behind larch, spruce, maple and silver birch, hid from view, the small stagnant lake which no one went near any longer because of the vigorous nettles growing on its banks.

Victoria and Robin were already there eating transparent slices of brown bread and Marmite. Nanny poured a weakly fragrant tea which Garbie knew came from China and whose smell got in the way of its taste.

They grinned at her. Tea made her clumsy. She could never get used to half a meal eaten at four-thirty. Until you were ten it was the last meal of the day and it was never enough. She stirred, and tried to adapt. Rotherbrook meals happened at rapid four hour intervals but nobody ever ate very much. The neglected plates of bread and cake shocked her.

'Take a pew!'

She'd told Aunty Betty how they left things, how they had bread already cut instead of cutting it when it was needed. Aunty Betty clicked her tongue against her plate. Garbie didn't know whether this showed disapproval or disbelief. She'd learnt at Rotherbrook to go a little hungry.

Robin was pulling out a chair for her. Victoria, wearing a boy's jersey and shorts and a yellow ribbon round her fluffy hair, giggled.

'What've you got a gymslip on for?'

'I haven't given the poor girl time to change,' fluttered Cissy, patting cushions. 'Sit down dear and let Nanny pour you a cup of tea.'

'Haven't you just *grown*!' crowed Nanny, gazing through her owlishly magnifying lenses with incredulity. 'It must be six inches at least.'

'Five and three quarters,' said Garbie and Aunt Cissy together. Nanny and Aunt Cissy agreed once more how remarkable this was and buried their teeth in cress and cream cheese sandwiches.

'But *why* are you wearing a gymslip?' persisted Victoria.

'*Darling!*' (A light reproof hindered by cress.)

'It doesn't show the dirt so much. From the trains.'

This struck Robin and Victoria as explosively funny.

'Garbie's quite right. It was very sensible of Mrs Beazley.' Cissy passed the sugar to Garbie who fished fruitlessly with the tongs.

Old Caesar the Airedale, now going grey about the face, came and pressed against her legs and sank down beside her. She felt better, and hoped she wouldn't sneeze again.

'I think brown is a perfectly filthy colour for school,' Victoria observed. 'Don't you hate it?'

'It doesn't show the dirt,' repeated Garbie hopefully, wishing her clothes didn't smell of mashed potato and gravy.

Her cousins collapsed so infectiously that Edward and Thom joined in, leaping up and down like puppies. Garbie began to laugh too. So, more hesitantly, did Aunt Cissy and Nanny. Jack Pendleton came down from his study and asked what it was all about, but the query started it all off again which saved anyone from explaining since they wouldn't have known what to say.

Jack met his family's amusement indulgently and pouring his own tea from the fluted silver pot said that it was a pleasure to see Garbie again. When she squirmed, a block of words impeding her tongue, he pointed out that this was an awkward age, and jovially pulled the nose of his younger son Thom.

'How are you getting along at school?'

'I don't know.' Garbie spoke rapidly staring at her nibbled piece of bread and honey. She adored her Uncle Jack.

'Have you thought yet about what you want to do when you leave?'

'I don't know.'

'I don't know,' echoed Edward and looked round for applause.

'Sit down,' said his mother.

They were all staring at her. She daren't eat her bread in case she had her mouth full when she was expected to answer. The voices were coaxing.

'I'm sure you thought of something you'd like to do ...'

'What's the thing you most enjoy doing ... ?'

Questions lit her brain up with flames. Aunty Betty didn't ask.

Her uncle was playing a wishing game; it wasn't real. Or perhaps it was. She couldn't think what to say. 'Mmmmmm ...?'

There was a figure on the bridge of her willow-pattern plate.

'Aunty Betty wants me to be a shorthand typist. Something clean.'

'Something *clean*!' snorted Robin, but a swift check round the family's expressions silenced him. 'There's a wasp in the jam,' he said, and flicked at it lamely.

'More tea, darling?'

'A shorthand typist eh?' Uncle Jack tilted his head back in serious thought. He was a handsome man with his eldest son's silky black hair – only his was turning grey.

'Where is Q?' sighed Cissy, feeling the teapot to see if it were going to be warm enough for her wonderful eldest boy.

'A shorthand *typist* ...' Uncle Jack seemed to be considering a global problem.

'But do *you* like the idea?' He turned his face to her. It was a preposterous question.

'I don't know.'

'There's no point in doing something you don't enjoy.'

She'd never considered the idea of enjoying work. You just did it and came home afterwards.

'I'd like to be a vet,' she said loudly without knowing why and dropped her eyes to her plate again. The wasp had come to settle on her honey, and it was all she could do not to drop the plate.

'AH ... !'

The other children lost interest and began to chatter amongst themselves, it helped the thundercloud of pressure to lift a little.

'It takes a great deal of study and determination to become a veterinary surgeon ...' Uncle Jack spoke so gently she knew it was in preparation for saying the possibility was quite out of the question.

'I don't really!' she cried abruptly to prevent his ever saying anything so cruel. The wasp's legs moved lasciviously over the honey.

'It takes a great deal of study and determination,' her uncle repeated quietly, 'but if you truly care about it and work hard for your exams there's no reason why you shouldn't aim to be a vet!!'

Now she knew she'd only ever suggested becoming a vet to please him. Most animals, reptiles and insects (like the wasp) frightened her. 'But darling,' broke in Aunt Cissy, 'Animals make you sneeze. You're allergic to them.'

'Yes,' she whispered gratefully.

'Pity!' murmured Uncle Jack. He sipped his tea ... (It embarrassed her that he should be spending so much time thinking about her.) 'Still ...' he went on, 'I think we must do something.' He laughed and put his cup down. 'We can't send you out naked into the world.'

She nearly died. Busily she began to prise a scab up off her shin.

'What do you think Cissy ... ?'

And they began murmuringly, to discuss over her drooped head, a future for her that was as arbitrary and as unchosen in its own way as Aunty Betty's was.

Quentin, washed and changed into a blinding white shirt, arrived for tea. Nanny collected the little ones and took them upstairs to wipe their hands and faces.

Freed from the web's centre Garbie gobbled her bread up quickly before the sated wasp returned and then sat still until told she could go. 'Well!' Uncle Jack got up. 'Well ... think about it. And let me know.'

Everybody was thinking about her future. Things had become quite different and worrying. She had come to the end of an age where things are what they are, where you like or dislike without dreaming to wonder why. She had come to the age of ambiguities without any of the weapons she needed to cope. There were alternatives.

'Thank you, yes,' she said.

Nobody said she could go so she was left sitting there alone on the terrace. Everybody else had a reason for leaving. She said she had a reason for staying.

'I'm thinking,' she told Robin.

The shadows of the tall trees lengthened across the grass till their tips nearly reached the terrace, and the pale warmth began to seep out of the sun although it shone still on the ochre wall behind her. Above, the children squealed as the soap got in their eyes. There was a comfortable clatter of washing up from the scullery. Victoria was practising on the piano.

For the first time in her life Garbie felt homesick for Dagenham. Dagenham law had been the only law and Rotherbrook was somewhere like the seaside or the zoo, a place that you could visit and go away from. But it was not like that after all. It was an alternative.

Small birds rattled and fussed inside the rhododendrons and her leg began to bleed where she'd picked it. She wished she hadn't said anything about being a veterinary surgeon even though it was a high expectation of the kind Mrs Crabbe would like.

When the last of the sunlight slid up the wall of the house and ran over the roof she went inside, avoiding people and hid in the library. It was a little room with one long window over-looking the paddock and it smelt of leather. Wistfully, she thought of the small scaffolded cherry trees of Atwood Avenue and the tufted, wall-to-wall carpeting of Aunty Betty's lounge. Even the big, surly brown pieces of furniture and the sharp, brass fender provoked longing.

The crocuses snapped shut in the dusk and a gong went for dinner.

'Excuse me Uncle Jack, I've had a think.'

She stood before him two days later in his muddled study and pulled at the waist of the pink dress Aunty Betty had made.

'I beg your pardon?' He smiled distractedly, thinking of the coming selection of a Labour candidate for Port Cawley. He took the coffee she'd been sent up with.

'Begging *yours*,' she said brightly, 'I'd like to be your private secretary.' She glowed with pride. She thought she'd pleased everybody.

Uncle Jack threw his head back and laughed, but seeing her sallow face narrow with hurt, he stopped. 'I'm most touched,' he declared. '*Most* touched.'

He thought of the hilariously funny letters Betty Beazley forced her to write and Cissy forced him to read. 'I don't know,' he said, smiling, 'whether I can afford a private secretary, but I've got a little tidying up you can do if you'd like that.'

'No,' she began, trying to explain. 'No, I mean ...' Her fingers fluttered in front of her mouth.

'Oh I see ...' He forestalled her. '... You mean, your *career* ... !'

She nodded.

'Ah ...' He looked serious and removed his glasses. 'Now then Garbie ... you don't think nearly highly enough of yourself, do you know that? Rushing away, hiding yourself ... We want to *see* you. See you enjoying yourself.'

Jack didn't realize that children like Garbie were not used to being cast adrift amongst the pleasurable scrap of hobbies. Children like Garbie had no idea what being left to their own resources meant; they were more used to tasks. She longed to do this tidying for him.

'Yes,' she said woefully.

He took her large damp hand and leant towards her, elbows on knees. He smelt comfortably of the country: of sacking and seed.

'Your aunt and I ... we've been thinking a great deal about your future. You're growing into a young woman now and you must have all that a young woman needs. We owe it to you!' He squeezed her hand and gave her a friendly smile. She dared to look under her lashes at him, but she couldn't smile back.

'Perhaps,' he went on. 'Because of the war and one thing and another, we haven't done quite as well as we might and you must try to forgive us ...' (another small squeeze ...) 'But we're going to make it up to you. Now, what we thought ...'

and he paused to let her see it was only a thought and she could argue if she liked, '... we felt it would be a thoroughly useful idea to send you off to a pleasant boarding school for a couple of years. I expect Victoria's told you, she's going to Cheltenham in September, well Cheltenham's all right ... Cheltenham's frightfully good in fact, but one has to think of a school in terms of the *pupil* ... Cheer up old thing, the world's not at an end!'

'No, Uncle Jáck.'

'So your aunt and I ... after due thought, and naturally nothing will be decided until we've had your views ... we felt the kind of place you'd enjoy would be somewhere like Dovedale Hall in north Derbyshire ...'

'Thank you very much,' rattled Garbie.

'You mean, you *do* like it?'

'Yes, thank you very much.'

'Jolly good!' He leant back, relieved and toyed with his spectacles. He had a wise, kind face.

'I have a syllabus here you might care to look at,' he reminded himself and ran his fingers through the small compartments of his desk. 'Well, somewhere, anyway.' He patted her on the arm. 'Jolly good then.'

She waited, hands behind her back, staring at her feet.

'Right!' Jack Pendleton replaced his glasses and swivelled back to his desk. 'Perfectly happy and everything aren't you? Oh, by the way, I believe your aunt is arranging for some elocution lessons. A pleasant voice is always an advantage, especially in a woman.'

He wondered if there were anything else he had to say. 'Ah! Before we do anything at all of course, we'll discuss matters with Mr and Mrs Beazley. They may not *want* you to go away! I expect they'll miss you dreadfully!'

He thought he saw now what had been troubling her. 'So don't you worry yourself about that, Garbie dear.'

'No.'

He turned back to his papers and his cooling coffee. 'I'm so glad you like the idea,' he said warmly.

There was nothing dishonest about Jack Pendleton's Socialism. It was just that his ideas grew naturally out of his own experience and background. By helping the have-nots he meant helping everybody to have the opportunities he enjoyed – a pleasant voice, a public school, a nice home and foreign holidays.

He faced up to the difficult facts. That it would take a long time economically to bring these benefits to pass. That he had a temperamental and personal difficulty ... he did not much care for squalor and stupidity. But then what reformer ever had? These were the very things that cried out for change.

'Ha-ow na-ow bra-own ca-ow,' said Garbie. The harder she tried, the worse it sounded.

'And once again!' Mrs Carstairs poised her baton.

'Ha-ow na-ow bra-own ca-ow.'

'I'm afraid shouting won't help. Just a normal voice please but plenty of lip movement!' And off they went again.

Cissy painted bitter aloes on the child's finger tips and sighed over her hair. 'You're just one of the unlucky ones who have to wash it two or three times a week,' she said and ran a despairing hand through the lank strands of weed. When Garbie stood up Cissy realized the girl was taller than she. 'What a magic beanstalk!' she cried with husky affection and squeezed Garbie's shoulders.

They bought her an Alice band and a grey flannel suit, a little loose-fitting, and stood round in a circle to applaud the vision.

'Doesn't she look divine everybody?'

'Not half bad!'

'Quite elegant!'

Garbie stood in the centre smiling fit to bust. She thought she looked really smart.

She wore it for Whit Week when they were taken down to the seaside. They went to Port Cawley where a Labour candidate was being selected. Jack had been told it would go down awfully well if his family were seen around the place.

It was still just possible to have a holiday at Port Cawley. The old town, not much more than a fishing village, clung desperately on to its disused harbour and whitewashed its face, but the brown postcards in the sweet shop had been there for ten years, some of them. To the west and spreading inland, dull cubes of architecture formed orange slopes along the valley. They fastened like farrow on to the chemicals factory.

On the coast, beyond the one small undamaged strip of sand, they were digging and drilling an artificial harbour that could usefully serve an oil refinery. The whole thing hinged on the main road slowly putting out a London sucker towards them.

Most people were delighted with the way things were going. Two or three farmers had been able to retire. Only the few men who still fished for a living would be puzzled four or five years later, to discover cankered and ulcerous oddities in their catch.

All this meant interesting social changes. 'A shift in the voting pattern,' as Uncle Jack described it. Tea parties and bazaars were on the decline while supermarkets and bright new pubs with fruit machines sprang up with the steadiness of adolescent sores.

Most of this escaped the children who had their photos taken dribbling white sand between their toes or leaping over the seventh wave. Quentin and Robin hired a small sailing boat to take them away from the world and Cissy built up a nice tan while Garbie hung for hours over rock pools.

Only Jack, facing the selection committee in the back room of the Baptist Hall (which smelt strongly of Three Nuns and antiseptic), observed the local implications and expressed his curiosity about the biological research station being developed up on the downs, no more than a mile from the chemicals factory.

It was his conviction that disarmament was vital now that Russia had her own bomb, which swayed the committee.

Three days later, his adoption was announced.

On October 25th, that year when the country, wearied by austerity, brought their beloved Churchill back into power, a swing against the trend was noted in Port Cawley. Sir John

Whitlock, local Conservative member on an unchallengeable majority for the past twenty-one years, almost lost his deposit.

Jack Pendleton had become a member of His Majesty's Opposition.

This brought a little popularity to the new girl at Dovedale Hall.

'He's my uncle,' she said. 'He's my uncle,' pointing proudly to a triumphant photograph in the morning's *Times*. The other girls, a friendly crowd, daughters mostly of wealthy steel and wool families for miles around, were warm in their admiration.

Garbie grew two more inches and became quite happy. Dovedale Hall, turreted and ridiculous, offered a curriculum that was well within her scope. Like all the girls she learnt a little French, the art of water pastry, the History of Scarlett O'Hara and a few acceptable snobberies.

5   23 December

The ward clock says half past six. Time creaks by. There are threads of liver stuck still between Garbie's teeth.

Across the yards of oiled parquet a black, religious crow hangs between Peg and Daisy's beds, pecking at wafers. They snigger quietly as they press their palms together in orison against their noses.

A screen is wheeled around Ethel Macready so as not to upset anybody. Especially the visitors.

Freddy will have found the note pinned to her door, though it's doubtful whether he will come. There are so many reasons against it. Snow is forecast on the radio; heavy falls in the south-east. And the train service, the nurses say, is poor. Besides . . . and her mind turns away from the other work he might be doing. She is used to men who come and go.

A trolley rattles in, its cups making an irritable sound.

The Reverend MacWhinnie comes to see her and asks whether he can stir her sugar.

'Back trouble eh?' he shouts and laughs as though he's made a joke.

Her mouth is too full of woody pips and gristle to reply.

'I hope everybody's being kind,' he goes on, edging slily towards some remark about this being the time of year for kindness. He has thick, nondescript features, greying hair and a tubular nose that seems entirely boneless. He is a lecherous man but has come to rely on God's forgiveness. One has to believe in one's product.

Garbie makes a blocked and gurgling response. Then: 'It's very nice to have someone to talk to,' she says in a tone that invites serious discussion.

Mr MacWhinnie is taken aback. Topics swing on a carousel

round his mind. The weather, falling church attendance, fêtes, Tottenham Hotspur, war wounds and Father Christmas, each subject safe for a particular category of person, spins round out of reach and wrong.

'Sit down,' says Garbie, and shakily, he does so.

'We can expect snow,' he says hopefully.

There is a pause while he feels to make sure his dog collar isn't back to front.

'What's your Christmas message going to be?'

'Oh ...' He shrugs. 'The usual.' He puts his hands on his knees with fingers splayed to stop any fidgeting.

'In my view,' she says loudly (though she tries to control the volume, knowing it to be a bad sign), '... in my view, the Church should be more openly political.'

'Ah ...!'

'For its own survival. The power of prayer you see is doubt-ful, if not totally unreliable in its effects. Action's what's needed. Action.'

'I do agree,' says Mr MacWhinnie faintly though he doesn't at all. He detests politics and thinks homosexuals should be hanged.

'After all, if anyone's got the money, the church certainly has!'

'They make tremendous savings on wages,' he cries, not fol-lowing her at all.

The two of them join in a gust of counterfeit laughter.

'So what's it to be?'

'Pardon? What's what to be?'

'Your message, naturally ...!'

'Oh ... forgiveness, kindness, goodwill, renewed celebration of Christ's birth ... love ...' The vocabulary of his profession becomes fallen egg-white in his mouth.

'Doesn't mean anything very much, does it?' she says morosely.

'I wouldn't say that.'

Garbie begins, without preliminary, to weep violently. Aghast, Mr MacWhinnie leaps to his feet. 'Can I get you a drink of water?' he jabbers as guiltily he spies the beating, starched white wings of Sister speeding towards him.

'What's all this?'

Nobody is capable of reply. Mr MacWhinnie rubs his fleshy nose with a nervous finger and finally mutters. 'It'll do her good to have a cry.'

Her vision full of love's neglected causes, Garbie sees brown babies too exhausted to cry, children murdered by the industrial filth cramming their mouths, homeless refugees driven into the sea, the transparent eyelid of poverty. She sees the East German boy mown down on No Man's Land, the Pope, clothed in white piety, pronouncing sentence in elegant Latin. *Humanis Vitae*. She sees a world wantonly allowed to bleed.

They let her grow quiet.

'That's better!' says Sister and straightens the bedclothes, the small act a very image of restored order. 'Perhaps Mr Mac-Whinnie will sit with you for a while.'

The gallery of straining necks shrinks back. Mr MacWhinnie crumples reluctantly into his chair. Pausing until he feels quite safe, he rolls back his upper lip in smile and says, 'We can expect snow?'

'That's right!' says Garbie brightly fighting her way towards the correct note. 'I've always been highly-strung.'

'Snow, for certain,' repeats the Reverend MacWhinnie.

The Reverend is perfectly right. Snow *is* falling. Flakes sweep in a dustcloud across the dark yellow night sky. Peg and Daisy press their bells in a frenzy till someone comes to prop up their pillows so they can watch it all through the windows opposite. They sit there with their earphones on, listening to *Does the Team Think?* and gaze peacefully at the flying torrents of flakes.

Viv James wiggles inside her plaster to stop an itch and prays the lanes round Rawley don't fill with snow and stop her family coming to fetch her. She goes through the list of things she has told them to buy ... chestnuts, chipolatas, muscatels, sweet sherry, extra bread, beefburgers for the little ones who won't touch turkey, a box of crackers, brown paper, string, a miniature bottle of brandy for the brandy butter. They can't manage without her she thinks and slips pleasurably back into her pillow.

Two nurses come into the ward carrying a small Christmas

tree, their navy blue coats powdery white and sparkling across the shoulders, their faces glowing pink from the effort of struggling through the snowstorm.

A tiny sigh of joy spirals after them.

(Mrs Crichton-Smith closes her eyes and speeds through the pine forests of Austria in a ringing sleigh, sable wrapped to the tips of her ears.)

The tree is secured in its practical bucket and looks very small in the long, high ward. Garbie can just see the nurses draping it with tinsel if she turns her head flat to the mattress.

They fix a glittering star to the top and thread small blue red and green lights through the branches which refuse to go on when plugged in. This makes them laugh. One of them calls out to Mrs Crichton-Smith, who is nearest, that they'll get some one to fix it. But Mrs Crichton-Smith is nearing a Schloss perched high on the mountain and doesn't mind at all.

The girls have brought a warmth with them, a little of the ordinary world outside which colours their murmurings . . . parties, presents . . . kisses they expect to get. Their eyes sparkle.

Suddenly the lights go on by themselves and there is a soft clapping of hands.

Garbie's neck aches with looking.

'Good night!'

'Good night!'

The nurses go, swinging their cloaks and blowing kisses. They glitter with melted snow and excitement.

'Good night ladies!' And the doors swing.

Like aged children they sit (or lie) staring at the fairy lights in silence, the rapture draining out of them. They were promised something better than this. Better than plastic needles and tinfoil pennies.

Small parcels bob on the branches (they have to be small or the branches would break). They are neatly wrapped and empty. They have a decorative function.

'Ah . . . Well . . .'

Daisy lets the little tree slide out of focus although she still looks in its direction. It's simply that her head's got stuck. She is listening to the seven o'clock news on her earphones and her eyes see nothing at all.

Pip. Pip. Pip. Pip. Good evening.

'Good evening,' mutters Daisy.

Here is the seven o'clock news.

Garbie stares at the ceiling and learns that the world is about its usual wicked business.

Two trains have collided near Walsall killing three people and injuring ten.

Restrictions on immigrant entry are not to be eased. The Russians have a rocket a million times more powerful than the one dropped on Hiroshima. Chieftain tanks have arrived in Israel. A dog can bark in tune to Jingle Bells. The police have not traced a missing child in Yorkshire. Suggestions in a White Paper for housing the homeless are not to be adopted and the world record for non-stop harmonica playing has been broken by a 63 year old grandmother of five who has kept it up for seventy-three hours and forty-two minutes.

'I beg your pardon,' she says. Mrs Crichton-Smith's neat head has appeared at the bedside. Her large eyes have retreated behind the bone.

'I beg your pardon?'

'I couldn't help overhearing.'

'Overhearing?'

'Not *eavesdropping* ...'

'No.'

'*My* husband was in public life ...'

'Oh.'

'... we travelled the world. Thirty-five years in the diplomatic service,' she smiles and sighs and touches her mouth delicately. 'From Puerto Rico to the Dardanelles. We lived in Vienna ... My son's there now.'

'In Vienna?'

'South America.'

Mrs Crichton-Smith has fastened a fine lace collar round her shoulders with a coral cameo brooch. She smoothes it lovingly. 'Are you much travelled?' she inquires.

Garbie hears the announcer saying the South East region

could be cut off by heavy drifting and wriggles her head free of the earphones. 'I was thinking of Paris or Rome only this Christmas . . .'

'Ah, *Rome* . . .'

'I'd like to try Majorca.'

'I once danced with Il Duce . . .'

'I . . .'

'I . . .'

There is a small, rainbow silence while they stare past one another.

'Of course, girls *these* days,' begins Mrs Crichton-Smith with the prettiest hint of a sneer, '. . . girls these days have careers.'

'I'm in public libraries. I was. Islington. I like libraries, I have a feeling for books.'

'Books . . . !' The eyes retreat further into an old dream.

'Ten libraries in twelve years I've been to. You see a lot of the world that way.' Garbie's stiff, conversational joints are beginning to ease. 'I had a proper training.'

'I have a book my husband wrote. *A Domestic Life of Agamemnon* . . . he was bitterly opposed to Arthur Evans, bitterly.'

'I think of the public libraries as a *service*, a real service to the public . . .' Garbie pauses. '. . . Of course, I'm not in public libraries any longer,' she explains, about to say she's found something with *tone*.

'Is it nearly visiting time?' asks Mrs Crichton-Smith peering at the clock in agitation. She likes to have someone to talk to when the visitors arrive so that she doesn't look as though she's been forgotten.

'Ten past seven,' says Garbie, 'I don't think my training was wasted.'

There is a distant banging of bedpans down the corridor.

'It's always something to fall back on,' persists Garbie trying to fight off a thin bile of fear in her throat.

'Ten past seven. Not long to go.' Mrs Crichton-Smith adjusts the rug over her stiffly plastered legs, examines her rings and inquires whether Garbie is much travelled.

'Chesterfield, Bakewell, Todmorden, Stoke, Harpenden,

Hatfield, Lambeth ...' concentrating hard, Garbie ticks off the places on her fingers. 'All those places I've been in public libraries. Occasionally a Carnegie library. It's stimulating to have a change of cataloguing systems.'

Mrs Crichton-Smith looks straight at her. 'How,' she asks carefully, 'did this interest begin?'

Garbie stares back uneasily, looking for the trap. She lets her eyes slide to a tiny straying thread in the old lady's fichu.

'How did it all begin, how did it start?' repeats Mrs Crichton-Smith firmly. She is threatening, but Garbie focuses on the thread and steadies herself. There is a terrible ache in her neck.

'Soon it will be a quarter past seven,' says Mrs Crichton-Smith impatiently and the danger of the direct question passes.

Garbie lets her stoppered breath escape, guardian still of her secrets.

People peck at you with their sharp little 'hows' and 'whys' trying to dig out private meat.

'Talk to me! Talk to me!' demands Mrs Crichton-Smith angrily (the visitors will be here at any minute) but now she's thoroughly frightened Garbie off. Yellow and suspicious, she's lifted her bedclothes up to her nose, over her mouth.

Surreptitiously, Peg scatters apple blossom talc between her thighs, just in case. 'Without hope,' she says, 'you're dead.'

Six pairs of eyes fasten wistfully on the door.

Into the ward bursts a wave of energy, noise and merriment. Five children all thickly wrapped in woollen scarves and hats break and scatter, followed by a tall, smiling man in a tweed cap. Whooping and squealing the children run up the ward, snow falling from their wellingtons.

Viv James's arms are open wide to withstand and welcome the torrent of kissing. Her husband has brought a little suitcase, and has lost control of the children. Like baby seals plopping one after another into the water they slither away and ride in the wheelchairs, send oxygen cylinders spinning over the floor and play tig round the Christmas tree.

Everybody watches the rescue of Viv James and sinks a little deeper into the winter waves.

Her bed is smoothed over, a warning oblong of ice.

Across the frosty stretch of grass a few nurses practise their carols in the empty canteen, giving themselves a faulty A on the piano. Hearing them, in the kitchens, Maybelline Odingu tears the last of the giblets from the turkeys and fills a brown paper bag with leftovers for the family.

Outside in the world, late night shoppers fight for a place on the bus and newspaper editors send out search parties for old people alone who don't mind a half page picture in the paper that might bring in a few postal orders. The office party is moving out of its sticky phase as middle range executives crawl round filing cabinets in pursuit of their secretaries and Jack Pendleton M.P., addressing a private meeting of the Thursday Group (a number of Labour Party members whose views on nationalization are interestingly out of line with those of their colleagues), is thrown off his feet by an explosion which seems to come from inside the drinks cupboard. He sees Hugh Bennett hurled upwards from his seat like an astonished Buddha before falling face down on the carpet.

'CHRISTMAS EVE AND ALL'S WELL!'

It is dark outside. Painfully, Garbie turns her head to look at the young nurse who's brought her morning tea. There is a faint warm smell of soiled bedclothes and bandages.

'They'll be taking a look at you today!'

'At me?'

'Yes. Here, slip this under you.'

'I'd like to make a phone call.'

'What, at six o'clock in the morning?'

'Oh.'

'And when you've done that you can rinse your mouth out with this.'

They come and look at you in pairs, marching two by two in identical white coats that are stiff with hygiene. They raise her legs one after the other to see how far each can be lifted before she's convulsed with a spasm of pain. It takes three of them to ease her over on to her stomach and then coolly, academic fingers examine each angry knot of her spine.

Her face, pressed to the mattress is wet with sweat.

'Very good!'

One set of fingers is replaced by another. Then another. They discuss the matter.

'What do you think?'

'Traction?'

'A lumbar injection? Float the spinal cord off with anaesthetic.'

'We must X-ray of course.'

They applaud one another and gather their notes.

Fear and pain fight for the upper hand. Her mouth, streaming with damp, is muffled by the mattress and prevents her shouting. Not that she could shout out loud anyway. Terror has always silenced her.

They pass on, leaving her lying face downwards, unable to turn over, unable to turn even her head because, when she tries to move her neck, all the wires scrape against sharp chips of bone. Her tongue lies, a useless flap of gristle against her teeth. She's heard of a woman who had a hole burnt in her intestines when they passed the bright radioactive beam through her. All the waste and fluids of her system seeped through, flooding the body with poisons.

Garbie's mouth opens and fills with feathers.

'Please ... please ...' she croaks to a passing shadow.

'Just a jiffy ...'

'Please ...?' Footsteps yelp urgently back and forth.

'I want to make a phone call.'

'Excuse me ... please!'

'Yes.' Palms rasp together with impatience.

'I need to make an urgent phone call.'

They trundle a telephone close to the bed and plug it in.

'What's the matter? Forget to get your letter off to Santa Claus?'

'No ... I ... it's got to be stopped!'

'Couldn't agree more, there's too much of it around!' laughs the friendly girl and wipes a bogey from her eye.

She doesn't like phones. They make her shout. She reaches

out a hand and a pain shoots down her back but she can't stretch far enough to dial the number.

'Please . . .?'

Peg and Daisy opposite are radiant with interest. They wave encouragingly to her.

'Please . . .!' she whispers.

Now the nurse is irritable. Her lips are pinched like bacon rind and she dials the number Garbie has whispered so fiercely she breaks a nail.

The number is ringing before Garbie remembers she promised Freddy to keep the number secret and her face burns red.

The telephone goes on ringing. By now the call has aroused so much interest in the ward she dare not put it down and disappoint them. In any case, she realizes with panic, she can't reach high enough to put the receiver back again.

Suddenly, there is a popping sound and a strange voice says 'Hello!'

Panic seizes her. 'Hello! Hello' she shouts.

'*Hello*!!' repeats the voice again.

'Hello! Hello! Is Freddy there?'

'Put your money in the slot,' says the·strange voice wearily over the popping sound.

She has no money. Helplessly, she lies with the receiver to her ear until the popping sound ceases and a steady buzzing begins. Two large tears roll down her cheeks.

Now she has a fresh crop of fears. Now she wants to know where Freddy is, what Freddy's doing. Fears combine like figures in a dance whirling so fast they make confusion. Outside, the snow falls faster, rising up the walls to the window ledges. Soon it will stick thick and dead to the glass while they play indoors with their radioactive rays and laser beams.

'The present you've got me . . .' shouts Daisy to Peg. 'What's it begin with?'

'Who says I've got a present?'

' 'Course you have, you mean old bag.'

'All right then. S.'

Daisy thinks about it and tries to grip the sheet. 'S ...' she murmurs.

'Smoked salmon is it? Silk pyjamas?'

Peg giggles.

'Saucy pictures? Cigarettes?'

'Think again!'

Ethel Macready rises from her long dream and believes herself dead. She has a glimpse of angels and all sounds are soft and distant like far-off steps in the snow. Two discs of light, two shining underwater shapes slip slowly towards the outer edge of her left eye and vanish. Now a scattering of quasars, pinpricks make shivering pains in her pupils.

If there is pain, she thinks slowly, I can't be dead. It's hard to tell where her hands and feet are. Then into this pale vault bursts a sound of living rage, a howl of protest like a thin, red, angry line advancing along the sharp contours of its graph. It is to her right. Dimly, almost a week away, she hears a voice say :

'What a lot of fuss! Over such a small thing!'

And she knows for sure she is alive. 'Well, bugger me!' she whispers to herself.

'What a lot of fuss! Over such a small thing!'

Sister is being patient, she knows Christmas puts an extra strain on her 'girls'. So she doubles her chin in kindly reproach as she might if she were coaxing a child. The cosy flange of flesh makes her face look as though it's on a life raft.

'Come along now Beryl ... It's only a little photograph ...' She puts out a hand.

Garbie tries to heave away but a liana of pain along her spine pulls her back.

'Has someone been telling you silly stories about X-rays?'

(Garbie's tongue wallows in glue.)

'Right girls!' Sister details her troops with a brisk nod of the head. 'One, two, three – up!'

(The tongue electrifies, lets forth a scream.)

'Goodness, gracious me! You'll have us all reported!' pants

Sister as her patient is raised and rolled on to the trolley. A cool linen sheet is pulled over Garbie, stretched and folded by four quiet hands. 'There!' says somebody. And she's wheeled away.

One wheel needs oil. It squeaks like a tortured nerve as they pass down dim corridors, left, right, right again, up a ramp, past a row of people, faces carved in patient waiting. There is a smell of adhesive and iodine and faintly steaming coats.

Although her stomach is liquid with nausea, Garbie has settled for a dull surrender. It is impossible to resist the things done for your own good, whatever Freddy says. (Freddy says resistance is the starting point of personality, but it's like trying to crack citadels with teaspoons.) She closes her eyes and gives in. The pain is less vicious that way. She can slide from one surface to another quite easily and even welcome the cool hand that gently smoothes her hair from her forehead.

Only when the great lamp is lowered over her and the woman in white hides behind a screen, leaving her alone between two heavy plates that might so easily, so readily squeeze the breath right out of her, do the birds begin to flutter on a confused mass of wing.

But it's nothing. The voice cries, 'All over!' And it's done. No flash of light, no roar of machinery. The damaging beam has passed quietly through her ... it's done. Perhaps the dust of Nagasaki deformed as peacefully as this.

Daisy has received a Christmas card. '... From the Staff and Management of the Cat and Fiddle,' she reads out slowly, her glasses slipping down her nose, 'Shall I read the verse?'

'Oh I like to hear the verse,' says Peg.

' "To you this joyous Christmas tide
Be love and friendship near.
The blessed birth of Jesus Christ
Was meant to bring good cheer.
All o'er the earth
The glad bells sound
To bring you joy my dear" ... Oh, isn't that lovely!' she murmurs as her glasses mist.

'Some people make a fortune writing tripe like that.'

'There's no poetry in you Peg!'

'I'd rather have a milk stout.'

'Don't get my juices on the run.'

'And a little dish of winkles. With a pin.'

'They'll have you for cruelty, Peg. What day is it?'

'Tuesday, Christmas Eve in the workhouse.'

'Tuesday, so it's boiled ham and prunes . . . How many Tuesdays we been here, Peg?'

'Twenty-four for me, twenty-two for you.'

'That's a bloody lot of prunes.'

'You're hurting my head!' Mrs Crichton-Smith reprimands.

The Hon. Mrs Lisle, Friend of the Hospital, has come in to do the ladies' hair for tomorrow's party. Mrs Lisle notes the angry glitter of the old lady's diamonds. The rings are loose on her fingers.

'Clumsy old me!' she tuts, and winds the fine grey hair more gently round the roller. 'Looking forward to your party dear?' Her vowels are shaped by razors.

Mrs Crichton-Smith, who thinks this is a silly question, says nothing.

'I'm sure you *must* be ...' Mrs Lisle reassures herself. (Her own mother is so wonderful for her age, so alert, so *particular*.)

'You're hurting my head!'

All manner of ungraceful phrases rise to Mrs Lisle's lips: she is not, most definitely not, accustomed to being spoken to in this tone of voice. She braces her neck against her pearls and decides to say nothing. The poor old things can't help it.

Nurses gather up the earphones. To make sure everyone listens to the carol service they say, but it's to cut off the disturbing stream of bad news, for Christmas is a jolly time and nothing is to spoil it. There's turkey and stuffing and a sixpence in the pudding. There are crackers to pull and jokes to read out loud to your friends, so we'll have a merry tune instead. Give us a note, nurse!

A pain killer for Miss Pendleton.

Pethidine flows through the needle into the veins and flushes all the little worries out. They float away, the rubbish of the ebb tides and leave her still as a rock pool. Lazily the hours slip through the glass vaguely marked by the changing angle of shadows. Meals come and go, there is an alteration in the footstep, in the rise and fall of speech. The snow, it is murmured, is falling again.

Garbie is still aware of anxiety, but without either shape or name it floats above her, a tethered kite obscured from time to time by passing clouds. It is easier to think of orchards.

The carol singers come in with mock lanterns made of silver paper and strips of sticking plaster. They group themselves, rosily flushed beneath their white caps, waiting for the right note on the recorder.

'O, little town of Beth-le-hem . . .!' they sing.

'How still we see-ee thee lie . . .!'

Peg and Daisy are smiling as though their faces will split, heads weaving, stiffly off-key. Where they can remember the words they sing them, where they can't they make them up or make do with something they do know. Daisy has hidden her card under her pillow so her friend can't pinch it and put it on her own locker. Beneath her breath she is singing 'Glasgow belongs to Me' to the tune of Good King Wenceslaus, she has forgotten she is going bald, has forgotten, just for a moment, that her knees are like yams and her toes so curled over she might as well be without them.

Sister waves at the old ladies to encourage their singing though she places a finger to her mouth as one small fair nurse sings the part of the page on her own, under threats of a rusty harmony from Peg.

The lights on the little Christmas tree fuse again but nobody bothers – they are entranced by the sweet uncertainty of the girls' voices and the way their song chains an infinity of Christmasses together, memories that merge and glitter in one single celebration. Their minds are crammed with friends linked round the piano, the popping of corks and crackers, wishbones and burnt little sausages, so dry they're hollow inside. Back even further, for the one great memory stretches to bumps on the landing and an extra, mysterious weight at the end of the bed, walnuts eaten in the dark of the morning, fingers so cold they are clumsy with knots, spitting sounds from the stove, the crowd of women in the kitchen, guessing games and the great Bible with its purple satin marker.

There is a last quivering note from the recorder, a rustling of music.

After the nurses have left the routine goes stealthily on, but the women are only half aware of their Horlicks and pills. Nobody tonight asks if their light can be left on longer, they are only too willing to slip from the waking ecstasy to sleep. Quietly the nurses tuck the sheets beneath their chins moving from bed to bed on tiptoe.

Staff tells night nurse who has just come on duty that should Miss Pendleton stir, she may, just for tonight give a further injection. Her notes, which she passes on mention that Mrs Crichton-Smith has mild depression, that Miss Macready's high temperature is beginning to fall, Daisy Arkwright has constipation and Miss Pendleton's results are through.

6 Reconnaissance

Garbie slipped through the public libraries of Chesterfield, Stoke, Todmorden, Lambeth, Ealing and finally Islington. There was little variation in the municipal scheme and smell so they merged peculiarly, dominated by the self-same supervisor wearing loose woollen garments and a man's wristwatch. It was everybody's ambition to get into the new Hampstead library but competition was terrific and Garbie was always being ticked off for reading on duty.

Calmly she passed from one area of irritability to another dividing her Bank Holidays between Dagenham and Rotherbrook until one day Uncle Jack nipped out of a debate and took her to tea in the Tate gallery. 'How are *you* getting on?' he inquired, gently dabbing with his hanky at some rings of fizzy orange on the Formica table top. 'I mean, are you ... *happy*?'

He took time to select the word and having selected it, felt it was wrong.

'Oh yes of course, Uncle Jack. How are *you* getting along? And Aunt Cissy? And the boys? And Victoria? I must come over one weekend soon.'

'Any time. Any time,' protested Uncle Jack.

'How about the weekend after next?'

'Yes, I'm sure that would be perfect. Give us a ring nearer the time, whenever convenient.' He smiled, folded his handkerchief and began to hum the Eton boating song while collecting himself for a fresh sentence.

'I will, I will,' his niece promised intensely! 'And there's only a month to Whit.'

'Only it seems to me ...' he went on, putting the handkerchief away and patting his pocket, '. . . that all is not well.'

'Oh?' she leaned forward, her concern repelling him like hot breath. He retreated, his gaze shooting up to the roof.

'Not with *us*!' he said hastily, and gave a little laugh, 'With ... er ... you. That is, with your situation.' He swallowed a little and laughed again to excuse his clumsiness, then got pushed in the back by a bearded couple edging past in their rainbow drapes. They were saying aggressively how deeply *intelligent* Richard Hamilton's work was.

'With *me*?'

'Oh, don't misunderstand me! I'm not voicing a criticism you understand ... we only want the very best for you.'

'You don't have to tell me that Uncle Jack,' said Garbie warmly, 'I know you do.'

She certainly didn't encourage him; in anyone else he would have suspected sarcasm but he saw she wasn't capable of it. She was smiling like an old, old friend.

'Well, it just doesn't seem terribly satisfactory, all these ...' Again he found himself searching, it was most unsettling. His hand strayed to his tie '... all these job changes and so forth. I'm thinking of work satisfaction, surroundings, people ...'

'I know just what you mean!'

'I have something in mind. The difficulty is, it does involve somebody's doing me a favour, you understand, and it would place me in a most embarrassing position if you left within a few months ... do you see what I mean?'

'You can trust me uncle!' Garbie winked gaily.

Hopefully he continued, 'I think the people, surroundings would be more agreeable, a wider range ...'

'Yes, well they're very nice of course in the Library, but narrow. Good natured but terribly *narrow*.'

'Are they?'

Garbie dropped two more lumps of sugar in her tea. 'Shockingly sweet tooth I've got!' she quipped and raised her cup in a kind of salute.

Jack Pendleton noted the marked growth in his niece's self-confidence and wondered wildly whether it were developing along the right lines. 'Well then,' he said again with inconsequent importance, 'this could be the very thing. With your

interest in current affairs, a news cutting library could be just
. . . your cup of tea.'

He ended weakly observing how easily one picked up Garbie's own expressions. '. . . At the Broadcasting Centre.'

Garbie's cup banged back in its saucer. Her mouth dropped
open and widened further, exposing ecstatic and quivering
pink tonsils. 'Oh!' she breathed. 'Oh, Uncle *Jack*!'

Her head seemed to flatten and her spine wriggled as though
she were a rapturous dog. Small, panting noises came from
her before she could finally speak.

'Oh, you are *good* to me! I don't know where I'd be without
you . . . and Aunt Cissy of course, well all of you, you're all
important to me. And kind. It's . . . I can't . . . I don't know how
I'll ever be able to repay you for all the kindnesses you've ever
done, the time you spend thinking about me, *worrying* about
me – there's no need for you to worry like you do, but that's
just because you're the kind of people you are. There just
couldn't be two better friends than you and Aunt Cissy. Well,
all of you. Do you know, when people say to me politicians are
all the same, you know, liars and cynics, I say, but you just
don't know my Uncle Jack. You really ought to meet him,
that'd be an eye-opener! And I tell them about you, you know,
all the wonderful things you've done for me and how there's no
reason why you should . . .'

'That's most kind!' Her uncle spoke in a strangled voice
and seemed to struggle to his feet. 'But it's no more than we'd
ever do for one of the family!'

'Oh!'

'Now!' He glanced at his watch, 'I must get back to the
House, for the foreign aid debate, but don't let me rush you,
dear . . . I'll write when everything's settled.'

But Garbie who was in a kind of trance, said eagerly that
she'd come with him. There was something about foreign aid
she wished to discuss.

'We've got real opportunities now,' explained Jack Pendleton,
gamely striding at a lion's pace along the Embankment. 'No
more of this piecemeal business. A concerted effort. International co-operation!'

Now his party was in power he found himself in a promising position in the Ministry for Overseas Development.

'... We want an end to these prestige projects. A more fundamental approach is needed in education, medicine ...'

'Yes, yes.' Garbie pursued her uncle at a half-trot on her rather flat feet. Her shoulder bag, clutched in her left hand, kept banging against her knees.

'... Aim to get the people really on their own feet. That's the thing!' he cried, waving to a colleague in a passing taxi. 'Yes, that's the thing!'

'Good thinking!' shouted his niece. Jack Pendleton turned with a weakly grateful smile, 'Glad you think so!'

'I'm right behind you on this,' said Garbie squeezing his upper arm with tremendous warmth. 'And I'd like to do something useful towards it myself. Perhaps I could collect money.' Because of the traffic noise she brought her face as close to his as she could. Jack Pendleton's eyes wandered forlornly round her earnest features and he moistened his lips.

'What a generous thought!' he said, and sank down, one foot in the gutter, beneath the force of his niece's enthusiasm.

The Broadcasting Centre marked 'a real step forward', as Aunty Betty put it, glad to have her niece out of libraries where she could see the opportunity for marriage was limited. 'I've always thought,' she said, putting it another way, 'that all the education you got at that nice school was put to waste in the library.' Aunty Betty glanced above the fireplace at the Sixth Form photograph – three close-packed rows of healthy girls, looking like a coach party who'd stopped off at a stately home. The stately home, a Disney affair, mullioned and turreted, swelled in the background.

'It really brought you out of yourself, that school,' she said. 'It really equipped you for *life*,' she went on approvingly, 'not for libraries.'

'Oh I don't know ...' remarked Garbie who had gone into libraries because of the cultural possibilities. 'There's a lot to be said for books.'

'All the same,' argued Aunty Betty, and stopped. She looked

again at the photograph, picked out Beryl, left of centre and nodded confirmingly over her cup of tea. 'You learnt a lot of useful things.'

Dovedale Hall educated its pupils on the basis of their future marriage to young men rising swiftly in the family steel firms. They learnt the latest in ballroom dancing and visited the Walker Art Gallery once a year. They grasped the convolutions of etiquette and were encourged in public speaking. Garbie had won an 'A' for effort in the art of conversation, though the woman who examined her and played the part of conversational victim marked her lower on execution.

'It developed interest in current affairs,' Garbie agreed. 'And I made some nice friends.'

The tea cups rattled like polite applause.

'Well perhaps you'll meet a few more now,' said Aunty Betty hopefully. She wondered if Beryl had ever had a boyfriend. At thirty-one, it was high time.

'You want to dress yourself up a bit,' she murmured.

'Oh, it's done a lot for me already,' said Garbie. 'The Centre. It's the people you meet. It rubs off, it's bound to. The discussions and so on. I mean you're bound to be quiet in a library aren't you? It stands to reason. There's very little brain stimulation once you've got the system taped.'

'I can see that,' replied Aunty Betty doubtfully, reaching for the tea strainer and pouring herself a fresh cup. 'But have you made a real friend?'

'Lots,' said Garbie, 'I like it there.'

She had taken her autograph book to work and all the girls came to admire the collection of signatures. They were always ready to take an interest, whether it was simply lending a pencil to stir the coffee with or entering into arguments about South Africa or the structure of the welfare state. She was happy.

She was happy, bent over the newspaper columns, swollen finger tip running down the print ringing the occasional word round with red biro. Every time the door opened, her head went up on a related mechanism to see if anyone famous had come into the room.

'Mind you,' prompted Aunty Betty, slicing open a scone and

spreading it carefully with Stork, 'I'd like to see even *more* of a change.'

'They talked about promotion prospects.'

'I mean *more* of a change . . .' repeated Aunty Betty, trying to catch falling crumbs.

'What more could I want – I've an active life, and as long as I'm busy . . . ?'

'I'm thinking of social activity.'

'Well, there's my social work, my town flat and plenty of job satisfaction. I've a lot to be grateful for.'

'No one'd quarrel with that,' conceded Aunty Betty, her mouth full. She thrust her tongue round her gums to clear them of dough. 'You have a lot to be grateful for.'

Sensing the devious approach of a complaint, Beryl added, 'I'd see you more often, except I'm so busy.'

'With your *friends* . . . ?' Cunningly, Aunty Betty waited.

'And my committees, yes.'

'Any special friend?' Carelessly, Aunty Betty reached for another scone.

'Well there is one . . .'

'Yes . . . ?'

'A really nice girl from Orpington, Shirley Dutton.'

'Oh,' said Aunty Betty, disappointed. 'Oh yes.' And in her disappointment, she allowed herself too generous a smear of margarine.

Shirley Dutton travelled in from Orpington every day on the train with her slimmer's lunch in a see-through carrier bag.

Shirley wanted to leave home.

'If we *shared* a flat,' said Shirley one day as they sat in the Roof Garden with their skirts raised as high as was decent, 'we could get something really nice.' She looked hard at Garbie. 'Something with its own kitchenette and shower. And a separate entrance maybe.'

It all sounded very pleasant : Garbie said so.

'Trouble is,' explained Shirley, nibbling her Ryvita in the smallest possible bites to make it last, 'my Mum and Dad think girls in London get bought up by white slavers.'

'That's ridiculous,' said Garbie, tucking a strand of hair behind her ear. 'I've lived here or hereabouts for years now, and I've never even met one.'

Shirley glanced at her, then went on: 'Now if they could *meet* you, it'd be a load off their minds, wouldn't it?'

'Would it?'

'Well yes. I mean if they thought I was sharing with an older girl, a sensible kind of a girl, a girl with an M.P. for an *uncle* . . .'

'Oh I see!' Garbie beamed and picked some fluff out from between her toes.

'And you'd like a better flat wouldn't you? It can't be very nice living in one room.'

'It's all right,' said Garbie.

'But a flat would be *better*, wouldn't it?' Shirley persisted.

'Oh! Oh, I see what you mean . . . well yes. It'd be lovely.'

'Why don't you come for Sunday lunch then?' Shirley's pretty little pink mouth and white teeth opened hugely round a Granny Smith.

'I was thinking of spending the weekend in the country. With my people.'

'Suit yourself!' Shirley shrugged and smiled radiantly at a young trainee producer who appeared on the roof carrying a beer and two ham rolls on his clipboard.

'But on second thoughts . . .' murmured Garbie, absently re-adjusting her slide . . .

'Oh go on . . . it's nothing grand, mind. Just a roast and two veg. But if the weather holds we could go for a swim in the afternoon, and my Mum'd be tickled pink to meet you.' The trainee producer backed round a corner of the skylight and disappeared apologetically from view.

'Why not then!' With a convulsive slap on her thigh, Garbie agreed. 'And that'll leave me free to visit some other friends on Saturday!'

Her other friends, a young couple she'd met through the anti-apartheid movement, were tied up on Saturday.

'We're absolutely up to our *eyes*!' declared Rose Birnberg over the phone.

Garbie could hear a lot of music and giggling going on in the background. 'Oh,' she said.

'Another time though!' said Rose.

'Fine. O.K. Let me know if you ever want any babysitting done!' offered Garbie gaily, and rang off.

That left Saturday unexpectedly free.

But Saturdays in Islington were always busy.

Down below her window, on the top floor of a narrow terraced house, Garbie watched West Indians hurrying to the Holy Church of God. They spent all weekend (sometimes from Friday evening onwards) in the Holy Church of God. The Holy Church of God was the Methodist Church Hall, built of reddish brick and dribbled with soot and white slogans. All she could read of them now was 'MOSLEY'.

A dull sun shone down making the men sweat. They wore suits with short jackets and shoes with long pointed toes, curiously deformed as though they walked all the time on the outer edges of their feet. Their collars made bright, clinical rims round their black faces. The women wore mauve, yellow and salmon pink. Their daughters wore straw hats and white gloves and scattered the dark street like daisies. When they started to sing inside the Church Hall Garbie could see the roof rock in a jaunty, irreligious way.

The woman from next door, Mrs Bonniface, crossed the road to walk in a noticeable manner on the opposite side, her feet crushing glass in the gutter. Garbie left the window and went to choose her weekend clothes.

She allowed herself a long time, wrote a prodigious shopping list and stuck plasters on her yellow heels so she could wear her new white summer sandals. Then, walking carefully, she went out.

A roar of holy bliss rose from the Church Hall.

'Downright bloody shocking! . . .' said Mrs Bonniface, going back to the market with two empty bags. 'What kind of pagan racket d'you call that?'

Garbie gave a hearty laugh as though someone had told her something harmless.

'Call themselves Christians do they?' Mrs Bonniface had dark, dyed hair and a faint growth of green fur on her upper lip. 'Voodoo more like,' she told Garbie, whose smile fluttered and revived in friendship.

'Oh they're Christian all right,' said Garbie.

Mrs Bonniface laughed at her credulity. 'Bloody funny Christians if you ask me ... killing chickens and dancing about with no clothes on!' She pulled the fine lines round her mouth together ... 'Black magic more like,' she declared.

'Oh I don't know,' said Garbie, but Mrs Bonniface pressed on:

'They move into your houses, fifty at a time, pinch your jobs, practise filthy habits *and* you can't understand a ruddy word they say ...'

'It's not their fault,' beamed Garbie.

'What do you know about it eh? I don't suppose you've had your job nicked like my Basil ...' Basil was a tired young man with a skin problem, who passed the day playing pinball in a Fun Parlour. 'There's nothing for him on the sites these days — and why not?'

She turned to nod to her eldest daughter, who'd come out in her rollers and slippers to hear what was going on.

'They've just not had our opportunities.' Garbie could feel her eczema coming on.

'Well they're not short of 'em now are they? Ah, you're all soft you lot. You don't know your bum from your cake 'ole.'

'Some of 'em's all right.' Sleepy Maureen spoke. 'That Sidney Poytych's not bad.'

'Oh well 'im, he *looks* like us don't he?' Her mother conceded a point. 'But it's not your Sidney Poytyeh or your Harry Belafonte you get round here. It's your basic, off-the-trees, nig.'

Garbie felt her face bulge. 'They're just the same!' she insisted.

Her neighbour cawed with mirth; 'You need your eyes examining!' she advised. 'If that's what you think. And I tell you something else ...!' She thrust her triumphant face forward and breathed gluey fumes up at Garbie. 'They don't like your sort neither!'

A twenty-ton truck groaned past and drowned whatever else was said.

Garbie trailed down the street to the transport café talking to herself and was forced to step off the kerb to avoid being knocked over by two small boys with a mongrel dog ducking and yapping at the end of a clothes line.

(Saturdays. But more difficult, Sundays.)

She got some milk from the machine outside the transport café. Two drivers behind the glass nudged, said something about her and laughed. It excited her. None of the rooms to let on the newsagent's board sounded right for Shirley, so she clutched her shopping bag and made for the stalls of Camden Passage.

The Victoriana and second-hand clothes smelt of mortuaries. Leggy girls buried into the piles and held things up against themselves for their boyfriends to see.

'Oh I must have it!'

'What do you think?'

Garbie tried a black satin jacket with golden pagodas on it. It was tent shaped and very large.

'Super!' said the young man behind the stall in plum velvet. She flushed and put it down.

She fingered stuffed birds and Georgian silver, pushed through the throng of people admiring one another's miniature dogs and arguing over where to lunch. It was eleven-thirty.

By midday the market was ankle deep in cabbage leaves. The air was full of market cries and selections from My Fair Lady flooding through a loudspeaker outside the radio shop. Women fought to disentangle the wheels of their pushchairs from one another and picked the fruit over to spot bruises.

Garbie bought herself an ice lolly and recommended Kiwi King in the three-thirty to the man in the sweet shop. 'Do you know of a nice room with shower and separate entrance?' she inquired.

'Why should I know?'

'I thought you might. Have you got the right time?'

'Twelve twenty-three.'

'It's just my friend is looking for somewhere to share with me.'

He shrugged and weighed lemon sherbet out into two-ounce bags.

There were blowflies on the butcher's meat and blood dried brown in the sawdust.

'Four pork sausages please!'

'Make it half a pound!' He put six on the scales, then buried his hands in slippery liver.

'Enough for one?' he cried and weighed it, cheating marginally over the price. The place was full of bereaved, the single and the separated. But things were changing all the time. In the shiny new Sainsbury's they sold garlic sausage and green peppers.

'What's this when it's at home?' muttered an old thing in a headscarf. It was Fanny Ann. She turned a purple object, cellophane wrapped, over and over between scaly grey fingers.

'An au-ber-gine. Au-ber-gine,' said Garbie and spelt it out for her.

'Bloody 'ell,' said Fanny Ann and put it back on its spotlit shelf. She shuffled off towards the cliff of Krispy Flakes, then turned and bared her teeth, as amiably as she could. 'Eh,' she said. 'Do you want yer stamps?'

A crowd of men gathered round the betting shop. A student sold *Peace News*. A mother showed England to her au pair and another mother, younger, festooned with pale children, felt the phlegm bubble green in her chest.

Garbie walked down Copenhagen Street looking in all the newsagent windows. She passed the council flats bannered by washing, down the Cally past the Public Wash-house and back up Pentonville Rise. There was a gap in the corrugated metal screen and she could see the bulldozers, digging out sores.

A great ball on the end of a crane swung towards a row of eyeless houses and smashed their faces in with the steady regularity of a playground swing.

The bricks slipped in a gentle spray of golden dust. They submitted gracefully, ready to die.

After twelve the demolition gang earned time and a half.

'It's a wonderful sight!' crooned the man with one eye.

'D'you know of a room would suit me and my friend ... A flat, I mean, with its own entrance?'

'If you stick around a couple of years,' laughed the man with one eye. 'They'll have just the job going up here. But let me recommend you and your friend don't get married. It's terrible from the tax aspect!'

'Oh ...' said Garbie and went up on to the waste ground where you could see the smoky saucer of London for miles and miles. The two boys were trying to train their mongrel dog to jump over an old iron bedhead.

At first it refused, its head pulling at an awkward angle against the tug of the clothes line and then it tried valiantly, twisting its ribby brown body in an effort to clear the obstacle. It landed, rolled over, and eagerly leapt to its feet wagging the hoop of its spine in hope of praise. The smaller boy hung hard against the line and the bigger one waved a biscuit above his head. Excitedly the dog crouched and trembled, barking for its biscuit. Then, as the boy hid it behind his back, the dog's ears dropped.

A long pink ribbon of tongue swung from its jaws.

Again the boy teasingly waved the biscuit bringing the dog to its feet. Its bark grew sharper with impatience and bewilderment. The boys laughed. 'Make him beg for it!'

The mongrel didn't know how to beg but was ready to please and tried, awkwardly balancing on his long, curved spine. He tumbled, catching the clothes line in his feet. When he stood again the merriment had quite gone out of him.

Up went the biscuit and down.

In the blur of brown Garbie saw yellow teeth. The boy went down screaming. The smaller one pulled with all his weight on the clothes line, but the dog had fixed itself deeply to his brother's leg.

'Gerr-off! Gerr-off!' The voice was high.

Garbie ran forward flapping her arms. The dog let go, snatched the biscuit and ran off cringing. It lay under a bath and watched with mean eyes.

'You asked for that.' Garbie hauled the boy to his feet. His face was streaked with grubby, blubbering trails. Roughly he rubbed the arm of his grey jersey across his eyes. 'Fuck off,' he said.

'Don't tease! Don't tease it! Of course it's going to bite you.' She was hot and shrill and still hanging on to him. He broke free of her.

'I said, fuck off,' he shouted. 'Fuck off or I'll do you!'

She backed, breathing heavily. She felt for her hanky in the sleeve of her cardigan and blew her nose.

The younger boy squinted at her curiously.

She stumbled away towards the dog and bent to pick up the loose end of the clothes line. The brown ears went down and a low rumbling came from the dog's throat.

'I'll set him on you if you don't piss off!'

She stood up and stared dumbly at the boys, her mouth working to separate the rubble of words.

'You ought to take that ankle to a doctor,' she stammered at length.

The boy bent down and picked up a sharp stone.

They stared at one another. Slowly he threw it up and caught it. Threw it up and caught it.

She walked awkwardly over to her pile of shopping, picked it up and left. A treacherous tide of moisture rose in her throat.

'I'd like my friend to see it first,' she said to the landlord, a man with a chin like cactus. 'It would be sharing you see.'

'Yeah.' He scratched his ear, knowing he'd have let the rooms to somebody by the end of the afternoon. 'You can leave a deposit,' he added hopefully.

'I'd rather my friend saw it first.'

'As you like.'

'Can I ring you?'

He gave her the number. 'A deposit'd be safer,' he said.

There were two other flats to see. She walked all the way up the Holloway Road because it helped the afternoon to go quicker. Her new sandals were killing her.

The first doorbell was answered by a woman who'd been crying her eyes out and showed her with melancholy pride how she and her husband had re-decorated the rooms with odd ends of wallpaper to give a contemporary effect.

'Very tasteful,' said Garbie.

The second one was the property of a Pakistani who said he liked white girls. He himself was married to one.

Worn out, Garbie returned to her own room, stuffy from the heat collected under the asbestos roofing, and typed a letter to *The Times* deploring the rise in rents in working class areas.

The walls of the church hall swelled and bulged with song. The members of the Holy Church of God beat their horny hands on their tambourines, till they could be sure Jesus himself would hear the glad noise.

Garbie drew aside the plastic curtain, jaunty with its sailing boats and wavy turquoise sea, to fill the kettle at the wash-basin and set it on the gas ring. Then she sat, elbows pressed painfully to window sill and watched the street. This room got the evening sun.

A smell of hot tyres rose off the road though the traffic fell away about six o'clock on a Saturday. Normally the lorry drivers roared and hissed their way down this narrow street to the caff at the end. You got used to the shaking of glass. One day a child would be killed unless the new people who lived behind purple, olive green and putty-coloured front doors, and grew geraniums in their window boxes, got up a petition.

In the room of the house next door, divided from Garbie's by powdery plaster, a man snored. In and then out. In and ... out. The air rattled rhythmically through the rusted metal of his lungs.

The kettle boiled. The clock ticked. Faintly she heard the signature tune of the television news from downstairs. And across the road they quivered in their joy of Jesus.

Five hundred pairs of eyes gleamed white as they turned towards her without ceasing their song. 'Jesu-us loves me ...!'

they sang, tongues trembling pink in their brown mouths as she hesitated in the doorway.

They reached to the ceiling in tiers. They sat on the floor, leaned against the walls. Behind the netball post was a blue and gold banner saying Girls' Friendly Society. Two people argued as to which of their seats Garbie should have.

'Praise the Lord!' shouted the small black man on the platform, his voice hoarse. The tambourines rose shuddering in the air.

'Praise the Lord!' wept the congregation. 'Praise the Lord! Alleluia!'

The little preacher man detached his gaze from heaven and let it slide over the white face, a sudden blob in the sea of brown.

'Praise the Lord!' he screamed. 'Praise the Lord!' His body went into a convulsion.

'Jes-us, Jes-us!' The sweat poured over him. 'Jesus is outside in the cold. He is outside my heart and he is cold and he is lonely.'

('Alleluia!' groaned the crowd.)

'He is out there and he wants so to come in. "Oh please," he say, "let me enter in your heart." He say, "let me enter in your soul for warmth and comfort. I is so so cold out here! And oh, Jesus, oh how he want to enter in ..."'

'Alleluia! *Alleluia*!'

'Do you have room in your heart?'

'Yes, yes, Praise the Lord!'

'Can he enter in out of the cold?'

'Yes, yes, Alleluia! Praise the Lord!'

'He is so happy, he say. He is so happy!!!'

'All-e-lu-ia!'

The woman behind Garbie fell to the floor groaning.

The crowd swayed and moaned, their eyes closed. A breath of wind shook the tambourines.

'Do you love Lord Jesus?'

'Yes, yes!'

'Do you love Lord Jesus?' Louder.

'Yes! Yes!'

'DO YOU LOVE LORD JESUS?'

YES. YES. YES.

The arms went up.

Garbie pulled her cardigan sleeves over her hands and hid them there. There was a hot, sour smell of excitement in the hall.

'Well, then. He say we must all love one another. We must all love and kiss our neighbour!'

The woman behind Garbie began to crawl on her stomach towards the platform. The children over whose feet she slithered took no notice.

'I love my brother ... And he love me ...!' They all began to sing.

The young boy next to Garbie shifted in his uncomfortable suit and pointed a finger for her at the song sheet. His lips were dry and wrinkled as lizards.

Some of the singers began to leave their seats and holding hands, wound round the perimeter of the hall in swaying dance.

'Oh, I love my brother ... And he lo-ove me!'

'And kiss our neighbours ...'

The snake of dancers encircled the hall. They broke off singing now and then to laugh and kiss a warm cheek.

'We live toge-ether in His Company!'

Garbie stared at the words and felt a languor spread within her. The boy holding the song sheet sang murmuringly.

'And Jesus beckons on the Jordan side ...!'

The crowd unwound into the dancing thread like a ball of wool.

'... To love us all He gladly died ...!'

She felt faint. A big brown woman in the dancing line paused and pressed honey lips to her face. A sweetness burst in Garbie's head. She turned to the boy next to her in his stiff suit and kissed him violently on the cheek. She felt a hot rush under his skin. He gripped the song sheet and turned his head away. A nerve shivered along his jaw.

Time to go.

*

'Pleased-to-meet-you!'

Shirley's mother wore a white spotted navy silk dress and a string of heavy, carved coral beads. Her hair, an unnaturally even chestnut brown was permed like a nylon bathing cap. 'Very gratified I'm sure,' she added aggressively. 'Aren't we Dad?'

She turned to Mr Dutton whose big oblong red face sat like a chimney on his formidable body. 'Oh aye.'

'Right then, well let's get off the doorstep and have a little chat in the lounge.'

Shirley kept nudging her.

'Would you care for a glass of sherry?'

They sat in an upright circle fingering the tiny glasses. The bristly upholstery tickled the back of Garbie's legs. Mrs Dutton played with a lace hanky stuck in the sleeve of her dress and announced: 'We're glad Shirley has such nice friends.'

Shirley giggled and quickly drank her sherry. She'd put her hair up revealing two burning and slightly protuberant ears.

'London is an evil city,' remarked Mr Dutton. His hands were like boiled bacon.

'That depends ...'

'Drug peddling and vice rings,' he asserted.

'Oh Dad, honestly ...!'

'I hope you don't mind rice pudding,' said Mrs Dutton.

The two bars of the electric radiator burnt hot, although the sun shone outside on the rockery.

'Evil is as evil does.' Garbie challenged her host.

'Exactly,' said Mrs Dutton. 'Would you go and turn the oven up Shirley?'

As her daughter left the room, Mrs Dutton leant forward and hissed: 'She's boy-mad you see. That's the trouble. Now a nice friend like yourself, well, you look just the ticket ...!' She paused to admire Garbie's grey jersey dress. 'And we know all about your good home don't we Dad?'

'Oh aye. Labour is he?'

'Labour yes.'

'I'm a Conservative myself.'

They sat round the shoulder of lamb.

'Try and find Miss Pendleton a lean slice Dad.'

Fat oozed through the crispy outside.

'Take your elbows off the table Shirley! And pass the mint sauce.'

'What does she want to go wasting her money on rent for, mother?'

'You've got to try and keep up with modern youth a bit, Dad. And Miss Pendleton here I know would keep an eye on her.'

'Oh I would,' beamed Garbie. She felt Shirley kick her viciously under the table.

'I've done a bit of travelling,' announced Mr Dutton heavily. 'I was out in the Middle East. I know what's what.'

'She's very young you see ...!' Mrs Dutton leant across her daughter to whisper to Garbie.

'I think I've got a flat!'

The news came as a shock. The Duttons froze.

'Great!' said Shirley. 'When can we move in?'

Mr Dutton thrust the carving knife under her nose. 'Just a minute young woman,' he said, 'just a minute.'

'Please help yourself to greens,' said Mrs Dutton rapidly, feeling for her handkerchief.

For a moment, Garbie was unsure which party it was best to please. She thought about it, swallowed a ball of phlegm that had collected suddenly in her throat, controlled the urge to shout and said: 'It's very conveniently placed for bus routes. Kitchen, sitting room, one bedroom, use of bathroom, cost of light included.'

'One bedroom?' Mrs Dutton's face relaxed and she turned to give her husband a meaningful look.

'*One* bedroom!' echoed Shirley. She glared at her friend.

'Oh well, one *bedroom* ...' Mrs Dutton repeated. 'Now you haven't any gravy have you? You can't go without gravy.'

'You look like a young woman who'd be particular in her habits.' Mr Dutton's thought processes arrived at their slow conclusion.

Sunday lunch became quite gay. Mrs Dutton chattered on,

wanting to know all about the furnishings at Rotherbrook and what clubs Garbie belonged to.

When the girls left to go to the Outdoor Baths she called after them : 'Don't swim for two hours at least. If you swim on a full stomach, you'll sink. I'll serve afternoon tea at four-thirty.'

Shirley sulked all the way to the Baths.

'Have you really found a flat?' she said at length, letting Garbie pay for her.

'Well ...' said Garbie and pushed through the turnstile as fast as she could.

'Eh? Have you?'

'Well ...' said Garbie racing for the changing rooms.

'Where is it?' shouted Shirley over the partition.

'Well ...' said Garbie and pulled on her rubber cap so she couldn't hear.

'We feel ...' Mrs Dutton passed a grey tongue over her lips. 'We feel that Shirley would be in very good hands with you. We'd like to inspect first of course,' she added. 'What do you say Dad?' She pulled the trolley towards her and cut into the pink sponge cake.

'Oh aye,' said Mr Dutton. 'And give us a decent sized slice of that cake will you?'

Somebody was boiling flannels in the house. She smelt it as soon as she put her key in the front door. There was still all of Sunday evening left.

There was only a week to go to Whit.

Whit week was fine.

At Rotherbrook all the conversation was about the war on world poverty. Uncle Jack's work was significant.

'Before the war you know, poorer countries, even the colonies really had to get along under their own steam. It took an earth-quake to get any aid in there. It's an appalling thought isn't it? Do you know how much money was poured into under-privileged countries last year from the West?'

'Can't think.'

'Guess?'

The younger people whom the Pendletons always liked to have around them glanced at one another seeking inspiration.

'Three hundred million?'

'Five hundred million?'

'No ...!'

'What then?'

He took a deep breath: 'Three *thousand* million!'

There was a whispering sound of muted gasps. Everybody turned to look at one another with amazement and pride.

'It always used to be said by Marxists,' Uncle Jack went on, knocking out his homely pipe against the dog grate, 'that the working masses would never succeed to prosperity and happiness without revolution. I think ...' he paused to give a modest nod, 'that we've proved revolution can be rendered unnecessary by caring and generosity.'

The young Labour League pressed their palms together in silent applause. Garbie too. She ached with pride in Uncle Jack.

Any time left over from discussion of tractors, dams and family planning was devoted to Victoria's forthcoming wedding. It was planned for the end of July and the reception was to be held on the lawn. Under canvas if it should rain, but that was more than Aunty Cissy could bear to think of. As it was, simple calculation was beyond her and the number of salmon, game pies, hams and magnums that could be accommodated on average by one hundred and seventy-seven stomachs, rose and fell like a balance of payments.

'You've over-calculated,' said Garbie, helping.

'I dare say dear, but it's better to err on that side,' sighed Cissy, thinking of the damage to her lawn. 'The hospital is always glad to have what we can't manage.'

She added two more names to her list, confusing the sums even further.

'What *colour*, I was wondering, Aunt Cissy, for the bridesmaids' dresses ...?'

'Bridesmaids' dresses ...?'

'I've seen a nice gold satin ... It would set Victoria off beautifully.'

'Bridesmaids ...?' repeated Aunt Cissy looking round for escape.

'I said to Victoria that I could give her a hand. Hold her train, you know ...'

'I'll give her a ring this evening,' promised Aunt Cissy faintly.

'When *I* marry,' Garbie went on. 'I shall keep it very simple.'

There would be, thought Cissy, sufficient roses from the garden to decorate the tables.

'I couldn't let you spend this sort of money on me,' said Garbie generously.

Cissy stared at her niece, a lozenge of ice slipping into her stomach. Mortified, she seized Garbie's hand. 'My dear child!' she cried, 'we'd always do the same for you ... of *course* we would!'

Victoria said she could do without help.

'*Please*,' begged her mother.

Victoria gave in to cream satin and gold shoes.

To her fiancé, Gerald Buckingham, as he made sadistic love to her in his Chelsea flat, she snapped that if there were one thing more likely to ruin the whole affair more than a three month pregnancy, it was her bloody cousin.

It took a gruelling display of virtuosity on Gerald's part to take her mind off the matter.

'We're tackling the land first,' said Uncle Jack. 'Land reform. Once we've got the land right, we're away. We're pouring in machinery, fertilizers, seed and naturally, irrigation schemes.' He paused to straighten a hunting print on the wall. 'And the wonderful thing is that this is an *international* project, the Americans are building a University and the Germans have submitted schemes for a teaching hospital. I can't tell you ...' and he was genuinely moved. 'How exciting it was to visit the villages of Awanzikwa and see the hope we've generated.'

He clenched his hands together and rose a little on his toes.

Later on, of course, there would be prospecting for zinc and copper deposits.

Obi Imbono, currently completing a postgraduate course at The London College of Economics, and a regular guest at Rotherbrook, adjusted his gleaming shirt cuffs. 'My country,' he murmured meaningfully, 'will become the envy of its neighbours ...' He glanced down to see if the whites of his eyes were reflected in the glossy toe caps of his shoes.

'Ah!'

'*Indeed* ...'

'*Trade* agreements are the things,' declared Uncle Jack evading Obi Imbono's gaze. 'We must use trade to stabilize relations. I look forward to the time when an African Common Market can flourish.'

'Jolly good,' said Obi Imbono, and knocked back his Scotch and water.

Edward, home from University for the weekend, wanted to say something aggressive and contradictory, but it was wasted on his father who took all arguments, even the downright perverse, as equally fascinating viewpoints to be fondly and patiently examined like moths or matchbox labels. Edward wanted to outrage his parents and found, in some elusive way, he was never allowed to do so. They smiled, stroked his hair, nodded thoughtfully, cast their eyes to the sky to ponder what he said, and gave him a cake in a tin to take back to University.

'I wish I could *hate* them!' he confided to Garbie, who was wonderfully easy to shock.

She clapped her hand to her mouth as if to protect herself from breathing in poison gas.

'You *shouldn't* ...' Her eyes were flat round pebbles. 'They're so *good* to you.'

'I know, damn them!' Edward picked up a paper weight and hurled it through the french windows.

Cissy, combing her hair in the room above sighed to herself in the mirror and murmured, 'I expect that's Edward working off his frustrations again. I hope he makes an effort at the wedding.'

The wedding was to take place on the last Saturday in July.

'I'll take the Friday off work so that I can come and help you,' said Garbie.

'Darling, that's sweet of you, but truly, you mustn't.'

'Oh I'm going to,' said Garbie firmly. 'You can't manage by yourself.'

Cissy was troubled again by the sensation of barbed wire scraping against her teeth.

To make up for it, she put herself out and drove to town with the idea of taking Garbie out to lunch and on to Hardy Amies' for a fitting. At the last minute she asked Victoria to join them.

'How are you getting on?' inquired Victoria energetically. 'Still enjoying the job?'

'Oh I've settled beautifully,' Garbie began, and then cut off to engineer the strands of spaghetti into her mouth. Cissy and Victoria toyed with their Coquilles St Jacques.

'. . . more my kind of people . . .' Garbie went on, '. . . more intellectually alert.'

'Have you made friends?' inquired Cissy. 'I should tuck your hair behind your ears, darling.'

'I'm going to share a flat with a friend.' Garbie went pink with pride.

'Going to share a flat?' Interest was expressed. The forks made a pretty tinkle on the plates.

'Of course it's difficult to find the right thing at the right price,' she said confidentially.

'Do you need some help . . .?' Cissy said with a touch of hysteria.

'Deary me no, you mustn't worry about *me* . . .'

She squeezed her aunt's hand.

'I *mean*,' she said, 'I know I could always come to you if I really needed help, I know I can count on you and Uncle Jack, but I do draw the line somewhere!' she gave Cissy's inert hand a final pat.

'Of course you can darling. I'm so glad you realize that.'

'Who's the chum?' Victoria pushed away the rest of her lunch. Pregnancy spoiled her appetite.

'A really lovely girl called Shirley. A real live wire. She keeps us all in fits in the office!'

'Sounds fun.'

'Oh! There's Macdonald Tennyson!' Garbie dropped her fork on the floor and waved vigorously at a beaky figure who'd entered the restaurant. 'Coo-ee!' she called, 'Mr Tennyson!'

A chill grey gaze circulated the room until the spot was located and Macdonald Tennyson, for twenty-two years the centre's most distinguished announcer, sighted Garbie. He smiled as if he'd just had two teeth filled.

'There!' She turned back to her relations, breathlessly, her face blotched with pleasure. *'There!'*

'I bet you look really smashing,' said Shirley. 'Quite the glamour puss. I say, Mrs Trotter, did you know Garbie was having her dress made by Hardy Amies?'

'Yes I did,' said Mrs Trotter.

'You must show us the photographs,' said Shirley.

'Oh yes, you must show us the photographs,' cried two of the other girls, giggling.

'I wish I could get married,' sighed Shirley wistfully, re-arranging a lacquered curl, 'I'll be past my best soon.'

'Men prefer mature women.'

'Speak for yourself Garbie Pendleton. *I'm* not going to wait till I find someone who loves me for my mind.'

'What sort of man do you want to marry Garbie?' The two girls in their short, bright summer dresses, quivered like butterflies.

'I need an older man, someone who'll understand me.'

'Not *too* old!!!' They smothered their laughter.

'No, not *too* old of course. Sex is very important.'

'Ooooh!'

'Second only to companionship.'

'Ooh! Mind what you're saying!'

'Girls!' Mrs Trotter looked up wearily.

There was a twittering of sparrows.

'Psst!' Poppy Denham leant along the desk, her hand to her mouth, 'Psst! Hey Garbie, do you believe in pre-marital sex?'

'There's no need to whisper,' replied Garbie loudly. 'We can be perfectly frank about these matters. Yes, I think free love is perfectly all right. In fact, for highly sexed people I think it is essential.'

'Why's it essential Garbie?'

'Repressed sex can have nasty effects on you.'

'Go on!'

Mrs Trotter threw an even wearier glance their way.

'Yes. Spots for example. And worse than that,' she added darkly.

'Worse than that? Oh what?' Their fingers were pressed to their lips, eyes dark as onyx.

'Psychological things. In the mind you know?'

'Are you highly-sexed, Garbie, would you say?' Shirley wore a grave expression.

Garbie tossed her hair and thought a minute. 'I have reason to think so,' she said at length. 'I mean we must be frank about these things.'

Faint splutterings eddied round the room. Garbie knew that sexual talk embarrassed young girls and that's why they giggled so much. She tried to set an example of openness. She was, after all, about ten years their senior.

'Well do you get it often then?' Poppy's friend Madge sounded concerned.

'I beg your pardon?'

'Do you *get* it ... often?'

'Oh, I see, yes. Well no. I'm saving myself.'

'Oh!'

'Free love is all very well with the right person.'

'Oh.'

She tried to imagine the right sort of man.

'I beg your pardon?' she said again. Poppy was saying something.

'You know who fancies you ...!'

A hammer struck hard in her pulse.

'No, I can't say I do.'

'Norman Entwhistle.'

'Oh really?' She tried not to look pleased.

Norman Entwhistle supervised the stationery stores having

worked his way up from messenger over a period of eighteen years. He had a dolorous moustache, halitosis and lived with his mother.

'Now *there's* an older man ...!'

'We could do with a new batch of notebooks and some paper clips!'

'Yes, we could, I was hunting high and low for paper clips this morning!'

Mrs Trotter, without raising her head, opened her drawer, reached in, took out a box of paper clips and put them down in front of the girls.

'Oh thank you Mrs Trotter. Just what I wanted Mrs Trotter. Couldn't we do with some new typewriter ribbons?'

Shirley had to loosen her belt, her stomach ached so much. 'I'd fancy him myself if he was just a bit taller,' she gasped.

'Here comes the trolley,' remarked Garbie collectedly. 'Let me go and get the teas.'

It gave them all a chance to relax.

'No, I'll pay for them,' insisted Garbie, setting down the cardboard cups on the desk. Her lost deposit had set her back a bit, but she didn't want to compromise Shirley by mentioning it. 'By the way Shirley.'

'Yes love?'

'About the flat.'

'Oh yes ...' Shirley pinched her lips together and fiddled with her curls. 'I've seen something else.'

'Oh yes?'

'*Two* bedrooms.'

'Can you pass my methyl cellulose tablets love, I'll take one with my tea ... Oh, my Dad'd never let me.'

'But!'

'I don't want to set them against me, do I?'

'I thought.'

'It wouldn't be right.'

'No.'

'Keep your eyes skinned though.'

'Yes, yes. I will.'

7   Provocation

The wedding guests spread out across the lawn, a gay scattering of petals and confetti.

Victoria had decided against a train, but everybody made a point of noticing Garbie.

'Ah, here you are dear! What a pretty dress! Garbie, do you know Mrs Clavering, Gerald's sister?'

Garbie changed her posy to the other hand and shook that of Gerald's sister. The white gloves felt quite empty.

'I must be a relation of yours now,' she said noisily. Everybody *was* talking noisily so it would probably be all right.

Mrs Clavering took a small step backwards. 'Oh,' she said, 'I'm sorry?'

'I'm Victoria's cousin!'

'Oh I *see*!' Mrs Clavering turned her handsome Roman face to Lady Riddle who'd made the introduction and laughed lightly, 'Something once removed then!'

There was a tiny pause. Lady Riddle looked round at the other guests.

'Aren't we lucky!' she carolled. 'To have such splendid weather!' She beamed at them both and re-adjusted a bow on her shoulder. 'Garbie,' she announced, 'lives all by herself in a London flat. Frightfully independent!'

'Ah!' Gerald's sister looked hopeful. 'Whereabouts exactly?' She smelt powerfully of *Madame Rochas*.

'Islington.'

'A lot of people seem to be moving that way,' she remarked ambiguously. 'There are some terribly attractive Georgian houses I'm told.'

'I don't live in that bit,' replied Garbie argumentatively, 'I live on the other side.'

'That's interesting.'

'To see life as it really is.'

'What a fascinating theory!' Mrs Clavering gently touched her face with her hand to make sure it hadn't slipped.

'Oh!' teased Lady Riddle. 'There's quite enough misery in the world as it is, without wanting to live in it.'

'We need reminding,' said Garbie fiercely. 'It's not enough to sell flags on flag days.'

She hadn't meant to be rude. A wound opened at the wedding. 'We try to all do our little bit!' The lips tightened in defence.

She could hear their decorations rattling. They would have preferred to talk to Obi Imbono; he was such a *gentleman*.

In her long dress, she ran away from them before she had trouble with her words.

'She's an orphan, poor little thing, that the Pendletons have fostered,' explained Lady Riddle. 'Ah! more champagne!'

'I think I'm going to be sick,' said Victoria.

'Oh darling, not here!' Gerald guided her away behind the marquee.

Colonel Naseby Smith was standing by the sundial in the rose garden. 'I don't like weddings,' he said as Garbie flew past. 'Could you get me something to drink?' Then, as she stumbled up the steps and disappeared between the yews, he mumbled, 'Bloody servants, all bloody rude!'

She washed her face under the tap in the scullery forgetting that she'd been made to put on eye shadow and powder, then drank two teaspoons of anti-histamine medicine to soothe the itchy feeling.

The bunting fluttered over the lawn set high above the leafy rise and dip of the Sussex countryside. Pink and blue hydrangeas, hollyhocks and sweet, scented stock framed the lemon, emerald, pink and white of the guests who drifted over the lawn like the sail of small craft. All the way up the drive the dark glittering metal of their cars stretched in a solid line.

Edward detached himself from the gathering and climbed

the terrace carrying a champagne bottle. He saw her face at the window and made a gesture of comic despair before disappearing from view round the corner of the house.

He joined her in the scullery, wiping the sweat from his face with the back of his sleeve. 'Bloody stupid clothes to wear on a hot day,' he said. 'Let's get pissed.'

The champagne bubbled gold in the glasses. 'Come on!' He pushed one glass towards her across the table and gestured to her to sit down.

'You look bloody awful too,' he said. 'What's wrong with your face?'

'I don't know.'

They drank in silence.

'They tried to get me to shave my beard off.'

'I know,' she said.

He rubbed the sparse growth angrily.

'I do believe my nicely brought up sister has a bun in the oven.' He laughed and swung his legs up on the chair. 'She's as green as grass shit.'

Garbie didn't mean to giggle, but she did. 'Pardon,' she said.

'I wonder if they know ... I daresay mother's got a good idea. Still it's not likely to rattle them much.' He gazed thoughtfully into his glass. 'I wonder what *would* get a reaction ... perhaps I should rape you.' He grinned and raised his glass under her nose. 'What about that?'

She blushed at the flattery and found a perverse giggle rising in her throat.

'Perhaps I'm the one who takes after bad Uncle Rikki,' he said, keeping his eyes on her. They were a little bloodshot. 'We still,' he went on, raising a finger to his lips, 'don't talk about him, not even to mention his posthumous decoration, whatever it was.'

She crushed her knuckles to her mouth to stop the laughter.

'Don't you ever think about him?'

'No,' she lied, her voice muffled.

'Oh well,' said Edward, 'I suppose it's all right ... Gerald marries my sister but Uncle Rikki gets expunged from the record. It just shows how much attitudes have changed in the last thirty years, doesn't it?' He was watching her closely.

'I didn't know he had a medal,' she said proudly.

'For gallant conduct.'

She caught at his irony.

'The family's been very good to me.'

He looked at her witheringly as she stared down into her empty glass. 'Oh yes,' he said at length, 'Oh yes.' Clumsily, he filled her glass.

'If I were you,' he said cheerfully, 'I'd want to smash their faces in.'

'You're tiddly,' she accused.

'Oh, piss off to Sunday School . . . !'

'I'm very fond of them.'

He laughed at her.

'What are you doing?' she said dully.

'It's the spirit of my generation.' He pulled a face and ran his fingers up her arm. 'Rebelliousness, ingratitude, surely you've heard about it?'

'Oh.'

'But then you're not my generation at all are you? You're about what, about a hundred years old?'

'I beg your pardon?'

'A little Victorian.'

'Oh!' she said with relief, 'you're teasing me!'

'No,' he answered, trying to make her look at him direct, 'I'm not the one who teases.'

He smelt of sweet, unwashed hair and danger.

'You're drunk!'

'I leave that sort of teasing to other people. Playing games, dressing up.' He plucked at the sleeve of her dress.

'They'll be wondering where I am,' she said, and touched her hair which had been put up for the occasion. The roots felt tender.

'You can't ignore me just because I'm drunk.'

He poured out more champagne and lifted his glass to fragment the clear gold rays in the sunshine. 'How much like your mother *are* you?'

She hesitated. 'We're both of us a good height. ... And fair, we're both fair ... I mean was ... She *was*.' Garbie swallowed.

'That's not what I mean ... as a *person*. What was she like as a person?'

'I don't remember.' (They must be wondering what she was up to. She grew sticky at the idea of letting them down.)

'Oh dear ...!' sighed Edward and got unsteadily to his feet. 'Talk about life's victims ...' He wandered over to the window and stared at the crowd on the lawn.

'Except, of course,' he murmured, 'it's not like that at all ... not a matter of victims and aggressors. Nobody's allowed to be an aggressor any longer and nobody's allowed to find out they're a victim. It's just an arrangement of top dogs and performing dogs.'

'Is anyone looking for me?'

'I wish you'd listen,' said Edward crossly, 'this is all for your benefit. Can't you see what I'm talking about, that some of us are educated to be top dogs – only it's called independence, self-sufficiency, or some other addled name – and top dogs help lesser dogs. Give them things, you know. Like culture and technology and *envy*. They create imitators ... they make dogs who walk on their hind legs, performing animals!'

He seemed terribly angry. She couldn't think how he'd got on to dogs. Redressing the balance, she said : 'To tell you the truth I sometimes think my mother was a bit stupid.'

He stared at her, breathing hard, then burst into laughter. 'Well,' he cried at length, 'I suppose you've answered my original question.'

'I wouldn't like it known,' she added anxiously, 'that I'd ever said such a thing because it doesn't sound very nice, especially of your own mother. And some things she knew a lot about. Like films, she knew who was in what film, and when it was made and what the story was ... she was very good like that.' She trailed away.

Edward sat down again and tried to speak. After a few inarticulate movements, he gave up. 'What good would it do anyway,' he said absently.

'You do say some funny things, Edward, but I expect it's

the University,' Garbie reassured him. 'Well, I've really enjoyed our little discussion, but I'd better be running along to Aunty Cissy or she will be cross with me for neglecting the guests. I promised I'd help.'

She stood up, scraping her chair on the stone floor. 'Well!' she said.

Edward's face was hidden by his arms both of which he rested on his upraised knees. He was totally still. Something about his shape made her wonder briefly whether he were crying but it seemed improbable.

'Oh well ...' she said again and made her way back down the dim, cool passage out to the garden. Outside it was hot. The heat bounced up off the terrace and made her feel her throat and nostrils were plugged with warm wadding.

Tiny wheels of conversation spun sugary threads round the guests; their mouths stuck together in the isinglass of gossip. She cleared her throat and fought her way through. 'Hello, there, Uncle Jack! How are you doing?'

He stared. He smiled. Tiny drops of sweat clung to his upper lip.

'Garbie,' he said, *'Garbie!'* He passed his glass from one hand to the other and tried to stand in front of his friends as though he were hiding them. The other men stopped their talk and looked at her too.

'My niece!' said Jack.

They nodded their greetings. Hugh Bennett, Denton Caldwell, Ben Digby and Sidney Herzog, members of the Thursday Group. All came from constituencies which raised interesting industrial and economic points of challenge to Socialist theory. They nodded again and slowly turned towards one another.

'We cannot afford,' repeated Caldwell, 'to alienate the trade unions ...'

'Having a good time?' asked Uncle Jack.

'Yes thank you.' Garbie's ear bent towards the background conversation, captivated by the sound of large ideas.

'... There is anyway, the growing gap between executive and members, look at the miners. One can discuss things quite reasonably with eight out of ten of the leaders ...'

'Had something to eat?' said Uncle Jack.

'Yes thank you.'

'... traditional points of disagreement like a fixed percentage of unemployed and curbing strikes by legislation ...'

'What about something to drink?' Uncle Jack could feel his smile beginning to liquify.

'I'm a bit tiddly already!' She giggled.

'Jolly good! ... And why not!'

'... must be more closely involved in the consultative processes. It's the only way ultimately of getting them to think like us ...'

'Have you met young Caldwell?' He seized her elbow and guided her towards a short, white-faced young man with heavy spectacles that made his eyes disappear in a whirlpool of glass. 'Why don't you show him the house?'

Garbie, spotting somebody in need of comfort, bared her long teeth : 'You look lonely!'

Cyril Caldwell reacted as though a revolver had been thrust between his shoulder blades. 'Not at all! I just don't like these ridiculous affairs.'

Somebody jogged him and he spilt a little of his drink. 'I suppose *you* like it,' he said morosely. 'Women do.'

'It's nice to get dressed up once in a while!' she said, hoping he'd notice her new dress.

He sighed hopelessly and muttered something.

'I beg your pardon?' She lowered her ear to his mouth.

'Nothing. Can you, I wonder, direct me to the lavatory?'

She packed him off and felt a little weak with drink.

The tent was stuffy with the smell of trampled grass and trapped air. One of the waitresses stubbed out her cigarette as she saw Garbie come in.

'Time to clear!' she whined, tying her apron a little tighter. 'Everything satisfactory madam?'

'Lovely thanks! Why don't you help yourself to whatever you want?'

Garbie took two asparagus rolls and went to find Nanny, who was having an angry exchange of child-care theories with the Claverings' nanny, a pert little thing in false eyelashes.

'Children learn by imitating grown ups. That's how they develop.'

'Children are one thing, grown ups another. They've got to learn to do what they're told – once you've lost control you're finished. They've got to have respect!'

'Oh that's terribly old fashioned!' laughed the Claverings' nanny gaily and delicately dabbed the moisture at the corners of her mouth as she'd seen her employer do.

'If I were your nanny, young woman, I'd put you over my knee ...!'

She darted through the guests, a fly on the flank of the behemoth. Hundreds of white gloves flapped signals or beat off the nuisance. Flap flap. Teeth snapped.

She smiled at everybody although their words were quite naked of meaning; sense had slipped off hours ago. Down one throat she spied rifles. Pressed against people the close-ups were so huge she could see every grain, every pore. The bristles on Sidney Herzog's chin sprang up in a black formation of spears. She was crushed to the palisades of Nanny's teeth, to the lustreless warheads of Cyril Caldwell's. They fired their sulphurous blanks and rocked her. Turning to Edward who loomed up out of the smoke she saw, or thought she saw, desolate Normandy trees in his beard.

As she fell through the film with the dry brown lethargy of a sycamore seed, the camera drew back to its new angle so that first hats, then noses, eyes, necks, bodies, legs, filled the picture. Their feet were dangerously close and vast, the size of Saracens. The heads, tiny. The shutter closed.

'... the heat!'
'... too much to drink!'
'Don't crowd too close!' Aunty Cissy's voice.
She could smell her sweet, vanilla and milk.

They put ice on her forehead then lifted her, four of them, and took her indoors to her baby bed in the nursery. Her feet hung over the end.

'Where are my gold shoes?' she demanded.

'Just relax. You mustn't worry yourself about anything.' Aunt Cissy drew the curtains and the sun shone a dull blood colour into the room.

Victoria came to say good-bye. She was wearing a pale, linen dress.

'What a scene-stealer!' she remarked good-naturedly. 'You should be strangled.'

'I do beg your pardon,' said Garbie. 'Cheeri-ho Victoria ... if you see my gold shoes, you might get them sent up.'

She heard the sounds of departure beneath the window. Slamming doors. The hiss and crunch of gravel. Goodbyes.

Then the sounds became more sporadic. A little chatter, the friendly squabble of magpies, the departing sound of exhausts; someone washing up in the kitchen, the scrape and rasp of metal garden furniture on the terrace, the hiss of the sprinkler hose and Aunty Cissy's voice crying out indignantly that the catering staff appeared to have eaten and drunk everything in sight.

She rose and drew the curtains. Outside the emptying lawn was bathed in the long, bronze rays of evening sunlight. Four men were taking down the marquee while two others were retrieving paper plates from the grass. The old black pony hung its head over the paddock fence watching them. The terrace beneath was now in shadow but she could hear drinks being poured and people settling themselves into the creaking wicker chairs ... Aunty Cissy and another woman, unfamiliar. The woman was talking about a whale washed up on the Kentish beach.

'Extraordinary! Left behind, stranded by the tide. It took eight of us to haul it back into the sea, pouring water over it all the time to stop it de-hydrating you know. And once we'd got it back, can you guess what it did ...?'

(Aunt Cissy must have shaken her head.)

'It headed straight back for the shore again!'

'No!'

'But it did ... It died ...'

Ice rattled in the glasses.

Garbie thought of the whale, this great sea creature with its silly lungs, longing to live (as it must have done once, in pre-historic times) with other lung creatures on the land. Or preferring to die there, rather than swim, misbegotten, in the ocean for ever.

'We'd done all we could to help it . . .'

'What an extraordinary thing . . .!'

'There was nothing one could do . . . we'd done our best.'

'I'm sure . . .'

She lay in the nursery and wept tears of amber.

The doctor said it was migraine and if it happened again to take the green pills and lie down in a darkened room until it had gone away. 'You ought to have your sinuses unblocked,' he commented. 'You snuffle a great deal, don't you? How old are you?'

'Thirty-two.'

'Mm,' he yawned. 'It's tension here.' And he tapped his high, white forehead.

But Garbie had already decided it was the result of sexual repression and began eyeing men in the street. She told Rose Birnberg, who was expecting her fourth baby, that either it was *that*, or the fact she had so many of the world's problems on her mind.

'Why don't you give up the one and take up the other,' said Rose, who was doing her painless childbirth exercises and didn't want to be bothered by Garbie.

'A person like me needs a lover.'

'Everybody needs a lover.'

'The thing is, Rose – and I know I can talk to you like this because you're a friend – I'm not at all clear on one point. Oh, I know how it's *done*, I know that. I'm very well up on technique. It is a question of the man himself . . .'

She paused. Rose took a deep breath. '. . . Procuring one, I mean. I suppose that what I need a little help with is *allure*.' She smiled hopefully at her friend.

Rose shuddered slightly. She was in no mood to discuss sexual matters with Garbie. She'd first detected this aversion in herself while working for the domiciliary family planning service. It was one thing explaining contraception to these women who crowded their apron hips across the doorway, but it was quite another when they insisted on straying from the strict, scientific point and describing to her (with a frankness she had thought was entirely middle class) exactly what their husbands did. It made her tighten her thighs together.

'I've got some pamphlets you might like to look at,' she snapped and while she was looking for them in the study, she made herself put half a crown in the Spastics Box for being nasty to Garbie.

She read them on the tube going to Dagenham.

The man opposite kept waggling his hands in his raincoat pocket. Garbie smiled at him because he was sick and he couldn't help it. He got off at the next stop.

'Hello, Aunty Betty.'

'How do you do, Beryl, nice to see you. Come in.' They held their faces briefly close.

Then they sat opposite one another in the unyielding armchairs and stared at the grate.

'I see you've got a budgie, Aunty Betty.'

'It's company. Guaranteed to talk in six months or your money back.'

'Has he said anything yet, Aunty Betty?'

'No. I've had him five months one week and three days.'

The room smelt of polish and Fresh-Air Spray. There were three large marigold heads in Colin's granite shrine. Except for the minute scratching of claws on chrome, there was no sound at all. The room was sealed off.

'I'm thinking of having my sinuses flushed out, Aunty Betty.'

'Oh yes.'

'I've brought some photographs of the wedding – and a piece of Victoria's wedding cake.'

'Let's have a look then.'

She was impressed. She looked long and steadily through her bifocals. 'It must have cost them a bit.'

'They said they'd do the same for me you know.'

Aunty Betty looked at her unblinkingly. A cataract had fallen blue and cloudy over her left eye. 'You've got to find a bloke first,' she remarked.

Garbie said nothing. She picked over the photographs on her lap.

'I know his face . . .' Aunty Betty peered more closely. '. . . that's Ben Digby our local M.P.'

'What about my dress though? Doesn't Victoria look radiant?'

'. . . It was Ben Digby M.P. came to our Christmas party at the Old Folk's and kissed me under the mistletoe.'

'Oh yes. Do you prefer me with my hair up or down?'

'Up's tidier. Yes, up.'

They sat quietly in a kind of peace.

'I've got your cake in my brief case . . .'

'They're out again at the works you know.'

'Official or unofficial . . .?'

'Oh unofficial of course . . . they wouldn't do anything the proper way!'

Aunty Betty was contemptuous. Uncle Arnold had been white collar before he left for the Home.

'Pay?'

'Pay, yes. What else. It makes it difficult for the women-folk. Half the men don't want to be out, but they're frightened.'

'It's for their own good in the end. You must try and grasp that, Aunty Betty. In the *end* . . .'

'Maybe . . .' She sounded disbelieving. 'It's the Commie lot they've got up there now, that's who it is. I get to hear. I don't speak to others much but I get to hear.'

'It's the struggle against capitalism, Aunty. It's inevitable, they say.'

'A fat lot you know about it,' said Aunty Betty. 'Put the kettle on Beryl, there's a good lass.'

'You ought to get out more,' urged Garbie when she came back, edging sideways through the door to manage the large tray.

Aunty Betty had removed her slippers and was trying to waggle the stiff toes. 'I'm all right,' she said.

But Garbie had found grease on the cooker. 'I'll take you up West one day,' she promised.

'*I'd* go, but my legs won't.' She picked at the cake. 'How long's this been in your brief case?'

'If you don't talk to people more you'll end up in the Home like Uncle Arnold.'

'I've never been a talker. There's too much rubbish talked ... they want a say in management at the works, that's what they're asking for now ... who do they think they are? They're ignorant, most of them.'

'It's only right, Aunty!' She felt herself growing breathless as her enthusiasms began to ferment. 'It's the way government's got to go!'

'And you with all that education inside you ... you should have more sense. Still ...' She broke a biscuit in half. '... still, there's some pretty funny goings-on altogether these days, look at the girls, it's a different class of student they've got now. Take everything for granted ... there's no gratitude.'

The word made Garbie's scalp itch. The word took her back twenty years when it was placed like a nail to her skull and slowly hammered into her head. Tap, tap, tap. Obligations, things owed, sacrifices made, gratitude ...

It took part of you away as if by surgery.

She said nothing because her tongue had suddenly soured.

'*I've* not had an easy life!' remarked Aunty Betty finally with a spurt of savagery. She stirred her tea as though the cup were full of egg yolks and sugar.

'Are you short ...?' It was the response which now came most naturally to her. It surprised her. She scratched her head.

'I can manage.'

Conversation lapsed. Garbie addressed the rest of her remarks to the budgie which blinked at her suspiciously.

Then it was time to put the television on. They watched Opportunity Knocks, the news and the Northern semi-finals of Come Dancing. One of the women fell over which made Aunty Betty laugh. The budgie fluttered off its perch in consternation at the noise.

'I'd better be off,' said Garbie putting on her coat and picking up her brief case. She left a pound note folded under the three brass monkeys on the sideboard.

'Very nice to see you, Beryl. Let me know how you get on.'

She walked the long way round past No. 1 Gate where the pickets were out waiting for the night shift. Only one of the tall chimneys flared in the night sky; the rest were dead, black masts. The placards read: 'Three Pounds More for A Living Wage' 'Fair Shares' 'Three Pounds and Workers' Councils' 'Give us a Voice and We'll Get the Rest'.

One man, trying to get through, was quietly punched in the stomach. A policeman standing a few yards further up the pavement, looked the other way. The man rolled in the gutter, clutching himself, one arm over his head to protect it from any further sly blows, then when none came, he scrambled to his feet and ran over to Garbie's side of the road.

'Red bastards!' he shouted, shaking his fist. 'Commie bastards!' There were tears of rage in his throat. And then he ran as fast as he could towards the pale green lights of the main street.

Tomorrow would be Saturday again and time to look for the flat.

She read her pamphlets in bed, memorizing the most popular positions, practising likely phrases on her pillow and learning that oral caresses were quite normal though she wasn't altogether clear what was meant by that. She'd always taken kissing to be quite normal.

'I'd give you my all!' she cried menacingly.

There was a knock at the door. 'All right in there?' called the old man from the next door room who kept pigeons in a shed out the back. 'Yes thank you, Mr Bean!'

She waited till the slow steps had gone slap, slap down the lino stairs to the lavatory before cradling her pillow again. 'Have your will of me!' she tried, having heard the words before somewhere. Perhaps from the lips of Margaret Lockwood in one of the period pictures Dotty used to love so much.

The prickly ends of the feathers got in her nose and made her sneeze.

Getting out of bed she made a peanut butter sandwich but lost interest in it and put it out on the window sill for tomorrow's birds. Two cats squalled in the street like men on bayonet drill and she went to cross another day off the calendar though she tried never to do that until the clock had actually reached midnight. Otherwise it was cheating. She switched on Late Night Extra, wrote a letter, and promised herself some evening classes in September.

The cistern was still moaning downstairs when she sat down in front of the mirror. It reflected the pile of unwashed dishes behind her, a slipping pile of National Geographics, the open wardrobe door with her few clothes fallen from their hangers. She felt, looking at her sallow image, that some wires had been crossed, others left dangling.

She also felt that you could, in the dark, at a distance, mistake her for Veronica Lake.

Ben Digby rang up his friend and colleague Jack Pendleton.

'Jack,' he said in his warm Geordie voice. 'I've had a letter from one of your relatives. Says she was a bridesmaid at your daughter's wedding, though I can't, to be honest, remember the face.'

'Oh yes,' answered Jack heavily.

'It's rather unorthodox ...'

'Yes, it would be.'

'Urging me to drop in on her Aunty ... Betty would it be?'

'Betty, yes.'

'Another relative of yours, Jack?'

'No, no.'

'And then raising the business of the trouble in the motor industry. Talking about a worker's council funnily enough.'

'Well I never,' said Jack.

'You know, we had them during the war, I can't think why we ever dropped them. In many ways we've gone backward. Anyway, Jack old lad, shall I deal with it? I just thought, if Aunty Betty was somebody to do with you?'

'No, Ben, you just carry on as you think fit.'

'And the other thing I thought ... what about a spot of golf?'

(Jack Pendleton, aware of his niece's increasingly wide interests, hoped to God she wouldn't soon include among them, the
development of chemical weapons. He began to wish he'd not
found her that job in the cuttings library and wondered whether
he could interest her in market gardening instead.)

'Getting anywhere with Norman Entwhistle?' questioned
Poppy Denham, her eyes round as moons.

'That'd be telling wouldn't it,' said Garbie, stiffly, slitting her
razor round the edge of a cutting.

'Because we've got something else for you if not.' Poppy
went on. She rolled a sheet of paper into her typewriter and
rattled a few words on it.

'What?'

'I've got it here.' She banged the carriage, and typed something else.

'About that flat, Shirley ...' said Garbie loudly. Her palms
were sweating.

'Don't you want to see?'

'I'm still keeping an eye out.' Garbie ignored Poppy and
smiled at Shirley's averted head.

'You think she'd show an interest when her friends are
trying to be helpful wouldn't you?'

'What is it?' Garbie rubbed at her eye which had suddenly
gone puffy.

'We're filling out a computer dating form for you, but we
need a little help naturally.' Poppy smiled wide to make her
dimples work.

'Oh I see.'

Someone began to sing 'Some Enchanted Evening'.

Hot gravel poured into Garbie's head. She wanted to make
a joke but everything was silted up.

'You will see a stran-ger,
Across a crowd-ed roo-oom ...'

'Come on now, let's have the benefit of your advice.'

'Find someone really nice for ... someone really suitable ...'

She laughed to join in their merriment.

'Now I *know* you're on the lookout for someone older, I've definitely heard you say that, so what shall we put?' Poppy tilted her head back to think hard.

'Ninety-two!' suggested Milly.

'Now don't be a silly-Milly. Ninety-two's ridiculous. *Eighty*-two'd be more suitable.'

Milly had her arms locked around herself to keep the laughter in. 'Now what about *size*?'

Milly burst.

'Don't be dirty, Milly. Pull yourself together. We're trying to help Garbie. This is a serious matter.'

Garbie looked round with a wild smile. 'It'd have to be someone tall,' she said, making her joke.

' "Some en-chanted even-ing" . . .'

'Shut up, Maggie!'

The butterflies fluttered around Poppy's desk.

'Have to be tall . . .'

'Tall . . . old . . . and . . . dead posh.'

'Doesn't say posh there!'

The paper went from one to the other; long, pink, red, silver, nails.

'Doesn't say posh, stupid. You've got to do it properly.'

'Upper class then. Put V., Upper class, will you! Income?'

'Over five thousand, definitely.' It was Shirley. She was pretending to be Garbie and was using a funny, affected voice. Garbie pulled at the neck of her jumper where the wool felt like wire and grinned round cheerfully.

'What does gregarious mean?'

'I dunno. Tick it.'

'Interests . . .?'

'Hunting, shooting and fishing!'

Shirley's voice really was funny. 'Oh you are funny!' said Garbie and looked round running a dry tongue over her lips.

'Religion?'

'None,' said Garbie.

'Oh you can't say that. Put Muslim and you might get an Eastern potentate.'

'Are you Caucasian?'

'I dare say. *Are* you Caucasian Garbie would you say?'

'Oh, ab-so-lutely,' nodded Shirley, rolling her eyes.

'How *about* an Eastern potentate, Garbie?'

'Oh super ... just the thing!' She tried to think of a joke about harems or elephants but nothing suggested itself.

'You wouldn't object to a black?'

'I'm told they've got a lot to offer!' The girls exploded. Garbie caught their meaning and explained it was just a myth. They looked at her archly and said, how would *she* know. They wagged their heads and sucked their breath in. It was a matter of climate she said, but they were scanning the questionnaire again.

She tried to fix her mind on something. She stared at the summer rain racing past the window, she counted the number of panes, multiplied the ones across by the ones down, tried to calculate the area of each one. She had chilblains like tubers on her toes which irritated even in August. Twenty panes. Twenty nines and a hundred and eighty inches. A hundred and eighty inches equal fifteen feet ...

She thought of the beached whale.

Fifteen by four was sixty. The total area of the total number of windows was sixty square feet. The rain made the sky dark.

'You need a pound postal order!'

'It's good value, just think ... at the very worst it's a free dinner ...'

The beached whale.

'... And at the *best*, there's no telling ...!'

The whale.

'*Tears!*'

'What you crying for, Garbie?'

'... It's only a game, that's all ...'

'I'm not crying.'

'Come on, blow your nose.'

'... Just a joke ...'

'I'm not crying. I never cry.'

'Just a joke ... that's all ...'

8   Alliances

'I'd ask you in if it wasn't for the muddle,' said Garbie, finding as they stood on the doorstep that here was a man tall enough for her to look up when she was speaking. A blade of wind left ice across her teeth.

'You shouldn't worry about muddle,' said Freddy. 'You can't shock me. I've seen everything you know.'

'Everything?' she echoed, searching his face for some possible defect.

'Everything?' she said again to play for time. His skin was dry and colourless but it was clean. He had a small moustache and quivering blue eyes. He was near perfect.

'You don't have to worry about *muddle*,' repeated Freddy encouragingly. He banged his hands together and looked down the deserted street to give her time. It must be three in the morning. 'I've never seen the stars so clear,' he said, looking up.

'Yes.'

'Well.'

'Thank you for seeing me home . . .' she began. She wasn't keen to lose him.

Down the bottom of the hill some heavy lorries groaned along the Cally. 'Beryl Veronica . . .' he murmured and the high pitched giggle bubbled on in his nose. He let the name simmer. 'Beryl Veronica . . . why *Veronica*?'

'Veronica Lake.'

'Oh, I see. I do see.'

They stood, staring at one another with disbelief and gladness for a moment while some woman screamed faintly in the night. Then Freddy turned his face away so that the light of the street lamp fell greenly across his face. 'I've seen you before,' he said suddenly. 'I've had my eye on you.'

She pulled at her hair, overcome. And then, unable to think of an answer, stared upwards at the green and red pricks of light from an aeroplane passing high overhead.

'I've seen you in the café.'

She pulled harder at her hair.

'I've seen you at the bus stop.' He made the bubbling sound in his nose again and shivered a little.

'What's your line?' she said coquettishly, trying to make conversation.

'This and that.'

'Oh yes.'

There was a silence.

'Mostly I'm a revolutionary,' he said modestly.

'Oh,' she said, taken aback, 'I've never met one before. I'm very radical myself.'

'I've travelled all over the world.' His tone was almost boastful. He pulled his coat closer round him. 'Only it's time to come back here.'

'I suppose it is,' she said hopelessly, feeling she was losing him.

'I know which room you live in.'

'Which?'

He pointed upwards to the top floor.

'How do you know?'

'I've seen you up there putting things out for the birds.'

'The sill's too narrow for pigeons,' she said. 'Only sparrows.'

'We might as well be friends,' he said.

'Mr Bean, next door to me, he keeps pigeons out the back. They mess everywhere.'

'We might as well be friends.'

'Yes, I suppose.' A pulse beat rapidly in her throat.

'That's why I dress like this,' he remarked suddenly.

'Like that?'

'To distract attention from myself. I have to be extremely careful.'

'Well you would, yes.'

She looked approvingly at the threadbare overcoat, the brown woollen scarf tied under his chin, the trilby. 'I'd appreciate it if you didn't mention me to other people.'

'I understand you,' she whispered, thrilling to the possession of secrets; she felt important. He was a mature man, of the right height. He had everything.

'I have my contacts everywhere. In the Government, the Universities ...'

'Yes.'

An icy gust of wind flew down the street lifting scraps from the gutter.

'Well, that's excellent then.'

'We might take a walk by the canal.'

'We might indeed.' He bowed, seized her hand in its woolly, Fair Isle glove and kissed it. 'Here's to the next time!'

'Yes please.'

And before she could say anything further or even suggest a day, he was off down the street at a half-trot, coat flapping, one arm raised in a farewell salute.

For two days she looked over her shoulder, searched behind every corner, but she couldn't see him. Then he turned up without warning, on a bicycle which he padlocked and leant against the area railings. Mrs Peabody's face gleamed at the basement window, like cream cheese in muslin, before she ran swiftly to answer the door.

She was going to complain about the bicycle but when she brought him up to Garbie's room, she said, 'There's a gentleman to see you,' quite politely. She paused for a moment to take it in, then mentioned that she liked to lock the front door at eleven. Her hands and arms were speckled with oat meal and herring scales.

Garbie had thought of a lot of things they must discuss over the past forty-eight hours, but they fell clean out of her mind. She stood scratching her right ear while Freddy circled the room. He wouldn't take his coat off but wandered round and round the confined space reading book titles and picking up photographs which seemed to amuse him. There was one of Dotty, a blurred snapshot taken at the seaside. She was wearing a striped bathing suit and her hair was blown across her face. There was one of Garbie in her bridesmaid's dress, standing stiffly on Quentin's arm and several small ones of the Pendleton family taken at different ages. She'd told him about her family.

'Would you like to see my scrapbook?'

'There's nothing I'd like better.'

He took off his hat and scarf to sit down before the gas fire and balanced the big book on his lap. His hair was a mixture of sand and white.

He read the cuttings, mostly about Jack's career and speeches, with deep absorption, running his finger down the paragraphs as he read and laughing softly from time to time. She put the kettle on and sat on the edge of the bed watching him.

'I've been there,' he said, tapping a map showing developments in Awanzikwa.

He'd been everywhere. Thailand, Malaya, Egypt, Algeria, the Congo, everywhere. He told her he couldn't settle. 'I've got the energy of a boy,' he said fiercely.

'Uncle Jack's very worried, the soil's eroded.'

'So I hear, so I hear . . . everywhere the same.'

'The dam wasn't built in time, you see.' She knew her facts on this.

'It'll be worse this year.'

'Tea or coffee?'

'You wouldn't have a little drop of whisky, would you?'

'If I'd known you were coming.' She was thrown into turmoil.

'Or even a dry sherry . . .?'

She remembered the beer she used for rinsing her hair. 'It's a bit flat,' she said.

'Never mind, never mind.' (He sounded a little irritable, she thought fearfully.)

It took him another three-quarters of an hour to finish looking through the scrapbook and then he sat smoking, sipping his dead beer, showing no sign of wanting to speak.

It wasn't going well.

'Would you like to listen to the radio?' Anxiously, she pulled at its aerial to recommend it.

'No thank you. When I've got some money you know, I'll take you out to dinner.'

'Perhaps I could cook something for you!' she shouted joyfully.

He flinched. 'I don't eat meat,' he said, 'that's how I keep my vigour.' He closed the scrapbook and put it on the floor. 'I collect sporting pictures myself.'

'So does Uncle Jack. Sartorious, Tillemans and so on.'

'No, no ... sporting heroes. Famous boxers, athletes ... I admire that sort of thing, don't you?'

'I don't know.'

'Perhaps you'd like to see a soccer game some time?' He didn't wait for an answer, but went on, 'I do like to see *fitness* ... you've got to regard the body as the enemy, do you see? It's out to get you in the end, discipline, exercise, that's the thing.' He delivered a right hook, then a left to the air. 'I could take on a boy half my age.'

She didn't like to ask his age, but he must be sixty.

'And then the mind.' He tapped his forehead and turned to look at her, 'A lot of men let their minds go. Inflexible. Got to keep up with the young, with the new thinking, that's the secret.' He smiled at her triumphantly and leant forward to pinch her cheek.

'I have some very radical ideas myself,' she said proudly.

'That's the ticket!'

'I always used to go on the C.N.D. marches.'

'The movement of protest!'

'I used to go with Uncle Jack.'

'Rules are there to be broken!' He was growing quite pink. His eyes quivered like mercury.

'I'm very fond of an intellectual argument,' said Garbie, settling herself comfortably on the floor.

'Ah! The time for argument is running out. Argument anyway is the exercise of the privileged ... *physical* language is the language of the people d'you see, they're excluded by argument. Depersonalized.' He ran a dry finger under his moustache. 'Resistance is the point at which personality begins.'

'I'm with you all the way!' cried Garbie. But he scarcely seemed to hear.

'All the world over ...' Freddy murmured, staring sightlessly at a pipe near the ceiling, 'people are enslaved by following the model of capitalist excellence. They're allowed the opportunities to imitate it up to a point, even acquire it up to a point – to a point where they can't even see how clever the manipulation is. They just don't see,' he said angrily banging his thigh, 'they just don't see until they reach for the citadel itself and then all the doors close!' He leapt to his feet and began pacing the limited space. 'I've seen black men pretend to be white!' he cried, narrowly missing Garbie's mug on the floor. 'I've seen them come to believe that they were white until the critical moment came when it was pointed out to them they were not, when certain privileges were still kept out of reach.'

'That's shocking,' sympathized Garbie.

'The more successful a democracy, the more successfully the lie is kept, d'you see? People fail to realize, they just don't *see*, how cunningly the system's fooled them ... one man, one vote was the cleverest con of all!'

'You ought to meet my Uncle Jack, you'd have a lot in common.'

Freddy stopped and laughed his funny, girlish, private laugh, 'Perhaps we would!' he cried and the idea struck him as hilarious. 'Perhaps we'd find we went to the same school!'

'You've got to give people their opportunities. Definitely,' said Garbie, feeling herself in close agreement.

'Give! *Giving* . . .!' Freddy pulled at his moustache. 'We still think of giving as a kind of patronage, something demanding obedience and thanks. Why should the people thank leaders for what's anyway theirs by right?'

'Why indeed?' she echoed keenly.

The gas began to sigh and gutter.

'Oh dear,' she said, 'do you have a shilling?'

His pockets were heavy with silver. 'I worked Green Park today,' he said. 'Not as good as the National Gallery, but not bad.'

'I expect the fresh air's very good for you.' She dropped a shilling in the meter.

'It's a way of keeping your eyes open. I've tried to work the sandwich board outside South Africa House, but the pigs move you on.'

'Oh dear,' she said again, and stood up smiling happily.

'You're really keen are you?' he asked.

'Oh yes,' she breathed, her eyes darting uncertainly to the sink.

'I wonder if . . .?'

'Yes?'

'I wonder whether . . .?'

'Yes, yes?'

'You'd be interested in the Movement?'

'Oh . . .'

'There'd have to be a thorough vetting . . .'

'Oh anything, anything, licking envelopes, anything, I don't mind!'

'. . . a security check, testing of attitudes . . .'

'I've done a lot of welfare work.'

'. . . you might break a few "rules", just little ones for starters . . .'

She was beginning to laugh and sank to the edge of the bed, squeezing her hands between her knees, rocking to and fro.

'. . . and then put it to the committee.'

The laughter whooped out of her uncontrollably, a kind of joy. She tore a strand of hair between her teeth to try and control indiscretions.

'We'll see.' He said before he was infected by the laughter. Restraints were scattered like ashes.

'I think . . .' she guffawed, falling backwards on the bed, 'I think you should be my lover!'

He flung his arms open, poised over an atom of thought. Then: 'What an excellent beginning!' he shouted, 'what a splendid idea! There's no time to waste!'

And he threw himself on her in a muddle of squeaks and hilarity. 'Sexual inhibition . . .' he whistled tenderly in her ear, 'is culturally repressive . . .!'

Mr Bean, head pressed to the paper roses on the wall, was spellbound with delight. Downstairs in the basement Mrs Peabody served fish pie to her son-in-law for supper and remarked that while there was no accounting for dress, Miss Pendleton seemed to have found herself a proper gent at last. 'A really educated person,' she declared.

In February, when the snow oozed grey in the city and lay in deep, diamond drifts round Rotherbrook, Cissy mentioned to her husband, that Garbie hadn't been in touch since Christmas.

'True,' he agreed, guardedly.

'It's most unusual. Perhaps something's wrong. Perhaps I ought to ring the Centre.' She twisted her knuckles in an agony of conscience.

'Oh, she'd have been in touch if there were . . .'

He looked up from his papers and silently, their eyes met. Cissy, embarrassed by the things she felt preserved by silence, looked away. Jack returned to his documents, shuffling them. 'There's too much drifting to the towns in Awanzikwa,' he murmured. 'We really must get the land right.'

'About Garbie . . .' Cissy began pulling the breakfast things over the table towards her, 'I sometimes wonder whether we've done the right thing.'

'Darling, I've more important things to think about just now!'

'Of course,' said Cissy meekly, taking the marmalade spoon from the bowl, 'I can always write.'

'One mustn't think of Garbie as a problem. She's an individual.'

'Of course,' sighed Cissy again and settled down to re-read an airmail letter from Robin in Australia.

Garbie made more frequent visits to Dagenham, even offering to dig over the iron square of earth and plant it out when spring came so there'd be no shortage of flowers for Colin's shrine.

'You needn't bother yourself,' said Aunty Betty, who'd covered the furniture with sheets and sat amongst the spectral lumps like a mourner. She'd taken the budgie back to the shop and exchanged it for a jereboah which she said she'd been talked into against her will. It smelt dreadful because she didn't dare take it out to clean it, just sprayed it with Fresh-Air.

Garbie arranged for two small boys from down the road to come and change the litter. Aunty Betty said they brought mud into the house, but she didn't try and alter the arrangement, merely said defensively: 'You're looking more and more like your mother.'

Garbie smiled secretively and bent her head to gaze at her greasy hem. Seeds of dandruff fell from her hair.

'I'm more concerned with inward matters,' she explained. 'Appearances are immaterial.'

'Not while you're in my house,' said Aunty Betty firmly and made her take her jumper off so she could wash it.

Garbie sat in the kitchen in her petticoat while her aunty tutted noisily above the suds. She hauled down the drying rack from over the stove, laid the pink jumper over it and muttered, 'You ought to watch you don't go the same way as your mam.'

'You're obsessed by appearances.'

'A little bit of obsession don't do nobody no harm. Did you know Dotty was exactly your age when she went?'

This mystical conjunction of figures lingered in Garbie's mind waiting to suggest meaning, but none emerged.

'One thing I'll say for your mother,' said Aunty Betty warningly, 'She never lost a job.'

'Oh,' sighed Garbie, tapping her foot in exasperation, 'you're entirely geared to the economic ethic!'

Betty Beazley gave her niece a quizzical look and put the kettle on to boil. 'Wait till trees grow money,' she said.

'And on the left,' said Freddy as they ploughed through the slush of Percy Circus, 'is the house of Karl Marx.'

Garbie, keeping up with difficulty in her fur-lined bootees, moved into a trot. 'Where are we going dear?' she panted.

'I'm taking you out to dinner. Just as I promised.' He tittered over his perpetual private joke.

'Can you afford it, dear?' she called nervously, reaching for her purse.

He stopped so she could catch up. 'I collected my assistance today.'

'Your assistance?'

'I sign on as an out-of-work television producer. There are no vacancies for television producers.'

'Oh.' She thrust a mittened hand through his arm and they continued towards the lights of the Euston Road.

'Anyway, the Movement meets major expenses,' he explained. 'My art work pays for the whisky.'

An arc of brown spray was thrown into their faces by a passing bus. Garbie longed to jump on it, but reminded herself the exercise was good for her, a mixture of physical training and spiritual mortification. She couldn't help squeezing Freddy's arm and saying. 'I'm getting to know all your little ways.'

He was too enamoured of his schemes and plans to take much notice. In fact he didn't speak again until they strode, heads down against driving sleet, past the glowing velvet windows of Charlotte Street. Behind the cold there were pockets of fragrance – of garlic and frying onion, spiced apple and steak juices. Drops of saliva burst on Garbie's tongue.

They stopped outside the largest restaurant, a tall white building with a little blue canopy outside. Beneath it, in his peaked cap and long military greatcoat, stood the commissionaire.

The commissionaire remained fixed to the spot. He rose to the tip of his polished toes and subsided again, still filling the doorway.

'Excuse me,' said Freddy.

Small bureaucratic eyes travelled from Freddy's trilby down the flapping length of his coat to his cracked shoes then moved across to Garbie's furry boots, and up. They rested on a face alternately purple and white like a turnip.

'Excuse me!'

'Have you booked a table?'

By some psychic signal the manager appeared, greased and glossy. He grasped the problem. 'Ah!'

'A table ...!'

'A table?'

'A *table*!'

'Ah.'

He stepped backwards allowing them over the threshold and fluttered through his book. Garbie's throat dried at the thought of being turned away. She wished she'd been given a chance to put on her seed pearls and ear clips.

Freddy spoke pleasantly to the manager. His accent bewildered the man who smoothed his hair with his hand to check all was as glossy as it should be. He found himself falling back on his professional promises and humility. He glittered his gold teeth.

Garbie followed Freddy's back up the stairs feeling the manager's desperate breath on her own. She allowed her coat to be removed and self-consciously smoothed her pleated skirt wishing she had on the jumper Aunty Betty had washed. Freddy surrendered his hat and scarf but said politely he would keep his coat on for the time being.

Still keeping her eyes bored in the small of his back, she followed Freddy across the restaurant to a dim, corner table. She heard a pause in the steady clatter of forks and spoons. Conversation slowed then accelerated slightly faster than before. She prayed he would take the seat facing the restaurant.

He did. Left with the menu, she dared raise her eyes to him. His expression was bland.

'We're being wonderfully insulting,' he said, pleased.

She lowered her stiff gaze to the menu again, feeling grape-shot in her back. Her spine began to hurt.

There was a nervous hovering of waiters.

'Tomato soup for two with a roll and butter each,' said Freddy. 'I take it the cost of the roll and butter is included in the charge of five and six?'

She locked her hands beneath the table to prevent her nails straying to her mouth and remembered desolate times when she'd eaten an artichoke with a knife and fork, whole, and another occasion when she'd busily helped everyone to a glass of wine before Uncle Jack had formally tasted it. She burned. Freddy was making the same error now. He and the waiter had a small, restrained fight over the bottle.

'I can manage perfectly well,' said Freddy coolly.

She was shocked that he didn't know how to behave.

Dabbling her mouth with a napkin she watched Freddy drop small pellets of bread in his soup.

'Are you enjoying yourself?' he inquired, adding loudly, 'We're being closely watched.'

'It's very warm,' said Garbie, choked.

'I thought it would be an interesting exercise, I know you're against this kind of thing.'

'I . . .' Her tongue swooned.

'It may sound cynical, though I promise you it's not, but the Movement likes to select young people at odds with their families. It helps them understand a little better the frustrations of the oppressed world. It is in essence, do you see, the same pattern of behaviour.'

'I'm very fond . . .'

'After all, a repressive parent is only one human preventing another from being himself.'

'They're very good to me!' she burst out, 'they spent a bomb on my Christmas present, a gold compact with enamel inlay.'

Freddy did not hear. 'It must make you angry being a woman,' he said, 'for precisely the same reason. Wooed and flattered and allowed to hold expectations as high as the opposite sex, only to find them ultimately withheld. . . . Ah waiter, the menu. Please could you translate the following into English.'

He took him through the entrées and then said he didn't eat meat. He'd like an omelette. Garbie said she'd like the same. 'Would you care for tomato sauce?' Freddy inquired of her. 'Bring it anyway!' he called to the waiter as she seemed to be having difficulty in deciding.

'You're very quiet this evening!'

'You must be awfully hot in your coat, dear,' she said with an effort.

'Come, come, you're not entering into the spirit of the thing at all! I've just been discussing the cabbalistic methods of exclusion, and here we have the perfect example! Manners are a part of the machinery. All ritual is hierarchical.' He poured her a little more wine and gave a courtly smile, 'Sometimes trivial conventions of this kind are the final defence. Now be a good chap and enjoy yourself.'

She understood. 'I do love to hear you talk, Freddy!' she cried and raised her glass to him, draining it defiantly.

'Good,' he said. 'Excellent,' he said. 'Let's get the orchestra to play "Knees Up Mother Brown".'

The request was borne to the musicians who conferred like hens over seed. 'Don't forget,' Freddy continued, while waiting for the music to begin, 'The ancient priestly sects who devoted their time to the pursuit of esoteric knowledge simply in order to preserve their power and mysticism. We haven't quite shaken their system off yet. Ah! Splendid!'

The music began. It was performed with so many trills and variations it was barely recognizable but the diners were not lost to it. Some plunged their faces deeply into their brandy glasses, some asked for their bills, and a few began to titter.

Freddy called for more wine and ordered the trolley of quivering fruits and meringue to be wheeled over.

'We'll have a little of everything shall we?' he said.

'I don't think I could,' she whispered faintly.

'Of course you will. This is a treat!'

He smiled at the waiter, who moved his mouth slightly. 'You see,' he said, bending his earnest attention on Garbie once more, 'The issue has become blurred with today's welfare state, widespread education, foreign aid programmes and so on. However!' he laughed, 'it doesn't fool all of us. Don't waste the marrons glacés. I wonder if they'd like me to sing.'

'Sing . . . !'

'A sing-song would be just the thing to get everybody enjoying themselves together!'

'I think I might be feeling rather faint.'

'I thought you wanted to be a member of the Movement.'

'I do . . . I do!' she cried despairingly.

'You'll have to prove your heart is in it.'

'I swear . . .'

'No lingering fondness for bourgeois tradition . . .'

'What would you like to sing?' she moaned weakly, and lay her head on the table.

He chose the Red Flag which drove the orchestra into a frenzied, competing performance of the drinking song from The Student Prince. Two large men with broken noses asked them to leave which they did. Garbie hurried past Freddy to the cloakroom while he stopped to shout 'Pigs!' at the clientele, then stood waiting for him at the bottom of the stairs to numbly congratulate him.

Her view of revolution was that love could change the world. 'I'll get you round to my way of thinking you see,' she said comfortingly as she nursed him home, but Freddy, absorbed by his own angry vision of the globe let the wine rise to his head and thought wistfully of hand grenades.

To show what she meant, she made him a hot toddy and brought it to him tenderly. 'You've got to keep your strength up,' she said, and stood behind him so that she could slip into her nightie and dressing gown without his watching.

Garbie saw a man who needed her help. She touched his hair tentatively, all her perilous instincts for rescue rising to a sweetness. 'Have you ever thought,' she murmured lovingly, 'of getting a regular job?'

Freddy choked a little on his hot toddy. 'Try and get it straight, old thing,' he coughed, 'I've no intention of being sucked into the comfort machine. Why else should I maintain this abrasive life style? Anyway, the Movement encourages a monastic level of existence . . . Not *altogether* monastic,' he added, rising to his feet to rub first her left breast and then the right.

Garbie undid the cord of her dressing gown.

Freddy thought hard of the saucy officers' wives who'd found him irresistible in the Far East over thirty years ago and thankfully felt his body respond to the memory.

'I do want to help you,' said Garbie, facing him, her nipples like walnuts.

He sank forgetfully on to the springs.

'You need me,' said Garbie, holding him.

'Yes,' he answered desperately, concentrating on his own battle.

It was a short, but triumphant skirmish. He lay, facing the angry knots of her spine. He ran a grateful finger over them.

'I was thinking,' said Garbie, her face muffled by the pillow, 'I was thinking I ought to take you down to Rotherbrook to meet my people.'

The finger peaused. 'Yes?' he said.

'What about Easter? I never miss Easter.'

'I ... er ... there's something else I have in mind for Easter.'

'Another time then?'

'Why not? Another time!' He laughed softly and continued his journey over the ranges of her spine.

Garbie rang her aunt the very next day.

'How nice to hear you!' cried Aunt Cissy, 'I've been wondering what you were up to!'

'Oh, this and that,' said Garbie darkly.

'Mm ... what exactly?'

'I'm not at liberty to disclose what exactly.'

'That sounds exciting!'

'About *Easter* ...' said Garbie.

Aunt Cissy was a bit odd about Easter.

'Jack's going away,' she said. 'I'll be on my own this time.' (Tactfully the Minister concerned had suggested a short mission to Awanzikwa over the Easter period to save embarrassment in the constituency. If his reports were accurate it would be as well for everybody.)

'Oh well, I'll come and keep you company!'

'Oh darling, how sweet. Actually I've half promised Victoria I'd pop over there ... the baby's due any time ...'

'What about Edward and Thom?'

'Thom will be climbing in the Lake District and Edward, well, Edward ... he's got some plans of his own.' There was a short laugh like escaping gas. 'He's got Finals to think of, of course.'

There was a long silence from Garbie.

'Are you still there, darling?'

'Oh,' said Garbie, 'Oh well, there's another month yet, I'd better come down before. I haven't missed Easter once in fifteen years you know.'

'No, I know darling, you haven't.'

'Next weekend then ... I've missed you all. I've missed not *hearing* from you.'

'I've been meaning to ring ...' Cissy felt under attack. She did so wish Garbie wouldn't let these long silences elapse on the telephone. Her breathing was still rather heavy. 'Next weekend would be lovely!'

'Next weekend then ...'

'Yes.'

'I might bring a friend,' said Garbie threateningly, and put down the phone.

Freddy said he'd have loved to come but he had to go over to Paris on business. He tried to make up for the disappointment. 'You might care to join me on the Easter march,' he said.

'Oh, I'm all for peace! All for more love in the world!'

'Topping!' he said and leant forward to wipe a smear of raspberry jam from her chin.

'I'm so sorry about Easter, darling!' repeated Aunt Cissy as they settled with coffee and Sunday papers in the drawing room after lunch.

'Oh that's all right,' said Garbie airily.

'Only Victoria's getting into such a state about motherhood, otherwise ...'

'Oh that's all right,' she said again, 'I'm going on the Easter March.'

The ceiling might have fallen in.

Jack Pendleton's newspaper came down like a thunder shower. A teaspoon fell on the polished floor and woke the dog who leapt to his feet to find the intruder.

'Which one?' A thin ray of winter sunlight caught Uncle Jack's glasses and refracted an angry beam into Garbie's eyes.

'Pardon?'

'Which one?'

'I'm sorry?'

'Which *march*?'

'You know, the peace march . . .'

His mouth taut, Uncle Jack re-folded his newspaper into four and jabbed his finger at a down-the-page news item headed 'Split Over Easter March'. He thrust it under her nose. 'Read that,' he ordered.

She did. It read:

In an effort to combat the steady decrease in the number of people taking part in the annual Easter March, this year's route may follow a different course.

Although estimates vary wildly as to the numbers involved, one group has declared its intention to march not to Trafalgar Square where the end of the march rally is traditionally held, but instead to the Government chemical and biological research station at Port Cawley.

The group claims it has strong support from the Radical Socialists and other extreme left wing student bodies. A spokesman said yesterday: 'The old Easter March has become totally meaningless. We want to make protest relevant. It will be a peaceful demonstration.

The Ministry of Defence in a formal statement issued last night said: 'Most of the research being carried out at Port Cawley is undertaken in the interest of public health. A small proportion of the work is devoted to defence methods. There is no plan to develop means of aggressive warfare.'

'*Which* march?'

'I don't know.'

'You don't know . . .!' He strode back to the fireplace, hands in his pockets.

Thom observed the action with his mild brown eyes. Thom was a poet. He never said very much.

Jack turned and saw the bewildered expression on Garbie's face. Indulgently he smiled. 'My darling girl!' he began, and reached for his pipe. 'My dear Garbie. Let me make this absolutely clear from the outset – I respect your freedom of thought, of opinion.'

'Thank you, Uncle Jack,' said Garbie rapidly.

'... This is after all the finest democracy in the world. I my-self ...' Delicately, he packed the tobacco, '... I myself know how passions can rage. I was an undergraduate at Cambridge during the Thirties, don't forget!' He paused to let the implications settle. 'Furthermore,' he went on, 'I *share* your views, I want you to understand that.'

'Yes, Uncle Jack.'

'Indeed, it is *because* I share your views, that I'm placed in this shockingly difficult situation. *Any* man caring to call him-self civilized loathes war.'

'Yes, Uncle Jack.'

'But, I have divided loyalties – no, let me put it another way! I have divided *responsibilities*! To my constituents on the one hand, to my government on the other ... This is a terrible posi-tion for a man to be in.' His voice was grave. Cissy, plucking the folds of her dress, ached for him.

'Many of my constituents,' he went on, 'feel as you do, as *I* do ... but I have to point out, sadly, that America is at war. America is an ally.' His voice drooped.

'Yes I know that, Uncle Jack,' said Garbie, not grasping the connection.

He held out a hand to his wife who rose and tenderly took his hand in hers. They smiled briefly at one another. 'We are a family,' said Uncle Jack simply. 'We must stand fast. We must be loyal.'

'Of course, Uncle Jack.'

'We may say what we like about one another's actions within the family circle, it is a part of loving to do so. But to the world, our front should be loyally, *lovingly* united. You, Garbie, are one of the family.'

He ended his plea.

There was a long silence and Garbie burst into tears. Her head was split apart by wilfully unconnecting ideas. But then the fragrance of logs burning, of the particular polish used, of the approaching vanilla sweetness that came with Aunt Cissy's gentle arms ... this fragrance of Rotherbrook rose in a beguil-ing mist.

'It's not a question, old girl,' repeated Freddy impatiently, 'of whether what you do pleases me or pleases your Parliamentary uncle ... that's a question of total irrelevance. This is an issue you're talking about, and really, old thing, that's something you've got to decide for yourself.'

9　On the March

The crowd stretched as far as their eyes could see. Black gas balloons with the white anti-nuclear sign painted on them flew high towards a racing sky like fat, comical birds. The winds of early April blew sunshine in fresh streamers across the downs of southern England and out towards the distant sea making fabrics flap like carnival ribbons and puffing away the zinc dust of winter.

People sat or lay on the grass overlapping one another in great waves. Some sang to a guitar. Some fed their babies. Some kissed. Others argued.

When the loudspeakers brayed directions over the common land selected as the southern starting point for the march on London, shifting patterns of movement rippled through the crowd. Banners divided between north and south.

In the midst of the crowd, as Garbie fought towards the coast end of the meeting place, she came face to face with Edward. They were jammed up together by a momentary crush on either side.

'Good God!' he said and brushed his beard on her cheek.

'Well I never!'

'You're not going to Port Cawley!'

'Why not ...?'

He was shifted round a little to one side by the crowd but his eyes stayed with hers in disbelief. 'Christ!' He raised his voice as they threatened to be parted. 'That's a bit below the old man's belt!'

'I thought,' she shouted as his face was drawn away between pushing shoulders, 'I thought you wanted to outrage ...!'

The thrust of the crowd pushed him back close to her again. She caught garlic on his breath.

'On the home ground ...!'

Their faces were so close they could have kissed. She drew his ear to her lips and bellowed: 'It's not a matter of pleasing someone. It's an issue that you've got to ... to decide ...' (They were prised apart then confronted again) '... for yourself!'

Like a twig in a mill race he was swept away. She saw his mouth making rubber toy words, then suddenly, the crowd divided, leaving her far at the back of her own faction.

A news cameraman, hanging overhead from a helicopter, panned across the seething common, catching the shadow of his own blades whirling the crowd to its opposite corners. 'It's a fair crowd going south,' he yelled. 'Pull up a bit, I'd like to see if I can get both lots on the road in one wide frame.

'It's a long way to Tipper-ary!' sang Freddy, his huge army boots crunching on the loose gravel underfoot. With the wind in his hair, an old gas mask and binoculars slung around his neck, a pack on his back and a banner in rifle position against his shoulder, he led his unit towards old-fashioned victory. He felt fit. He felt magnificent.

At their front marched a row of six police. Behind them, for three-quarters of a mile, stretched a weaving line of banners. (From a distance, as they followed the curving line of the countryside the march had a medieval silhouette of crosses and ploughshares.) There was a piping of music, a billowing of bright clothes and flying hair. As the day wore on, skins grew pale gold in the wind and sun.

Here and there were more blackly clad people who might have marched north. But they'd turned their face to the sea and made new pledges.

As the sun moved to its height and the hills grew steeper, the singing and chatter lost its tempo. Instead breathing rose and fell in heavier concert.

People came to their doors in the villages – women carrying children who waved, old men straightening their Boer backs as they heard a tramp of feet beyond their failing line of vision. There were few stragglers.

The march was deliberately circuitous, skirting towns to keep the main coast roads clear, so it followed the line of fields still brown with winter sleep and fringed by leafless birch and beech. There was a warm scent of waking soil and grass.

The column wound between a chalky cleft and climbed again to find itself on the outstretched breast of the land. Slowly, they passed, small and black across the horizon and descended back into their dream valley.

From the top of the hill Garbie could look for miles across the landscape in the clear air and see the dark oval of pine and yew concealing Rotherbrook. She steadied her shoulders on a line with those of the marchers to both left and right, kept her eyes on the head of the man in front and found herself moved to tears by the single spirit that bound them, all two thousand of them.

Freddy wouldn't take a bus back to the nearest town when the first day ended. He camped. He liked camping and was good at it, shouting out instructions for himself as he erected the small tent, spread the ground sheet and unrolled the sleeping bags. He was proud to have carried the load on his shoulders all day without tiring.

'I dare say I'm the fittest fellow here!' he cried, as, stripped to the waist, he stretched his bleached bony arms. There was a deeply scarlet division between his neck and his chest.

A few others camped in the field set aside for them by a dubious farmer. Freddy inspected the camp and nodded approvingly here and there, speaking to the other young people making a place for the night.

He came back carrying his map. 'Another day and a half's march!' he calculated sitting down and slumping between his long, crossed thighs.

'You'll need this to keep your strength up,' urged Garbie handing him his favourite fig bar. 'You must have a minimum of 2,000 calories.'

'We should attack at thirteen hundred hours Sunday, April the fifth . . .'

'What did you say, dear?'

'... In a manner of speaking, that is ...' He bit his fig bar clean in half. 'The attack is purely spiritual.'

'I see,' said Garbie, unwrapping a miniature pork pie.

'Tactically, the time is not right for violence ... to be effective, moral protest should first provoke a disproportionate violence ... that's the time to leap.'

'I don't hold with violence of any sort.' Garbie was passionate about that. 'It thoroughly upsets me. After all,' she added with a triumphant grin as she made a logical deduction, 'that's why we're here isn't it? *Because* we disapprove!' She went on smiling she was so pleased with herself.

Freddy picked fragments of fig bar abstractedly from his teeth and continued to gaze at the fading sky, 'Violence,' he murmured, 'can be highly moral. It can also of course,' he acknowledged, '*kill* people. But violence d'you see in revolution should not be thought of as either massacre or martyrdom ... I hope you're following my line of thought ... violence in revolution is different in kind to imperialist violence in war.'

'Either way Freddy dear, you're dead – and that's the important thing.'

'You're not listening,' he reprimanded. 'Now pay attention there's a good chap ... I was saying, violence in revolution is different in kind. It is *not* directed towards capitalist ends ... it is a freeing of the spirit, a psychological necessity if the true personality is to be restored. Not so much a killing of the enemy, d'you understand, as a killer of the alien, adopted personality. There is, I assure you, a major, philosophical difference.'

'Oh Freddy!' she sighed, enraptured. 'I do so love *ideas* ...'

'I'm rather fond of them myself.'

The stars came out and put the birds to silence. It was bitterly cold. 'A nip and a kip,' recommended Freddy, whose camp fire had been only a minor success.

She climbed into his sleeping bag. 'You don't mind, do you?'

He tucked her head in the crook of his elbow. 'There!' he said rather briskly. He smelt of sweat dried in the fresh air, reminding her of sun and hay and horses.

They didn't talk about their love-making unless he had a

minor direction to give. Garbie kept her eyes closed, sealing in her ecstasies and even, beneath the eyelid, exaggerating them. Freddy was straightforward and quick, afraid that he wouldn't, amazed that he could. He had to concentrate very hard.

He groped beside him for the flask and drank a little whisky.

'Do you love me, Freddy?' murmured Garbie, her face pressed to the sharp blades of his rib cage.

'You're a good sport,' he said, and he squeezed her arm warmly.

They started early.

In the village gardens the sun shone pale gold through daffodil trumpets and the showers of forsythia. Scarlet japonica bells festooned the low stone walls where children sat in silent wonderment watching the marchers pass. Cows bumped alongside, ineptly herded by a toothless man in a cap who wobbled by on his bicycle unable to stop grinning.

At Ashinghurst, a larger place where Saturday morning market brought a temporary halt, they met more than curiosity.

'Long-haired fags!'

'Yellow-bellies!'

'Bring back conscription!'

One boy, his hair cropped so close it made visible shadows on his scalp, pranced beside them, leering.

'Mother-fuckers!' he hissed, his tongue loose and yellow pollened, 'Student shits!'

He made Garbie uneasy. He kept jostling her.

The police moved them on, carrying out their duties with fixed indifference, while a television cameraman took his lens over those who raised their fists.

Attack drew the marchers together; they shooed off the enemy. There was no longer any need to talk together.

At the front, high above the others waved Freddy's jaunty head. 'It's a long way to Tipper-ary!' he sang more vigorously than before.

On Sunday, a profound sense of excitement drew the caterpillar segments of the march together like a pliable muscle.

'Will your feet last out?'

'Only four more hours!'

'Watch out for the fuzz!'

Except for the undercurrent hum of expectation, a silence fell over the march. The clouds seemed to Garbie to speed faster out to sea, to accelerate their own pace. At the front, immediately behind their police escort, were six drummers dressed in black, the pigskin surfaces of their drums taut and ready. Ahead, a camera car with a tripod fixed to the roof crawled slowly up the road, its backward eye unblinking.

They rose over the penultimate hill, legs white with dust and paused to check their numbers. Gulls flapped out to greet them.

Beneath and beyond, the road flew away gathering itself for the last green rise to the station. It sat, squat and imperturbable in the high noonday sun, its glittering silver domes giving it a Byzantine invulnerability. The sight of it and its odd, suggestive shape, brought a religious confusion into the fierce Easter spirit. It could have been Jerusalem.

Two thousand people faced the sun. The drums began to roll. The sound made Garbie's palate dry. She started violently when a banner next to her cracked and billowed in the wind.

Adjusting his binoculars, Freddy noted an ominous absence of enemy troops on the north wall. No sniper positions, no speaking flash of sun on glass. Disappointed, he put the binoculars away and moved, propelled on by the force of people behind him.

And then, as they leant to the final climb, everybody saw three low buses draw out from behind the building. Before they'd even stopped, black uniformed figures spilled out and spread swiftly in front of the high brick wall and silver painted gates.

A sigh travelled through the column.

Garbie's heart was beating so fast she could barely breathe. She had a sudden, horrid vision of the march, unable to stop, driven on by a drumbeat, pulping brick and stone and flesh beneath its feet. She saw it go invincibly on, taking its torn flags over the cliffs and into the sea. Then somebody next to her shouted and the image went.

At three hundred yards the uniformed figures grew faces.

Slowly, each pink dab produced a mouth, a nose, two eyes. Panic stricken, Garbie saw that the alien troops were family men, but the machinery of legs moved on enmeshing her.

Two hundred yards to go.

One hundred. Bones fused in iron construction.

She saw the eyes and mouths more closely – slits filled with arrows.

The notices read : 'Keep Out.' 'Keep Out.'

She felt anger rush sweet and clean as water.

KEEP OUT. KEEP OUT. Each letter two feet high.

There was a rumble of machinery speeding up, shouting, a quickening drumbeat. From the rear of the march a tidal wave began to roll forcing the front to flow before it. She was carried by it.

The black arms linked.

GOVERNMENT PROPERTY. PRIVATE.

The notices danced as she was rushed towards them and then the force accelerated, scattering its outer margins. She was flung clear and went rolling over and over down the slope. A few scrambled to their feet and ran again towards the main core of the march, running frantically as if for cover. They ran past her and she sat alone on the grass.

Above the churning heads and shoulders, above the shouting, the big white notices stood firm. But still the marchers kept coming like a river entering its delta. Still the struggle at the forefront was going on but even from where she sat, she could sense the heart going out of it.

Feebly at first a chant began. But it was taken up louder and more loudly. 'Open Up! Open Up!'

The disorganized group at the front fell slightly back to link arms and add to the chant. 'Open up!' 'Open up!'

The police stood firm. No one was pushing them now. The citadel was intact.

Behind the high walls, the buildings rose silent to the sky, the silver domes austere.

'Open Up!' 'Open Up!' 'Open UP!'

The police smiled. A good natured lot, it would say in the papers.

The police smiled. The tabernacle still housed its vicious secrets.

Slowly, in wave after wave, the marchers sank down, arms upraised, voices hoarse and failing.

It was a pleasant afternoon on the downs with the wind rising salt and fresh from the sea. An ice cream van painted with Mickey Mouse and Donald Duck figures approached in the distance, its Greensleeves bells faintly dissonant. People had their photographs taken.

The police allowed a petition to be received at the gate asking that the station should be subjected to open visits by the public. It would be given to the Director who was away for Easter.

The chanting sank on an exhausted spiral as people lay down and kicked their boots off. Garbie sat bolt upright unable to see Freddy. Fear, anger, bitterness, excitement curdled and began to cool. She no longer knew what she felt.

Like fallen petals, the marchers subsided. They lit cigarettes, dropped silver paper on the grass, struck occasional chords on their guitars. Defiance became tame.

'We shall overco-ome.

We shall overco-ome! . . .'

Beneath the unblemished brick walls their song bloomed prettily.

She felt cheated. That's what it was. She felt cheated.

'Miss Pendleton?'

She opened her eyes and saw a black shadow stooped against the sun's glare. 'Miss Pendleton?' it repeated.

'Yes?' She sat up, gratified.

The young man crouched beside her, trying to avoid the resting marchers and breathed on his Biro. 'Peter Taylor, *Daily Chronicle.*'

'Pleased to meet you.' She nodded amiably.

'I wondered if I could have your views . . .?'

'My *views* . . .?'

'That's right!' He bent back his spiral notebook and poised himself politely.

She noticed somebody taking her picture and smiled coyly. 'Cheese!' she said and wound her hair behind her ear.

'. . . about the purpose of the march?'

'Oh.' She stared blankly and looked around for Freddy. 'Oh, well, in a democracy, you know . . .'

'Yes?' He smiled encouragingly.

'We have to defend our rights!' she shouted triumphantly. '*Fight* for them . . .'

'Yes, fight for our rights,' she repeated for the benefit of his slow shorthand.

'Ah. You feel strongly . . .'

'*Violently* . . .' she agreed.

'What rights would they *be*?'

'Um . . .' She looked about frantically and her eye caught the notices. 'Er . . . to be included in . . .'

'I see, do you know what's going on here?' He gestured towards the research station and narrowed his eyes hopefully.

'They say it's for our own good . . . health. . . .'

'Have you any reason to believe they're manufacturing CS gas for America?'

She stared at him, her mouth open. She longed to be knowing. ' I wouldn't be surprised,' she said.

'But do you *know*?'

She shrugged, laughed, and picking a blade of grass, sucked it staring at him equivocally. He gave a small, corresponding laugh and wrote something down.

'It gives a great sense of brotherhood,' she remarked. 'All this.'

'How does your er . . . *family* feel about "all this"?'

She shrugged again and turned away to spit out the chewed grassy pap.

'I mean,' he said leeringly, drawing closer, 'I am right in thinking Jack Pendleton was elected on a disarmament ticket . . .?'

'Oh he's very *anti*. . . .'

'Anti "all *this*"?' The young man liked to speak obliquely. He too, felt better for secrets.

'You could say. Would you like to take my friend's photo?'

'In a little while perhaps. In the meantime, Miss Pendleton . . .' and he blew again expectantly on his Biro.

They went home by train. Garbie said : 'I wanted to have
my photo taken with you,' and nodded sleepily, 'it would
have made a nice memento.'
'Spiffing!' sighed Freddy and contentedly kept up his un-
musical blend of humming and giggling all the way to Victoria
Station while Garbie snored.

MP's Daughter In Protest, said Monday's *Daily Chronicle,*
beneath a picture that Garbie didn't think showed her at her
best.

Garbie sat in a taxi amid the hot, ill-temper of the rush hour and glowed, peaceably. She'd been back in the office two days now since the Easter break and still congratulations flowed in.

They shook her hand. They asked if they had the pleasure of addressing Beryl Veronica Pendleton, assistant librarian and demonstrator extraordinary. She was even asked for her autograph by Ewan Christopher, the ace reporter.

She'd bowed, she'd blushed, obliged.

Freddy rang to say : 'F. here. Jolly good show !' and rang off.

They asked would she like to cut out and file her own news story.

'But why?' persisted Shirley. 'Why on earth did you say you were his daughter?'

'I never did,' said Garbie, too paralysed with smiling to stop.

Victoria had telephoned and invited her over to Chelsea for drinks. 'Take a taxi,' she said, 'Mummy says she'll pay.'

Garbie hoped somebody would be standing on the doorstep with the money in their hand. But when the taxi stopped outside the little white house wreathed in trailing plants, nobody was there.

'You did say fifty-two?' yelled the taxi driver when there was no movement from the passenger seat.

'That's quite right.' Eventually she had to pay herself.

But the incident flustered her, so she was puffy and inclined to drop things when Victoria answered the door. 'Hi !'

'Hello. Thanks very much for asking me over to see the baby. Is he nice? Did it hurt?' She edged in knocking a spindly table with a Chinese pot on it dangerously awry. Victoria steadied it with a cool, white hand. 'Come in here a minute,' she said, and stepped into a tiny dining room. 'It's a *she* by the way, Prunella, Prune for short because that's what she looks like. I'm going to give you a stiff drink.'

'Thank you very much Victoria. I hope you're going to look after the child yourself until the age of five – during the formative years – it's absolutely vital. I say, if you don't mind me saying so, this is a jolly small house isn't it?'

Victoria ignored her, pouring some previously mixed drink from a cocktail shaker. 'Vulgar but powerful,' she said, handing it to her cousin. 'Come upstairs when you've drunk it and I'll introduce you to my well trained Nanny.'

Garbie sank the drink while still gazing round. 'I thought Gerald was rolling in it.'

'He is. Come along.'

They entered the drawing room on the first floor, Garbie remarking how peculiar it was to have the lounge upstairs. She was a little put out that Victoria didn't seem to have noticed her picture in the paper and was thinking of ways to get round to the topic.

Cissy and Jack whirled round from the long windows with strained smiles of welcome.

'What have you got on your feet darling?' cried Cissy faintly.

'My feet? Oh, well ...' she beamed meaningfully, 'socks and sandals are so much more comfortable after all my marching!' She gave a jovial wink.

'Marching!' echoed Jack and took a hurried sip of gin to help clear his throat.

'Good trip Uncle Jack? Nice weather?'

'A little trouble in Bahziah ...' He coughed again, sipped again and added uncomfortably, '... the unemployment is rather higher than expected, very hot, yes.'

His commission had been met in Bahziah, the capital city, with a little more than warmth. The whole affair had hurt and unsettled him and he hadn't even caught up with the time changes. 'I do so loathe flying,' he snapped, 'One leaves one's wits behind!'

Garbie laughed boisterously, and noticing nobody else did, sat down.

There was a pause in which everyone wondered how best to begin. Garbie slapped the arm of her chair, raised her empty glass and was about to drink to the airline's sending Uncle Jack's wits on after him, but failed. She somehow got stuck with mouth open, glass in mid-air. Finding it a difficult moment to ride she decided it would be less noticeable to massage her feet.

Quite suddenly, as she was bent to the task, she heard the sound of fury breaking. A tree rushed through the foliage of the jungle and struck the ground. A squall of hysterical parakeets arose.

'Pardon?'

'Offensive ... Intolerable ... Ungrateful ...!'

Uncle Jack seemed to splutter over his gin.

'Pardon?' she repeated, benignly.

'How dare you!' he shouted, 'How dare you!'

Garbie stared. She had never seen him angry before. Never. Moss clogged her throat.

'After all we've done for you!'

A sudden shutter revealed Aunty Betty and closed again. 'You have no right to opinions! You have no right to discuss things you know nothing about!'

The fungus spread along her tongue, stopping speech. She had an urge to throw herself on the floor at his feet and howl, but the floor itself seemed to be splitting open.

'Why?' wailed Aunt Cissy's voice, 'Why did you say you were our *daughter*?' And then she clapped her hand to her mouth with a faint cry.

'Oh leave her alone.' Victoria took a cigarette from the silver box, and snapped it shut.

She felt her own fragment of floor separate from theirs, the fissure widening as she drifted away. She put an arm out towards Victoria but the space between them was too great.

'After all we've done for you!' repeated Uncle Jack more violently than before.

And then a change took place. As she seemed drawn away to a further and further point of terror, the sensation stopped and all her frightened, sucked out pipes began to fill with a warm, sullen oil.

'You wouldn't yell at Edward like this,' she heard herself say quite clearly.

Jack Pendleton's face went red, then white. Speechlessly he tried to find an answer that could be critical without being cruel. Privately, passionately, he wished Garbie were capable of making out an intellectual case for herself. He could cope with a well constructed piece of theory however unacceptable in itself.

He looked at her, at her clumsiness and ugliness. At her wide open, imperfect mouth. At the graceless way she sat. And something in him despaired. Not of her, of himself.

He took his handkerchief from his pocket and pressed it firmly to his brow, mouth and cheeks. Everyone in the room was aware that something profoundly unsettling had happened to Jack.

They watched him sit down without speaking. Cissy grave, Victoria curious, and Garbie woodenly sulky.

The ormolu clock on the mantelshelf ticked religiously.

'I think,' ventured Jack, pressing his handkerchief to his mouth as though he might be sick, 'I think ... I'm beginning to wonder ... I think maybe I am an *academic* socialist ...'

There was a long silence terribly disturbed by the clock, the soft groan of King's Road traffic and the steady tap somewhere of metal on stone.

At length Cissy re-folded her hands on her lap and swallowed gently. The ash fell off Victoria's cigarette on to the cream carpet.

Jack's lips moved but they were too dry to speak. He moistened them with his tongue and tried again. 'We must all love one another,' he said forlornly. And as he said it, he knew the generation believing that was already brought to an end by its own fatuity. Love alone was not enough. Faith, hope and charity, he thought bleakly.

But his wife heard him with relief. She placed her hand over his.

'Is that it, then?' asked Victoria pungently.

'You wouldn't have shouted at Edward like that,' repeated Garbie aggressively, pleased with the effect. But nobody took any notice of her this time. Attention had passed to Jack.

The ormolu clock struck the half-hour.

'Get me another drink V, there's a dear.' Jack stretched out his glass. Then he looked apologetically at Garbie. 'We haven't been altogether fair to you,' he said, 'I'm sorry.'

'You're just *saying* that!'

Everyone jumped. But the resentment had taken hold and Garbie was reluctant to let go now.

'I think you might ...!' Cissy began indignantly, then stopped.

'You're just trying to pacify me!' she shouted.

'Don't push it,' murmured Victoria pouring gin into her father's glass. 'Let me take you to look at the Prune.'

Garbie was on her feet glaring. She could see what they were up to. And then, suddenly, she couldn't. They sat in a calm semi-circle, sipping their drinks, faces like alabaster. She shook her head and the dust cleared. 'Okeydoke!' she cried gaily and banged her glass down on the small rosewood table. 'O.K., well that's cleared the air a bit eh? We'll all feel better for that I wouldn't mind betting!' She beamed at Victoria. 'Let's have a dekko at your little stranger then!' And she shuffled out backwards.

Victoria followed with a dry expression.

'Oh dear!' said Cissy trying to smile.

Jack felt absurdly, that a dangerous moment had passed. That somehow, in this impeccable, family room, a fundamental had been threatened. He couldn't have said so, it would have sounded ridiculous. 'We must be kinder,' he vowed.

'What did you mean ... *academic?*'

'Oh ...' He shrugged. 'I've just been a little shaken, that's all. The crowds in Bahziah.'

'What did they *really* do?' Cissy knew he'd made a small thing of it.

Jack smiled sheepishly. 'They tried to overturn our car,' he confessed.

'Tried to overturn the car! Why on earth would they want to do that?' Cissy was horrified.

'Oh, you know how it is ... there has to be a scapegoat.' He didn't mention they'd carried sticks and knives.

'Oh Jack! ... And now Garbie!'

'And now Garbie ...' he nodded. In Bahziah he'd had a sense of totems falling. 'We must be nicer to Garbie.'

'She's made things awfully difficult.'

'Yes, poor dear.'

'I wish she could be more ... more ... *tactful.*'

'Political, you mean?' Jack laughed, 'she doesn't understand.'

'No.'

'We must make allowances I suppose.'

'Bring her into the home more.'

'Help her to see ...'

'Improve her clothes perhaps, her hair. Get her face done ...'

'It might be wise for she and I to be seen ...'

'Appearances can make a world of difference.'

'... seen together here and there.'

'What darling?'

'I said I think it might be an idea ... Cissy darling?'

'Yes?'

'How many Palace garden parties have you been to?'

'Oh heavens, five, six ...'

'Enough?'

'Quite enough.' She laughed.

'Do you think, Garbie ...?'

'Oh Jack! She would be thrilled!'

'Cissy my angel, I do love you so!'

Freddy laughed when he heard about the row and scowled when he heard about the garden party. Then he laughed again. 'You've got him rattled!' he crowed, 'You've got him rattled!' He chewed his moustaches frenetically and said he'd give her a little outing himself.

They went to see The Wildest Show On Earth on Clapham Common. Freddy loved circuses. It was a grey Saturday after-noon with stubborn buds still on the trees, not that the queue cared tuppence for the toothy cold. They punched each other in a friendly way, listened to the soccer match on their transistor radios, stood on their heads and blew bubble gum bubbles. There was a smell of animals and the sweet, burnt sugar of candy floss.

'You want to stand up for yourself old thing. Can't you see what they're up to?' Freddy could spread suspicion like the plague. He made her feel stupid that she couldn't see now. She'd thought she could, but she didn't know. She was going to the garden party.

'It's not,' said Freddy, 'that one minds your going to the garden party. One only minds your *wanting* to go.'

'I don't want to upset anybody.'

The queue moved forward.

'I'm glad I made you wear your woolly,' said Garbie, and shivered.

Two warped tumbling dwarfs and a sequinned lady with huge, firm thighs and pointed toes came out on to the little platform to entertain the crowd while it waited. The lady, whose spangles were puce, tossed Indian clubs in the air.

'I love circuses!' said Freddy.

Garbie scratched behind her ear and stood on tiptoe to see. 'You know,' she said affectionately, placing a hand on Freddy's shoulder and pausing to brush away a little dandruff, 'You know it gives me a real thrill to do little things for you.' She puckered her lips in full-blown kiss. 'And another thing,' she went on, with a giggle, 'being with you, makes me feel quite *petite*.'

She meant feminine.

'I don't need coddling by women,' sulked Freddy.

They shuffled forward in silence. He jingled the coins in his pocket vigorously and then apologized. The sparkly lady did a cartwheel and stood up for applause. The drums crashed.

'I used to do a double somersault myself before the war,' said the woman behind to no one in particular. She had a dead paw on her lapel.

'There *is* something . . .' said Freddy.

'Yes?'

But he thought better of it.

She wanted to be included in the game. 'Anything!' she

promised eagerly, 'I'll do anything!' Her mind dwelt wistfully on fried eggs, knitting patterns and Fairy Liquid lather. The womanly fondness for slavery made terrible tangles with a strategy for freedom.

Freddy clapped her reassuringly on the shoulder. 'We'll make a man of you yet!' he said.

They passed through the flap and sat on cramped wooden benches. 'There's nothing like a good circus!' Freddy had recovered his humour and rubbed his hands together. It excited him, being in a crowd. He was enthralled by men eating fire, by toes wobbling on a tightrope, way beyond the arc lights. He was impressed by bodily perfection and discipline.

A brassy band began to play. The children roared. Freddy roared. Garbie sat in a chill of disapproval, hanging on to her bag. Round and round went the spotted ponies in their pink plumes, the tottering bears, cherry-nosed clowns, swaying elephants in Fred Astaire hats, a hoop of doves, tumblers, drums, a red-eyed bull. Round and round they went till the small ring bulged.

They slipped a cage round the ring and let in the lions. Sleepy and sullen they reached for their pedestals, pretending to yawn, longing to eat their trainer's head. The trainer had a glossy crest of hair, gold teeth and tennis shoes. He threw contemptuous scraps in the lion's jaws and bowed.

'It's cruel,' said Garbie, disgusted.

'Watch the trainer! . . . Watch his control! . . . Watch how he plays with danger!'

'Look at his whip,' said Garbie.

She offered Freddy a mint lump, but he was absorbed. He clenched his hands with delight when the lions snarled and the trainer tickled their noses.

'Perfect control,' said Freddy. 'Totally fearless . . . you've got to be in the pink of condition to keep so alert.' He was excited by recklessness.

The fluttering doves interested him less. When the middle-aged women oohed and aahed, he turned to Garbie and said: 'We discussed your application.'

'Yes? What did they say?'

'They were quite pleased by the march, but they want something more.'

'A gesture. A commitment ...'

'I'm not quite clear ...'

'A little outrage.'

His attention was distracted by a toreador teasing his bull. 'Look!' he demanded, his face rapt, 'A thing is only worth doing if what you stand to lose is your life!'

Glumly, Garbie watched the manoeuvres. She couldn't imagine fighting a bull. The man insulted the animal. She thought of melancholy chimps pouring tea and the corrupt scraps lying in the lion's mouth.

'Could you suggest something?' she whimpered as her mind refused to budge beyond collecting boxes, a jumble sale and letters to *The Times*.

'Aaaaaah!' sighed the crowd as a horn tore the red cloak.

'It's only a trick,' said Garbie suspiciously. 'It's not really wild.'

'Wild enough,' whistled Freddy, 'You can never be sure.'

It made him feel young.

The bull was chased away, kicking its heels in a mixture of fury and animal exhibitionism. Out came the spinning clowns with their wide crimson smiles.

'What kind of thing?' persisted Garbie.

And she followed Freddy in the hope of an answer.

She followed him to his room in Euston.

'Another time,' he said. 'Meetings, interviews, arrangements of various kinds.'

She hung about outside the front door.

She followed him to the Farmer's Arms.

'What kind of thing would you advise, if asked ...?' she said, but his reply was lost in late Sunday morning laughter and talk.

She followed him to Speaker's Corner. He went on his bicycle, she went on the bus and searched for him across the grass. There were sheets of daffodils in Hyde Park.

She found him, but couldn't get near enough to repeat her

question, as already he'd collected a sizeable crowd. She was forced to the back and when the old regulars bawled out: 'Speak up!' she couldn't hear a word.

Using her elbows, she pushed and wriggled against the backs. Freddy's head stuck vulturine out of his large, black woolly. His arms whirled like catherine wheels and the veins stood out on his forehead. Garbie strained to hear but his words were drowned for her by the nextdoor speaker whose message was that God Is Protein. Eggs, cheese and milk got confused with freedom.

Freddy glared at the spectators, row upon row of Sunday pork, soft with indifference. He forsook persuasion.

'You ...!' he yelled, shaking his right fist. '... Petty bourgeois! ... You *mimic* men ...!' (Not a movement.) '... You ... *droppings* of capitalist complacency! ... You inert *waste*!'

(A few nudges and upraised hands, but it was all in an afternoon's sport. They took the abuse as entertainment. As vaudeville.)

'Haven't you got any angry blood in you?' (No response.) 'Have you forgotten the Luddites!'

'The who?' piped a voice.

'... So proud that you fought for your country! So *proud* to have fought when your generals told you to! So proud to have marched blind into war at the order! So *puffed* with pride!'

'Oh-oh-oh what a luv-erly war!' sang someone at the front.

'You think you fought for honour? For glory? For freedom? ... You fools! ... You fought ... to uphold ... the imperialism that enslaves you!'

'Give us a kiss comrade!'

But Freddy thought peace was a terrible state to be in. 'With your small slaves' minds! With your small slaves' hearts ...!'

'Better than your big mouth bruvver!'

Amusement began to bind the crowd. They were pleased with themselves. They enjoyed the mild spring sunshine.

Garbie tried to wedge her way through the thick bodies and clouds of beer.

'Mind who you're shoving,' said someone and trod on her foot.

A man in braces with a belly over his trousers, like a flow of hardened larva, cupped his hands to his mouth and bawled: 'Your time's up Number Seven! Back in the bin with you!' His friends creased themselves.

'They let 'em out of a Sunday afternoon,' he explained to them. Garbie shoved him in the stomach and left him winded.

'Workers? ... Call yourselves *workers*! ... I'll tell you what you are! What you really are! ... You're grubs in the arse hole of capitalism!'

The women in the crowd hid their faces and giggled in fright.

'... Feeding on their fundament ...!' He was dancing with rage. (Garbie had a good view now and could hear quite clearly.) '... Bloated with bourgeois crap!'

There was a stirring among the married men who took the arms of their wives.

'Watch your language bruvver; there's decent people here!'

Garbie turned angry, protruding eyes upon hecklers.

'So corrupted by your own greed you don't see, don't hear! ... Dupes! ... Pap in the capitalist gut!'

'Troublemaker!'

'The old nutter's harmless. Take no notice.'

'The time is ripe! We will rise! ... We will take the oppressor by the throat ...!'

Lethargically, they cast about in their minds for enemy shapes and found mainly benevolence.

'You are fit ...'

'Put a sock in it!'

'For ...'

'Go home.'

'... only one thing!' Froth at the mouth, eyes white with hysteria, Freddy reached for his flies, seized his penis and let forth a thin amber trickle on the ground.

'Hey! Hey!'

'Ha! Ha!'

The crowd split in two, half protesting, half hooting with laughter. But the sun shone and the wood pigeons gurgled and the laughter won. Nobody even bothered to call the police. Garbie, trapped in the sea of hilarity shouted indignant defences which went unheard. Over the wheezing and screeching and tear wiping came the one clear cry that Protein was the Life Force and present in all.

Freddy had vanished.

'Was that the sort of thing you were meaning ...?' she inquired at the earliest opportunity. Her eyes were oily with admiration. She clung to his elbow as he went speeding off to Waterloo to observe the comings and goings of trains.

'Was it something like that you had in mind?'

'Hurry! Hurry!' cried Freddy and she pounded up the platform after him, hair flying.

'You've only to ask ...' she called.

Reaching the far end of the platform, Freddy took notebook and pencil from the end of his satchel and wrote something down.

'... Only to command ...' gasped Garbie, reaching him.

Freddy took a small green flag from his satchel and raised it as the engine driver moved past. He lowered it. 'Synchronize watches!' he ordered.

They examined their wrists.

'Fifteen hundred hours, forty-nine minutes and two point five seconds, exactly!'

'Excellent!' said Freddy. 'Now I must go home and prepare myself for a lecture tour of the universities.'

'But ...' began Garbie, breaking into a lope again, 'I wanted to ask ...'

They handed in their platform tickets.

'There's a great deal to think about,' said Freddy, 'a great deal to arrange.'

'Yes,' breathed Garbie and unexpectedly began to dream about the garden party.

11 Spring Offensive

In May, as blossoms broke, students from Edinburgh to Bristol locked staff out of their offices and daubed ancient walls with the catchwords of anger.

The Holy Church of God ceased praising the white Lord and found a black one, far more beautiful. Guns were discovered buried close to the Ulster border and three men arrested. The Royal group of docks lay idle. Millwall tenants forced their way into County Hall and were held responsible for the death of the lift man who fell down a day later from a sudden heart attack. Most surprising of all, Bob Dylan songs rose from a column of bank clerks marching across Westminster Bridge in grey worsted suits and twin sets.

Garbie's razor flashed faster and faster round newspaper columns reporting other people's outrages and she longed wistfully for one of her own. She felt in a vague way, that if she failed to take advantage of the time laid aside for revolt, a whistle would blow and she'd find herself on the side of resigned, unhealthy shadows. It was all one wanton puff of the dandelion clock away.

Her friends in the office said it was awful in a place proud of its police force and its free speech. Mild old people got quite angry. They could only see plastic bubbles with slogans painted on them and cheered anybody who wagged their finger from the pulpit.

The *Financial Times'* index fell by four points and when Jack Pendleton tried to make his voice heard among the desperate speeches in the House, everybody brushed aside the question of sabotage in Awanzikwa. They certainly hadn't the time to debate a planned return of the tsetse fly.

There was no word from Freddy so Garbie did some babysitting for Rose Birnberg while she and her husband Leo went out to organize a happening in the evenings.

'The final scene,' Rose explained, 'is where we all take our clothes off, go and sit in the laps of the people in the audience, and kiss them. The trouble is, at the Living Arts Centre, the audience rather enjoys it.'

'What a shame,' said Garbie.

Freddy had not returned by the end of the month, so she went to Dagenham.

'They're all out again at the works,' said Aunty Betty, 'I don't know what things are coming to.' Some pressed flowers fell out of her book. 'They ought to bring back conscription.'

'Oh Aunty ... !'

'It's no good giving me your funny ideas ... goodness knows where they come from with all your advantages.' She reached for her solitaire board and said huffily, 'There's too much nudity.'

'You should be proud of your body Aunty.'

Betty Beazley glared through her milk-blue eyes. 'Your Uncle Arnold, I'm proud to say, never saw me with my clothes off. And another thing. I thank the Lord Colin didn't live to see it.' She adjusted the sleeves of her cardigan. 'There's that many poofs round here these days, I'd have been afraid to let him out.'

'Oh Aunty ... !'

'That's enough body talk from you, young woman.'

She was easily diverted by the Buckingham Palace Garden Party. 'A real honour for the family,' she said. 'Will you try and get a photograph? I'd like to have one next to Colin's in a nice frame. Will you speak to the Queen?'

'You realize the monarchy's defunct, don't you Aunty Betty?' remarked Garbie, 'I wouldn't go, but it might be one of the last opportunities to see a living monarch.'

'Maybe,' said Aunty Betty absently, 'you'll need a new dress. I'll run something smart up for you.'

'All right then!'

'A silk perhaps, or a nice length of crêpe ...'

'I had a fancy for black taffeta.'

'... or taffeta then. You're too young for black.'

They agreed on turquoise. 'Yes, you'd suit that,' said Aunty Betty.

She brought out her work-basket and cracked her knees to get busy with her tape measure. 'It takes me back,' she said. She was happy. 'Do you remember the parachute silk?'

'Twenty years ago?'

'Twenty years is it? ... D'you know,' mused Aunty Betty, her mouth full of pins, 'you're the same age your mother was when she met with her accident?'

The connection again imprinted itself, as if anxious for meaning. 'If she'd had your advantages ...'

'What then?'

'She was just took advantage of ... that was her trouble. She was a bit simple, your mother.'

'Simple ... ?'

'You want to watch you don't get took advantage of ... a girl like you.' Aunty Betty measured her from wrist to armpit and said again carefully, 'A girl your age wants to look out.' Her eyes wrinkled like dried apple rings.

Garbie looked wildly round the room at the dull ginger lumps of furniture, the faded galleon wallpaper, the sixpenny jar on the mantelpiece. A cobweb festooning the picture rail had escaped Aunty Betty's notice. There was a grey patch of damp on the ceiling. 'Did you know,' she said, 'that they're giving away tin openers with four labels from Typhoo tea packets?'

'Men,' persisted Aunty Betty, 'are likely to take advantage of a girl of your age.'

'Have you heard the first cuckoo yet Aunty Betty? It's about time don't you think?'

'I only mention it because of your mother. How low do you want the neck?'

Garbie looked at the opaque eyes only six inches away from her own. Over her aunty's shoulder she saw a bluebottle settle on the newly turned out tin of luncheon meat, pink in its yellow blob of jelly.

'I'm sorry?'

'About here? ... or up here?'

'Oh ...'

'A little Peter Pan looks very nice. Very dainty. Or you could have a V with a little modesty vest tucked in ...'

'All right, all right,' said Garbie meekly.

'Which?'

'Either.'

Cissy rang to show there was no ill-feeling. Garbie mentioned that Aunty Betty was making a dress. There was a small pause. 'Oh,' said Cissy, 'I thought I'd buy you something. Something simple.'

'It'd be a waste.'

'You mustn't worry about the money darling! Why don't you let me?'

'There are some *people*,' said Garbie heavily, 'who can't afford a pair of shoes.'

'Very well, dear,' murmured Cissy, crushed, 'We must lunch some time.'

The pollen count was extremely high on the day of the garden party, otherwise it was perfect.

Garbie was ready dressed by twelve sharp. She'd had her hair done by Maureen's Coiffeuse and her scalp felt stiff. The lacquer made her sneeze though the French pleat she thought was chic. She tried not to spoil it as she clipped on the half moon of turquoise feathers she'd bought very reasonably at the Oxfam shop. The sharp little points dug in behind her ear.

Freddy surprised her by calling round.

Nervously, she pirouetted. 'How do you like it?'

He started irritably, 'I don't know. I don't know anything about that sort of thing.'

'I'm not really obsessed by materialism!' she cried frantically and plucked at her voluminous skirt, 'but I do like the sound it makes.'

Freddy began to cry.

'I'll take it off!' she gabbled, a terrible pain boiling up in her chest, 'I'll take it off if it upsets you!'

He bent over his knees and wept noisily. The shoulders of his speckled overcoat jogged up and down.

Garbie ran to put the kettle on and poured whisky into an egg cup which she thrust in his hand. Then she patted him on the head and said, 'There, there, don't cry!' But he did.

She hung about, touching things until he'd finished. She buttered two slices of bread thinking they might help somehow. 'I never cry,' she said kindly as his sobs died away, 'it makes me feel ill.'

'I'm losing my hair!' he wailed, refusing to look at her.

'That's all right ...'

'I'm losing my *hair*!' he raised a desperate, watery face.

'It'll just be the summer moult ...'

'Look ... !' Savagely he tore at his head and removed two sparse handfuls of his peppery hair. 'Oh God!' he hiccupped and began to weep again.

'It'll be all right. My grandmother wore a wig.'

'That's not the point,' he moaned and thought of all the field marshals and generals who'd kept their hair past seventy-five.

'You won't leave me will you?' he wailed in a moment of weakness, clutching at her skirt, 'I've still got the vitality of a man half my age!'

'Of course not,' she smiled, 'nobody would ever *guess* you were ...' And she remembered she had no idea how old he was exactly.

'What's this?' he barked, suddenly aware of the taffeta he had gripped in his hand, 'what on earth are you wearing?'

She sulked a little, then he made her sit down, held her knee tightly in his dry old hand, told her how much he appreciated her and reminded her to be sure of getting her uncle's views on the student problem. 'Nothing so useful as the unofficial view,' he said. 'Can't trust anything but the horse's mouth. Can't trust anybody these days, that's why, of course, the membership business takes so long. You've got to be certain.'

'Oh I do understand.' Garbie stood up and looked down at herself. 'You don't think the rosettes are a bit on the showy side do you?' she asked doubtfully. Aunty Betty had placed six round the frill at the hem and two at the neck. Garbie plucked at the puff sleeves and smoothed her waist. There was a smear of butter on the skirt which Freddy tried to remove with Dab-It-Off.

'Would you like to read the invitation?' she asked. And gallantly, just to please her, he did.

She hung her matching dolly bag on her wrist, pushed her feet into painful white shoes, then sat next to Freddy on the bed in silence. A lorry rumbled past outside.

'It's all right,' she said at length to reassure him.

'Oh, I nearly forgot!' he cried and plunging into his satchel took out a very small camera. 'The reason I called!'

She stammered her thanks.

'You might,' he urged, 'like to have a photograph taken, with a nice view of the rear aspect behind. That would be most unusual. There's a time exposure mechanism here.' He showed her and put the camera away in her bag. 'Discreetly done of course!' He smiled, and banged her gently on the shoulders, 'I believe there are flamingos in the gardens. And now if you don't mind, I'll kip down for a little here. I've been on the go all night.'

'If anyone knocks,' she said, tucking him up, 'don't answer.'

'Mum's the word!' he winked, and fell peacefully asleep.

Jack Pendleton swallowed hard when he saw his niece. 'Ah!' he said. And again, more boisterously, '*Ah*!'

She kissed him fondly and wagged her finger at him. 'What a disgrace you *are* to me!' she cried playfully, 'You're covered in dog hairs!' And she gave him a brisk pummelling.

The gates of the palace stood open wide to let in the flow of guests and their sleek, black cars. Garbie sank back in the deep leather. 'It's really wonderful, isn't it,' she commented warmly looking about her and bowing her head to a policeman, 'to have a Queen who lets the common people into her home!'

'Rather!' yelped Jack.

When they got out of the car, he steered her firmly across the courtyard and into the drawing room that opened out on its far side, to the lawns. They moved past several people he knew, at tremendous speed.

'The carpet's a bit threadbare! But isn't that nice though? A really *homely* touch! I must tell Aunty Betty.'

Already the lawn was filled with the open mouthed in their new clothes. The indifferent, the seasoned guests, arrived later on.

They descended the shallow steps from the terrace.

'Now what do we do?' She looked around her shamelessly trying to spot celebrities.

'We're supposed to chat. Mingle,' he gazed at his trouser legs and cracked his knuckles, hating himself.

'That reminds me!' She tapped her forehead and drew her face closer to his to whisper, 'I'd like your views on the student problem.'

He gazed at her helplessly, found a speck in his eye and murmured, '*Which* problem?'

'Oh come on now! You can't play the innocent with me! The *protest* problem.'

Jack Pendleton adjusted his carnation and wondered which side of his niece were the more difficult to cope with, the helpless or the assertive.

'Oh,' he said dismissively, 'students will be students.'

But she persisted.

'Well,' he shrugged, 'if we educate young people to think for themselves, we can hardly grumble when they do, can we?' and thinking he may have said the wrong thing, he took her elbow in an effort to get her walking about. He was afraid someone might come up to them if they stood still.

'It's only natural after all,' he tried again, 'idealism in the young.' He felt himself perspiring and headed for the bushes bordering the lake. 'And how's your own fierce sense of idealism coming along?'

'I like to take a lively interest. It stops the mind from going dull.' She smiled at him gratefully. 'It's always a treat to have an informed view like your own.'

She made him feel mean. 'I can't pretend,' he told her more confidentially, 'that I sympathize with all their ideas ... not that,' and he laughed, 'not that it's always easy to tell what their ideas are! I'll have to do a spot of brushing up on them if I'm to do a radio talk about it all next week, won't I?' He thrashed about for a sympathetic point to make, 'But I admire the sense of *commitment* in our young people, that's what I find so attractive ... Some of the things of course,' he went on, moving briskly through the rhododendrons, 'some of the things that get said and done might be better conceived, but it's all a matter of trial and error isn't it? I was impatient with practical difficulties myself as a young man, it always seemed that Utopia was only over the next hill and the sole factor preventing our arrival was the stupidity of old men. But there we are!'

And making the common mistake of thinking the problem was one entirely to do with youthfulness, he retired into a rueful contemplation which he hoped concealed any hint of irritation with the hooligan element in the Universities.

'Hello there!'

Denton Caldwell and Hugh Bennett popped up guiltily from behind a clump of pampas grass.

'What a pleasant surprise!'

'I think you've met my ...'

'Ah! Weren't you the one who ... ?'

'It's the political firebrand unless I'm very much mistaken!'

She pulled a face trying to look modest. Then all three men spoke at once.

'Just discussing one or two ... !'

'Must get back for the Weights and Measures division ... !'

'Must be getting on for tea ... !'

'Ha! Ha!'

'Why don't you run along darling and see the Queen?'

'Oh, I shouldn't like you to miss it Uncle Jack.'

'I think I can bear it just this once!' he whinnied and gave his friends a sidelong wink.

'I'll give you a yell if I see her coming.'

'Not to worry!' he called as she went loping off towards the crowds gathering at the back of the Palace.

When the Royal Family appeared on the terrace, all the old timers raced off to the tea tent to get the best of the chocolate cake, while the newer and more eager borough councillors and their wives bunched themselves together for a close peek, prevented from any vulgar pushing closer only by a sense of what was proper and the fact that their heels were sinking in the grass.

Her hands waving in their large, white minstrel gloves, Garbie found herself a space and strained forward. Taller than most, she had a clear view of the small figure in apricot silk, so much smaller than she'd expected that an offensively watery lump lodged in her throat. She'd tried to fix an image of carbuncular rings, stout calves and arbitrary orders in her mind, but however hard she tried, she quite openly gave, together with all the other women round her, a faint communal 'Ah-h-h! ...'

The small figure with its practised smile moved down the line, pausing occasionally. When she laughed, nothing moved, as though she were afraid her hat might fall off. The smile was unfaltering. It moved equitably over the open, coarse-grained faces of her subjects. It passed level with Garbie's chest and moved on. Garbie fought her way down the line, white gloves protruding spasmodically between people's thighs and arms, her face now way above the ears of the crowd, now craning round their elbows.

Jack observed the ripple of movement, the flashing gloves, the turquoise feathers and asked Denton Caldwell if he could name the aircraft flying overhead.

'... a return to law and order!' sang Caldwell, his eyes momentarily dazzled.

The gloves and feathers were professionally observed by the Queen and her private detectives. Smiles dried to a film. They'd heard rumours of agitation in the outside world.

'*Tea!*' snapped Jack Pendleton smiling with all his teeth, and he pulled her backwards out of the throng. Falling back on popular vocabulary he heard himself claim, 'There's nothing like a nice cuppa.'

Her yellow skin was glistening, there were brown stains on her chin and she said: 'Hang on a tick!' while burrowing in her dolly bag. 'One for the scrapbook!' she hissed thrusting a small camera into his hands. Then she posed expectantly, gloved hands clasped and her large feet bent into the ballerina's third position.

'I ...'

'Ready!'

'But ...'

'Are my eyes all screwed up?'

Something sank inside him. But nobody seemed to be looking.

Rather than argue, he gave a furtive look to either side, glanced through the viewfinder and clicked the shutter rapidly over a brief image of his niece placed diagonally against a tipping roof. Guiltily, he fought with the drawstring on her dolly bag trying to replace the camera.

Two large men, looking hot in their morning suits, stepped out of the crowd and gently eased him away by the elbows to listen to him with ominous patience.

Applause trickled politely across the lawn and women friends began to gossip together, twisting pearls around their ancient necks. Claws snapped over the last of the chocolate cake and Uncle Jack was released from conference with his friends. He was incapable of speech.

'Where are we going?' inquired Garbie, propelled at great speed by a hand in the small of her back. There was a choking sound.

'I know,' she said, with an unconscious blend of humility and viciousness, 'that people don't always want me around. I do know that.'

'You mustn't talk like that!' he shrilled, thinking how one lied to the dying. How they knew one lied.

'I know I'm different,' she went on, ignoring him, 'I've had to learn to live with that.' They were climbing the terrace steps two at a time.

He didn't want to hear of disability. 'And a very dull place the world would be if we were all the same!' He pinched her upper arm with a kind of warmth.

'But I thought that's what you wanted Uncle Jack! For everyone to be the same!'

'In a manner of speaking ... !'

They fell into the waiting car. It was stuffy and smelt of saddles.

'But I don't understand ...' she insisted querulously, and sneezed.

'Who does ... ? Who does?' lamented the politician and drew her attention, as they passed St James's Park, to a pelican with a broken wing.

When they drove into Trafalgar Square they found traffic halted and hooting as crowds of yelling students flocked from the Square across the road and towards the Strand. Summer tourists stood on the steps of St Martin's and hung over the parapet of the National Gallery gazing entranced at the surging spectacle. Two people ran past the bonnet of the car carrying a banner between them.

' "Expulsion means Dictatorship",' spelt out Uncle Jack, leaning forward from his thickly upholstered seat. 'How interesting. Drive on, would you!'

Slowly they crawled round the Square to the Strand side. Students were still pouring out of the Square. As they halted at the traffic lights, fists beat on the bonnet of the imperturbable Bentley.

'Well, well ...' remarked Jack faintly, recalling the terror of his recent trip to Bahziah where hands had rocked the car and made him slide, ridiculously from side to side. Black faces, pressed angrily to the glass, had obliterated every inch of sky. He looked warily at his niece who seemed to have developed an uncanny knack for involving him in incident. She was shining.

The chauffeur, anxious to get round the Square, hooted and started to slide forward. He provoked fists, shouts and cat-calls.

'Steady on!' called Jack. He coughed and remarked that he'd expected all this to end when exams began.

'Two students were expelled,' said Garbie, hypnotized.

'Yes, I realize that, but they were making life extremely difficult for those who wanted to work, the majority in fact ... we can't have that sort of thing, can we?'

She refused to comfort him by replying.

'I mean, if laws are broken ... laws, rules, are for the protection of the majority. I think you can move now Bartlett.'

But he couldn't.

Jack tapped an evening newspaper on his knee ... He'd always accepted youthful exuberance – nothing wrong with that, but he hated the excess of fanatics.

The car again began to move, Jack heaved a sigh of relief. 'At last,' he murmured to his niece who, he suddenly perceived, was fighting with the door handle. 'For God's sake!' he shouted, 'be careful!'

She stumbled out, the door swinging. Another car braked and hooted. Then she was gone, across the road and into the river of people. The Bentley gathered speed and accelerated towards the House, while Uncle Jack flung himself across his seat to grab the swaying door. 'Not even a thank you!' he shouted to himself. 'Not so much as a –' And the M.P. fell on the floor.

Feathered and flounced she was stuck like a lonely ostrich in the midst of stampede. Shoppers were flung into doorways holding their screaming children high above the wild current that surged down the Strand, towards the Aldwych and into the narrow bottleneck of Houghton Street, where police horses nudged into one another showing the whites of their eyes as the roar approached.

She lost a shoe and was carried on, exhilarated; an atom of anger with no direction except the one on which she was involuntarily borne. For Garbie now, no matter what, an angel sang.

It was dusk when she arrived at Freddy's room.

Freddy's room was in a basement down six black steps in one of the ragged streets behind Euston.

Cypriot children still played hopscotch on the warm, darkening pavements and flecks of soot sailed like burnt paper into eyes, mouths and windows.

Freddy was busy giving a class to a visiting American. So

she sat down quietly on a spiky plastic stool and proudly gathered her torn skirts.

'First raise a local issue, applicable to other areas, states or campuses. Do you follow me?'

'I'm right there with you!' enthused Bruno S. Kreutleburger morosely, rubbing his large, brightly capillaried nose. He was balding, came from Buffalo, where he studied creative writing and carried a gun. He wore a sweat shirt which clung damply to a swollen breast and stomach and had the words Superman Can Save printed on it.

'Keep the protest rumbling till disproportionate reaction's provoked. That broadens the sympathy and divides the government.'

'Right on!' nodded Bruno S. Kreutleburger.

The room was always dark because of the low ceiling and the area wall outside the window, but Garbie liked it. 'It's got a cosy feel to it,' she'd said when first invited. She meant, exciting.

There were posters of Che and Mao on the walls and one magazine picture of Martin Chivers, a typewriter, a tin of Fru-Grains, whisky, newspapers, glue and bits of model aeroplane all over the table. On the floor were Freddy's sleeping bag and a bottle of green milk. It was covered in a dull yellow, speckled lino that didn't quite reach to the skirting board. Brown tufts of newspaper stuck out of the gaps.

'The harsher the repression, the broader the sympathy. Opposition intensifies.'

'It's beautiful.' Mr Kreutleburger shook his head disbelievingly, 'the simplicity . . .' he said, 'it's poetic. But can it work?'

Taking a waxy-toothed comb from his pocket, he began, reflectively, combing his hair.

Freddy wiped shreds of cheese from his moustache. 'I,' he said proudly, 'have helped lots of young men like yourself. The method has been tried and tested.' He raised one leg on the chair and leaned forward along his knee. 'The philosophers,' he whispered, 'have studied my technique.' He let this sink into Mr Kreutleburger's absorbent cortex. Then he stood up again and flexed his shoulders. 'It's a matter of military intellect and experience,' he added, betraying briefly a preference for strategy rather than ideology.

Garbie listened in a state of enchantment. The words held for her the same awe and incomprehension as the ornate Latin of a Catholic service. It was a language designed to comfort the superstitious.

Bruno S. Kreutleburger was handed a number of pamphlets and his free copy of *One Dimensional Man*, which he paused to read out aloud.

'Tophole!' said Freddy. 'Now let me help you to an aperitif.'

Eagerly, Garbie poured.

'Your dress!' observed Freddy. 'It seems damaged.'

'Yes.' Trying not to smile, she stood holding out petticoats. 'I lost a shoe too.'

He stared at her feet. 'Did the garden party become violent?' he inquired, hope sneaking like a light across his face.

'A horse trod on my foot.'

'Excuse me,' said Mr Kreutleburger slowly, 'a *horse* trod on your foot?'

'Yes.' Shyly, she nodded.

'A *horse* trod on your foot at a garden party?'

'At the College!'

'A horse trod on your foot in College! Oh, you British!' sighed Mr Kreutleburger admiringly, you're really out of sight!'

Garbie tried to get it right. She explained while Freddy listened intently, dropping cheese into his mouth. When she finished she was so overcome by pride and the effort of speaking at length, she couldn't help whistling Camptown Races.

Freddy considered the obstacle of police horses. He drew one on a piece of paper, and pinned it to a green baize board.

'The rear is the most vulnerable,' she said, studying it carefully. 'One must direct the attack to the hindquarters if possible.' He thought about it, picked his teeth and congratulated Garbie. 'You might be able to help us tomorrow,' he said.

'Excuse me.'

'Yes?'

'Excuse me, but I'm on duty tomorrow.'

'Duty?' echoed Freddy, his blue eyes shrivelling, *'Duty!'* he repeated.

And she hung her head.

Across both ends of the semicircular street which separated the College buildings from the main road, police horses stood like statues. There was an occasional, gentle clinking of ceremonial bits, the lethargic swish of a tail.

It was hot, but the cloud hung low and broody. The heat brought on Garbie's migraine which had at least given her a truthful excuse to stay away from the office. It was the kind of day that leaves gritty London dust between the teeth.

Down the gutters of Kingsway limped the Happy Wanderers, shaking a collecting box and playing an asthmatic version of The Saints. A model girl with eyes as strange as spaceships and wearing a rattling net of silver plastic discs was photographed handing them a coin. Or another silver plastic disc.

Garbie stared at her own reflection in the insurance company's window. She was, she thought, turning sideway slightly, as tall and slim as the model girl. She forgot her geodic joints.

Small, morning clusters of people passed this way and that, some pausing to peer between the horses' flanks at the night's miracle with sucked in breath. Garbie, trying to look like a housewife, walked on tiptoe to study the new steel gates hanging across the College entrance like an eight foot grille. A card suspended on an amateur piece of string, said quite simply, CLOSED.

The police kept one leather hand on the reins and stared over her head.

Most of the students who'd arrived for their ten o'clock lecture were dull, baffled creatures burdened down with books. They began whispering doubtfully among themselves. Some left. Some waited without having good reason to wait. Casually, Garbie sauntered past for the ninth time and studied other roof tops.

At half past ten, behind the swell and roar of nearby traffic, came the faint but steady sound of chanting. A pulse kept time in Garbie's ribs. With each fresh fall in the traffic noise, the chant came louder. Three regular beats. The horses tossed their heads and shuffled their hooves softly.

A woman gathered her Peke in her arms and fled.

Under the hot grey sky, through busy city came the poles, the pennants, the cry.

'O-pen up! O-pen up! O-pen!'

Disembodied faces hung in constellation behind the glass. There was a trembling of hands.

'O-pen up! O-pen up! O-pen up!'

The traffic began to pile up in knots and swathes while private drivers made disobedient manoeuvres round the trouble. People ran across the zebra crossing, then walked swiftly against the tide, heads turned back to see what would happen. The newspaper seller, sitting beside his box on the corner of Kingsway, spat and shrank into an angle of the wall.

'OPEN UP! OPEN UP! OPEN UP!'

They swept round the corner, a rebellious and unbuttoned army. Like flood water they poured round buses, stranding them in this bubbling rush, filling the Aldwych and lapping high up the enclosing walls.

Garbie stood a second, dazed by the suicidal force unrolling towards her and then it was over. They were on top of her, carrying her forward to the front of them, straight towards the quivering chests of the horses.

Involuntarily, she fought every last, small inch of the way, her feet straining against the road surface. She was probably shouting. Her arms crossed high in a mixture of religion and protection, she scraped onward, elbows foolishly exposed to blows. She caught the warm, straw stench of the horses, saw their muscles move the light, glimpsed an eye rolled whitely inwards and then was thrust powerfully against a massive scapula. In a clear, brief moment of panic she knew she was going to be crushed between two sweating, muscular masses as the beasts staggered backwards carrying her with them. She saw a boot, a spur and then, her head forced downwards, an artillery of sparking hooves. Her feet pedalled the air trying to skip over pain. Her fists were occupied with their own, different business, attempting to prise the shoulders apart.

Something landed and smashed a few yards ahead on the ground, loosing a tongue of flame. With a scream of energy the horse on her right bounded forward, its tail alight. As it went, the spur travelled across her cheek and she burst free under a sudden torrent that forced her to run four steps on her knees.

Dizzy, weaving sideways and swooning a little on to her finger tips, she crawled, then loped forward, a surprising, salty trickle of blood leaking into her mouth. Ferociously, she made her weak and whining muscles take her towards the swarm of people who'd leapt or stumbled over her and thrown themselves in a growing crowd, against the gates.

Unable or unwilling to look backwards, she could tell from the sounds that nobody else had escaped the line behind her into the street and she knew the police barrier must have closed tightly together again. On feet as big and stupid as asbestos mats she tottered towards the students who thrust themselves again and again upon the gates. The shouting of the mob behind her was halfway across the world; a cyclone tearing up the archipelago and whirling it into vanishing circles of air.

Two policemen who'd been on duty beside the gates and had snatched the first boy through the line, pinning his arms behind his back, were now engulfed and fought a retreat that was human and angry and nothing to do with the law. It was a street corner battle, all blood and teeth and youth. Their helmets had fallen off. Garbie passed them, kicking one a few rocking inches further away.

She hung on to the battering ram of bodies, eyes closed, letting herself be carried back, then hurled forward with terrific force. Somebody was screaming. She glanced up and saw through sickening perspectives, white knuckles stuck to the bars as though an electric current held them there.

She hung on, teeth clenched against a muddy rise of vomit and rode the great leviathan. Endlessly, it seemed to carry her back and forth, back and forth, until there was a sudden metallic crack and the gates of the citadel snapped from their hinges. There was a massive, inward rush and the metal buckled underfoot.

Trying to keep her head up, Garbie was swept through the entrance. Her mouth, popping like a goldfish, reached up for air and then she was rolled off the edge of the mob as it made a curving movement to the right and up the stairs.

She doubled up, gasping and stumbled forward while the rest of the tide raced away from her. Reaching out her arms to stop herself falling, she staggered against two swing doors and plunged into a large, dark auditorium whose invisible floor fell steeply away beneath her. Hanging on to the wooden backs of the chairs for support, she sank into the narrow space between two rows of seats.

She stayed there, head uncomfortably lodged against something metal and tried to drag the last shrivelled scrap of breath from her lungs. Slowly, as her panting subsided, she heard the sounds beyond herself, beyond the swing doors. There was only a desultory clatter of footsteps on the marble floor of the entrance hall outside. A faint rumble of movement overhead, the odd shout. And beyond the brick, away in the street a pale, but steady moan of anger.

Then she became frightened.

She was, she realized, alone. Her skin, no longer in crushed contact with other skins, turned cold. Triumph, plunged into vinegar, wrinkled.

It was dim and quiet in the lecture theatre. Things slowly assumed confident shapes and she knew she didn't belong. The lectern, the table were thick, yellow wood. Water stayed solid and unsparkling in the glass jug. I don't belong, she thought. I don't belong.

She was a trespasser. The word was full of biblical terror. Her mind ran hysterically over the possibilities. Breaking and entering. Wilful and malicious damage. Other people's property. She had, she realized weakly, committed a criminal offence.

Crouching very still between the wooden seats she felt her heart ticking like a large red, alarm clock. She wrapped her arms round herself to muffle the noise of it, and then, in this awkward, knotted pose, she shuffled herself slowly forward out into the side aisle. Then she paused and listened, her ears stretched out like radar saucers, hunting for signals.

Nothing. Moving half an inch at a time, she crawled to the doors and then, after another pause, scraped one open with a finger tip, pressing her eye to the narrow vertical of light. The roar from the street swelled a little, but the hall seemed silent and empty. She swivelled her eye, opened the door a fraction wider, then rapidly hauled herself to her feet. As she did so, a shout from above made her scuttle through the gap, into the hall and straight down a flight of stairs to the basement.

Her feet panicked over the stone steps, two, three at a time, down, through a door at the bottom of the flight and into a long corridor with a concrete floor and other passages opening off it.

A weak light came from bulbs, spasmodically lit, but she could see it was deserted. Somewhere, a machine hummed and clicked.

Half-searching for a back way out of the building, she crept forward trailing weak fingers along the wall while the colossal clock in her chest raced towards a ringing time. All her other limbs had gone curiously light as though fear had sucked the bones hollow. If she were to let go of the wall for one instant, her feet would lift away from the straight line and she would be buffeted with weightless indirection from one wall to the other.

Overhead, the low grey pipes gave a whispering gurgle, making her jump and move more quickly towards the end of the corridor. Here it branched left and right into two identical corridors. Increasingly swiftly, she passed down the right hand passage, her hand twisting on every handle as she went. None would open.

There were red arrows pointing in no particular direction. Wildly, she followed them, not caring any longer how noisily she released the door handle as she passed. Each door had an opaque square of glass covered in wire mesh and a random number.

Salt tears ran into the cut on her cheek and made it sting. Unable to see clearly, she sped from one right angle into another, growing bigger every moment and banging her knees, her elbows against the corners.

She felt like a rat under the floorboards, an intruder. A laboratory rat in a maze proving some witless experiment. A snapping, scuttling rat, suspicious of traps.

Her mind forgot what it was running from, let go of cause and fixed itself massively instead on escape. Faster and faster, she flew through the corridors, the handles snapping horridly behind her and then, suddenly, one sprang open. She was almost past it before she realized, then she reversed, slipped into the room and slammed the door shut.

There was an abrupt sense of stillness.

It was not a pleasant stillness.

There was a sense that this room, or something in the room, had been waiting for her. The metal racks of books stood very black, very quiet. The books were old, many of them damaged but others, some of them too big to hold comfortably, were bound in fine leather.

The room hadn't any of the dusty warmth of Bakewell library, or Lambeth where there were biscuit crumbs inside the Enid Blyton books and guilty squiggles pencilled in biographies. This was a treasury of books, a reference store of the world's esoteric philosophies.

Garbie moved along the rows, running her finger absently over the spines. It was an instinctive touching, something she'd always done in Bakewell, Chesterfield and Todmorden. A way of drawing calm and comfort. She passed to another row and saw, as her finger slowed its progress, that every single volume was in a foreign language.

Greek, German, Latin, Hebrew, Russian, French and Sanskrit; all the knowledge of the earth set down in hieroglyphs.

She stopped. She frowned, eyes down. Something flickered in her like suspicion. A feeling that she was being watched through some high-placed spyhole.

Moving clumsily as she always did when she thought someone was looking at her, she ran over to the wall and tried to reach one of the two barred half-windows, set high up against the ceiling. Her fingers slipped through the dust of the sloping, cream-painted brick sill. As she stood, staring upwards, wondering whether to jump, she grew aware again of sounds that had never ceased. Of the lowering movement of a crowd somewhere outside in the street, not very far away. The sound gave Garbie hope. She jumped and touched the bars. She jumped again and this time seized them, her feet dangling some four inches from the ground, but she had to let go because the effort hurt her arms so.

A pair of pinstriped legs walked past the window. They were such orderly legs they were immensely cheering. They disappeared to lunch. They were the kind of legs that told Garbie without having to look at her new, waterproof watch, that it was one o'clock precisely.

She felt better. She still stood, wanting to jump up at the window although she knew there was no way out. It was simply instinctive like the yearning of potted plants to grow towards light as though they're magnetized by the sky.

Shouting broke out. And then a low, stirring sound, followed by a collective thunder. As Garbie gazed transfixed at the window, more legs passed. First at a hurried walk, then a loping run and finally, her light was blacked out by a tumbling flight of drumming, dissociated legs. Caught in the moving thicket of the strong, the slim, the white legs, she glimpsed the slender flight of ostrich and impala. They ran as if pursued by forest fire. The wall shook with their pounding. Books shifted uneasily in their metal racks.

She turned away, and pressed herself up against the wall, arms and fingers outspread like a crucifix. Her heart had almost stopped in horror at the thought that she wasn't even to be captured, but far, far worse, was going to be left alone, ignored.

The abandoned books, drooped. One fell face downwards on the floor, loosing a few of its coded pages.

Wilfully her mind spun out its panic stricken stream of images like a faulty computer spewing tape. She thought of castles squatting bland over their dungeons. She thought of bars and keys and dying flesh. She thought of stone a foot thick, of forgetfulness, of deafness and indifference. She thought of the luxury of monuments and the prisoner's mocking square of sky.

Pressed fiercely against the wall she stayed, hypnotized by

her own imaginings, until slowly she realized the drumming sound was just an insistent beating in her own head and that outside the window above her there was nothing but the regulated noise of milk vans and the domestic gear-change of deliveries.

She swayed away from the wall, wiping her cheek with the back of her hand. She saw the blood was still wet. Her smeared knuckles reminded her of the Rotherbrook children coming home from their first hunt, daubed on both cheeks with the blood of the fox. They were so proud they slept all night with the blood drying in brown crusts on their faces. She smiled a little to herself and felt braver.

The passages ran into one another empty and quiet. Doubtfully she stood plotting her escape route. She rubbed her nose hard and tried to establish a bearing – the windows of the storeroom had given her some idea of which side of the building she was on, but direction slipped round her head on a roulette wheel.

At a flapping trot Garbie worked her way round the perimeter, resisting short cuts until she came to the door which divided her from the stairs to the ground floor. All was quiet. With a small whimper of relief, she pushed her way through and crept up the stone steps.

Her arms were gripped and twisted.

'Now then, now then!' cried a deep voice with enjoyment, 'here's another young rat come up out of its hole!'

And then his grip slackened.

The police officer looked close into the stained and melted face and saw something he hadn't quite expected. He frowned. He couldn't put his finger on it.

'I'm not a student,' she sobbed, 'I'm not a student, I don't belong here ... I ...' She raised her raw eyes and the police officer saw the cut, the lines, the boiled potato skin. He saw a silly spinsterish woman.

'Got caught up did you?' he murmured sympathetically, then repeated with more assurance, 'I see, you got caught up.'

She nodded, strings of mucus swinging bloodily from her nose.

'You want to go to the out-patients,' he advised, kindly letting go of her arm.

He saw her past the constables on the door where the gate swung broken against the wall.

'There'll be twenty-odd of them up at Bow Street in the morning!' he shouted cheeringly after her, adding, 'Madam.'

She trailed down the street deep in broken glass and horse dung. A torn banner lay face down on the road flapping gently in a low breeze that had begun to stir. The police who still stood across the end of the street in a barrier let her through with no more than a curious glance. Some of them had streaks of flour and pips on their uniforms.

Two red buses swayed past, their tyres flattening paper, egg shells and a pink straw hat. The newspaper man sold noonday editions from his safe angle of the wall and a small boy scattered peanuts for the pigeons.

Swiftly, the city had restored herself, sunk in her nice wadding of routine.

Garbie unrolled the tip of her tongue and tasted the sweet salt of blood. Just to make sure.

12 Escalation

'Coo-ee! It's me!'

Heads turned, shocked by so presumptuous a claim.

They were having drinks to celebrate Victoria's wedding anniversary. They wheeled in formation. A family group.

Quentin had come down from the estate in Scotland inherited by his wife Emily, whose massy, chestnut hair he now stroked, while thinking malevolently of white-skinned boys. Cissy clung to his other arm, drowned in admiration.

'Hello all!'

She advanced and the magpies flew off the lawn.

'Ha!' A hand protruded in welcome. Other people fingered their drinks and let the conversation drift warily.

'You should have let us know ... !'

'Your face darling!' Cissy dropped her eldest son's arm.

'. . . free to come down!'

'Your *face*!' she repeated, aghast.

Garbie touched her healing scar with pride. Freddy had called it her badge of membership and made her count the white seams of old wounds puckering his own body.

'Just a scratch,' she said, and stood grinning, winding up her new, waterproof watch.

'Been in *another* scrap!' Jack tried to make his words sound playful, harmless.

Garbie stared at him chewing her underlip thoughtfully. 'I've been wanting to ask,' she said, 'were you tortured, by any chance, during the war?'

Jack laughed jovially. 'What a funny thing to think about on a day like this!' To humour her, he drew her aside and whispered, 'What'll it be – gin or fruit cup? The Japs gave some of the boys a pretty bad time you know.'

'I've been reading a book on brain washing,' she said by way of explanation and let herself be led towards the drinks.

'You must meet Emily, Quentin's wife.'

The Honourable Emily's great feature was her torrent of hair. Beneath it her pale green eyes popped and her chin fell away into her neck. She was rumoured to be one of the wealthiest women in the British Isles.

'Are you fond of horses?' ventured Emily vaguely.

'Very!' Garbie gave her imitation of a stallion whinnying.

'Jolly good!' said Emily. 'Do you show at all?'

Somehow she'd got Garbie confused with stables. Maybe it was the bush shirt and baggy corduroys she was wearing.

Cissy bore down in a flutter of white linen panels and diverted her niece. 'Come and see the baby rabbits,' she urged, wondering how to suggest that Garbie leave Jack alone. 'How are ... *things*!' she exclaimed.

'Oh fine, fine ... I have things in hand.'

'That sounds exciting!'

'One gets by,' said Garbie using the family pronoun.

Cissy remembered all the things she'd promised. Hair appointments, facials, theatre tickets and a trip to the Zoo. 'Life,' she cried, pulling at her beads, 'is so much better now for young people than it was when I was a girl!' She thrust a baby rabbit into Garbie's arms. 'Were you planning to stay for lunch?'

'Thanks very much,' said Garbie.

A soft breeze stirred the curtains at the open windows of the dining room. The family, casually aware of their easy dynastic links, moved round the oval table picking at tomatoes, ham, beef, crisp yellow lettuce, peppers and fennel. Garbie sat doggedly in a corner, tuned to suspicion. It was a contagion caught from Freddy. It had the effect, like a fever, of finely distorting all images.

They were looking at her. They were not looking at her. They whispered frequently to one another, dropping passwords into a chain of ears. '*Do* help yourself, darling.'

But she refused to be budged and shook her head violently.

'I do hope it doesn't leave a nasty scar, darling. I can't think how it happened.'

'I don't mind.' It was her diadem, her nonpareil.

She swallowed two anti-histamine tablets with her glass of wine.

The family swayed and bowed like lilies turning their trumpets into one another's shade, exchanging the royal buzz of bees. Garbie took a small notebook and pencil from her pocket and noted down their cryptograms.

'Since you *ask* ...' confided Victoria to her mother, '... I do think she's looking a bit odd. And I don't just mean her appearance, though heaven knows whether we're meant to think she's Fidel Castro or a Chippenham dog breeder, but then, apart from that ...' and she sucked in her fine cheeks thoughtfully, 'I always have thought she was a bit ... well, *borderline.*'

'*Hush!*' said Cissy, 'Hush! ... now come on Garbie dear, you know you love fresh mango!' And scooping a little of the flesh out with a teaspoon, she popped it into Garbie's mouth. 'There! Of course you like it. Edward will be down later this afternoon and you'll be able to gossip about revolution together!' She smiled and passed on, a draught of costly scents.

Angrily, Garbie drank from the glass Quentin re-filled for her. He stood, looking down at her unsmilingly, 'Who can you be fighting now?' When she refused to answer, he shifted his weight, raised his own glass and shruggingly sighed, 'Ah well, here's to peace and prosperity anyway. Especially prosperity.' He slid away.

A white butterfly fluttered through the open french windows and caused a moment of stillness. They were caught, golden arms upraised, creamy silks and linens falling in stiff pennants, an unpolluted, levitical group amidst its crystal and silver. The pause seemed long to Garbie and the ensuing burst of chatter, more rabbinical than ever.

Emily was speaking in her quivering voice of hocks and dishers; Thom of anapaests. Gerald and Quentin made a long rally of par values and floating exchange rates. Cissy murmured of Silesian scrolling and the Prune gurgled. Tongues grew the five points of pentangles.

Garbie shrank back, the hard, carved oak of the seventeenth-century chair snapping at her shoulder blades.

'*Really!*' sighed Victoria, wandering past, peeling a pear, 'I honestly can't think why you want to embarrass everybody so by sitting in a corner as if you had some nasty disease!'

And, dropping the long coil of peel into an ugly, Chinese funerary jar, she stepped out on to the terrace.

The others slowly followed her out in ones and twos. Quentin held a thin cigar between his fingers and kissed the egg-like forehead of his wife as he passed by, murmuring about relativity. 'Everything,' he was saying, 'has an abominable context. There is nothing either plainly good or bad.'

Garbie noted the remark down and followed them out on the terrace. There was a general easing into wicker chairs, a clink of cups and liqueur glasses on the parapet.

'It breaks my heart to think of it,' sighed Cissy, 'but I'm afraid it will have to go.'

'Oh no!' said Quentin quickly.

'It's so expensive to maintain, darling.'

'Rotherbrook is everything,' Quentin argued firmly.

Garbie gazed out at the rich sweep of summer flowers and caught the idle zither of insects.

'By September, there'll only be your father and myself.'

'Cut down in other ways!'

'A small flat in town and a cottage in the country perhaps ...'

'Oh no!' cried Quentin emphatically.

'I agree,' said Garbie. She looked beyond the flower beds to where the tall poplars, larch and beech concealed their lake. Down there, at different times of the year, grew irises and king cups. In the evenings, you could hear the frogs sing.

'Why,' she said, 'don't you turn it into a home?'

'A home?' Quentin made a choking sound.

'For the handicapped or the deprived?' Her eyes shone.

'Ah ...' murmured Jack with a polite interest.

'Oh. *That* kind of home ...' sighed Cissy, '... I hadn't thought about that.' Now that she had, the thought filled her with despondency. She picked up the cat and plopped it in her lap.

Jack tried to be gentle. 'These days of course,' he said, 'we prefer to treat people within the community, in their own homes. Keeping the family intact wherever possible.' He laughed, slightly embarrassed and twirled a celandine between finger and thumb. 'Research shows, well, research shows that it gives them a better chance of ... finding themselves. Normalizing.'

'I know what you're getting at,' remarked Garbie, meaning nothing in particular. She saw their heads jerk towards her on strings. She beamed round, her confidence and enthusiasm swelling.

'All the wheel chairs, all the conversions ...' Cissy spoke faintly.

'Well just the underprivileged then, like the Stepney kids, remember?'

'Ah, yes.'

'Them, dear God!' Quentin expostulated. 'Who was it, Trevor? Yes, Trevor, I found him shitting on the carpet!' He gave a yelp of sour mirth.

'Hush, darling!'

'Really, Q!' Jack lowered his brows in disapproval.

'How funny!' squeaked Emily. 'Why don't you ask the SPRE?'

'The who?'

'The Society for the Preservation of Rural England.'

'Now there's a good notion!' nodded Gerald, fearing he might be asked for a donation. The market wasn't too good.

Garbie, momentarily lost in memories of the Stepney children, barked, 'Do you remember the stables, Quentin?' and giggled.

'No,' said Quentin sharply, a faint blush rising.

'What about the stables?' questioned Emily eagerly, thinking they were back to her favourite topic of conversation.

'Games,' said Quentin irritably. 'Garbie's war games.'

'Pillaging, looting and rape!' shouted Garbie, rocking back and forth on the parapet, her fist stuffed in her mouth to stop a tidal wave of laughter.

'What did you say, darling?'

'The place would be ruined,' persisted Quentin, keeping an

icicle eye on his cousin. 'Vandalized and re-converted. Nissen huts on the lawn in no time at all.'

'Oh I don't know ...' someone protested feebly.

'For God's sake!' Quentin killed his cigar savagely. 'When everybody finally is working a two-day week on a minimum wage of fifty pounds let's at least leave them something agreeable to look at in their spare time!'

Jack attempted to say something but his son cut him short. 'The trouble with your kind of dogma, father, is that it involves such a treacherous amount of destruction.' He finished his brandy and stared at the distant trees.

Jack tried again to say something that would steer a safe course between progress, factories, motorways and the common good, but this time was rescued by the maid's coming to tell him he was needed on the phone.

Garbie pulled eagerly at the tiny rock plants growing between the crevices. 'The flower beds could be turned over to vegetables,' she enthused, 'and the paddock's just about right for a football pitch!'

'Not so fast, darling.' Cissy brushed her hair lightly back from her forehead, then resumed a frenzied stroking of the cat. She gave a short laugh to the assembled company, and said, 'We can none of us keep up with Garbie's ideas, not even Jack. Oh look, V! I think the Prune is going to cry.'

Anxiously everyone peered at or moved towards the wicker bassinet, its white muslin folds rising like petals. Victoria picked her daughter up.

'Of course,' said Garbie, 'you wouldn't get such a good price from the Council, but think of the satisfaction!'

She tried to give an encouraging smile and looked menacing.

Cissy took the Prune from her daughter (who removed the cat) and curled the fine wisps of baby hair behind small ears. 'There,' she crooned, and rocked her. 'I should so like to think,' she went on in a singing tone, 'that the Prune would grow up to see all *this* ...' And she raised her head to gaze palely at the sunspilt trees and grass and flowering shrub.

'... helping people less well off than yourselves ...' persisted Garbie dreamily, speaking without a heritage to preserve.

Gerald said he was going to look at the gun collection and excused himself.

'... bringing light into the world's dark corners ... !'

'Oh do shut up,' said Victoria. 'Can't you see you're upsetting Mummy?'

'I'm only ... !' she began indignantly.

'It's a family matter, not a political matter.'

The gates slammed. Garbie's mouth was crammed with air bubbles. She gasped, gulped, tried to rally, but in that moment of unresounding silence, Jack returned and sat down heavily.

The cat leapt out of Victoria's arms and bounded into a flower bed below. The hollyhocks rustled and wagged.

'Something's wrong!' Cissy knew.

Jack let his head droop on to his hands, muttered something incoherent, then without looking up, said, 'Now what do we do?'

'What ... !'

'What ... ?'

'What is it?'

'Mambele's stopped the elections, declared a state of emergency.'

'What does it mean?'

'Heavens!' said Emily, her green eyes turning pale jade. 'Who's Mambele?'

'The Prime Minister of Awanzikwa,' explained Garbie loudly.

'It's a blackmailing move.'

'What else do you know?' asked Quentin.

'It seems the polls were not going in his favour ... he's given out the usual thing about rigging and so forth, and imprisoned both the King and the Opposition leader. Or they've disappeared at least. Dear God ...' And he let his head fall again on his hands. 'The man's crazy.'

'Or clever,' said Quentin.

'Or clever.' Jack gazed at his outspread fingers. 'I only hope South Africa's as embarrassed as we are ... we don't want them all fleeing there, nor do we want South African aid pouring in.'

'It all sounds terrific,' cried Emily. 'All Rider Haggard stuff.'

'He's trying to suppress Communism, that's what it is!' shouted Garbie indignantly and began pacing a short distance up and down the terrace.

'That's not the point,' Quentin let thin baleful streams of smoke escape from his nostrils. 'He's trying to squeeze more money out of Britain – he couldn't give a fart one way or the other about Communism as such, only in so far as it represents opposition. As a matter of fact the opposition would probably be more successful at wringing aid out of us, since I dare say we'd respond more readily faced with pressure from China than we do with South Africa on their doorstep. Mambele's just too comfortable to go, and unfortunately he's got about two thousand South African nationalist refugees in the country.'

'Exactly,' groaned Jack.

'Of course,' said Quentin cruelly, 'the country's in a bloody awful mess thanks to the aid you did give them. A hydro-electric power station's just the thing for people who can't afford electricity!'

'Oh Q that's not fair!' Cissy raised the baby to her shoulder and beat it furiously on the back.

'Oh that's nothing, just a start!' Quentin smiled at his mother benignly. 'The farmland's eroded, there's not enough money to develop industry in ths towns, and naturally the one thing they all need when they're unemployed is an O level education with a working knowledge of Lord Byron.'

'You must judge your father by his intentions!' cried Cissy angrily. She looked from her stooped and silent husband to her handsome, sneering son. 'His intentions were always good,' she said defiantly. 'What can be done if the Government simply hasn't got the money?'

'I judge, on the contrary, by achievement,' smiled Quentin faintly. 'There is no other measurement of any value.'

'Anyway, my darling,' Cissy tucked the Prune into the crook of one arm so that she could reach towards her husband with the other, 'anyway, you mustn't think of it as your responsibility always ... You advised, that's all. In the early stages.'

Then she turned again towards Quentin, a quivering Portia. 'Besides,' she said, her lips whitening, 'the death rate has gone down and the birth rate gone up!'

Quentin laughed outright with rare and genuine mirth. 'Oh really!' he said. 'That's wonderful.'

Jack remained bent and still looking at no one. One did all one could and it was never enough. One felt it personally and woundingly. 'I hope Obi Imbono's all right,' he murmured.

'I daresay Obi Imbono's behind it all,' said Quentin airily.

'Oh nonsense, he's well to the Left.'

'Oh, when,' sighed Quentin re-lighting his cigar, 'when will you realize that these labels ... left, right, far left, are so many idle ideas for academics to play with after lunch. Politics, especially in a place like Awanzikwa, are practical. Opportunist, if you like. *Dear* father ...' A brief flash of genuine fondness gleamed through Quentin's exasperation, '... if only you'd accept that politics is *business*, at its most effective with the best Board in control, then you and your fellow politicians would waste less time trying to square your consciences somewhere between dogma and real life.' He let a pause elapse, but getting no response, pressed on. 'Obi Imbono understands that perfectly well, but you can't allow yourself to think that he does. In your framework it would make him a sinner, and black sinners are most embarrassing. Well, you're being ridiculous. The man is attuned to a perfectly honest ethic of efficiency. It makes for considerable consistency.'

'I can't bear to hear you talk like this.' Jack rose, tight-lipped.

'Sit down and finish your coffee,' said Cissy more sharply than she meant. The baby tried to push a finger up her grandmother's nose.

Allowing a perfect ring of smoke to escape, Quentin tapped ash from the end of his cigar and developed his view. 'The reason your Party has failed, if I may say so, is not because you've lapsed from faith on occasion, but because, in a sidelong shift towards consensus politics, you've paid too little respect to efficiency. Faith leads people towards ideas they can't fulfil and consensus leads to bungled execution.' Quentin was quite relentless and enjoying himself enormously.

Garbie stared from one to the other, her understanding and loyalties totally confused.

'I wish,' said Jack, straightening himself, 'I wish, Q, I could believe you *cared* more.'

'What on earth does that mean?' Quentin laughed lightly. 'What kind of sentimental rot is that? Caring, like daily baths or a good wine at dinner, is a luxury of the non-needy. Caring has to be effective to count, that's all I'm saying.'

'He only does it to annoy!' sang Emily, her thin fingers playing glitteringly on the air.

Jack stared at his son, frightened by the wicked glint of truth in what he was saying.

'What are families for if you can't have a good argument?' Garbie waved her arms cheerfully at the subdued group, but they paid no attention.

'*And*,' persisted Quentin, his narrow face taut with suppressed amusement, 'and now all that hydro-electric power is redirected towards and paid for by South Africa, what do you do next?'

There was a moment's hesitation. 'I *suppose* ... morally ... one must break off relations.'

'Morally?' scoffed Quentin. '*Morally!*' He stretched a languid hand towards Emily's head and stroked it gently. 'If, of course, Mambele had *lost* the election, as he certainly would have with unemployment as high as it is, you'd have been faced with a much trickier moral problem when that old Maoist Kimberere came to power. It remains to be seen whether his supporters can organize a revolt. So *morally* you're so hung about with millstones you can barely move! And so ...' he crossed his legs with arachnid elegance, '... and so the answer is, to break off relations is it? To dive into the diplomatic bolt-hole?'

'We have to show disapproval.'

'But I thought *caring* was your concern.'

'As indeed it is!' Jack's heart was pounding unnaturally fast. He felt he might be terribly ill at any moment.

'Daddy,' said Quentin softly, dangerously, 'there's going to be bloodshed in Awanzikwa.'

'Not necessary at all!' Jack discovered he was shouting. It was dreadful.

'Oh Daddy! ... oh Daddy ... !'

'Careless talk costs lives,' remarked Victoria rising to her feet and take the Prune from her mother. 'You're a naughty fellow Q.'

Even when sense escaped Garbie, atmosphere transmitted itself. She had thought herself in a war zone, but Victoria's voice, the way she pulled her brother's ear, turned it all into another game. The change of mood enraged her. She stamped her foot, needing to shout about something. Then stamped again, her head swinging frantically east and west in an effort to coax the anger up and out. She felt the veins behind her eyes turn red.

Helpfully Victoria banged her on the back. 'That should shift it!'

The family swung to and fro, a blurred crescent of beads, united by a mutually breathless smile as they waited.

'Something's stuck.'

'Bang her on the back again V.'

'Water! Fetch a glass of water.'

They sat motionless, shouting their instructions, hands crossed.

Like nausea, it finally, thankfully, rose: *'It's all your fault!'* she screamed. 'It's all your fault!' And she dropped, crouching and coughing to the ground.

'What do you mean?'

'I didn't hit you too hard did I?'

'... Removed all the fishbones ...'

'It's nothing to do with Jack, dear, it's the Foreign Secretary's business now.'

Cissy bent over her, a blonde shadow. 'You must be careful where you place blame ... do get up darling ...' She helped her to her chair. 'I know you feel very deeply, about ... but do try ... not to *spoil* things ...'

She was given a glass of water, patted, asked if she would care to lie down.

('Try not to spoil things . . . !')

She began to understand. She sat on a chair, hands dangling between her thighs, watching ants and beetles run between the cracks of the paving stones. Her eyes tried to transmit something of importance to her brain but the whispering gestures on the margins of her vision distracted her. She wanted to ask them questions to which there were clear answers, and would have done were it not for the fact that her torn and elocuted tongue seemed to speak an elliptical language that grazed past their understanding. Garbie shook her head to clear it of vapours.

Jack, too, was being poured into a chair and offered water.

(Surely it was Quentin who had spoiled things?)

Murmurings of love bubbled about Jack. Mothy kisses brushed his face. The women crooned over his wounds.

Quentin, unmoved, re-crossed his legs. Passed a cigarette to his father who rarely smoked, unless in crisis. Cissy lit it for him.

'Darling Jack, you look quite white . . .'

'Give me a moment . . .'

'Your pulse!'

Victoria turned towards Garbie, tall and contemptuous. 'Why did you have to do that! Why do you always have to make a scene!'

Raising her hand to her eyes to shield her disbelief, Garbie strained to fathom expressions blackened by sun. '*Me?*' she repeated, trying to smile in a friendly way, *Me?*'

And she turned towards Quentin to see if he would put right the confusion. He stared back, his eyes as cold and unblinking as a cayman's.

Involuntarily, her hand rose and pointed a finger at Quentin. She jabbed speechlessly at the air, then seeing the still, black ring about her, she withdrew her hand from its accusation and slowly turned it till she was pointing at herself. Three times she tapped her finger against the thorny sternum.

'Me!' she repeated. And then again, more softly, knowingly, 'Me.'

(A mess of glued shards from among the black earth and the

creeping things, those tabooed, abominated creatures of the Bible.)

And she roared with laughter.

'Relations broken,' read out Freddy from the *Evening Standard*. He whinnied discreetly. 'Well,' he gurgled, 'A chap couldn't really ask for anything better.'

'Better?'

'In, as it were, a manner of speaking, *better* ...' He glanced warily at Garbie and spread his arm across the newspaper page to stop the breeze blowing it away. They were sitting in the gardens of Lincoln's Inn Fields, watching the tennis and eating hard boiled eggs.

('As much part of the scenery as possible,' Freddy had explained which accounted for his own tennis shoes and enormous, flapping cricket flannels.)

He screwed his monocle back into the socket of his eye and read on:

Diplomatic relations were broken off today between Great Britain and the independent state of Awanzikwa. This move follows the announcement last week of a one-party state led by self-termed President Joshua Mambele after he suspended elections and declared a state of emergency.

Awanzikwa, a member of the Commonwealth, became independent in 1967, and has recently been negotiating terms for a three year aid plan with Britain.

King Julian, until now constitutional head of the state, which is modelled exactly on the British Parliamentary system, is rumoured to be confined in Bahziah Gaol but the whereabouts of Mr Bengi Kimberere, leader of the Nationalist opposition party, are as yet unknown. King Julian, who was known to favour Mr Kimberere's party (which was expected to win last week's elections) is an ex-Sandhurst officer.

So far there have only been small, scattered outbreaks of violence, but white families have been seen crossing the border into South Africa in great numbers ...

Freddy adjusted his MCC cravat with an air of satisfaction.

'*Cracking* situation ...' he declared. 'I'll wager your Uncle Jack's got some interesting things to say about it eh?'

227

'What's the time?'

'Thirteen hundred hours, fifteen minutes. We'll take up positions in forty-five minutes exactly.' He re-wound his watch and called out 'Shot!' to a burly, scarlet barrister who'd just served an ace. 'You will,' he went on, 'understand of course, if I keep very much in the background.'

She squeezed his arm tightly.

'Nervous?' queried Freddy tenderly. 'Even the best chaps are you know. You have to be bloody stupid – pardon the French – not to be afraid.'

'Yes. No. I don't itch like I used to though.'

'Itch?'

'As I used to ... With nerves, hayfever ...'

'Ah.'

'Not with you beside me, Freddy!'

'That's enough of that corporal!' he said huskily.

Two young men walked by with a poodle on a lead. It had gold toenails. Freddy winked at them. 'Two of the members,' he whispered to Garbie. 'Splendid cover, don't you think?'

'Could have fooled me,' admitted Garbie admiringly. She snuggled a little closer to Freddy.

Although she admired him, although Freddy had now superseded other heroes in her narrow landscape of life, Garbie didn't quite believe everything he had to say. It didn't matter that he teased, exaggerated or even fibbed a little. This small, uncertain area excited tenderness, just as his secrets excited a feeling of complicity even when, like most of them they went unshared. But today, she felt, on the day of the putsch, she would know for certain. She would know whether all the hints of numbers, plots, positions, were true.

'Forty minutes,' he said, looking at his watch.

'Forty minutes,' she echoed, checking hers.

Beyond the trees, the traffic roared. In front of them, sounded the steady pat of ball and racket. The square itself was a shady pool of idleness slopping over with the slow business of crosswords and eating sandwiches. Garbie fingered her fading scar.

'You're sure the police change shift at two?' she asked.

228

'Absolutely.' Freddy straightened the gleaming seam of his cricket flannels. 'And in any event, there's only a small nucleus of twenty-five on duty, now that Finals have started,' he gave a gurgling, uncorked laugh. 'You can't beat the element of surprise in attack.'

'Attack!' She rattled the staccato syllables against her teeth. '*Attack!*' She tried it again with some relish and then added, with a doubtful glance at Freddy, 'Whack-o then!'

'Indeed.'

When the clock struck its two peaceful hours across the quadrangle, a secret, subterranean life rose to the surface of W C2. People unfurled from their benches, slid out of parked cars, put down their tennis rackets and streamed out of the pub. Two huge removal vans pulled away from the kerb and turned round the corner leading to the back entrance of the College. Other passers-by became suddenly aware of a silent, oddly casual army on the move.

They came up from the Embankment, out of cafés in the Aldwych, away from bookshop counters. The traffic sounds sank to a whisper as everyone and everything paused to watch this extraordinary communion of people. They flowed together, falling in shoulder to shoulder. No banners, no shouting. Just the purposeful tread of feet.

Garbie fell in step between a man in tennis shorts and another in a neat, single breasted charcoal grey suit. The silence was powerful, awesome. Onlookers, puzzled by the unusual confusion of dress, pressed away from them against the walls. Even the traffic, halted by the thickly moving river, failed to hoot. The city was stunned by the spectacle that flowed around it.

Not until they rounded a corner towards the rear entrance of the College and Garbie saw the abrupt, appalled expressions of the police did she feel that faint, uncertain stirring of serpents in her stomach.

For a moment, the police stood in frozen attitudes of defeat and then they combined to make a brave black barrier which strained, then split under the avalanche. They were cast up, black corks, bobbing on the indifferent torrent as the demonstrators pouring in from both ends of the semi-circular street finally, densely, encircled the entire block of buildings of which the College was a part.

As bodies crushed more tightly in upon one another, a vast, roaring breath was expelled, blowing pigeons from their parapets. And then followed a louder, angrier roar like the waking of an ancient beast as, with one movement, the crowd pushed again towards the newly mended gates. People began to scream.

Momentarily, there was an hysteric babbling of a walkie-talkie radio in Garbie's ear as she was squeezed up between the wall and a police officer. They passed one another by with a rough, scraping movement and Garbie had to struggle to keep upright. If anyone were to fall, they would be killed.

Garbie, fighting to keep her feet on the ground saw that, just as they had pincered in on the police, they too could be trapped in this tunnel. There would be no air left. Her lungs began to pucker and cling like plastic bags as she was drawn back then hurled forward in a further wave that cracked the gates apart. Forced by the current towards the bottleneck of the gaping doorway, people were flung aside against the walls, faces ripped across with fear.

'Look out!'

A pair of glasses flew through the air, a handbag bounced across the shoulders like a ball. Something split open and bled.

'Ah-h-h!'

Now all the movement came from the back of the crowd. Sweat turned sour with terror as they were swept towards the open gateway. She felt her feet trample over flesh. Saw Freddy's head rear briefly above the crowd to her right as she burst between raw hinges into the building.

Now they swarmed everywhere shouting instructions. Doors were smashed, voices raised. She put her hands over her ears to shut out the howl of bells and let herself be propelled up the stairs. They passed a girl vomiting on the second floor.

At the top a meeting was hastily being called together in a lecture room where a few people nursed cuts or slumped exhaustedly. Others ran to the windows to see what was happening down below.

Police were flooding into the street, truncheons swinging. They fought, two to a student. One ambulance had already forced its way below, its blue light revolving like an angry eye, and another was slowly parting the crowd at the far end of the street. She saw a stretcher carrying someone, neither man nor girl, their face a pulp of blood. She saw a boy fall, bent over on his knees clutching his groin. She saw anger, hate.

'They'll come in and get us!' quavered a red-headed boy pushing past her to the window. He looked dreadfully young. His skin was delicately white and unshaved.

'Not at all!' cried Garbie reassuringly slipping on her black arm band and rolling up her sleeves. 'They can't do a thing unless the authorities give them orders.'

'We're trapped!' whined the boy, turning his pink jellied lips and eyes towards her.

'We're in occupation!' said an American rather sharply, overhearing them talk.

'We're in charge of the key building.' He pulled his forage cap further down over his eyes and turned on his heel.

The red-haired boy gripped the window sill and began to cry.

'Chin up!' said Garbie, and gave him a friendly nudge.

'Oh God!'

'It's a victory,' she said hopefully and looked away as she caught a quizzical stare being focused upon her. (The students were busy doing things, saying things, making things behind her.) 'It's all right,' she said to the boy. 'It's very good in fact. You've got to make sacrifices.'

But he blubbed on thinking of slaughter in the streets below. 'Why can't it be done through the proper channels?' he wept, and his little hands with their baby-pink nails scrabbled over the sill.

'Keep your eyes skinned,' ordered Garbie, 'since you're here.'

A Black Maria pushed forward. People were bundled endlessly inside as if it contained a machine grinding them into small, easily-packed pieces. 'There are bound to be a few bruises.'

Police stood six deep at either end of the street facing a crowd that chanted 'Out! Out! Out!'

An upraised voice came through the thin partition from the meeting door: 'We've stormed it! We've taken over!'

'We're trapped,' wailed the red-headed boy.

'We're now in control!' bawled their leader next door.

'They're bound to get us in the end.'

'We've got to hold our positions until the authorities can be made to agree to our terms!'

'They'll *always* get you in the end ... There are more of them.' The red-haired boy wet his trousers.

'Oh honestly!' said Garbie. 'You are spoiling things.'

A girl was being dragged, kicking across the road. She lost a shoe but they put her in the van without it. One ambulance closed its doors and moved off, bell clanging. The street grew dark with police.

'OUT! OUT! OUT!'

Downstairs, workmanlike, but tense, they'd made a barrier of steel filing cabinets across the doors. She wandered about, unquestioned, trying to find Freddy. Everywhere people were gathered in groups talking and arguing exultantly about individual rights and freedom. She hung about on the edge of circles ready to say something.

'Hear! Hear!' she hooted faintly once or twice, and glanced towards the barricade of cabinets surprised no effort was being made to hurl them down. Angry voices still shouted outside.

One group made plans for the occupation as busily as a social committee at a tennis club, dispatching girls to the canteen to find tea bags and sliced loaves. Freddy was not there.

In a ladies' lavatory on the third floor they found the caretaker who only agreed to come out from behind his locked door if they promised to let him safely out of the building. He was lifted by his armpits, dangling, clubfooted and lowered from a ground floor window into the street. Then they began to chop up desks and chairs to board across the windows. Garbie gazed at all the purposeful activity, remembered the air raid shelter behind the buildings where Dotty had sat, rocking beneath a table, and asked a boy with a shaved head and dark glasses who was methodically ransacking files in the Registrar's office, whether there was something she could do to help.

'Who are you?'

She stared at the round black discs and slipped a thumb nail between her front teeth. 'A supporter of the Movement,' she gabbled, her thumb in her mouth.

'A what?'

She repeated herself.

'Oh.' He sat himself down at the desk and stretched his ear lobes thoughtfully. 'Oh, an alien. You should really be scrutinized!' He released his ear lobes brutally and asked, 'Do you have some proof of membership?'

'I didn't bring my handbag with me. I – I, my application is before them now.' She smiled confidently, and pointed to her face. 'This is my scar.'

'Mmm,' he said. The dark glasses stared blankly.

On the verge of saying her Uncle was an M.P., she restrained herself and leaning forward across the desk, shouted: 'Friend of Freddy's.'

The effect was surprising. He relaxed and removed his glasses. He had a marked squint. 'Oh *well* ...' he said. 'I see.' And he smiled somewhat to her left.

'You haven't seen Freddy have you?'

'Not in here. He wouldn't come in here,' said the boy a little sharply.

'No, of course,' she said uneasily. 'I saw him outside though. I'd like to help.'

'Report to Ops HQ, committee room 143, fourth floor.'

'You're very kind,' she backed out.

In committee room 143 they discussed procedures to be followed if under arrest. In committee room 145 they agreed on the line to be taken. The college authorities were acting illegally in refusing access to students. In committee room 147 a motion was put to the vote. Seeing the hands rise, Garbie raised hers. The motion was passed. Garbie found herself moved to tears by the sense of unity and comradeship. They all sang the Red Flag.

At a quarter past five, the commotion which had died down in the street outside flared up again, as a van with a loud-speaker crawled in front of the building and broadcast a message that bounced off the high narrow walls and made it hard to discern.

'If an orderly evacuation of the college premises takes place now, no further action will be taken. If an orderly evacuation ...'

There was laughter and cheering. People leant from the windows and gave a slow handclap.

'... no further action will be taken. If an orderly ...'

Clap ... clap ... clap ... clap.

The red-haired boy slithered downstairs, two, three steps at a time. He found and fought for, an unboarded window. Hands tossed him up, juggled with him, threw him through the window. Heads, trailing like tangled flowers over every ledge, watched and hissed as he picked himself up off the pavement, and ran, agonized, into the ranks of police.

The van turned and came back again past the barricaded front entrance.

'... evacuation of the college premises takes place now ...'

(She could defy anything.)

The van stopped. Everybody hushed and waited to see if they had another quisling to excrete from the building. But there was nothing. Shouting broke out jubilantly mixed with whistles and catcalls. Every single student hanging from a window could see blood on the street.

The van slunk out between the police.

Victory was sweet. The more so for being unexpectedly swift and easy. The bully boys had collapsed like pricked balloons.

'Once we're inside they can't do a thing.'

'They can't arrest five hundred people!'

'The Principal wouldn't dare arrest his own students.'

They were as exuberant as young wives whose recipe had worked first time by following all the instructions carefully.

'Tomorrow we'll ask the authorities to come in for discussion.'

Everybody nodded, bright-eyed and eager. If everything else worked why shouldn't the men in gowns troop meekly in when asked?

They passed from one to another in triumph. They kissed impulsively. They held the world as small and innocent as a tennis ball between their hands.

Somebody squeezed Garbie's fingers and passed on to take another hand in a chain of speechless congratulation. They were adults surprised to be adults. They had moved from words and ideas to possession.

Garbie sat on a desk, arms wound round her legs, trying to suppress a luminous burst of laughter and the twitching of her toes. Within the space of an afternoon she had seen popes and captains boiled down to vaporous grit. A young man with a golden cloud of hair placed a quiet hand on her head as he passed by. A friendly pressure. She made the leap into an enchanted circle of friends who were allowed to touch; not the powdery whisper of relations but a touch of real salute and greeting. This passing stranger's hand, neither sexual, nor polite, moved her. It was beautifully careless. His hand hadn't lifted her by the chin to seek out a landing place on the dangerous landscape of her face. It hadn't dropped away, duty performed. It didn't bless or patronize or lie. It just accepted her.

'Tea?'

A pot as big as a bird bath was brought into the room. Falling to the floor in a smiling, cross-legged circle, they shared their cups. The chatter was constant, ebullient and quiet. Garbie felt utterly at home.

'Jesus Christ!'

The shout, coming from an upper floor, fell like a sword through their circle. Everyone leapt to their feet and rushed to the nearest window.

Down below streamed a column of dark figures. Garbie blinked, unable to place them in space or time. They carried medieval shields, had robot faces with goggle eyes. As they swarmed with the silent speed of ants, she ducked.

'The fuzz!'

'*Gas!*'

'Gas?'

'Oh sweet Jesus, no! They can't!'

She was unable to move, but remained bent, her arms doubled over her head. All round came the scattering crash of feet and breaking glass.

Down below, arms were raised, poised, swung back.

Gas! thought Garbie dumbly, *gas* ... and something in her corroded with bitterness. She had a glimpse of judges, dons and politicians trying to hide glittering claws in the black folds of their fustian. Then glass flew everywhere.

She clapped her hands to her face.

She seemed to be a single tongue of fire. Flame melted her eyeballs, streamed down her throat, sunk molten pipes in her lungs. The lungs bubbled and blistered. With one hand across her eyes, one across her mouth, she swayed away from the window bruising all her bony angles against wooden corners as she tried to find the door. In her darkness fire streamed in through every pore. Even the tears hurtling down her face burnt like lava.

She fell through a space and crawled blindly over other bodies in what she felt was the right direction. It was a pit of sighs and screams. She pulled herself over somebody who clutched at her and shrieked for water, but coughing and choking, she crawled on wildly trying to escape the heart of the furnace.

Gropingly, she found the staircase and somehow pulled herself to her feet by clinging to the banister, then slipping, tumbling her way down an endless and uneven flight of stairs. Through torn retinas she saw now and then, the blur of a falling body, hands tearing at eyes and then her own barbed lids scraped shut over the appalling, bloodless battlefield.

Still pushed on by the weight of wailing people behind her, she was sick in a hopeless, scorching rush. She daren't put a hand to her mouth for fear of leaving her eyes exposed and the vomit trickled over her chin and down her neck.

The descent was timeless, but eventually the floor beneath her feet was even. Dimly, she saw beside the broken barricades, a girl pouring a paper cup of water over her face. Then screaming, she hurled it away ripping open the corners of her mouth with her nails.

Dizzy, sick, unable to breathe, they reeled out in the street, instinctively raising their arms to shield their heads as the unhorsed knights advanced behind their shields. Too ill to avoid the swinging truncheons the evicted swayed in a muddled line against the wall, feeling their way towards the end of the street.

There was only a soft moaning. No shouting, no crowds, no traffic. The buildings rose, implacably dark and empty towards a dying sky. Instinctively, like weary turtles, those who didn't fall on the pavement, went south, towards the river.

She was aware of ringing ambulances arriving alongside, aware of people being seized as they stumbled on, aware as her lungs dried to ashes, of a hatred so deep and so savage, she was shocked by the potency of her own unmapped emotions.

'You don't look too good!' observed her colleagues in the office as she sat, next morning, green-faced amongst the newspapers.

'That's a nasty cough you've got there. You should have taken another day off.'

She thought they were mocking her and scowled at them.

'Only trying to be sympathetic,' they said, affronted and went murmuring away like swatted flies. She turned her shoulders towards them and wheezed accusingly, but they drowned the sound by rattling violently on their typewriters.

The headlines were equally divided between the college incident and the situation in Awanzikwa; most editorials were critical on both counts. The nation wearied by months of juvenile behaviour on the campus was now, it was informed, shocked by the ill-considered use of CS gas which no amount of provocation could be said to justify. The authorities had placed themselves fairly and squarely in the wrong. The university was a place for debate, a place where staff and students might learn from each other. The *Telegraph* asked that serious thought should be given to the Principal's continuing in office.

'Staring into space never brought the moon any nearer!' cried the supervisor in Garbie's ear. Then, catching the rattle of rusting phlegm, ordered her to go home.

The sun hung low in a hot swaddling of cloud over Pitt Street. There was a smell of burning incinerators and fermenting hops. Fanny Ann found a pair of plimsolls in a dustbin and scratched her crutch with the heel of one of them. It was dinner time and chips sizzled in splashing fat.

Except for the mewing of kittens in the basement, the house was quiet. Garbie picked her way over discarded clothes and stained sheets to the little enamel topped table beneath the window where she found a single piece of lavender notepaper given her by Aunty Betty. She sat down and began to write a letter to *The Times* neatly underlined in red and heavily cross-referenced in which she drew attention to the British manufacture of CS gas.

13   Disengagement

There was a hot sigh of August dust outside the window in Pitt Street. For weeks the sun had drooped in the same sullen position. All the plants had died in the municipal gardens and were now bent over, brown and creaking. They had put tables with umbrellas in the garden of the pub. People sat there gladly, but they were much too hot to talk.

In Garbie's room, the heat stuck to the ceiling and caught flies. She and Freddy lay naked on the bed, breathing slowly.

'I mean,' she said, turning her head towards him, 'I mean we're different you and I. Different, aren't we?'

Freddy had sore red marks on his shoulders where his satchel and binocular straps had rubbed him.

'The chosen few,' he agreed.

'You've taken the very words!' She gave him a warm, homely smile, tugged his moustache playfully and said, 'Do you think we'll be in the history books?'

Freddy reached for his half eaten Marmite sandwich and gloomily observed. 'There's only one proper place for a name ... on a headstone.'

'Oh you mustn't talk like that!' It was hard sometimes trying to guide Freddy away from death. 'You're not going to die!' she cried with a pinch.

'I'm not keen.'

Half the time Freddy believed he was immortal, but now and then something worried him.

'Tell me about the Clay–Liston fight,' she urged to jolly him up, but he wasn't to be persuaded. Garbie looked down the gorgonzola length of her body to where the skin hung on the tent poles of her pelvis.

Together they listened to the slow, brown drip of the tap. 'The storm clouds are gathering,' murmured Freddy.

'It's been a really hot spell all right!'

'I wasn't referring to the weather,' he said irritably.

'Oh.'

'The anger's mounting.'

'Well, it's awful at the moment ... what with the wage freeze, high taxation and overcrowded classes,' she rattled in agreement.

'And the refugees.'

'Most of all, the refugees.'

'The anger's rising!'

'It's very exciting,' sighed Garbie, picking a segment of rind from her navel.

Their hands travelled absently down one another as they considered what might happen next. Freddy, trailing the sticky skin, the contour of a nipple, sensed the rightness of time, the need to move before, possibly, the Government took steps to help or even admit the refugees.

'Mustn't lose the advantages,' he murmured to himself. And then suggested, turning his gaze on Garbie, that a little intelligence work would be appreciated. 'Because of the recess,' he explained, 'it's hard to know what's what. I was just thinking that a visit to your people might not be out of place.'

Garbie leapt off the bed muttering mixed-up words. 'Could you repeat that?' asked Freddy.

'No, I said.'

'No?'

'Yes.'

'Why?'

'*You* know!' She went over to the sink and turned the tap full on. She stuck her face in the flush of tepid, iron-stained water. It felt like fur. '*You* know,' she repeated, standing up, catching drips of water on her tongue.

The Times hadn't published her letter, but she'd written it and that's what mattered. She felt as if she'd struck a blow against Rotherbrook. She couldn't go.

'Come now!' Freddy's voice shrilled a long way off.

She stiffened her arms and clenched her fist. 'A lot of things ...' she cried in agitation, meaning reasons why not. She flung clothes in the air trying to find something concealing to put on.

'Oh come on!'

Her lips were jammed together and her face hidden in a tugging flurry of prune-coloured cotton.

She ran away from the pleading sounds. As she got half way down the stairs, she could hear Freddy's plaintive, reedy voice asking for a small sacrifice. At the bottom of the stairs on the hall table, next to the plastic primula she found a post-card addressed to herself.

It was from Greece, from Athens. Sky and Acropolis dazzled one another. 'Wonderful cruise,' it read. 'Much needed rest. Putting on weight. Grey old England far away. Returning end of August, see you then, love Cissy and Jack.'

She tore it slowly in two.

They were very, very brown. Cissy wore a heavy gold chain on one wrist which she kept playing with. 'How absolutely lovely to have someone to meet us as soon as we got home!' she said, straining the links of her bracelet. Avoiding her niece's steady eye, she added with a note of apology, 'It was a last fling you see ... Now Rotherbrook's on the market.'

They all gazed morosely at the yellowed grass and baked earth. The air was spinning with midges.

'There've been record temperatures on the Air Ministry roof,' remarked Garbie.

'Really!'

'It makes one so irritable,' complained Jack who hadn't felt irritable till that moment. Now his skin felt gluey and covered with small crawling things. He struck at his arm. 'It's got to stop soon,' he muttered.

'How one longs for the Aegean ... the dark sea, the clear air ...'

Cissy longed too, to keep her home. It had saddened her, coming back to see the parched earth and ailing shrubs; as though the house had prematurely sensed neglect. She couldn't forget the massive golden ruins of Tiryns and Mycenae, the plundered grave-shafts, and the strange city on the island of Rhodes that stepped resignedly down the hillside and into the sea until it disappeared. Greece had been full of sorrow for Cissy.

'The Aegean!' she heard Garbie cry scornfully. 'The Aegean! A fine time to go off on your holidays!'

Cissy glanced at her husband. He seemed to be dreaming, shaded by a massy overhang of honeysuckle dipping from the golden stucco. He woke slowly, aware of attention directed on him.

'Yes,' he said, 'it makes one very irritable . . .'

'Don't you know what's been going on here! In Awanzikwa!'

'I'm sorry?' Jack passed a hand over his forehead, bewildered.

Cissy intervened. 'It's no good shouting at Jack, dear!' She was losing patience with this kind of thing. 'I don't think you're being altogether fair.'

'Fair?'

Outraged by such a word, outraged by their obstinate taking of a holiday when a holocaust burned at their backs, Garbie foamed speechlessly at her aunt and uncle.

'We're very tired . . .'

'Tired!'

'Do stop repeating everything dear,' wearily Cissy reached for her bag and took out a small spray of cologne. Deliberately, she aimed it behind each ear with a tiny, aggressive puff.

Desperately, Garbie wiped cobwebs off her mouth and tried to make sense of her fury.

'It's a very reasonable concern,' whispered Jack automatically, closing his eyes again. 'I do believe it's hotter here than it was in Athens.'

'But what are you going to *do*!' burst Garbie.

Uncertain what she was talking about, Jack slid back behind his eyelids in a lethargic escape from the heat.

'I don't think it's any of your concern.' For the first time in over thirty years Cissy began speaking to Garbie as she might to one of her own children. But it was too late. Garbie had grown accustomed to the allowances they made, to the kindly deceptions. She spluttered hysterically.

'I'm sick and tired of all this meddling, all this trouble-making,' warned Cissy.

'But don't you *see*!' shrieked Garbie, drumming her fists on her thighs.

'Always pestering your uncle . . .'

'Oh I don't mind, Cissy darling . . .' murmured Jack sleepily.

'Behaving like an overgrown adolescent . . .!'

'But don't you *care*!'

'Of course we care!' Cissy rose to her feet, her eyes throbbing with anger. And then in the rush of sentences that followed she let loose one dangerous word that flew apart from all the others like an isolated and accurate bullet. '. . . *ingratitude* . . .!'

Then she turned on her heel and left, her heels clicking across the paving stones like testy little silver hammers.

Garbie sat with a clean round wound beneath her heart and found the snivelling, helpless recitation bubbling over the edge of her lips . . . '. . . Nobody could have done more, been kinder, given me all I ever had . . .'.

As suddenly as the flow had begun, it ceased. Her tongue turned renegade. She remained very still, looking at her Uncle Jack. His head hung loose like something out of a butcher's shop. One hand fluttered apologetically. 'The heat . . .!' He spoke slackly without raising his head.

In the silence that followed, his defensive cell of privacy became uncomfortable. He got up. 'Excuse me,' said Uncle Jack and went to find his wife.

House martins fluttered out of the eaves, a scythe swished. The long view of the Sussex countryside lay still and cracked under a high yellow glare. Garbie felt a pain in her back as the tension eased. She moved and split a beetle underfoot. Then, gathering up her brief case, which held a laboriously copied list of Uncle Jack's engagements to the end of the year, she strode painfully down the drive.

At the gateway, overgrown by brown fern and meadow-grass, she hesitated, then turning away, firmly set her back on Rotherbrook.

On the train journey back to London, it began to rain. Two hot-faced girls, their fat, dangling little legs packed into pale sausage skins, noticed it first. They'd been talking in earnest whispers about personal freshness.

'Oh, bloody hell, look at that!' said one, pointing at the brightly faceted explosions bursting on the window.

'Oh eh, it'll bugger up me hair,' said the other, nodding her dough face in sympathetic exasperation.

One huge drop flew through the open window and struck Garbie between the eyes. Her skin grew cool, then cold. A sudden rash of goose pimples, purplish and scaly ran along her arms. She clutched her briefcase on her lap and felt the flower of pain unfold its scarlet petals at the base of her spine. She smiled to herself.

It was a good wound. It marked for her, the place where the twig had been broken from the trunk, from the old black walnut; a clean break. The pain would heal.

It was an end to makeshift grafts.

She could fight off the attacking swarm of good intentions, gifts, kindness and their atrophy of gratitude; it was a clean, strong break.

As the train swayed dangerously fast round a bend, she caught the excited sound of her own heart, the one ugly, honest valve her benevolent technocrats had not been able to improve upon. It was the only certain sound of existence, and faint as it was, the train picked it up, pounding it out a thousand times on its headlong rush back to the city.

Cissy kept urging Jack to see a specialist and wrote a letter to Robin in Australia expressing her fears. Immediately she wrote another one telling him to ignore anything she'd said in the first.

'You will go, won't you?' she said to Jack.

'Whatever for?' he answered irritably, arranging pebbles in colour sequence.

'We've all got to face up to the fact sooner or later ... it's just the sensible thing to do that's all. A check up.'

'I feel exactly the same as I felt when I was thirty,' he lied.

Jack didn't wish to see a specialist because he didn't feel ill. He hadn't a single symptom that would interest a doctor. He just felt gloomy and tired.

'But you know how women are,' he said to Denton Caldwell, 'you know how they fuss.'

'I think we need a change of leadership,' remarked Denton Caldwell and the view acted like a mild tonic. It prospered in Jack's head and helped alleviate the heavy sense of ... *disappointment.*

'Is it just me,' he said to one after another of his friends in the Thursday Group (they were the only people he could talk to frankly any more), 'or have things changed?'

'Both,' they replied sadly, for they suffered a little from the malaise themselves.

Until now, Jack had always thought of the future as a glad and ever-widening space. Now he had a sense of an end to things. There was Rotherbrook, that saddened him. And yet, as soon as his affairs could be ordered, he longed to leave England altogether, and travel with Cissy to more dreaming places ...

He was saddened by the amount of government Socialism seemed to involve, saddened by people seeming to be less, rather than more free, saddened by the greed that he'd watched grow out of affluence.

Cissy pursued him. 'You're not sleeping,' she accused, grey herself with sleeplessness.

'I need very little sleep,' he snapped.

To Hugh Bennett he confessed that he now thought hopefulness was a young man's virtue. A young man's privilege. 'There's no time left for building new, great bridges in the mind,' he said.

'I've been thinking a change of leadership might do a lot for us all,' said Hugh Bennett.

Neither man mentioned the matter of the Awanzikwan refugees which was driving a jagged line through the Party, but both silently observed the link in thinking.

'I'll certainly turn it over in my mind,' conceded Jack.

All the random gusts of anger sweeping the country had become greedily, mutually fixed on the Awanzikwan problem. Jack accepted fewer and fewer invitations to drink or dine with his friends outside the House because he knew that at some juncture during the evening, he would be harried and abused about it. As it was, he could only repeat the Party line that immigrant quotas for the year were over the mark already and since it was better to try for a proper settlement with the country concerned, there was no sense in offending them by granting entry or asylum to what, at the latest estimate, amounted to nearly three thousand refugees.

'When the war ended,' he sighed to Cissy, 'there seemed so much that could be done. It was a time of hope, the whole country felt it, pinned their hopes on us. In 1945 I thought we were going to build a Jerusalem.' He smiled regretfully and pressed his mouth to his knuckles. 'There was too much stacked against us then ... we were terribly inexperienced. But *this* time! After the election in 1964, I really thought, really believed ...' his voice trailed away.

Cissy made a loving sound and touched him lightly on the hair.

'And yet you see!' he went on, renewed, 'and yet God knows, I'm still on the side that thinks people should be helped, not the side that thinks people should stand on their own feet.' He drew his wife round so that she was facing him. 'When it's all over,' he said, 'when it's finally settled, we'll sail away to where the sun shines and stay there for ever.'

'How could we?' Cissy withdrew her hand but spoke fondly, 'for all sorts of reasons how could we? There's Garbie for one thing ...'

'Ah!'

This too, was part of his sadness. Garbie had grown for him into a personified reproach of his whole career. She stood for failure. A failure in himself.

'We really shouldn't worry so much about her!' He spoke jovially because he didn't want Cissy to worry. But he felt a weight like an albatross swing on his own neck.

'She's not really capable of looking after herself, standing on her own feet ...'

'Nonsense! She manages perfectly well ...' As if to prove the point, Jack added 'We don't see her for long stretches you know.' His voice faded guiltily.

'... It's not often enough ...' Cissy exerted gentle pressures on the links of her gold bracelet. 'She's getting very ... odd. All these sudden ...'

They gazed past one another on silent diagonals.

'What else can we do?'

'What happens when she gets older? What does one do then?'

They considered the prospect numbly. Then incautiously Cissy burst out: 'I sometimes think we should never have interfered!'

Jack was shocked. 'What! Left things as they were? ... You can't mean that. What! All the poverty, neglect ... the lack of dignity!'

'No,' said Cissy. 'No, of course I don't really mean it.'

They retired behind their wanton, guilty lips and thought of other things.

Swans flew in a flapping, humming line across the trees outside. 'You *will* go and see the specialist won't you, my darling!' pleaded Cissy after a little while.

Towards the end of September Garbie too paid a visit to the specialist. 'It's the pain,' she said, 'in my back, you see.'

The eminent man stared at his client (dressed as far as he could tell in a Cuban guerrilla outfit) and wrote something down to still his suspicions. It was an alarming time for Jews.

'You were recommended,' said Garbie politely and then, because silences embarrassed her, added, 'I'm not complaining. In many ways it's a healthy pain, even you might say, metaphysical.' She smiled generously and shortened the strap of her shoulder bag.

'But you want to get rid of it,' stated the back man flatly. Without seeming to, he searched her outline for hand grenades.

Garbie looked stumped. 'I suppose I do,' she acknowledged,

and then as all the nerve ends in her back squeezed through an electric grater, gasped out 'Yes! Yes!'

Fastidiously, he picked his way through her khaki garments, while the blue jowls of his face drooped in deeper suspicion.

'*I* can find nothing whatever wrong,' he announced. 'But I suggest you see this friend of mine.'

And he wrote her a note with a weary, squeaky pen.

The friend lived only a few doors away and looked exactly the same. The likeness was unsteadying.

She'd put off the appointment twice because it had so far cost ten guineas to find nothing whatever wrong. Then she got a fit of sneezing which acted like a pulley on her spinal cord, tugging it rapidly over the rocks of her vertebrae, so she broke into the money she was saving as a membership fee.

'Come in,' mumbled the twin.

Staring at the rimless glasses, the same solemn and swelling nose, the same loose blue flesh around the chin, she felt her way cautiously round the edge of the room.

'It's all right,' he nodded. 'Lie down. Relax.' And he indicated a table covered in sheets.

She turned her mind forcefully to other things while he examined her. To the prismatic lights of the chandelier, to her newly determined commitment, to iodine stains and the nature of the outrage she had to perform to free herself spiritually, for Freddy still demanded an act of personal revolution. (The office had asked her not to wear her uniform to work though they no longer objected to trouser suits.) She thought of medals, explosions, syringes, scalpels, and gas clinging like pale weed to people's faces. Of martyrs and the terrible pain in her back.

'You want to keep it . . . ?' inquired the twin.

'Pardon?'

He repeated himself in a tired fashion.

'I believe,' she began courageously, 'that one can learn to live with pain.'

'. . . Or shall I book you in . . .?'

'That it can sharpen one's appreciation of life ...'

'I shall require a specimen.'

'... but it's interfering with regular sexual activity,' she ended on a loud burst.

'It shouldn't,' he said, 'that's an old wives' tale.'

She stopped. She looked up at the enlarging planet of the face suspended above her. The mind popped. 'I'm sorry to be such a nuisance,' said Garbie, 'but would you mind re-capping?'

Patiently, he went over his findings.

'I wonder if I could have a drink of water?'

He fetched her a glass of water with a blueish tinge and a dental taste. Slowly, she sipped it, resting her weight on one elbow. 'Are you saying,' she said eventually, weighing her words with dignity, care and disbelief, 'that I've fallen for a ... that I've got a bun in the oven!'

The gynaecologist, second cousin of the orthopaedic surgeon, sat down heavily with a sense of defeat and gratefully finished the remainder of the drink his patient offered him.

She stopped off to tell the Birnbergs who gossiped wildly after she'd left, racking unlikely corners of their imagination to try and identify the father. 'But who, possibly, who on earth could it be?'

Garbie, proud, secretive and shy, had said it was immaterial and billowed home to Islington as big as a galleon.

'And how could she not have *known*!'

'She said her mind was occupied with higher things.'

From their first floor window they watched her disappear over the rise of the street and rolled their eyes to signal despair.

She was singing as she climbed the stairs. She put cheese in the mousetraps to trembling minor chords of The Messiah, and removing an old brown Brillo pad from the saucepan, heated water for a cup of tea.

There was another dead snap of wood from the tree as she swung closer to freedom for she felt, suddenly, far less need of Freddy. To calm herself, she sat down and shakily began to cut round a picture of Paul Newman in the *Daily Sketch* and stuck it in her scrapbook together with Uncle Jack's most recent speeches. They were getting shorter and bleaker all the time.

Wind rattled the window frames and blew chip papers down the street outside but the gas fire hissed with excitement as her mind swooped over a crowd of magical elements all scrambling to be re-connected. Vivacious, glassy structures erected themselves springily in her head like fine laboratory tubes filled with thin, bubbling chemical colours.

There was the element of Dotty, the element of similarity. 'Like mother, like daughter!' Aunty Betty would sigh when she knew. (Garbie felt suddenly close to Aunty Betty, closer than ever before.) Genetic repetitions rose green and volatile in the glass bulbs until she was *Dotty*. Or Dotty doubled. Even Dotty immortal.

Between them they'd survived the doodle bugs. They'd survived crumbling walls and slipping roofs. They'd been picked out of the rubble to the sound of incredulous applause, part of that nation whose photographs decorated modern histories, smiling people crawling with arms raised, thumbs up, out of holes beneath broken beams and bricks. They were a cheerful part of survival that dragged its legs out of holes and grinned into the camera.

Scissors snipping frantic paper fringes, she pressed on with the towering construction in her head, becoming more and more excited as elements matched, unlikely properties linked, waste vaporized and left behind the small, hard granules of proof.

The hours had flowed past, drifting into lamplight, drifting through the steamy juices of other people's summertime until the pips of the ten o'clock news hiccupped faintly through the wall from Mr Bean's bedsitter. Amidst a mounting, mesmeric pile of snipped newspapers, Garbie sat refining her discoveries. By midnight (and the melancholy sound of the national anthem from next door) the elaborate piece of work was complete. Where factual evidence was weak, she'd made deft joins with superstitious circumstance and they withstood all strain, as elastic, secret and sustaining as religion.

*

Freddy's secrets became less enviable. She had her own. She sat clustered around them and watched Freddy unroll maps of Whitehall and Westminster. Tenderly, beneath the table, she stroked her stomach overwhelmed to find again, and again, that sufficient had been left from the well meant surgery of Rotherbrook for her to reproduce herself. Craftily, she smiled at Freddy who let his monocle drop and cried: 'Long time . . . no joy!'

'Meaning?'

'How's your back?' He stared at the ceiling and screwed up his eyes, waiting for her.

'Slap and tickle?'

'*Absolutely*!' He opened them, beamed at her and blushed.

She laughed and pushed her nose to one side with her fingers. They laughed together. He sat down and skewered a match between his teeth. 'You're very cheerful!' he piped and nodded encouragingly as if he wanted her to tell him why. But she wouldn't. She grew fat on her secret and let the amusement rumble delightedly round her.

Freddy was wary. He had a sense of hidden arsenals and tried to beguile her.

'Ticky-ticky-ticky!' he cried, leaning across the table to paddle his fingers in her arm pit.

She doubled up, face squeezed and wet with mirth.

'Chase you!' he squeaked, 'twice round the guardroom!'

And they leapt up, two weaving things with brittle joints, almost forgetful in their windy dance. But she wouldn't be tricked. She kept her secret, like she kept the remnants of pain, flowering proudly inside herself. The only person she wanted to tell, with whom sharing any longer meant anything, was Aunty Betty. Even her prejudice seemed homely.

Garbie guided her aunty creakingly down Pitt Street. 'There's that many blacks about,' observed Aunty Betty, 'it makes me wonder if I've come to Africa.'

The wind tore at them and they stopped to gain breath.

'They've got British passports, a lot of them,' cried Garbie and drew her aunty away as a cat shot between their legs and disappeared down the basement.

'It's how they got hold of them I'd like to know,' Aunty Betty was enjoying herself. She'd not had a day up in Town since bread rationing ended. In spite of her legs she'd stood over the stove making some fudge and brought it up in her basket together with a tin of spam and some lemon curd.

They stopped in front of the brown, peeling door. 'It's right at the top, Aunty! Forty-three stairs!'

'I'll never do it,' said Aunty Betty, determined nothing should stop her.

'Anyway,' she added, swaying slightly as Garbie released herself to struggle with the front door key. 'There must be places where they'd be better suited.'

'Hang on to my arm!' cried Garbie as the door swung open. Clouds of cat's lights rolled up from downstairs.

They struggled to the top. Garbie pulling from the front, then pushing from behind. Aunty Betty paused on the landing and felt her heart. 'I've tried to tidy!' she heard her niece say as she wriggled past her and opened the door.

Though the shapes of Betty Beazley's vision were dim, there was a familiarity about them that struck her like a shock of cold water. She took an unsteady step forward, clutched on to the end of the bed and whispered, 'Eh ... this, eh ... it could be Dotty's!' She gripped the bed end tightly with one hand and put her basket down on the floor. 'Beryl!' she called out shrilly, 'Beryl?'

But the girl was round the corner of her vision clinking metal on metal, banging cushions. Particles of dust zithered into the sneezing membranes.

Blood was bursting through Betty Beazley's head in hot spurts. Since nobody invited her to sit down, she sank herself into a chair which seemed to have something like a tropical helmet already on it. She felt weak.

'I'm just warming the pot,' said a familiar voice.

Aunty Betty freed her neck of its hot circlet of fox and took in the shadowy streams of books, shoes, brown paper, spilt wax, frayed wire, eggshells and orange rind. 'It's not good enough,' she whispered faintly, 'it'll never do.'

'I've run out of sugar,' called Dotty, 'do you mind?'

'Haven't I told you!' The old woman's voice grew a little stronger, 'Haven't I *said* ... where's your pride, your self respect?' She bent and picked something up from the floor, kneading it between her hands. It was a greyish pink jumper.

'The trouble I had making it ...' whimpered Aunty Betty, and the silvery tears flowed over her cheeks.

'D'you mind fig biscuits or do the seeds get stuck in your teeth?' The voice was raised above a jet of water.

Aunty Betty turned the jumper over and over, rubbing the wool lovingly between thumb and forefinger as the tears ran salt down her face. 'It's no place to bring up a little one ...' she murmured, as Dotty edged into view carrying a plate of biscuits.

Garbie frowned guiltily and sat down nibbling a biscuit trying to remember if she'd said anything careless already. The time wasn't quite right. 'Nine weeks to Christmas!' she said, trying to change the subject. And she scratched her head.

Aunty Betty realized her mistake and changed her tone. 'Look at it!' she snapped, brandishing the jumper, 'you've learnt nothing.'

The lino gaped, mice rattled through the joists.

'I'll not be going to Rotherbrook this Christmas though,' said Garbie, ready to begin her explanations.

'All they've given you, all your advantages ... a nice school, lovely clothes ...'

'They'll ask me of course.'

'I'd hoped for better than this ...' The old woman's head drooped like a broken wing.

'I'll just leave the tea to brew.'

'Why ...?' demanded Aunty Betty pettishly, 'why isn't it better ...?'

She felt old and disappointed and her legs hurt. 'I've told people about your flat in town.' She sounded petulant and cheated.

'About Christmas,' tried Garbie again, 'I might go to Paris with a friend.'

'Paris!' Aunty Betty had lost faith. She clucked in disbelief.

'Or possibly Rome . . .'

'Rome!'

'Probably Rome – you should really go to Paris in April, they say . . .' *April*. Garbie paused. The baby, it said on a blue card she'd been given, was due on the seventeenth of April. But it didn't mean anything. The secret was in her head, not some other, irrelevant part of her body; a growth of self, not another separate being.

'I'll be sixty-nine in April. Seventy, the April after . . .' Aunty Betty watched the tea come black out of the pot and spoke sadly.

'And in two weeks it's Remembrance Day!' stepped in Garbie swiftly, seeing Aunty Betty might get morbid. All the same, she hadn't meant to mention Remembrance Day.

'I can't bear it.' Aunty Betty spoke softly, needing help.

Sensing it, seeking more distractions, Garbie thrust some brochures in her lap. 'I thought,' she announced loudly, 'I thought I might do a package tour for my holidays next year. They're very reasonable – do you know you can go to Spain, all in, for fourteen days from thirty-seven pounds ten shillings. Or, more exciting, off the beaten track, two weeks in Dalmatia from forty-one guineas with your own bathroom en suite . . .' She spoke rapidly.

'You say that every year.'

'I always have my hands full, people needing me for things. It makes it difficult.' Nervously, Garbie poured more tea, slopping it.

'Could you show me the toilet, dear?'

'Half way down the stairs. You have to take your own paper.'

While she waited, Garbie wondered how best to get round to telling. Then she thought of other topics it would be all right to discuss over tea, cancerous substances in white bread and (a favourite amongst the girls in the office) the proper length for a skirt. It was thirty-five minutes before she went to see whether Aunty Betty needed any help up the stairs.

Aunty Betty sat on the toilet slumped against the back pipe, a wad of tissue paper in her hand and a fixed, final look of disappointment on her dead face.

'What a good thing,' said Mrs Peabody made triumphant by the justification, 'that there was no lock on the door. It must have been Fate broke it.' She lowered her head in a more seemly way. 'Poor old thing. It was the final effort.'

She wasn't pleased to have a corpse in the house but she knew what to do. She made tea and phone calls and put Miss Pendleton's torpor down to shock.

Together they pulled Aunty Betty's knickers up to make her decent and shook hands with the doctor who had the body taken away.

'I wondered how she was going to get home,' said Garbie vacantly and went upstairs for a quiet think.

She sat until the gas ran out then, absently feeling in Aunty Betty's basket, found the fudge and began to eat it lump after lump while she tried to consider what it would be like not to visit Dagenham any more. Something had gone terribly wrong. Although she'd said she might go to Rome for Christmas, she'd planned to go to Aunty Betty's. Now there was nowhere to go. Except, of course, she told herself, Rome. Or possibly Paris.

There was a knock at the door.

Mrs Peabody stood there, viscously sympathetic, holding a minute glass of brandy. 'I thought you might be needing this, dear,' she said. And while Garbie looked at her blankly, she peered round her shoulder at the state of the room. Her lips tightened momentarily as she spied the need for one of her warning notes, but propriety telling her this was not the time, she bared her orange teeth in a neighbourly way. 'For medicinal purposes only,' she said, and waited till her tenant had drunk the brandy down.

'You're looking a bit on the waxy side,' she commented before going back to her cod's heads and boiling handkerchiefs in the basement.

Garbie closed the door on her, opened the tin of spam and sat in bed eating it hungrily as though desperate to digest the last of Aunty Betty now the worst had happened.

Other people professionally saw to the remaining details. The funeral directors were simperingly efficient, dropping a watch, rings, a ten shilling piece and a return Tube ticket into her hands while looking the other way. And Mr Corbishley, the solicitor, told her firmly he'd relieve her of all worry by disposing of the property, while calculating swiftly the percentage to himself.

'I thought I might like to live at Number 23,' she said wistfully, but Mr Corbishley found a dozen good reasons against it. 'The money will come in useful,' he wheedled, and she realized abruptly that indeed, it would. Rose Birnberg's pamphlets stressed the cost of everything.

When she told Freddy she'd be going to the funeral, he said, 'Have a good time then,' without pausing to look up from his flags and diagrams.

She was the only one there when they lowered the box in above Colin and Uncle Arnold. She was all that was left on that side.

She stood, with her collar growing damp, amidst the slanting rain and gravel heaps and as she gazed down at the disrupted earth, she had a vanishing and disloyal desire for the warm vistas of Rotherbrook.

The funeral notes died away. Instruments were reverentially lowered.

Jack Pendleton stood stiffly at the window of his office in Whitehall as the moment came for the two minute silence, and gazed down the broad street towards the Cenotaph. Beside him, Denton Caldwell stood equally erect. They were rigid, not with any martial respect, only with apprehension.

Below, in the pale drift of bitter rain, old men's heads creaked. A great national silence fell. The two men standing together inside the government building allowed themselves to breathe out, eased their shoulders.

Too soon. A roar, deep and distant, rose and spun towards them in a typhoon of contempt.

'The fools!' hissed Denton Caldwell in his blunt, north country voice. 'The bloody fools!'

The ranks of old soldiers, ranged geometrically beneath them, remained quite still. Unfalteringly, the royal family stood together. There was a faintly perceptible stiffening of shoulders from the Cabinet, otherwise the only obvious movement was that of a life guard's horse which nervously backed three paces. Jack's ears picked up the faint rattle of a sword.

The common roar, fragmenting into a thousand different angers, seemed to be drawing nearer.

'Haven't they got any bloody feelings whatsoever! Can't they see what a rotten, senseless time this is to pick!'

Jack, still observing the two minute silence, was unable to answer his friend.

'Just two minutes out of the whole year, that's all! Just two sodding minutes!' shouted Caldwell. He fell into a heavy breathing and jingled the coins in his pockets. 'Ah well! At least there's enough of the metropolitan force out there to give them what they deserve. They'll not break up the proceedings *altogether*.' He felt in his waistcoat for his watch and checked the time. 'Serve them right,' he said, 'if they used a bit of gas again. Gas! Good God, they don't bloody know what gas is – some of the old fellows down there could tell 'em!'

The formal (and disturbed) silence came to an end. Thankfully the brass struck up, as artificially tuneful as if they were performing on a northern pier. A few heads turned eastwards out of curiosity.

'They'd never dare use gas again,' observed Jack quietly.

'Pity.'

'It was indefensible last time. It swung a lot of support behind them, too.'

'Aye, well,' commented Denton dryly, 'it was a bad miscalculation.'

Jack spoke through his teeth, 'That's all that's wrong with

them now,' he said. 'Miscalculation. It's their strategy that's wrong – not their thinking.'

'Steady on,' cried his friend, trying to sound amused. 'That's not what you'd have said three months back.'

'No,' said Jack slowly, 'no, perhaps not.'

Regimental reds and golds began to flutter sickly in the rain. Jack gazed down at the black parallels and the scarlet heaps of wreaths and said bitterly, 'What, after all, does a war ended twenty-five years ago, or even one of over fifty years ago, mean to them now? They're quite right, war is disgusting. What *did* men die for?'

'Come off it, Jack!' Denton Caldwell gripped his friend by the shoulder. 'Come off it laddie! They're not even on about *that* war!'

Crushed between tall black buildings, the crowd flowing from Trafalgar Square, tried to force its way up Whitehall. Now their political anger was wildly spiced with frustration. Placards and banners reading 'Genocide in Awanzikwa' 'Admit Refugees' 'British Arms in Awanzikwa' 'End War' became useful weapons, beating down upon and knocking awry the navy helmets of the law.

Garbie, hair dripping and well to the fore, punched a boy policeman who tried to seize her arm. 'Bugger off!' she screamed, 'I'm an expectant mother!' He let go, clutching his nose from which slid a vivid stream of crimson.

She paused to look with pride at the damage she'd done before being forced away by thronging pressure from her right. Feet barely touched the ground as the growing, bursting crowd swayed this way and that, all the time edging a little forward nearer and nearer the formal mourners in their medals, the more important of whom were being bundled untidily into waiting black cars. 'Corruption!' shrieked Garbie, wading into the billows of the mob 'End corruption!'

It seemed to Jack that the tempo of the band had increased to an undignified degree. What was quite definite was that the rear of the police lines could be seen moving slowly but steadily backwards into view.

'There must be thousands of the bleeders,' said Denton Caldwell, shocked.

The two men gazed silently at the sliding line of defence and then Denton Caldwell said : 'By the way ...'

'Mm ?'

'You know there's been a lot of talk about the leadership ...?'

'Well, yes.' Uncomfortably, Jack put his hands in his pockets without taking his eyes off the scene outside.

'He's got wind of it.'

'Oh yes?' (A concertina-like shuffling of the ranks was going on.)

'I hear ...' and Caldwell paused to allow room for doubt, '... he's got a scheme to pre-empt it. To use the refugees as a reason for going to the country, or worse, to take a referendum on ...'

'*What!*' Still Jack couldn't look at anything but the incipient chaos outside. But his mind suffered a shock.

'... sacrifice the Party rather than himself.'

'I don't believe it!' said Jack in a low voice. But in a way, he did. In a way, it was the Party that should be judged, not an individual.

'We'd never win the next election,' he said.

'Oh come on now!' Denton Caldwell laughed. 'What a time to start laying bets . . . Still I'll lay you ten to one against we do.'

'I think not,' said Jack.

The Old Contemptibles wheeled and turned, forced to keep pace with the eager brass. Some fell out of step, giving the impression of a queue jostling for Cup Final tickets. In the swirling rain their medals made a dull sight. 'Don't give up yet!' Jack heard his friend Denton say and he answered the friendly clap on the shoulders with a thin smile. For he sensed, growingly, that the immediate cause for this march was only a cover for other discontents. This wasn't a student problem they were dealing with any longer.

'That's just it,' he said sorrowfully. 'If one believes in any-thing at all, one can't give up. One has to go on doing the same thing, believing the same thing hoping that one day it will work out right even if ...' and he looked away from the crowd for a moment, '... even if, it does mean defeat.'

The truncheons were out.

(There'd been a serious underestimate of the police numbers needed and it was difficult to bring up reinforcements until all the people attending the service had been dispersed. Out of pride, the old soldiers were refusing to hurry as fast as they might.)

The march, made, some thought, in the name of peace, had become surging and violent and embattled. Middle aged women, forced for the first time in their lives to do something, anything that would give vent to feelings they little understood, were becoming hysterical as they were swept and whirled against rock, their hair dragged in streamers across their faces by windy spray. An elderly man whose heart had stopped in fright two minutes before, was still being borne, battered and upright, along by the crowd.

Garbie knew it was different. It was in savage and terrible earnest. People were shouting for their lives.

Faintly, in between bursts of storm, she heard the tinny retreat of martial music, its tone flattened and wheedling in the rain. Then the human roar closed up the gaps and she raised her arm across her face.

Still the police fought for control, falling back inch by inch like a dyke wall until the mob reached the deserted Cenotaph. As the tide rolled imperviously on, the thicket of white banners, their letters running in the rain, were spattered with a new scarlet.

Wreaths were caught up, tossed up, cast helplessly on the waves of shoulders like the forlorn memories of sailors drowned. They began to disintegrate until the crowd and the air and the street were covered in poppies, the flowers known as the survivors of the field.

Up above, on the third floor of their building in Whitehall, the two men were unable to speak. In horrified, immovable silence, they gazed down at the reddening tide racing below them.

Jack, surgingly overwhelmed by his dreadful sense of an end to things, found himself weeping. The pain in his heart rose to his throat, and his eyes and overcame him totally.

Turning abruptly away from the window, he reached with blind fingers towards his lapel, searching for the emblem he knew he'd fastened there, and finding it, he tore the poppy from his coat, crushed it in his hand and cast it down upon the floor.

14   A Sense of Victory

Garbie was having a wonderful time.

She picked her way carefully, keeping close to the shop windows and the walls in case anyone from the Centre should spot her and tell.

She wore the collar of Aunty Betty's squirrel coat tightly fastened round her neck to keep out the biting fall of sleet which darkened the late November afternoon and made the pavements slippery underfoot. Soon the sky would be quite black against the garlanded lamps and dipping angels.

Her parcels slowed her down (the ones she'd felt she could carry). The others, Liberty's and Harrods had obsequiously promised to deliver. On either side a home-going crowd pushed by, heads down, finally indifferent to the red, green, orange and blue commercial stars of Christmas. They winked above their hopeful arrangement of furry slippers, asbestos gloves, saucy ash trays, indoor watering cans, nylon hair-bands, paper-weights, plastic inkwells and breakable toys, all caught in a torrent of rusting tinsel.

She'd spent wildly. The bank manager didn't mind about the overdraft for Garbie had explained her inheritance to him. Smiling and bobbing he'd plunged his hands in the drawers and lifted out little paper bags of money and wadges of pound notes snapped round with rubber bands which he pushed across the mahogany towards her.

'I'm only interested in seeing the best, the very best!' she'd shouted at all the assistants, her eyes shining like meteors. And the girl on cashmeres, seeing the woman in her dead aunty's squirrel coat had brought only the second best to get rid of the stock.

In a surge of gay malevolence Garbie bought gifts for

Rotherbrook to make them all feel guilty. It never crossed her mind that the most bitter thing would be to buy nothing at all. Large and overladen like a stockbroker's Christmas tree she bored from counter to counter demanding to see everything. Rejection was as enjoyable as purchase itself. For Uncle Jack she chose a naked green Negress in large reproduction. *Bonsoir* toilet water in two-litre bottle the shape of the Post Office Tower for Cissy, a hip length cardigan in maroon and ochre cashmere for Victoria, matching head rests for two of Quentin's cars, an abstract fibreglass sculpture for Edward, a bound set of the *Reader's Digest History of the English-Speaking Peoples* for Thom. And to Robin in Australia, she'd already airmailed premium bonds.

Her heart clattered with uncontrollable excitement. The man in deliveries, noting the gleaming eyes and the high colour, asked for some form of identification and swerved his lustrous smile from left to right.

Now, her hot face icing under needle-pricks of sleet, she crept past the Centre which blazed like a liner in a storm and hoped she'd not be seen. She hadn't been to work for weeks.

She searched the corner of St Martin's Place outside the National Portrait Gallery. The pavement was trampled wet without any chalky traces. She stood up, head above the slanting crowds searching for a similar protruding landmark, but Freddy had gone. The traffic swayed past on wet tyres and people hurried for their trains.

She leapt for a bus.

'Standing room only!'

Passengers fell off the 75 like cicadas. Garbie clung to the rail and winked at a Sikh who pretended to study the bell system. To show she didn't mind or hadn't seen, Garbie whistled Moon River.

At Euston she jumped off and ran through the maze of back streets. They swam with the smell of liquid yellow curry and pink paraffin. She peered into lit basement windows and a face peered back. She unhitched herself from the railings and scurried off to another where the leaves turned black in the drains.

'Give us two bob!' whined an old man, unshaven and hidden inside his duffel coat. His back fought off the attacking sleet.

'I'll give you four!' laughed Garbie, diving into her bag and he went off giggling at her, the loose soles of his boots making a splashing sound.

Freddy's light was on. He was in.

'Yoo-hoo!' She ran down the steps, pausing with a yelp as a sudden impertinent spasm caught at her back.

Freddy opened the door just a crack. His nose came scenting round. 'Who's there? Who is it?'

'Give you three guesses.'

'Oh yes?'

'It's me. Little me!'

'Ah!' he opened the door wide. 'And a jolly good evening to you!' he barked, 'Just in time for cocktails.'

'I've been hunting all over!' She took off her curling wet fur and shook the drips from her hair. 'Oh!' she cried, 'you've got company!'

A short, pasty-faced young man with glasses and a sluggishly growing moustache sank into a deeper corner of Freddy's G Plan settee. He gave her an elliptical look and picked furiously at the varnish.

'Company yes!' said Freddy who never mentioned names for security reasons.

'Hello!' said Garbie, advancing heavily, 'I think I know you.'

'I don't think so,' said the young man quickly lowering his face almost to his feet, 'I don't think so,' he said again.

'You're among friends,' advised Freddy drawing the curtains a little closer.

'No! No. Don't tell me!' Garbie tapped her chin and gazed upwards. 'Let me think ...!'

'I don't think so,' said the young man again, emphatically this time.

'V's wedding!' she shouted, 'V's wedding!'

'I beg your pardon?' He continued to look away as if someone were taking blood from his arm.

'*Caldwell!* Cyril Caldwell!'

The pale skin drained deadly white. 'Oh my God,' he said. He swallowed and took the large, lilac hand she offered to him.

'New recruit,' said Freddy. 'Different cell. What's your poison?'

Looking upset, Cyril accepted tonic water. Garbie, confident and afloat still on the buoyancy of spending, took whisky and stretched herself out on the sleeping bag. 'I was just wondering,' she sighed luxuriously, 'how'd you like to spend Christmas in Paris, dear?'

'I'm not sure I'll be free.' Freddy drank his whisky rapidly and settled down to run through Cyril's reading list. 'This is a crash programme you understand. Pity, can't be helped.'

'Oh, the crowds!' yawned Garbie. 'Still, I like to get it all done early.' She wriggled her throbbing toes and tried to get her back comfortable. 'There are some lovely things in the shops this year,' she said wistfully.

'You'll have to be sworn in at next month's meeting because of all this,' explained Freddy to Cyril. 'That's when Miss Pendleton's membership comes through.'

'I beg your pardon? Come again!' cried Garbie, sitting up straight and hurting herself, but Freddy was steaming on. 'This must be my perfect day!' she said and sank back.

'In fact, it *is* my perfect day – there's no doubt about it ...' She found a feather and stuck the small, sharp end of the quill into her gums. '... even if prices have *rocketed* this Christmas ... It's really wicked for some,' she said to no one in particular. The two men were deep in their briefing.

'Miss Pendleton here has played a vital part in the arrangements ...' concluded Freddy with an indebted nod in her direction.

'Only too delighted!' she beamed with a smile so ecstatic it tried to fly from her face. She wished she could think of something nice for Freddy. He was difficult to choose for.

There was an interval of silence. Cyril Caldwell twisted his glass round awkwardly. Then Garbie said, 'I didn't know you ... you were *involved*.'

Cyril gave a laugh like sticky tape being pulled off a rough surface. 'Well!' he cried, 'Oh well ...!'

'Absolute secrecy!' warned Freddy.

'Of course.'

They sat through a further stretch of silence until Cyril strained to his feet. 'Good,' he said, 'that's excellent.' And he looked flappingly about him for a coat or a pair of gloves.

'Ah!' Freddy slapped his thigh and with a watery ripple of laughter got to his feet crying. 'Well don't forget now old boy . . . a bit of this, a bit of the other . . .' And he drained his glass.

'Yes . . . yes.'

'My one indulgence,' explained Freddy unscrewing the whisky bottle, 'A man has to have just one. Otherwise . . .' and he poured a little more, 'otherwise, we like to maintain a life style of moderate poverty. Simplicity, we like to call it. We have a scheme in fact . . . any material goods, you know . . .' he smiled encouragingly, '. . . tape recorders, hi-fi, electric mixers, anything of that nature, we recommend should be sold off and the proceeds donated. The Movement . . .' and he laughed at the joke, 'requires a little capital.'

Cyril pulled off a loose button and laughed too.

Freddy stretched out his hand. 'We believe in mind *and* body,' he stressed, 'plenty of exercise, including sexual activity.'

'Yes.'

'It's culturally liberating.'

'Yes, yes I know.'

'Well, that's it then.' Freddy increased his grip on Cyril's hand. 'Good luck old man.'

'Thanks.'

Cyril stumbled over a hole in the lino and left.

'Fancy meeting him,' mused Garbie. 'It's a small world!' She lay back on the sleeping bag and studied with pleasure the smoky boas on the low bulging ceiling, the sharp lingering spray of an orange Freddy was peeling. 'What's the official position on marriage?' she inquired.

'Monogamy?' Freddy shrugged and moved to the bookshelf, trailing a finger over the titles, 'Culturally repressive.'

'That's what I thought,' she said proudly.

266

Freddy removed a book and looked up 'logistical dependence' in the index.

'How old *are* you exactly?'

He stiffened. Even to count the years frightened him. He was no age. He was the continuing present. There were times even when Freddy believed himself to be abstract, all ideas and nothing else. He had a conviction, an Oriental fancy, that by cutting off all bodily needs like food and sleep, he could be released into an unpolluted gas of thought.

'You can tell me . . . go on!'

He replaced the book he held and seized another, his favourite. An illustrated history of sporting heroes.

'I bet I can guess. I bet I can guess *exactly*!' Her voice sounded dangerous.

Freddy flipped through the pages merging the faces of Joe Louis, Zatopek, Bannister, Mortenson, Clarke into a single expression of glorious pain. The pain of self bursting out of its limits.

'I bet . . . I bet you're sixty-five exactly!'

Freddy stared fiercely at Gordon Pirie. The expression of agony and victory combined could so easily be that same expression of violent death. Something in the coincidence appealed to him. Below, ran the dull bubble of Garbie's voice.

'You would be about that . . .' she was saying.

He thought of how he would have enjoyed being a team manager. How good he would have been. How cunning and full of stratagems.

Garbie passed away from the personal. Freddy felt himself relax. She spoke harmlessly of black power and choked canals, of cyclamates and tuna fish and refugees, topics he could cope with in the blowing regions of his mind.

They spoke to one another in newspaper paragraphs, in the prose of part remembered books and borrowing what they saw to be the mechanisms of human intercourse, they made their brushing contacts. They were confident in their narrow knowledge of one another.

Garbie sighed at the papery touch of skin as Freddy lowered himself on her thickening form. 'That's nice,' she murmured hitching up her skirts a bit. 'Make yourself comfy.' And she patted him gently on the bottom.

Then, as he sank thankfully into her, letting his breath escape in her ear, she cried out in her bliss: 'What can I possibly buy you for Christmas, Freddy my dear!'

The Hon. Emily insisted on doing her Christmas shopping in London.

'I can't see why,' said Quentin, but agreed to go with her.

'I couldn't go on my own, not possibly. From all accounts ...' (she meant the television news) '... the place is swarming with angry mobs!'

'All the more reason for staying at home,' yawned Quentin, without pressure for he'd thought of ways of passing the time.

He endured it from Fortnum's to Liberty's then made his escape to an address he had in Greek Street. It was from there, one hand still toying idly with the young man's testicles, that he called his father and arranged to meet.

He left Greek Street with plenty of time to spare. He wanted to walk despite the cold and the crowds. He needed to walk off his savage sense of elation lest it affected the way he dealt with his father. Quentin loved his father with a despairing exasperation and knew, that in talk together, it was the exasperation, not the love that showed.

The wind blew meanly down St James.

He cut across the Mall, past Horse Guards' Parade and the deserted park. Leaves blew into desolate drifts against the railings. The trees were blackened and bereaved by December. Quentin, glancing at his watch, saw he was still far too early for the appointment and briefly resented leaving the flat in Greek Street twenty minutes before he need have done. To pass the time he went into the Stranger's Gallery and watched his father.

An Opposition member spoke incoherently about war loans or lime pits. He seemed to juggle cherry stones between his teeth. Opposite, on the government front bench, the Prime Minister who had earlier that afternoon answered questions about the refugees, unpicked a loose thread from his trousers. The member for Port Cawley sat two benches behind garlanded in private thought. Quentin smiled.

His father had aged recently. His neck had developed a stiff hinge that accidentally gave him the air (when he moved his head) of a man who found hearing increasingly difficult. His now completely grey hair was either thinner or cut more closely to the head. Probably the latter. A slight frown, once an occasional, attractive alteration to his face, now characterized his expression, raising one eyebrow quizzically higher than the other.

My God, I love him, thought Quentin.

The Honourable Member concluded his string of obscurities and sat down. The Speaker motioned to somebody else on the Government side. Quentin's attention shifted lazily (and critically) to the standard of dress on the Labour benches when a sudden disturbance behind made him turn his head.

In a flurry of contagious movement he saw a pasty-faced young man with glasses and a wretched moustache rise to his feet babbling hysterically. Then with a wild lack of aim, he hurled a black object over the gallery, down into the body of the chamber.

Around him people leapt to their feet, but Quentin, unmoved by the commotion, followed the trajectory of the object which landed, streaming smoke, on the green carpet and rolled a little towards the Government side.

Most of the front bench scrambled away, clinging onto or banging into one another in panic. For a fraction of a second only the Prime Minister remained still, hypnotized by the rising plume of smoke in front of him.

As the Prime Minister suddenly rose and walked at a hasty but controlled step out of the Chamber, Quentin saw his own father belatedly move, blocked by a writhing knot of M.P.s trying to climb over one another. The knot burst and Jack Pendleton clapped both hands to his face uttering a soundless cry of disbelief before stumbling after his colleagues out of the door.

The gallery was in turmoil. As Quentin turned to see the

young man being hauled, struggling, out of sight, he felt his own skin sting as though struck by acid.

'A young man about, oh ... mid twenties, doughy complexion, glasses, dark hair, and a ...' Quentin drew a descriptive finger over his upper lip, '... a *form* of moustache ...' He tapped his chin puzzling over the nagging familiarity of the young man's face.

'That it should happen *here*!' Jack Pendleton paced to and fro, rasping his hand over the back of the leather chair as he passed it. They'd escaped to the empty smoking room of a club in St James's.

'In the Mother of Parliaments you mean?' Quentin sounded amused. 'Or in this country?' He flicked his lighter on and off and trimmed the flame. 'It's been a long time coming you know,' he said. 'We must get over the idea that only barbarians fight one another and assassinate their Presidents. That such things are just an unseemly feature of past history.' Quentin snapped the lighter shut and looked up at his father. 'On the contrary,' he asserted, 'it's only just beginning. As in so many things today, we're actually rather behind the fashion.' He gave a concealed smile.

'The third incident! The third explosion in five weeks!' Jack moved like a caged-crazed animal. 'What, *what* in heaven's name do they hope to gain by it ...?' He came to a halt and leant against the back of the chair, wrists dangling. 'Dear God,' he said shaking his head, 'we got our Civil War over and done with three hundred years ago.'

'Phase one,' corrected Quentin, 'that's all it was. What a static view of history you do have, daddy.'

The word 'daddy' made Jack suspicious. (Quentin used it to salt wounds lightly.) Speaking as if to soothe, he said, 'Still, we mustn't exaggerate ... the act of a single madman is scarcely Civil War!' He dabbed at his sore eyes. 'How would you describe Cromwell then? Revolutionaries need to be a little mad. They need to lack humour.'

'No. Well. I've never been very keen on Cromwell either.' Jack laughed uncomfortably and renewed his pacing.

'Do sit down father ... all this restlessness ...' Quentin retired into languor, leaning his head back against the chair.

Reluctantly, Jack obeyed. The portraits of statesmen gazed down on them, foggy and despondent. Father and son stared into their drinks.

'At least they've got the man.'

'The *boy* ... yes, they've got the boy.'

Beyond, in the hall, the ancient lift landed and clattered.

'Emily? And the children ...?' Jack tried.

'Prospering.'

'Ah.' Jack nodded, satisfied, then burst out: 'But they've nothing to rebel against, not really! I know things aren't perfect, but there's nothing *really* to rebel against!'

'Ah. You think not.'

'Oh nonsense, Q.'

Another pause. Then: 'My God! A hand grenade could have killed both front benches!' Jack was very nearly sick.

'Indeed.'

Jack clutched his head between his hands. 'Why?' he cried, '*why*?'

Quentin made an exasperated sound. 'Who started this war?' he demanded.

'War? War? What do you mean, *war*?'

'You hadn't noticed ...?'

'Oh you and your silly riddles!'

'It doesn't admittedly have all the usual features of war as you know it, that could be why it's escaped you ... but it is war, just the same. The battle for survival.' Quentin knew he was playing with his father but he couldn't help himself. Quibbling, contradictions, perverse logic, all these lifelong weapons came involuntarily into play to scratch and spoil the Oedipal wisdom.

'Oh,' countered Jack, vaguely irritable as he reached for his glass. 'I suppose you're talking about pollution. Everyone is.'

Quentin laughed.

'*Is* that what you're talking about?'

'Not altogether,' said Quentin equivocally.

'What then, what?'

'Well, put it another way if you like,' (Quentin played luxuriously with his ideas), '... call it the doorstep salesman theory of politics ... the promise of quality stuff, the real thing ...'

Jack blew his nose fiercely.

'... whereas what you've really been marketing is a vulgar, second-rate production of the real thing. The teak cocktail cabinet with machine made Queen Anne legs.'

'If I understand you,' said Jack, not at all certain that he did, 'that's a bit harsh.'

'Oh a lot of people are very happy with the imitation. Being vulgar, second-rate reproduction people, they're completely fooled by it. They have a comfortable and totally erroneous impression of having improved themselves.'

'My dear Q,' sighed Jack, thinking he did now understand his son's elliptical mocking manner, 'you simply can't deny that today's working class lad,' (he used the word 'lad' with a shadow of self consciousness) 'can make good. Look,' he added desperately, searching out the newly gilt mouldings of the ceiling, 'look at ... at the pop world, the fashion world ...'

He was cut short by a sour laugh. 'Fashion!' sniped Quentin, 'I'm glad you mentioned that. That's an excellent example,' and smilingly, he paddled his finger tips together, 'of the Uncle Tom success story. A kind of political before and after.'

Jack choked a little on his drink. 'You're being grossly unfair!' he protested, unwilling to open up his own argument if it simply meant feeding Quentin's perversities.

'Well,' yielded Quentin, 'there is a *nicer* way of putting it. You could say people are being killed with kindness, with your politics of kindness.'

A steward slid into the room to empty ashtrays. Jack signalled for more drinks and suddenly felt exhausted. 'God knows what you're talking about ...' he complained peevishly and thought of the years he'd spent listening to his growing sons' arguments with a silent, flattering politeness, gently suggesting alternatives here and there, until, unknowingly, they'd been coaxed to a reasonable consistency of thought. Now, he felt Quentin was too old for persuasion. Too old to be won back.

He was frightened of losing his son completely, but knew, if he tried to follow Quentin's cunning trails he would be tricked and made to look foolish.

'God knows,' Quentin was saying nastily, 'what manner of damage you've done with your kindly politics, with your ethics, with the better life you so love to talk about.'

'I hope you're not ...' (Perhaps, thought Jack hopefully, Quentin was *joking*.)

'People must have health, wealth, justice. People must not die, people must not starve ...'

'Of course.'

'Not just our own people, but the people of the Third World.'

'Precisely.'

'*Exactly*.'

'Quentin, if you're about to embark on some fascist line of thought, I'd rather ...'

'Which line I wonder, is ultimately the more compassionate, mine or yours?' Quentin managed still to suggest indolence, but it was the feigned approach of a predator. 'What your kindly politics have done,' he went on, 'is to increase with the most lavish, irresponsible promises of education, equality and so forth, is to increase expectations. Unfortunately, there's a shrinking ratio of opportunities to all these innocent and growingly high expectations. You've created not only a taste for more and better, but suicidally, a belief in the absolute personal right to more and better which you frankly can't hope to satisfy. You've built, almost wilfully, a situation of such appalling frustration, that something has to break ...' Quentin raised his hand as his father made to interrupt. 'You've failed,' he went on, 'you've failed because you've tried to force the spiritual ethics of the early Christian church into a world that can't politically, any longer, contain them.'

'You're trying to say my morality's out of date!' (Still Jack hoped for the moment when his son would say he was only joking but he no longer felt sure.)

'Yes, if you like,' answered Quentin. 'Your morality's unimpeachable in the short term, in terms of slowly moving change, in small communities even. But globally, it won't do

273

at all.' He put his drink down and leaned forward as if genuinely wanting his father to perceive something of importance. 'Can't you see,' he pressed, 'that the emphasis you place on the individual, on his right, on his duty to strive towards a greater prosperity, is the envious ethic of war? And that, to satisfy the kind of envies you've created, people will kill one another?' He paused to regain a cooler note. He covered his mouth with his hand for a moment. 'Except that's not all, there are more complex factors entering in ...'

'Not all!' echoed Jack with strained jocularity. 'It's enough!'

He didn't wish the steward, who had returned with his small silver tray, to sense cracks in his composure. The steward performed his elegant gestures. Not merely elegant, thought Jack, his eye now narrowed in suspicion, even arrogant.

He used the pause to plot a change of subject and snatched recklessly at an opportunity to draw Quentin's hostility into a more amiable current. He leaned forward: 'By the way,' he said, 'please, I must ask you to keep this to yourself ... not a word to your City chums ... there's a likelihood of an Election in the early spring ... the P.M.'s feeling cornered.' He squirted soda into both glasses, pleased to have achieved the conspiratorial.

'Yes,' said Quentin, 'I'd heard. You'll lose of course.'

'Oh.'

For a moment Jack was more disappointed by Quentin's knowledge than he was by his judgement. Then: 'I know,' he said.

'You surprise me!' Quentin did sound genuinely surprised.

'For all the wrong reasons.' Jack picked up his brandy and swirled it unhappily.

'Because people panic. They want law and order, they want peace. They ignore all the other things.'

'Oh yes, for a while. Some of them do. But I doubt,' pressed Quentin, drily back on the offensive, 'that your Party, as it is, will ever return. You're finished.'

'That's absurd!' With an effort, Jack sounded mellow.

'Not at all. A spell of strong Tory government should stimulate just the polarization necessary.'

'Necessary for what?'

Quentin took the time to light a fresh cigarette. 'Necessary for the *war*,' he said as though repeating something obvious to a small child. 'As I said before, there's a complex range of feeling to be drawn together. Quite apart from the faction who want the prizes you've promised a damn sight quicker than you can ever hope to give them, there's a growing number of people who see that the very objects you've put in the display windows of your good life are destructive and ugly and lethal. Some want them all the same just because they've been *promised*. Oh, they'll fight for them because they're the only emblems of excellence they know, they've been thoroughly taught. Success *can* only be measured by the possessions of a consumer economy. It's always possible of course that they, like so many before them, will get safely sucked up into the cut-price world of middle-class values, though if they do, they won't want a Labour government to look after them. But the rest,' and he paused to reflect on the rest, 'well, perhaps they do see that the *effluvia* of affluence if you like, will kill them off completely. Not just psychologically, I don't mean that. Much more important, I mean, physically. A case of the biter bit, rather ...'

'Ah!' observed Jack triumphantly, 'Now you *are* talking about pollution!'

Quentin laughed, 'Oh, all right then,' he conceded.

'And that *is* something,' countered Jack eagerly, 'we can deal with.'

Quentin's laughter swelled slightly. 'You imagine, daddy,' he said, 'that pollution is building a factory on green belt and that counteracting it is appointing a Minister who'll refuse permission to build because of the amenity value of the surrounding area ... Don't you see, it's the factory itself that's suspect? Wherever you put it.'

"You can't possibly achieve better standards without economic growth,' Jack, more confident, spoke dismissively.

'It's no use, is it?' said Quentin softly.

'No, *please* ...' Jack apologetic, recovered his patience and urged his son on. 'Please!'

Quentin looked at him quizzically and drew on his cigarette. 'Tell me something,' he said, exhaling thoughtfully, 'did you ever, as a young man, read Georges Sorel . . . ?'

'*Réflexions sur la violence?* . . . Yes, yes . . . we all did. I seem to remember he regarded Britain as a special case, a place that didn't respond very well to having its system smashed.'

'He also said something to the effect that capitalism itself has to give birth to the situation which will overthrow it.'

'Did he? . . . yes, I suppose he did . . . well?'

'Well, capitalism has delivered. It's given birth to waste, filth, poison, fumes . . . things that don't exclusively threaten the working class. It really doesn't matter any longer from which standpoint you proceed, you're bound eventually to arrive at the idea that the system's due for overthrow . . . No, wait!'

Quentin fended off his father's rising protest. 'Whether you're a worker, a student, or simply a lover of the White Rhino . . . all these people, whoever they are, knowingly or otherwise, are undergoing a massive repulsion for this Jerusalem of yours, especially its Satanic mills, the lot – everything it produces and everything it's come to represent . . .'

'You're wildly over the top Quentin, I must stop you. Of course people want change . . .'

'They don't want reform, daddy. They're going to astonish themselves, a lot of these people, by finding out it's revolution they need. Even your gentle eaters of organic wholemeal bread – you *can't* change things for them any more, not in your system.'

'No, no, no . . . it's too melodramatic. The majority of people want very simple things. Justice. Fair pay, a fair reward, a fair chance to better themselves and as to improving the world around them, well, all sorts of excellent things are going on already. We are alerted to the problem you know, Q!' Jack leant back in his chair with an amused, bewildered gesture, 'I don't know,' he said, 'a moment ago I thought you were going to shock me with your Right wing view. Now you've managed to shock me with your Left wing view. I scarcely know where I am!' Uneasily, beneath his amusement, Jack sipped at his brandy.

'Well, there you are, you see,' countered Quentin ironically, 'maybe I'm a living measure of what I mean. A Sunday preservationist turned anarchist.'

So it *was* a joke. Jack allowed himself to laugh out loud. 'Not you!' he protested.

'I want none of it,' replied Quentin slipping back into the role expected of him, 'I intend to live comfortably as I can, for as long as I can, as far away from other people as it's possible to be.'

The two men settled more easily into their drinks, leaving a pause for tension to evaporate.

'Still,' said Jack at length, ceding a point, 'I'll go this far with you. I agree that we've failed this time ... but I don't see us going the way of the dodo. Not yet!' He drank with relief at his own conclusion.

Quentin, unable to escape himself, said obstinately, 'You've left it too late. If you'd taken your chances in '45, even managed to hang on in '51, you might just have squeezed through. It's too late now, you've been overtaken. You mean nothing to people born after the war.'

'You exaggerate Quentin ...'

'I think I must,' Quentin allowed a thin smile. 'It is, after all, a matter of survival.'

'Come now!'

Quentin, sliding from one area to another in his obliquely sadistic way, had succeeded in unsettling Jack again. And yet, for all his son's bitter snares, Jack felt in some way, moved. As though Quentin had not attacked him, but shown a brief, truthful glimpse of himself and let his concern shine naked. But then, he thought, the habit of wariness rising to protect him, I could be wrong.

He smiled comfortingly, shifted his hand on his leg, began to say something, stopped, and then remarked, 'The *real* trouble at the moment after all, is the question of the refugees – that's what most people are steamed up about. Understandably ...'

277

He smiled with the hopeless air of a man whose three-card trick has failed.

Quentin gave a small, self-deprecating shrug and scarcely bothered to say, 'It's just a symptom.'

'A symptom?'

'They understand the feeling of perpetual mirage.'

Jack took a quick, thoughtful draught of his brandy and soda. 'Look,' he urged, leaning forward, 'let's be honest about this. The standard of living in this country ...'

'Of course, of course!' Quentin rose to his feet impatiently and then, apologetically.

Both men gazed inwardly on some private matter. A gong sounded faintly from upstairs.

'You do exaggerate don't you Q ...?'

Quentin smiled bleakly down at his father. 'Always,' he said.

A steward came in and with muffled hands drew the heavy velvet curtains together cutting down the street sounds to a strangled blur.

'Well ...'

'Must go ... Emily will have rung all the police stations in London.'

'Give my love to Emily.'

'Of course.'

'I'm so glad you're both coming down to Rotherbrook for Christmas ... It'll be the last.'

'Yes.'

Jack locked and unlocked his fingers desperately. But he could think of nothing relaxed or intimate to say to his son.

'Well,' he said again, then added hopefully, 'Perhaps you and I could meet before then?'

Seeing what his father desired, Quentin felt for his pocket diary. 'I'll be down a couple of days before Christmas! ...' he said, hunting for the date, '... the twenty-third. Why don't we meet for dinner then and travel down together ...?'

Jack consulted his own identical diary (both put into their stockings by Cissy a year ago).

'The twenty-third ...' he murmured, running his finger down the page. 'Oh!' he cried with genuine disappointment, 'I've

278

got a Group meeting that night. Perhaps I could ... I wonder ...'
He hesitated, wondering whether to put it off, then felt, repri-
mandingly, that his urgent need to talk to Quentin was probably foolish. It was all too late. 'Never mind Q,' he said, 'there'll
be plenty of time to talk over Christmas, won't there? I'm so
glad you're coming. It's probably the last, you know ...'

And, formally, father and son shook hands in farewell.

15 Survival

Pigeons rapped with their beaks on the iron ground of the municipal gardens at the end of Pitt Street. A lean orange cat sat beside a crack in the ice of the ornamental pool waiting for a goldfish to come up for air. In the butcher's window across the road, turkeys swung by their claws, a clamp of plastic holly around limp necks which swayed slightly every time someone came in to spend their Christmas club money.

'You'll be going away for Christmas I dare say! That's the way to do it, have someone else wait on you hand and foot!' The butcher slipped half a pound of purplish mince into a plastic bag and stood on a cockroach beneath the counter.

'Going away, yes!' echoed Garbie with a pale gentility. She pulled at the wrists of her long suede gloves.

'Very nice! Verr-r-y nice too ... and where'll you be going?' He added the last, seeing she didn't want to leave.

She stared at him, at his belly, bloodstained and fading up to the throat. He gave a quacking laugh and cracked a lamb carcass open from the anus.

'Paris, Rome ...' she said. 'Nothing's finalized yet.'

'Paris? ... Rome!' he repeated, impressed.

She spent much of her day, deep in the luxury of choosing. The brochures were beginning to look tired.

'Yes,' she whispered and left, taking care not to jar the bones in her back as she crossed the road.

Freddy would be too busy to come, but it mattered less and less. Her body grew warm round its extra companion.

She stopped at the kerb to take a delaying breath and looking down the cold hills that lay between Pitt Street and Euston, decided not to visit Freddy, not even to find out about the membership. He would tell her all in good time. And Cyril too. Poor Cyril dangled his legs from a bench in Brixton where he was awaiting trial. His father's offer to stand bail had been rejected. Cyril faced a charge of attempting to use an offensive weapon in the Palace of Westminster and the services of the most expensive psychiatrist in London were being sought.

She crept into the safety of her room.

Webs grew across the windows, thin veils between her and the Holy Church of God whose blackish brick vibrated with growing devotion. Something in her saw and knew their aggressive note. And when she'd tiptoed across the road to see better and they'd gently, politely, closed the door in her face, she drew back into her own warm, small cell at the top of the house, and watched through the web with a kind of understanding.

So she sat.

The shadow of her profile rippling on the web, she sat contentedly with the gospels in her ears, a good, green fruit in her womb, writing Christmas cards to three hundred and fifty people she knew. Love and best wishes from G. Pendleton went speeding out to people in public positions, or people who'd appeared on television the night before; to the entire staff of the news division at the broadcasting centre, many of whom had left since Garbie was last seen regularly there.

She did go out. She went daily to the bank in Upper Street where the clerks gave nervous, glittering smiles as they pushed her winnings over the counter. And then, the scissor-pain snapping occasionally at her back she passed from one gaudy shop window to another, happy to be talked into some irrelevant purchase which she could yoke, after several hours' pleasant thought, to one of the names on her list.

Mrs Peabody was writing a note on her high standards, her good name, her certificate of hygiene when she received a matching chrome hearth set and coal scuttle sellotaped into escaping mauve tissue. No matter that Pitt Street was (unbelievably) a smokeless zone. The note was filed away in a Coronation biscuit tin.

Rose Birnberg, too, was overcome, to find on her doorstep, a gold wrapped tablecloth hand-embroidered by the witless women of St Jerome's with the shapeless names of anyone they could remember. The enclosed card declared it was for 'Two good friends'.

'Oh God, how *awful* ...!' said Rose, guilt-stricken. 'We'll have to ask her round to dinner.'

'If you do,' observed her husband Leo, 'you'll have to use the tablecloth.'

'Oh God,' said Rose again, 'how *awful*!'

So there was no loneliness. She fixed the cards that came in reply with drawing pins to the wall. Each pin entered Mrs Peabody's soul as it pierced the wallpaper, but what could she say? She told her cat, as she threw slops out of the back area, that she would end up a ruined woman, but she smiled at Miss Pendleton in the passage. Miss Pendleton had taken to paying her rent a month in advance.

Miss Pendleton bought a round in the pub on the corner. The Barmy Arms always contained plenty of people willing to have a round bought for them. They patted their greasy knees for Garbie to sit on (sometimes she did, swaying towards them her mouth swinging loose with happiness) and invited her to join them in a song.

> 'Roll me o-ver,
> Roll me o-ver,
> Roll me o-ver
> In the clover
> And do it again!'

The saloon bar was harsh with cigarette smoke and the smell of steaming raincoats.

'You're a fine figure of a woman. Did ye know dat? A fine figure!'

'I've got my points.'

'You've got your points. Dat's true enough, you have. And you're very civil wid your money.'

'A proper distribution of wealth.'

'Very proper, you're right dere. A very proper distribution. Now would you join me in a little drink?'

'Let me.'

'You're very civil.'

She knew no pleasure like it. Her purse crackled and rattled and emptied only to be replenished the following day. On her rare exits from behind the webs, people smiled and bowed in the street. Mr Sweeny, the bank manager deferred his mealy warnings till after Christmas. Mr Bean received bells and hoops and mirrors for his pigeons and though they were not performing birds, he invited her in for cocoa.

The invitation from Rotherbrook had not arrived. This left a sense of minor discomfort, like a corn or ingrowing toe-nail. (A distant rub one could cope with.) But she longed for the joy of turning it down.

Frost turned black on the roofs as she sat behind the web, adrift in her daydreams, listening with half an ear to news of Cyril's appearance in court and arguments about the need for bullet proof glass in the House.

'They just assume I will go,' she thought to herself as she wondered whether to ring Rotherbrook and gazed at the spilling orange paper sack of parcels. But the pain pulled at the twanging wires in her back and she pictured them all, staring dismayed upon her empty place at the table.

The ice dripped in a weak noonday sun and the pipes burst in the outside lavatory. She sang a few snatches of John Brown's Body and cleaned her teeth on the toothbrush she kept for Freddy. She thought about him, neither yearningly nor anxiously, but she thought about him. She thought about the thinning, speckled hair, the scars, the black crustaceous toes, the odorous bloom of alcohol, the eyes that faded on some distant object and thought, not that they were passionate lovers, but a pair of lovers unlike any other.

She scraped a dead insect from the wall, and formed a conclusion that their love was no sucking, malignant affair, but something that turned one's face out upon the world. A love that weaned. She padded the circumference of her room, finger tips touching the live plaster, trying to define the size and shape of her world. She contained the child, the room contained her; it was a gestating time. Anticipation made her quiver.

Sitting with Paddy's hand on her knee she watched Match of the Day on the television set fixed high up against the ceiling of the Barmy Arms. She picked Paddy's head out of her lap and winked at the butcher who'd dropped in for a quick one. He strained inside a tight navy blue suit, burst a button from his dazzling shirt and sorrowfully raised his glass to her. 'Got your arrangements sorted out then yet, duck?' he cried.

She rolled her eyes to indicate a globe of secrets and he tipped his Guinness merrily into his chest.

In Chapel Street market dusk came early as the stalls switched on their fairy lights. A man tossed twelve plates in the air and caught them all again without any breaking. Irritability filtered out of the shoppers and they had their pockets picked as they offered up their baskets for oranges, nuts, apples, sprouts, holly, small firs, and spices. Gas balloons on rigid strings got in people's faces and tangerines split underfoot but a gaiety survived as everybody weaved in and out clutching their children, even hoisting them cheerfully on their shoulders amongst the balloons and noisy carols crackling from the radio shop.

Garbie re-tied her head scarf with the hunting scenes on, elbows pressed tight to her chest in the crush, and beamed round like a nodding doll. 'Peace be with you!' she called to anyone who cared to hear. 'Peace be with you!'

They were used to that kind of thing in Chapel Market.

'Isn't it all *characterful*!' shrilled a voice raised on spa water.

'Isn't it too divine?'

'Peace be with you!' insisted Garbie.

'Oh Alexander, did you hear that!'

They swept on, lifting their carton of whelks up high. A dog squealed as its paw was trod upon.

Up above the stalls in the cramped brown houses, Dora pencilled her eyebrows in heavy right angles and remarked that business was booming.

'It's the age of affluence,' observed her friend.

Garbie saw two small black boys steal a handful of almonds and patted their terrier heads as they wriggled past. 'Peace!' she said.

They were playing 'Noel' on the pub piano to collect pennies for the blind.

The sky turned ink-blue and shoppers struggled home or fell into the pubs for the first one of the evening while their kids clung to the wall outside. They were drinking Black Velvets and port-and-lemon.

Behind them they left sagging canvas and empty boxes. The old regulars wrapped in their sacks moved slowly through the waste of peel, picking over rotten fruit and seeing if they could still crack nuts between their teeth.

One old creature bound round with string, reached out a hand and touched Garbie. She stepped back a little from the stench of poverty; a disquieting blend of dried urine and grief. 'Spare us a tanner for a cup of tea,' mewed the old woman.

The pub door burst open.

> ' "Fear not!" said he
> For mighty dread
> Had seized their troubled minds.
> "Glad tidings of great joy I bring
> To you and all mankind!" '

The door closed behind another customer.

'Here!' said Garbie tearing two of the remaining notes from her purse, 'I'd like you to have this.'

'Bugger me!' said the old woman faintly.

'Your need,' said Garbie tenderly, 'is greater than mine,' and she walked away stiffly as pain gripped her back.

The sooty, ill-wrapped old woman watched her limp home between the street lights. 'Bloody snob!' she spat and turned towards the pub. For it was old Fanny Ann and Garbie hadn't recognized her.

There was a message from Freddy. A piece of exercise book paper, folded and refolded into a tight two inches square and bound round with a yard of sellotape. 'Will call tomorrow or

Wednesday,' it said. 'Urgent business.' It must be about the membership. She leant against the narrow hall wall and suffered the urgency of her own affairs. She was barely able to pull herself up the staircase. The automatic light switch kept going off before she reached the top of each flight and left her in darkness slit only by the lasers of brightness under other people's doors. Each landing smothered the old fog of boiled cod with fresh scents. Sage and onion stuffing, incense, mulled wine and the dark, cooking richness of fruit cake. The steam rose to the top of the house and, clinging there, streaked her door with damp as, slowly and painfully, she reached to open it.

The room was so icy and glittering with condensation the walls felt like the skin of an old, fevered man. Sweat burst out on her own brow as she struggled towards the bed and swooned on it, exhausted. She lay until she quivered with cold before she could face the ordeal of getting beneath her blankets.

Fear nested in her throat like a mouse.

Turning her head with difficulty, she calculated from a calendar that hung above the sink that there were three days to Christmas. Just three days.

Practical concerns shot through her thoughts like a winter sun piercing holes in the cloud. Everybody in the house would leave. Mr Bean had already gone. She'd seen him bundled that afternoon into the back of his daughter-in-law's black Anglia and swept off to Chorlton-cum-Hardy. Soon they would all have finished scraping and stacking their pans, brushing their dancing shoes, strapping up cases and leaving for wherever it was they'd been born. All except for Mrs Peabody in the basement, a wild, deaf distance away.

The weather crept in through cracks in the window frame freezing all objects into their places. Although she still wore her clothes, Garbie shivered uncontrollably beneath the harsh grey army blankets.

Swaddled as she had been in dreaming philosophy, panic gave her thoughts a sudden clarity. The pain itself lost its cloudy symbolism; images of a branch snapped from a tree became merely, concentratedly, pain. Survival, a decorated theme in her head, became a matter of immediacy.

People left to go to their parties. Bang, crash, click, went the doors, one after another, each new one more hollow than the last.

She could go to Rotherbrook.

The thought landed with a thud. A sudden rush of snowy pillows, steaming drinks, smooth hands on the sheets and stories being read out loud passed through her head.

It would be the last Christmas at Rotherbrook.

At Christmas, Rotherbrook was fragrant with wood fires which scorched the skin. There was always music. A thin, sweet celebration threading through the house giving a ritual grandeur to dull chores. The dark house rustled and popped softly with the tearing of paper, sighs, slippered feet. Quietly, on the floors below, mouth organs and musical boxes were tested. Everybody lay in the warm expectancy of darkness waiting for Aunt Cissy's alarm to go off before rushing in and out of every room exchanging and comparing gifts. The small ones. The big ones, solemnly wrapped, lay in a sliding, multi-coloured cluster beneath the tree in the hall. It was the biggest tree she'd ever seen in a private house anywhere, drifted with gold and white angels, tiny silver bells, pink sugar animals and real candles that burned leaving a sharp, enchanting scent of melting wax and paper.

And afterwards, after the kissing and the wonderful discoveries they ran into the crystal air, into cold sunshine which changed the creamy yellow tones of the stucco into clear, lunar brilliance. Long pine shadows reached across the frosted grass. There was copper in the horses' coats. Their breath escaped in curving white plumes.

Sometimes, if there were ice, they skated, before tea, long red scarves and shining sprays unwinding behind them. And all day long it seemed, church bells rose from the valley.

Or sleepy with wine, you lay down and dawdled through new books. You sneezed at the faint warm smell of dogs and drank endless cups of China tea in a darkening afternoon. Butter melted on the toast and you admired new bracelets on the women's wrists. You ate raisins, let truffles melt upon the tongue. You were tickled by a cousin. Played games.

You slept.

She woke, having dreamt lasciviously of her home, to a chill darkness broken only by two orange cubes of light from the street lamps hanging on the wall. The dreams lay like warm silt in her mind and lingered treacherously on until she slept again, this time till morning.

The frost on the windows cast a white light across the drooping room which showed it must be nearly ten o'clock. Like a tiger, the pain lay concealed until she moved her head towards her stopped watch, then gave itself sharply away.

As sleep shrivelled away, the day's needs stood exposed. She was hungry. She needed a wash, needed to go to the lavatory. All these moves took thought, took time. Ten appalling minutes slurred past before (by hanging on to bits of bed, table and sink) she was able to get to her feet. She stood for a moment, nauseated by the scything pain that cut her legs away from their joints.

It took fifteen further, bad, minutes to get down one flight of stairs to the bathroom. Like Aunty Betty, she found herself stuck on the seat.

A door banged. The last pair of crêpe soles squeezed across dangerous acres of lino. The front door crashed shut. A carpet sweeper was being rattled to and fro somewhere.

At Rotherbrook they would be only too glad to lift her, wait on her, wash her. It was only three more flights down to the phone.

Freddy would come, she told herself sharply. Freddy would come. He had left a note saying so. He would come. He would quite literally, help her stand on her own feet.

She waited, the hours doubling, trebling in length. Occasionally the phone rang downstairs and Mrs Peabody's refined tones filtered up to her. Once she tried shouting out, but the slippered feet shuffled off and sank into the silence of the basement.

She thought of nothing. Panic narrowing into the single, unspoken scream to be saved, she lay rigid, focusing blindly

288

on the dead flies blackening the opaque bowl of the light above. Her breath rose vaporously in a coldness so intense even the sheets close to her body remained chill and old plates, piled in a half full sink of water, were locked in ice.

All the sparkling thoughts, whose complex connections and revealed mysteries had companioned her through past weeks, came to a feeble halt when brought nose to nose with the urgent need to survive. She required, not a dazzling theorem of life, but a human being.

Above guitars and tambourines, the Holy Church of God laid a claim to Jesus.

Their halleluias repeating faintly in her ears, a woman down the street gave birth to a coffee-coloured son. A goldfish, forgotten by its owners, turned over and floated belly upwards to the surface of the tank. In Rossendale Square, behind Pitt Street, a Nigerian slit the throat of his third wife and butchered her neatly till she fitted into a cardboard box he'd saved from Sainsbury's, which was wrapped and found its way into the Christmas post.

Not one of them, least of all the goldfish, needed a theorem of life, yet men walked about wearing them like eyelids they could pull down at will.

The clock stopped.

She knew Freddy would not come.

Or, as she put it, *could* not come.

It was only one of the certainties she had about Freddy. The other, growing slowly but more substantially with each new day, was more exciting.

But then, it wasn't theories about Freddy, it was Freddy she needed.

The light began to fade on the ceiling and she wondered where to go.

Mrs Peabody found Miss Pendleton littering up her hallway at half past four in the afternoon.

'May I ...' she inquired, baring her wicked gums to smile at the prostrate figure on the floor, '... presume to know whether anything is wrong?'

'I was trying to dial 999.'

The smile froze, 'I don't want trouble in my house ...!' Mrs Peabody began, but then, discovering she was not to be sued for loose stair rods or worn lino, gladly put herself out to ring for an ambulance herself.

'It's getting to be quite a habit!' she quipped as she waited for someone to answer.

Among the things the kindly practical ambulance men put into the overnight case she'd already, long ago, packed, was the blurred photograph, framed in passe-partout, of Dotty.

'It's a comfort to have your nearest and dearest beside you,' he said, and tucked a red local authority blanket around her rigid, awkward shape.

> 'It's one, two
> Buckle my shoe!
> And *three*, four
> Knock at the door!'

All the patients who are able gleefully imitate Sister's mime. She thinks she is amusing them. (She is.) She's limbering them up for a bit of a party. It's all on the National Health.

> 'Five, six
> And pick up your sticks!'

she whoops.

The snow outside is steadily falling cutting them off, so what does it matter any longer. Peg and Daisy, tittering weakly after a stout, each shut an imaginary gate. 'Got to humour her,' whispers Peg.

'Got to maintain every appearance of normal life,' breathes Sister heavily later on to a student nurse. 'Not let them feel left out.'

For the time being she flails her navy arms and darts her small pink eyes into every corner seeking out participation. The patients are mildly disorganized, missing cues or leaving certain actions out altogether (partly because of their disabilities) but her staff, trim, flushed and obedient, repeat:

> 'Ten, eleven.
> I'm in heaven!'

To illustrate the point, Sister smiles beatifically and spreads out her arms to indicate her gathered flock.

'Bloody 'ell,' burps Daisy.

They've brought in one more patient from another ward to swell the numbers. They are a little nervous of having her there. Mrs Thomas is not altogether 'with us', but it seems cruel to leave her alone so they've shouted into the great, green cave of her ear that it's Christmas Day, that there're games and puzzles from ten on, then a bit of a sing-song followed by grace and Christmas Dinner at twelve sharp. *'Have you got that, Mrs Thomas?'* And she nods, staring out through tiny black pupils which gave her a shrunken view of the world. She has a pink plastic comb stuck in her long, thick grey hair where she began to make herself look pretty, but forgot.

'Nurse! Nurse!'

Garbie calls out. She is wearing a paper hat because the old girls couldn't wait till dinner when they saw the crackers in their box and insisted on pulling them at half past nine in the morning. The nurses helped, tugging a little on the barnacled arms. Garbie's hat is large and yellow and has a skull and crossbones on the front. It is so large, it lies still on the bed allowing her to turn her head from left to right inside it. She would push it up a bit, away from her nose if only it didn't hurt so much to raise her arms. 'Nurse!' she calls again with already that whining note the dependent develop out of unconscious resentment.

Loosened a little from the bemusing effect of the drugs her spirits have descended like weary birds on the ashes left in her womb by the radioactive X-ray beam. She sees the child in black and white like a grim photograph of war, its head thrown back, its little limbs splayed wide by shock. It's hard for her to think of the child as living still and yet this morning for the very first time, as the nurse wiped her face with a hot, wrung flannel, she felt a light flutter. It flutters now like a small fist weakly knocking on a door for help. Or maybe signalling the obstinacy of life. She can't think clearly what it means; she is too full of sorrow.

('Seventeen, eighteen,
I'm still waiting . . .')

The chant tugs her at the edges. Pulls her wilfully towards the resilient irritations and pleasures of the ward's narrow life.

292

'Nurse!'

The nurse, plump and grey as a pigeon, waddles at high speed to the bedside. They know now what the problem is and they're as kind as they can be.

'I've told the engineer!' she whistles, anticipating another complaint about the disconnected earphones.

'Then I'll have somebody else's.'

'But you've got plenty to listen to already!'

> 'Nineteen, *twenty*!
> My plate's empty!'

(There's a rattle of shouts and claps.)

'I'll have somebody else's.'

'Eh, you want to join in don't you!'

Garbie doesn't answer, but her sallow face turns a slow, petulant red. She needs to hear the news.

Whispers, whispers, Sister says it's all right now. No danger now. So they plug her in and she crawls up close to Emperor Rosko. The staff cast an anxious eye and crush their lips at one another to show their sympathy.

The old ladies, unwisely, are allowed another drink. Even Ethel Macready is glad to be alive now they've taken the tubes out of her nose. Urged by the staff, she claps her hands approximately in time to the music and sings in a reedy voice.

> 'Here we go loopy-loo!
> Here we do loopy-lay!'

A small group of doctors or medical students comes in, their stethoscopes swinging cheerfully. They smile at everyone. One awkwardly joins in for a couple of bars then abruptly stops and turns away to examine Daisy's glass.

'Drinking again you wicked old thing!'

'If I'd got the money I'd be an alcoholic, lovey. Can't think of anything nicer.'

He laughs and tweaks her chin.

'You're assaulting my friend,' shrieks Peg. 'I'll have you struck off.' And she blows him a kiss. She's glad to be wearing a magenta purple hat. It covers the bald bits. The young man wanders away before she can touch him and speaks to Mrs Crichton-Smith.

She stops singing. 'I hope one of your men will do the carving,' she says.

'Of course. All aspiring surgeons have to, as part of their training.'

'I think that's rather personal,' she says, offended.

'What?'

'Cutting up old birds.'

'I never . . .' He shakes his head and backs a little.

'I know what you were getting at!' she shouts at his re-treating figure. Sister comes scurrying up to remind her of the words and replaces the pretty blue hat which has somehow fallen off.

Words have got round that Mrs Thomas is syphilitic and that's why she looks as old as she does.

'I'm not having her bum on my bedpan,' says Peg.

'What makes you think your bedpan's exclusive to your bum?'

'No, straight up, you can go blind.'

'What's it matter anyway . . .?' sighs Daisy, suddenly weary.

The smell of approaching dinner rouses everyone. Even Garbie tries to raise her head as the trolly sweats close. Mr MacWhinnie stands guardian beside it and bows his head over white palms.

'. . . May the Lord make us truly grateful!'

To show their gratitude they keep their heads down a frac-tion of a second longer than Mr MacWhinnie. Mrs Thomas has to have hers lifted up again and a white napkin is tied, bib-like, round her neck.

'Turkey, sausage, stuffing, sprouts and spuds.' Peg ticks off the items with her knife to check she's missed nothing. Every-thing is sealed in beige gravy. 'I've not tasted turkey in five years,' she whispers and can hardly bear to taste this now because she'll have, eventually, to finish it.

The cheery nurse with red hair and white eyelashes stands over Garbie and pops potato down her throat. She chatters on but Garbie, with her mouth full, finds it too much of a struggle to answer.

'We had the party last night! *Great* ...! Do you know Dr Salmon? No? Well, he's – more stuffing? He's married of course, three kids, but still ... Do you like the Rolling Stones ...?'

It's like the end of everything to lie helpless on your back having food dropped into you.

'Is this you?' With a yellowing sprout poised on the end of a fork in one hand, she picked up the photograph in its passe-partout frame. 'It's quite like. Where was it taken?'

The sprout descends.

Her mouth closes round it. '... My mother ...'

'Mother? Well ...! Two peas eh! We've all got red hair in our family.'

The food falls faster and faster without intervals for chewing, sausage, stuffing, custard, currants, gravy all get clogged round a sixpence hard in its centre.

There's a shout as Mrs Crichton-Smith wins a hard fight for the wishbone.

'What've you wished for, lovey?'

'A round the world trip by P & O?'

'A man of your own?'

'A fully automatic self-switching cooker in white enamel?'

'I want to die!' cries Mrs Crichton-Smith.

'Oh you are a one!'

'What a tease eh!'

'Right now girls, one more chorus!'

Garbie nestles up to her earphone and catches the end of the 12.30 news flash which says a man is helping police with their inquiries into Thursday's bomb incident in Whitehall, the north-west of Scotland is entirely cut off by snow and two tiger cubs have been born at London Zoo.

> 'Knick-knack paddy-whack,
> Give a dog a bone!
> This old man
> Is rolling home!'

There's a small tot of cherry brandy for one and all from the

Friends of the Hospital. Soon, nobody will know *where* they are.

'. . . Rolling home!'

Garbie is very still.

As stealthily as air filling out a parachute, jubilations creep into every corner smoothing out the collapsed and wrinkled depressions. Her thoughts (ornate, forked, interstitial structures) can take in a fragment of fact like this and find a place for it. Shapes and colours swirl, eddy into other amoeboid patterns and finally, accommodate the new factor. She is full of certainties, like the insane.

She knows.

Knows why her membership has gone through. Knows Freddy. Knows Dotty and Dotty's daughter. She knows revenge, knows freedom. Knows everything.

She is full of knowing.

She lies very still.

Cissy shakes her furs and walks with a forced tread down the long, antiseptic corridor. She has dressed with particular care to keep her mind steady, but the silver fox is sinking under the weight of wet snow and her hair which tends to frizz in damp weather is bursting round her face in a spiked halo of whitening-gold.

As she pushes through the swing doors, a moving hiss travels round the ward.

'Visitor! Visitor ...!' And they wait poised, to see which bed is to be selected.

There's a rush of trotting feet as Sister surges forward and takes the visitor by the arm. Garbie, wrapped in earphones and a pirate hat, neither sees, nor hears.

They talk rapidly. About what the consultant said, about the best method, the right approach.

'Poor Garbie!'

Poor Garbie turns and freezes at the unexpected face dangling over her. Rage, joy and terror obstruct all speech.

'I've brought you some flowers.'

She sees wreaths. Lilies.

Cissy hangs, doubtful, with her gifts, then lays them on the bed and takes a long time removing her gloves. Her hands emerge flashing with precious stones and ornaments. The skin is looser on them now. She sits, disturbed to find her face level with Garbie's. They are at whispering distance. 'What ghastly weather!' she says.

There is no response whatever. Garbie thinks her aunt has come to accuse her. She stares, head awkwardly on one side, a smell red, cold sore at the corner of her mouth. The yellow hat covers her forehead and gently Cissy pushes it back. 'I *am* sorry,' she says softly, then realizing Garbie can probably only hear the thin jagged ribbon of music faintly escaping from the earphones, she removes the hoop of metal.

'If only you had come to us,' she murmurs wistfully. 'We thought you . . . you seemed to be . . .' and she turns away slightly to whisper, 'it's my fault for being angry.'

Garbie pushes the sixpence out of her mouth with her tongue. Still she can't think of anything to say. Can't be certain what Aunt Cissy's doing here. Suspiciously, she hangs on to silence.

'The hospital rang.' Taking a tissue from the top of the locker (her eye briefly and curiously caught by the photograph) Cissy picks up the sixpence with it and quickly lays it down. 'They said . . . they told me about your back. *Poor* Garbie!'

The pause is filled with flowery scents. 'You should have come to us!' Cissy bursts out, not meaning just now, for Christmas, but 'always, when you need love and help and understanding!' She halts, unable to bring herself to talk about the trouble, and then pressed on by Garbie's unremitting stare, breaks into a clumsy smile and says, 'You're not the only patient to be visited . . . I'm having quite a time!' She has tried to make a joke of it and failed. It is not a joke. 'Jack too,' she says slowly, 'Jack has been hurt.' She bites her lip as fear for his injuries bursts upwards on a jet of tears.

Playing with her gloves, twisting them over and over her fingers, she hears Garbie speak for the first time.

'Hurt?'

The sound startles her.

'*Hurt?*'

'An accident ... an ...'

'Not dead!'

It's a statement, not a question. Cissy is repelled by the sharpness of the consonants. '*Hurt,*' she answers rapidly. 'Badly hurt. How did you ...?'

'I heard something on the radio.'

Garbie has become suddenly cunning. It is the effect of her own fear. Releasing Cissy from her stare, she is torn away to the odd sensation in her head – as though a frantic animal were racing round and trying to retrieve some hidden object. She is shaken loose from the safety of her certainties and quite lost for the proper way to react.

The theory, captive in diagrams and special logic was that he would vanish, be obliterated. The enemy, an abstraction that could be removed with a sixpenny school rubber was to be destroyed.

'I told them not to let you listen!' Cissy is saying, wringing her hands.

Garbie cannot look at her she is so frightened. The theory is wrong. He is hurt and she doesn't like that, doesn't want it. Instead of a vanishing gust of smoke, she sees intolerable images of blood, pain and splintered bone. She sees it is her fault. She made it possible with her spying and resentment.

'My poor Garbie! There, there! It's all right ... he'll be all right. In a few weeks, they say ...' Ashamed and moved, Cissy presses her cheek to Garbie's. How unfair, how cruel of me! she cried inwardly, to burden her with this as well. 'We must be grateful ...' she urges, her mouth caught in the yellow hair, 'we must be grateful he's alive!'

Garbie encounters the word 'grateful', strains over it, and feels her thought turn a corner. 'Yes!' she says, 'Yes, we must.'

She is glad. But his pain is her fault and her mouth dries.

She is on a precipice and knows it, feels a swindling wind tug her back and forth. Screwing her eyes tightly shut she buries her face deep into Cissy's dripping furs until the very weight and texture threaten to smother her, and then, violently, she pulls away.

298

Cissy, half-sprawled across the bed, makes a wrong inter-pretation. 'They've got the man responsible!' she cries, stretching out to save Garbie.

Garbie stares through eyelids narrow as traps. It couldn't be, wouldn't be, Freddy. Freddy is so careful not to be caught, not to be seen. Freddy wanders invisible like a burning draught through people's imaginations.

Of this, she is fixedly certain. Her shaken inner constructions re-assemble themselves.

Like a natural interval, the tea trolly arrives. They have iced the cake in concrete and the old women struggle like dogs with their bones rather than be beaten by it.

'Have you heard a word of what's been said?'
'I haven't been listening, Daisy love. I dropped off. Booze'll be my ru-i-in.'
'There's summat rum going on I tell you.'
They re-adjust the aerials of their ears.

Cissy takes the feeder from the nurse. 'Let me!' she offers, and pours tea down Garbie's throat. They're both glad of the tea-time distraction. They need to recover and consider what else is to come.

Keeping the spout firmly between Garbie's teeth, Cissy wonders how best to start. She is so tired. For two nights she's barely slept and yet, dragged down by worry, her thoughts for Jack have manned a frontier between herself and sleep. A steady tramp tramp over the same unyielding stretch of ground. Now she doubts reality; she can't even remember if all the presents were properly labelled or whether the family's been fed. In the midst of her mind she recalls the tree surgeon gazing up at the black walnut and saying it could be saved for a while by scaffolding, but she can't remember making the journey here, can't remember the turns taken, the signs fol-lowed. She remembers only a white and blinding landscape that seems itself to be an extension of her dreaming wake-fulness.

Garbie hasn't noticed the silence. So full is she of philosophy and detection she barely knows her jaws are grinding on the grey icing. The hump-backed foetus knocks in vain.

'Well now ...' says Cissy hopefully. 'Well now ...' she begins again, trying to launch herself. 'They seem to have discovered the cause of the trouble!' She stops, caught by the absurdity of this diagnostic remark. '... Your back ... your back I mean ... Does it hurt *dreadfully*?'

She stares into the rotating jaws and feels for a second as though she too, is being sucked and pulped between the great teeth. Glancing over her shoulder, she leans forward and whispers, 'The *baby* ... the baby is lying on the spinal cord.'

There is no flicker of response. The eyes maintain their dull and steady stare. Shaking herself free of their numbing beam, she bursts forth: 'Who? *How*! ... Who is ... *responsible*? Who is the father?'

She doesn't realize how readily she had assumed somebody uncaring and cruel is responsible for this. Falteringly, she repeats again, '.. the father?'

'... my father ...' Garbie is smiling venomously. She is luminous with outrage.

'The *father*?' insists her aunt, made almost angry by fear. She tears at her rings, grinding them painfully back and forth over her knuckles.

Softly, Garbie is laughing. Murmuring atonally to herself she is making her brilliant connections, '... Freddy ... Frederick ... Freddy ... Rikki ... *Rikki!*'

'I beg your pardon!' Cissy leans closer to catch what her niece is saying. A sweet and wicked drift of powdered scents spills over Garbie and she strains to remember her loyalties to Dotty. 'Frederick – *Rikki*!' she shouts conclusively, making public her outrage at last.

Puzzled, distraught, Cissy only partially sees a connection, thinks the girl is struggling for her father's name in the confusion. '*Richard*,' she says, 'your father's name ... Richard. You remember ...' She passes on to other things, to suitable names for children, to favourite names and family names, indifferent to (or unconsciously avoiding) the sudden halt of the circling jaw, the opaque eyes abruptly filled with swirling particles as though the sea bed has been disturbed.

There is no clear realization. Only a creeping tide sliding round her tiny, vanishing island. A slow, relentless, sense of panic.

Faiths and theories are tossed like weed in the tide. The water runs in sucking furrows dragging fragments of shell and unloosed limpets with it. And she, alone on her shrinking patch of sand clings to the one remaining means of survival.

'But we must face facts ...' Cissy is saying. (Cissy, a small figure on the distant shore.) 'We have to be sensible.'

The wind carries these dangerous words. A lifeline that could pull her under.

'It is all arranged,' says Cissy.

'It is all arranged!' drifts the small voice hinting at safety.

Cissy has spoken to the surgeon, discussed personal fitness, the radioactive risk to the child, the threat to mental stability. 'It's a minor operation,' she is saying, beguilingly.

What is she saying? Garbie looks at her in terror.

'It's simply to remove the pain. The possible damage to your spine ...'

'No!' she cries. The cry is a groan of despair as she feels the last strand of survival snatched from her hands. 'Oh no ...'

Now Cissy is speaking rapidly to try and cover the sound. 'You must trust us. Trust our judgement ... It's for the best, I swear to you ... for the best. You can't be allowed to suffer so ...'

'Suffer!'

'We shall look after you, always ...' And Cissy pauses, trying to free herself of the feeling that a lifelong weight has been hung round her neck. But she and her kind cannot bear to see suffering, cannot bear the guilt it places on them.

The water rises swiftly round Garbie, threatening to engulf her, but while she can still speak she again cries out, 'No!' and hears her own, fading note.

'The pain will be taken away.'

Despairingly she gabbles to her aunt: 'I can stand the pain! I don't mind the pain!'

But her aunt who is wise, who has discussed the patient's ability to bear and rear another human being with the surgeon, is forced to be persistent.

'For your own good,' she says kindly, 'we must get rid of the cause of the pain.'

'I don't *mind* the pain!' Defiance is reduced to a whisper. It is only a matter of time now. The water flows over her almost peacefully and carries her like the sorry whale, in towards the shore. To a kind of safety. To a certain death.

Her hand is taken. A sweet vanilla-scented cloud droops over her. 'We shall always look after you, do all we can for you.' Cissy presses her face to the damp, salt skin and lets her guilt go free.

It is all over now.

The sad cetaceous beast dries and dies upon the shore.

(But the ocean swarms with other, breeding, creatures.)

Garbie, crushed by the sheltering weight of her aunt's wet furs, slips into a kind of tranquillity and watches the images fade. The battling Holy Church of God mingling blackly with young whites and refugees march past in a pageant that turns grey and then, like an exposed piece of film, white with only dabs of grey before running off the reel altogether.

Although Aunt Cissy murmurs gentle things in her ear, she has a sense of silence.

She has surrendered.

A tender hand cups the back of her head as the terms and conditions of this new treaty are softly uttered. Muffled by expensive fabrics, jewels and fur, Garbie (dumbly) remembers her manners, 'Thank you, Aunty Cissy,' she whispers, stiffly obedient, the silver fox laying hooks in her tongue. 'Thank you, Aunty, for everything . . .'

And the older woman, raising herself slightly from the still body, smiles the length of the blank white ward, glad at last to have done the right thing.

More about Penguins
and Pelicans

Penguinews, which appears every month, contains
details of all the new books issued by Penguins as they
are published. From time to time it is supplemented by
Penguins in Print, which is a complete list of all
available books published by Penguins. (There are well
over four thousand of these.)

A specimen copy of *Penguinews* will be sent to you
free on request. For a year's issues (including the
complete lists) please send 30p if you live in the United
Kingdom, or 60p if you live elsewhere. Just write to
Dept EP, Penguin Books Ltd, Harmondsworth,
Middlesex, enclosing a cheque of postal order, and
your name will be added to the mailing list.

Note : *Penguinews* and *Penguins in Print* are
not available in the U.S.A. or Canada